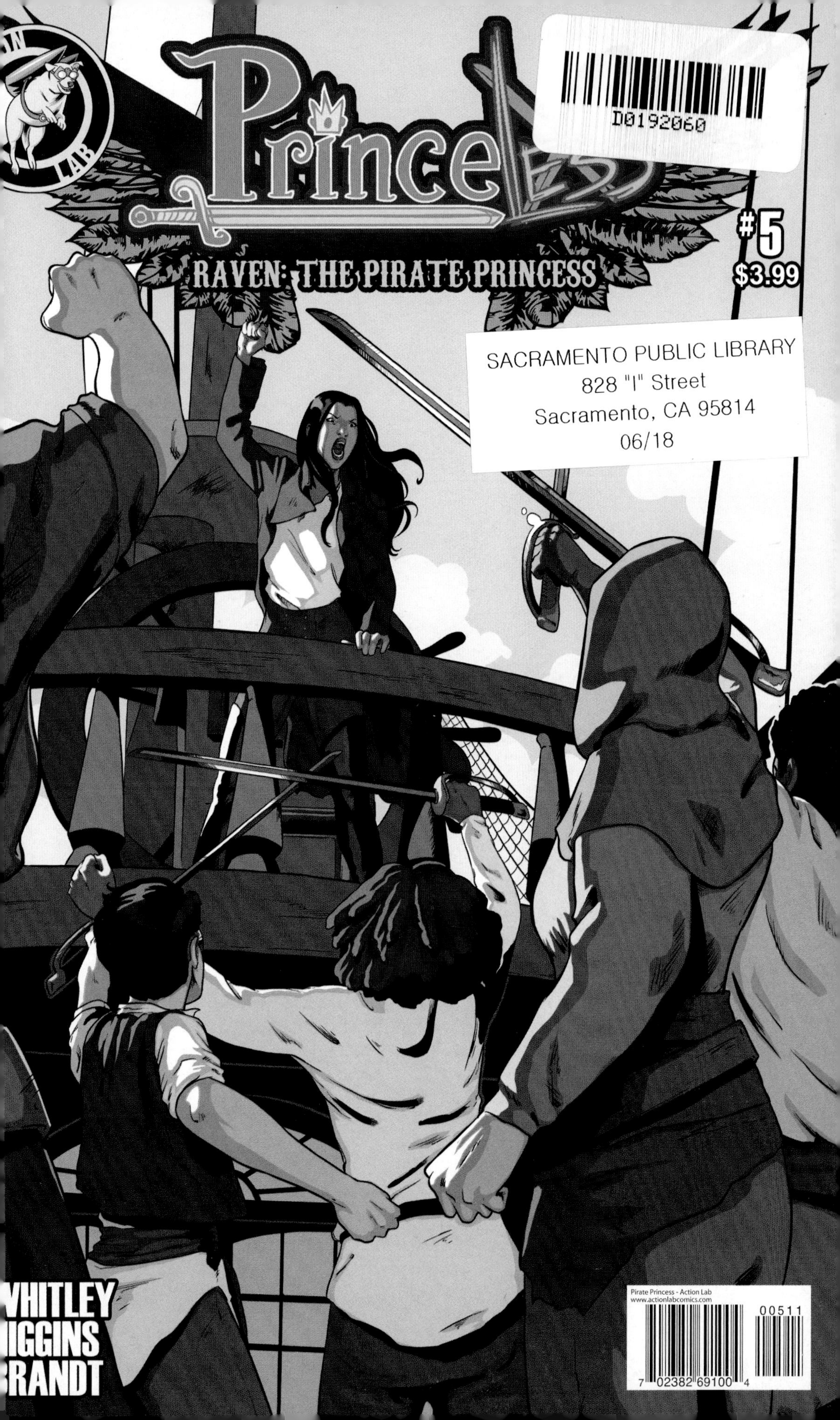

Princeless
RAVEN: THE PIRATE PRINCESS
#5
$3.99
VHITLEY
IGGINS
RANDT
Pirate Princess - Action Lab
www.actionlabcomics.com
00511
7 02382 69100 4

ACTION LAB

A

FROM GARY TUR
CARLOS GOM
AND TEODORO GONZA

Mage

FEATURING COVERS BY
JONBOY MEYERS AND
JASON PEARSON!

AVAILABLE IN FINER STORES EVERYWHE

Into a realm of magic and savagery comes a mysterious boy washed ashore. His is a
lone survivor. Befriended by an apprentice magi, her quirky mentor, and a metal golem
together they are Kai's only hope to stay alive long enough for rescue. Prepare yoursel
for a d20 RPG adventure with an all new twist.

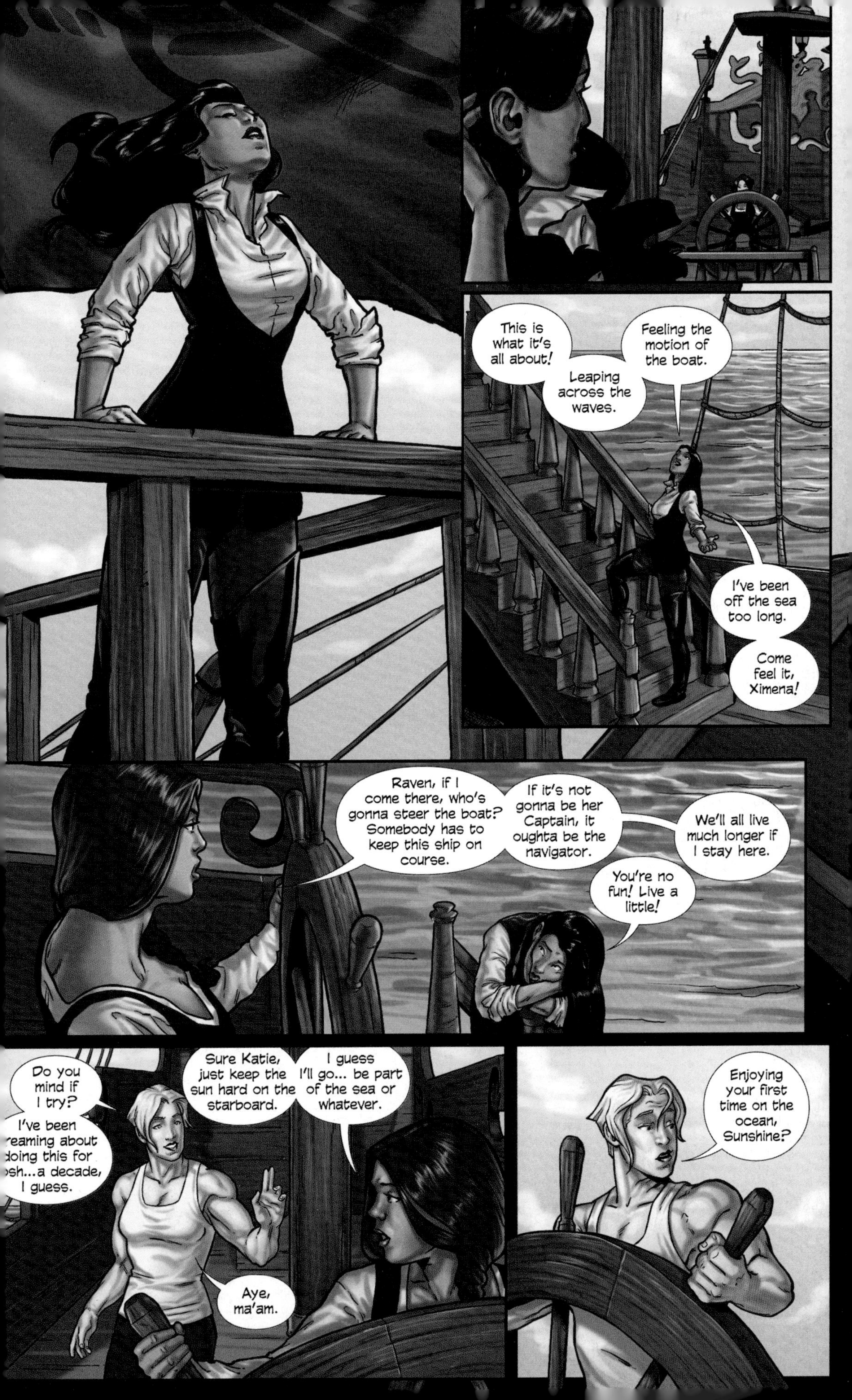
This is what it's all about!
Feeling the motion of the boat.
Leaping across the waves.
I've been off the sea too long.
Come feel it, Ximena!
Raven, if I come there, who's gonna steer the boat? Somebody has to keep this ship on course.
If it's not gonna be her Captain, it oughta be the navigator.
We'll all live much longer if I stay here.
You're no fun! Live a little!
Do you mind if I try?
I've been reaming about doing this for osh...a decade, I guess.
Sure Katie, just keep the sun hard on the starboard.
I guess I'll go... be part of the sea or whatever.
Aye, ma'am.
Enjoying your first time on the ocean, Sunshine?

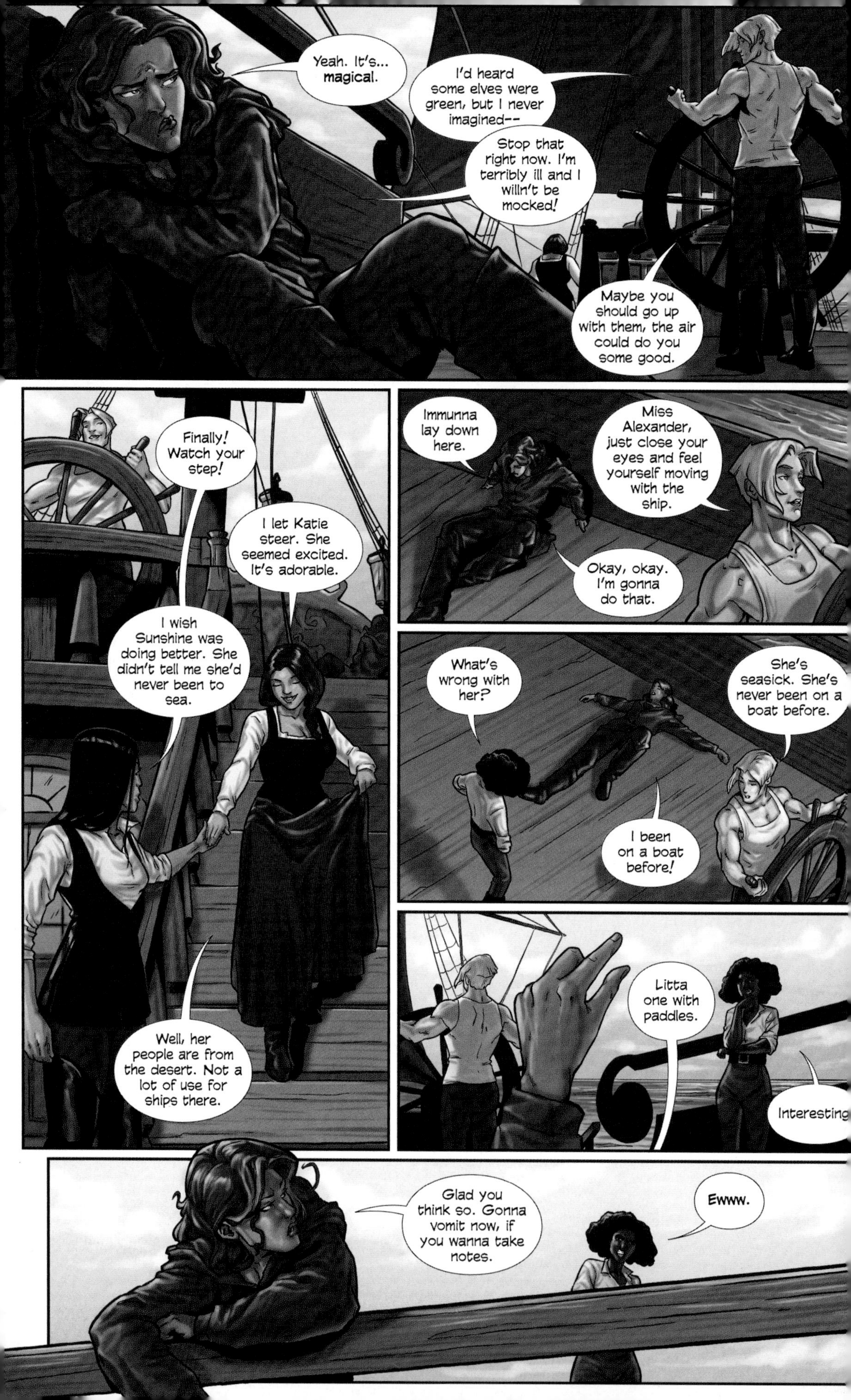

Yeah. It's... **magical**.
I'd heard some elves were green, but I never imagined--
Stop that right now. I'm terribly ill and I willn't be mocked!
Maybe you should go up with them, the air could do you some good.
Finally! Watch your step!
I let Katie steer. She seemed excited. It's adorable.
I wish Sunshine was doing better. She didn't tell me she'd never been to sea.
Well, her people are from the desert. Not a lot of use for ships there.
Immunna lay down here.
Miss Alexander, just close your eyes and feel yourself moving with the ship.
Okay, okay. I'm gonna do that.
What's wrong with her?
She's seasick. She's never been on a boat before.
I been on a boat before!
Litta one with paddles.
Interesting
Glad you think so. Gonna vomit now, if you wanna take notes.
Ewww.

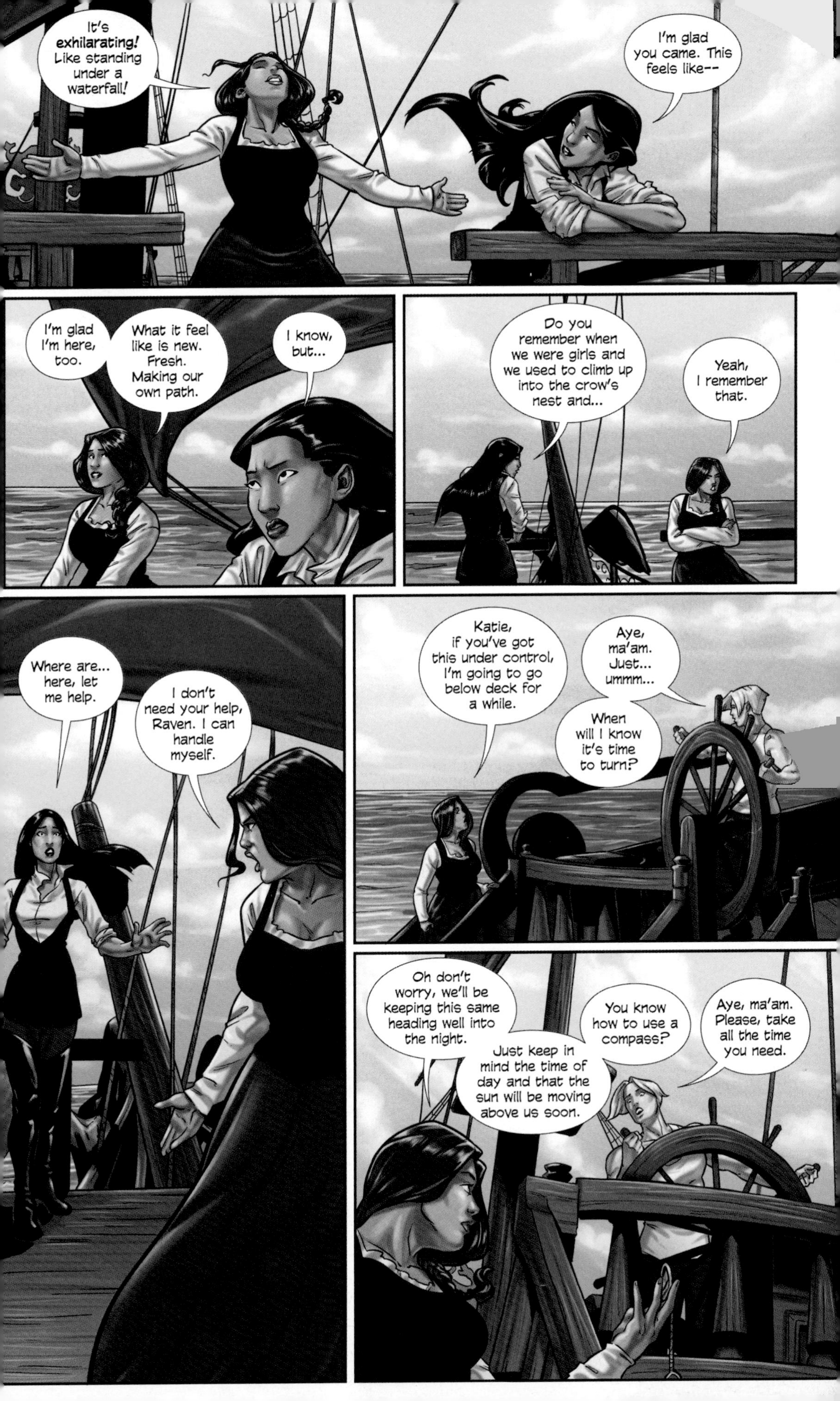
It's **exhilarating!** Like standing under a waterfall!
I'm glad you came. This feels like--
I'm glad I'm here, too.
What it feel like is new. Fresh. Making our own path.
I know, but...
Do you remember when we were girls and we used to climb up into the crow's nest and...
Yeah, I remember that.
Where are... here, let me help.
I don't need your help, Raven. I can handle myself.
Katie, if you've got this under control, I'm going to go below deck for a while.
Aye, ma'am. Just... ummm...
When will I know it's time to turn?
Oh don't worry, we'll be keeping this same heading well into the night.
Just keep in mind the time of day and that the sun will be moving above us soon.
You know how to use a compass?
Aye, ma'am. Please, take all the time you need.

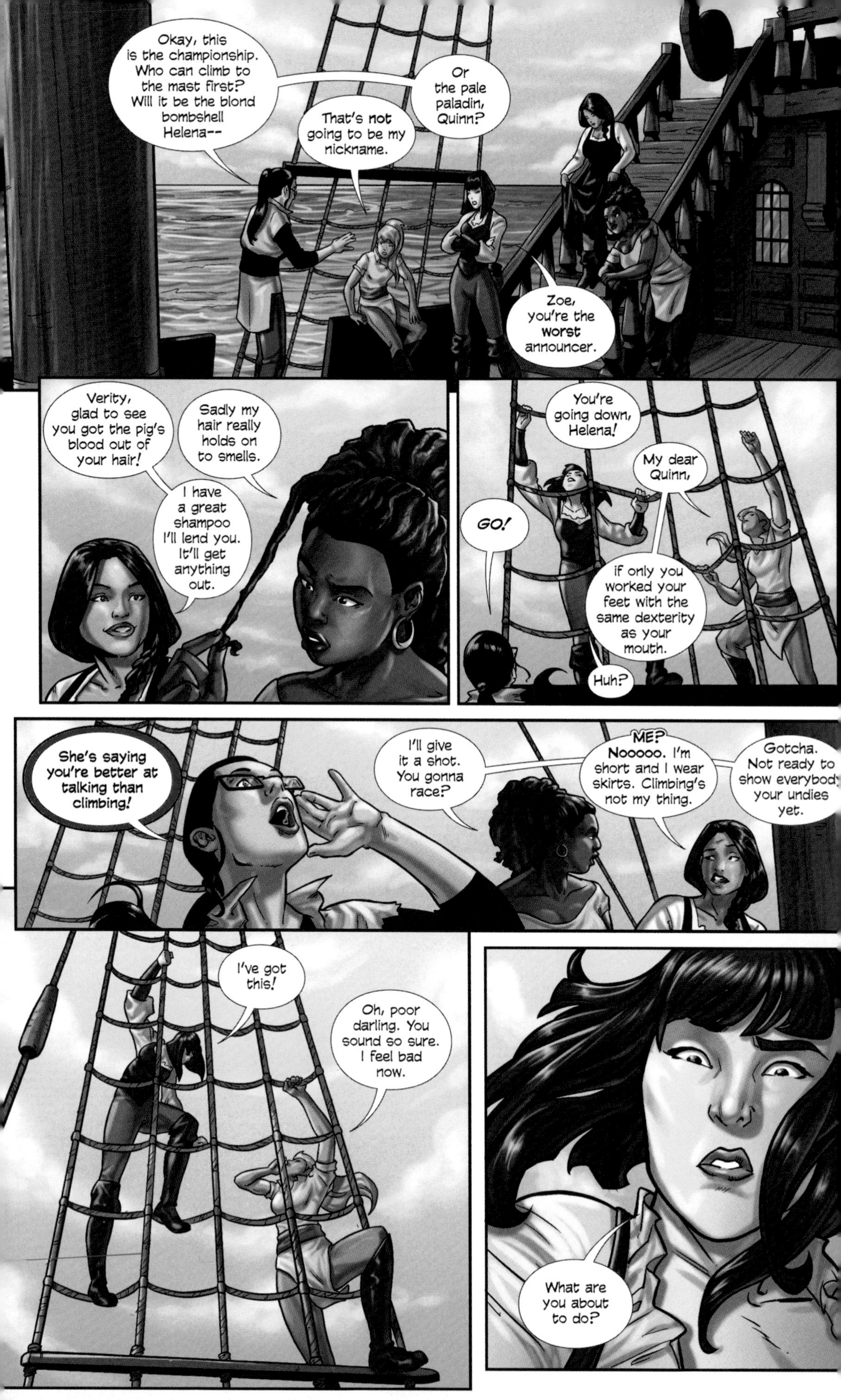
Okay, this is the championship. Who can climb to the mast first? Will it be the blond bombshell Helena--
That's **not** going to be my nickname.
Or the pale paladin, Quinn?
Zoe, you're the **worst** announcer.
Verity, glad to see you got the pig's blood out of your hair!
Sadly my hair really holds on to smells.
I have a great shampoo I'll lend you. It'll get anything out.
You're going down, Helena!
My dear Quinn,
GO!
if only you worked your feet with the same dexterity as your mouth.
Huh?
She's saying you're better at talking than climbing!
I'll give it a shot. You gonna race?
ME? Nooooo. I'm short and I wear skirts. Climbing's not my thing.
Gotcha. Not ready to show everybody your undies yet.
I've got this!
Oh, poor darling. You sound so sure. I feel bad now.
What are you about to do?

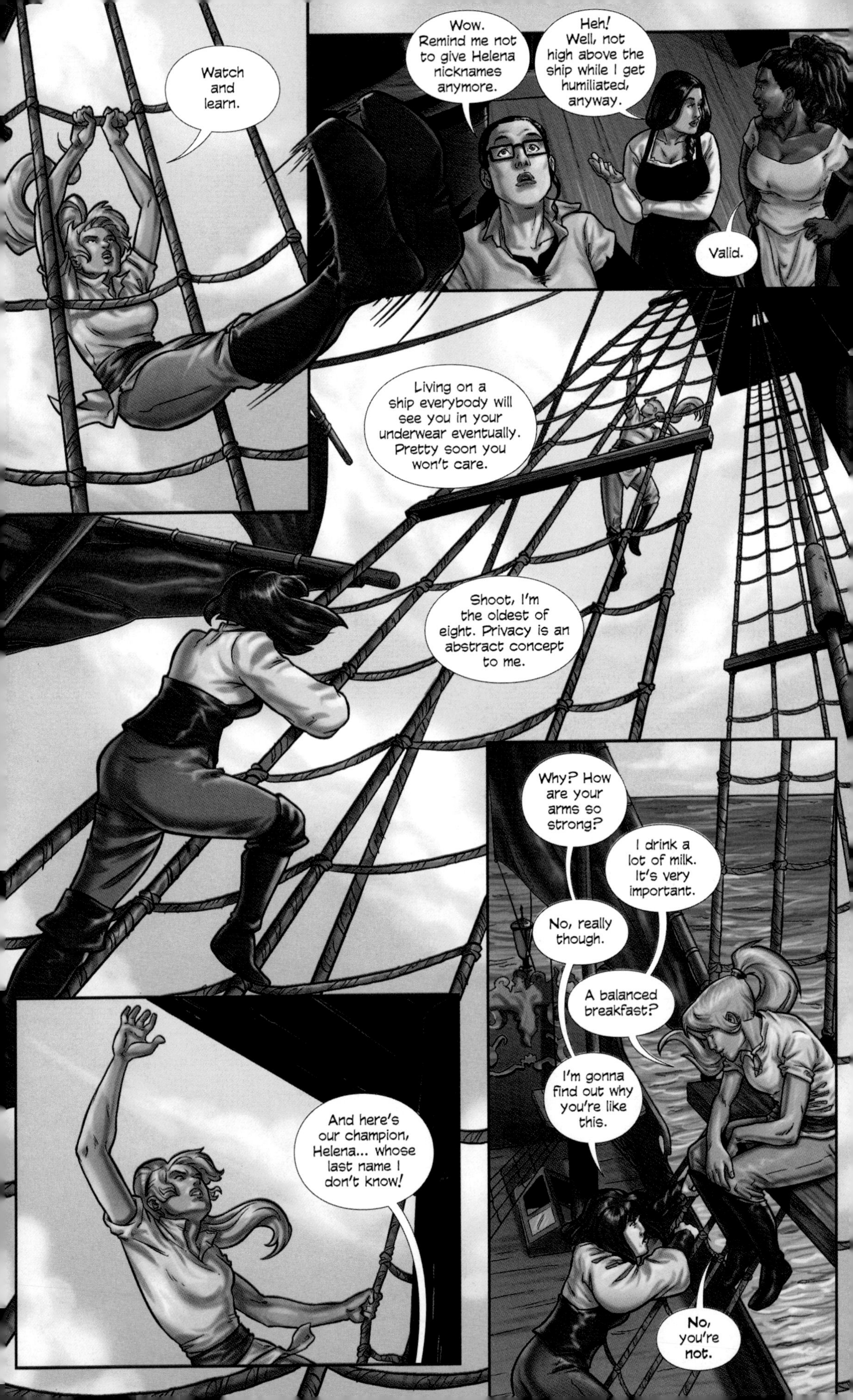
Watch and learn.
Wow. Remind me not to give Helena nicknames anymore.
Heh! Well, not high above the ship while I get humiliated, anyway.
Valid.
Living on a ship everybody will see you in your underwear eventually. Pretty soon you won't care.
Shoot, I'm the oldest of eight. Privacy is an abstract concept to me.
And here's our champion, Helena... whose last name I don't know!
Why? How are your arms so strong?
I drink a lot of milk. It's very important.
No, really though.
A balanced breakfast?
I'm gonna find out why you're like this.
No, you're not.

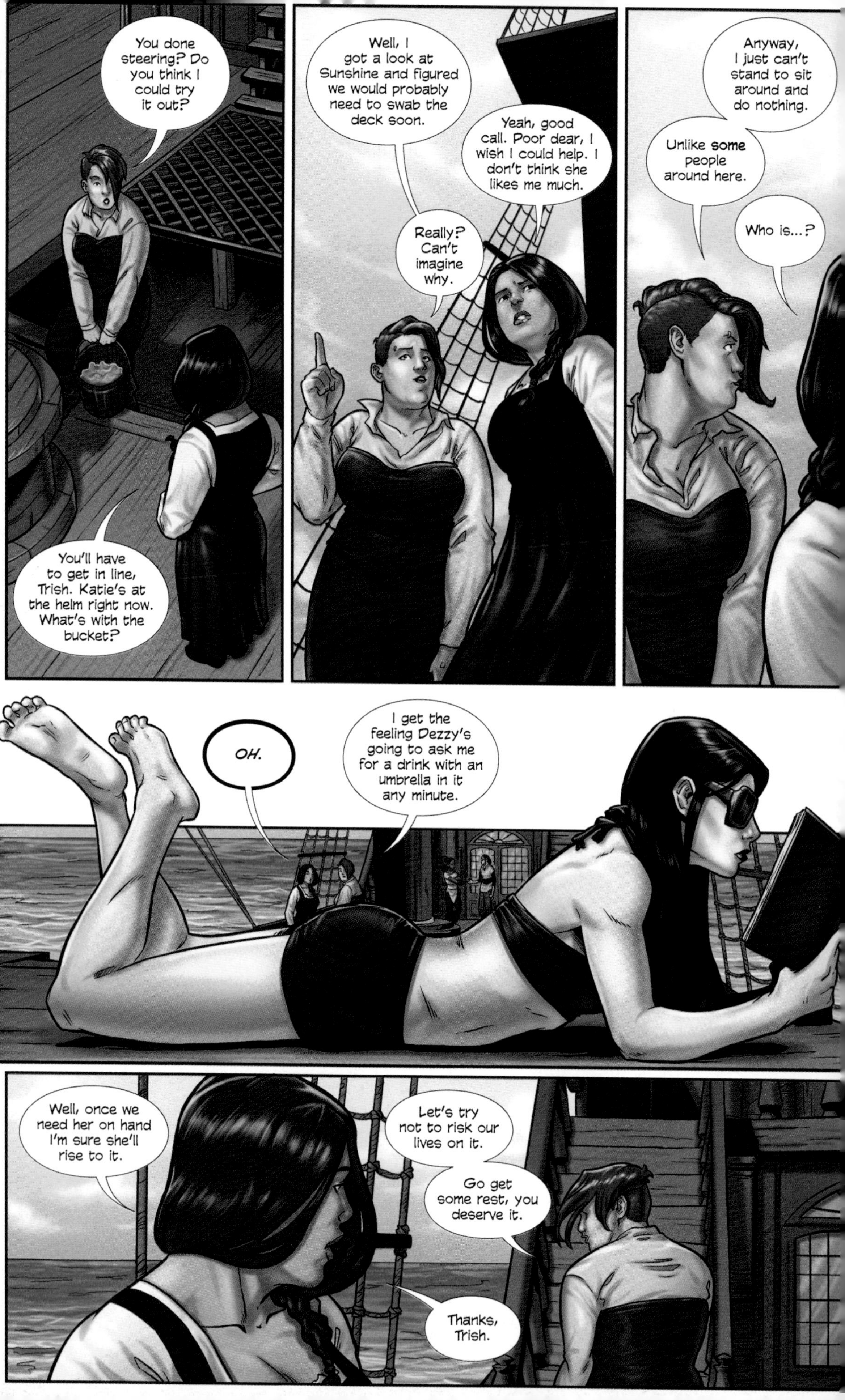
You done steering? Do you think I could try it out?
You'll have to get in line, Trish. Katie's at the helm right now. What's with the bucket?
Well, I got a look at Sunshine and figured we would probably need to swab the deck soon.
Really? Can't imagine why.
Yeah, good call. Poor dear, I wish I could help. I don't think she likes me much.
Anyway, I just can't stand to sit around and do nothing.
Unlike **some** people around here.
Who is...?
OH.
I get the feeling Dezzy's going to ask me for a drink with an umbrella in it any minute.
Well, once we need her on hand I'm sure she'll rise to it.
Let's try not to risk our lives on it.
Go get some rest, you deserve it.
Thanks, Trish.

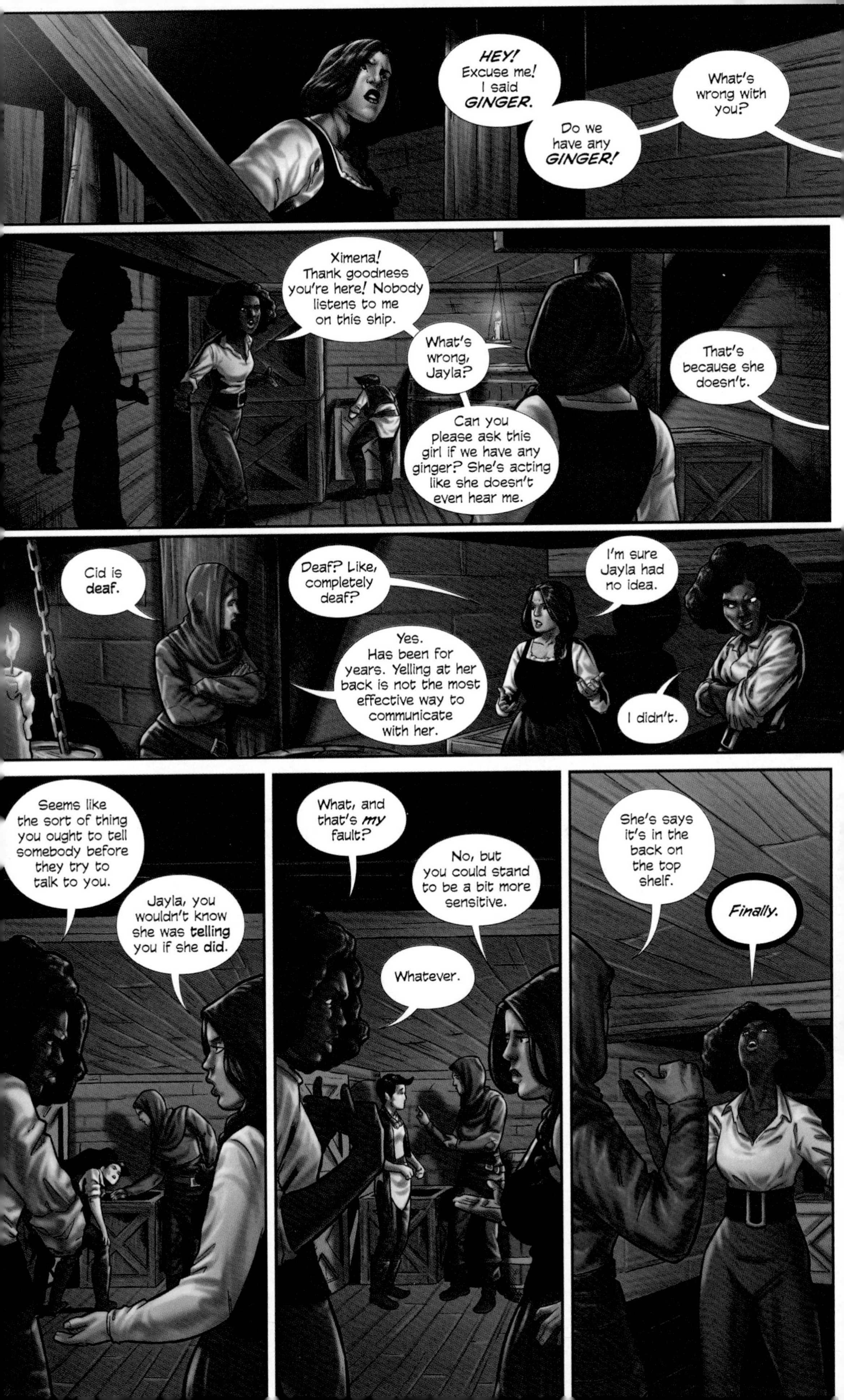

HEY! Excuse me! I said GINGER.
Do we have any GINGER!
What's wrong with you?
Ximena! Thank goodness you're here! Nobody listens to me on this ship.
What's wrong, Jayla?
Can you please ask this girl if we have any ginger? She's acting like she doesn't even hear me.
That's because she doesn't.
Cid is deaf.
Deaf? Like, completely deaf?
Yes. Has been for years. Yelling at her back is not the most effective way to communicate with her.
I'm sure Jayla had no idea.
I didn't.
Seems like the sort of thing you ought to tell somebody before they try to talk to you.
Jayla, you wouldn't know she was telling you if she did.
What, and that's my fault?
No, but you could stand to be a bit more sensitive.
Whatever.
She's says it's in the back on the top shelf.
Finally.

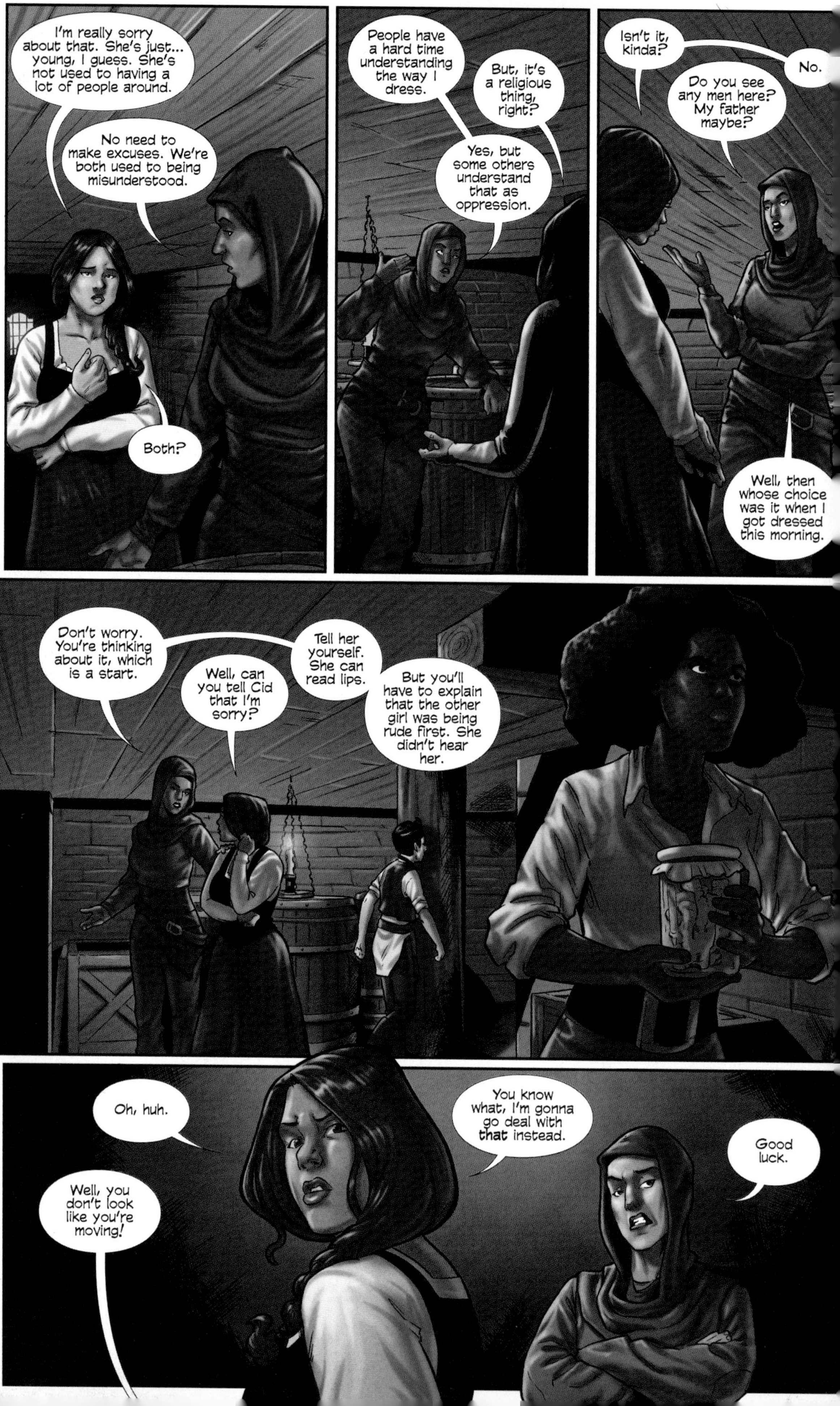
I'm really sorry about that. She's just... young, I guess. She's not used to having a lot of people around.
No need to make excuses. We're both used to being misunderstood.
Both?
People have a hard time understanding the way I dress.
But, it's a religious thing, right?
Yes, but some others understand that as oppression.
Isn't it, kinda?
No.
Do you see any men here? My father maybe?
Well, then whose choice was it when I got dressed this morning.
Don't worry. You're thinking about it, which is a start.
Well, can you tell Cid that I'm sorry?
Tell her yourself. She can read lips.
But you'll have to explain that the other girl was being rude first. She didn't hear her.
Oh, huh.
You know what, I'm gonna go deal with **that** instead.
Good luck.
Well, you don't look like you're moving!

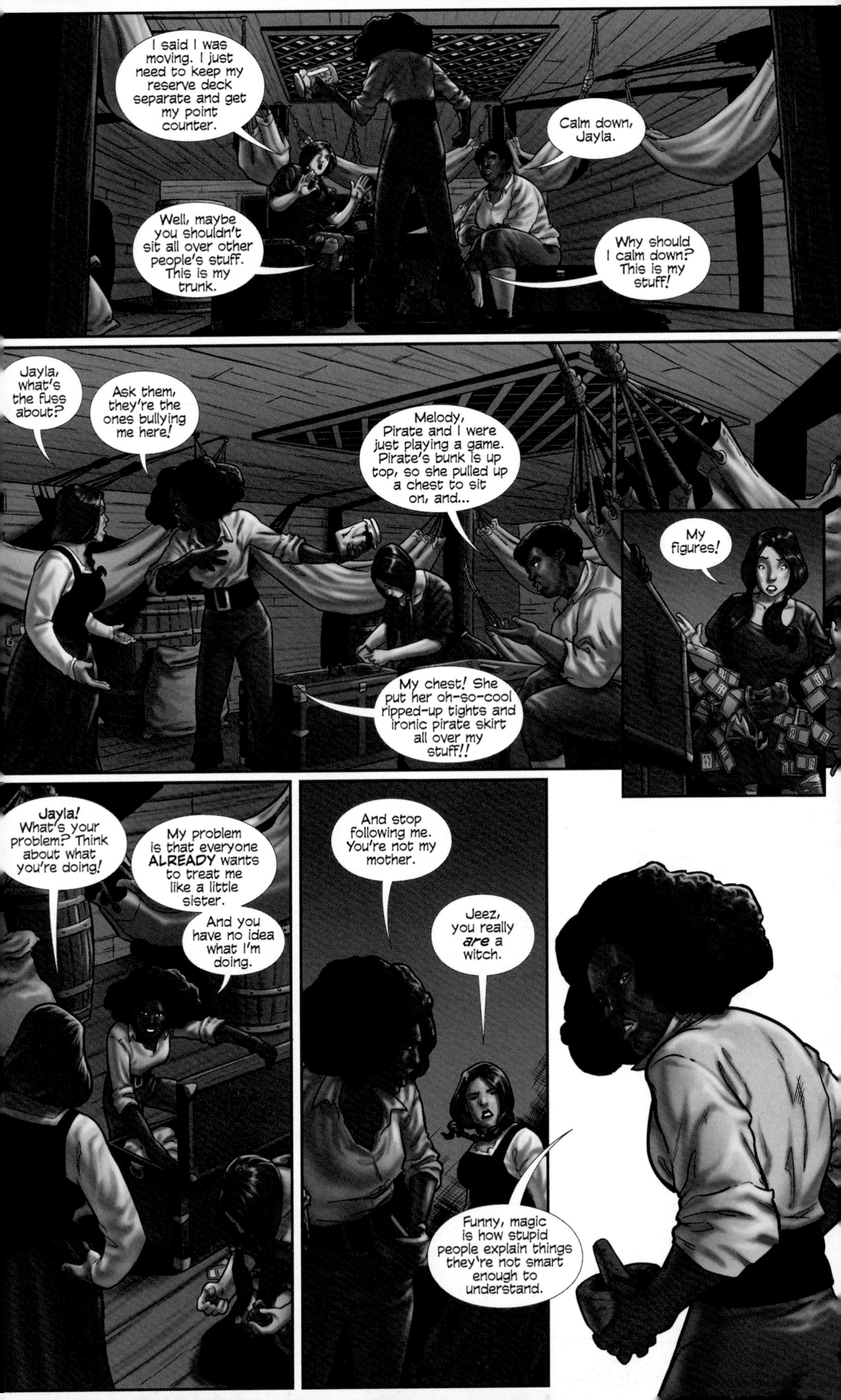
I said I was moving. I just need to keep my reserve deck separate and get my point counter.
Calm down, Jayla.
Well, maybe you shouldn't sit all over other people's stuff. This is my trunk.
Why should I calm down? This is my stuff!
Jayla, what's the fuss about?
Ask them, they're the ones bullying me here!
Melody, Pirate and I were just playing a game. Pirate's bunk is up top, so she pulled up a chest to sit on, and...
My chest! She put her oh-so-cool ripped-up tights and ironic pirate skirt all over my stuff!!
My figures!
Jayla! What's your problem? Think about what you're doing!
My problem is that everyone ALREADY wants to treat me like a little sister.
And you have no idea what I'm doing.
And stop following me. You're not my mother.
Jeez, you really *are* a witch.
Funny, magic is how stupid people explain things they're not smart enough to understand.

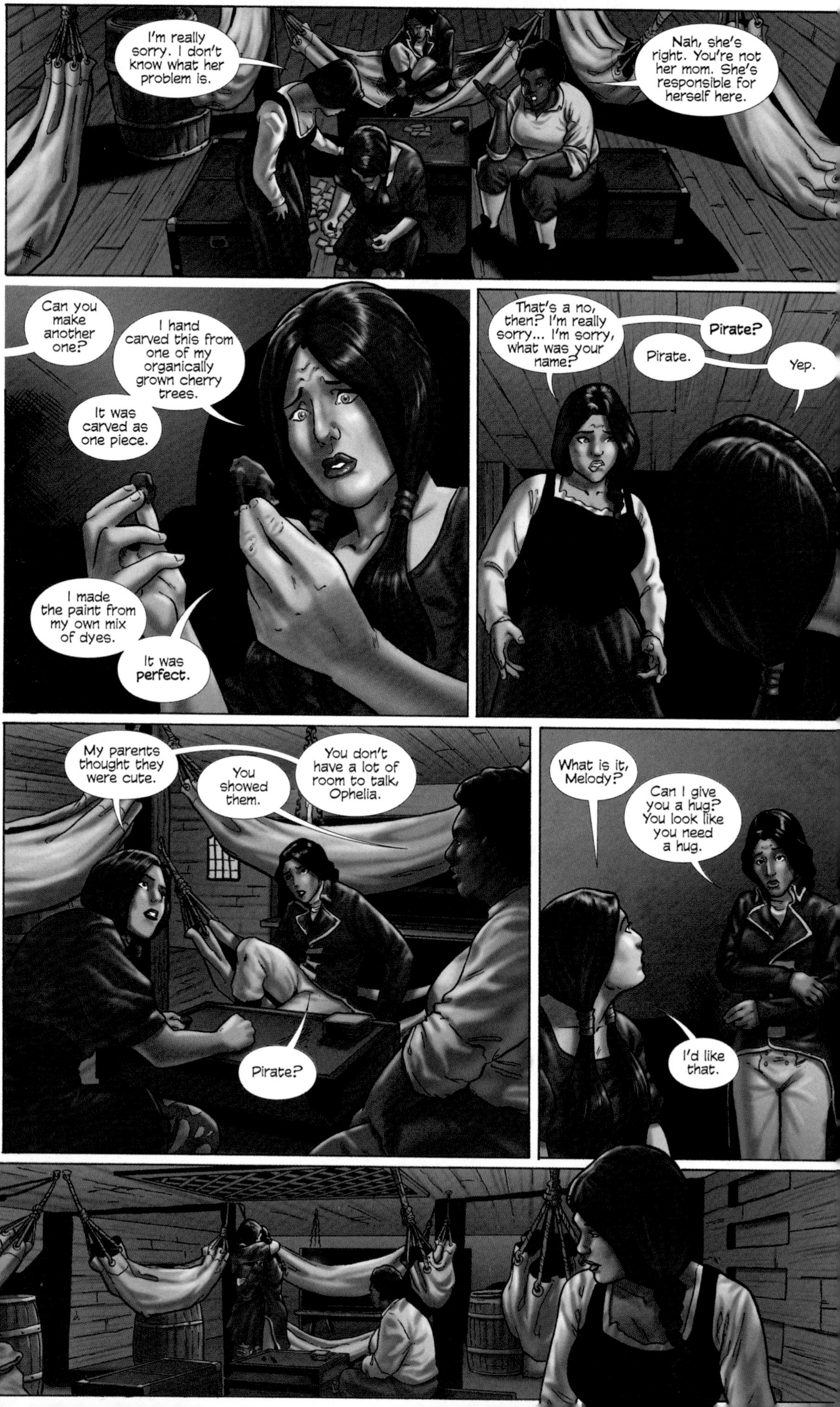

I'm really sorry. I don't know what her problem is.
Nah, she's right. You're not her mom. She's responsible for herself here.
Can you make another one?
I hand carved this from one of my organically grown cherry trees.
It was carved as one piece.
I made the paint from my own mix of dyes.
It was **perfect.**
That's a no, then? I'm really sorry... I'm sorry, what was your name?
Pirate?
Pirate.
Yep.
My parents thought they were cute.
You showed them.
You don't have a lot of room to talk, Ophelia.
Pirate?
What is it, Melody?
Can I give you a hug? You look like you need a hug.
I'd like that.

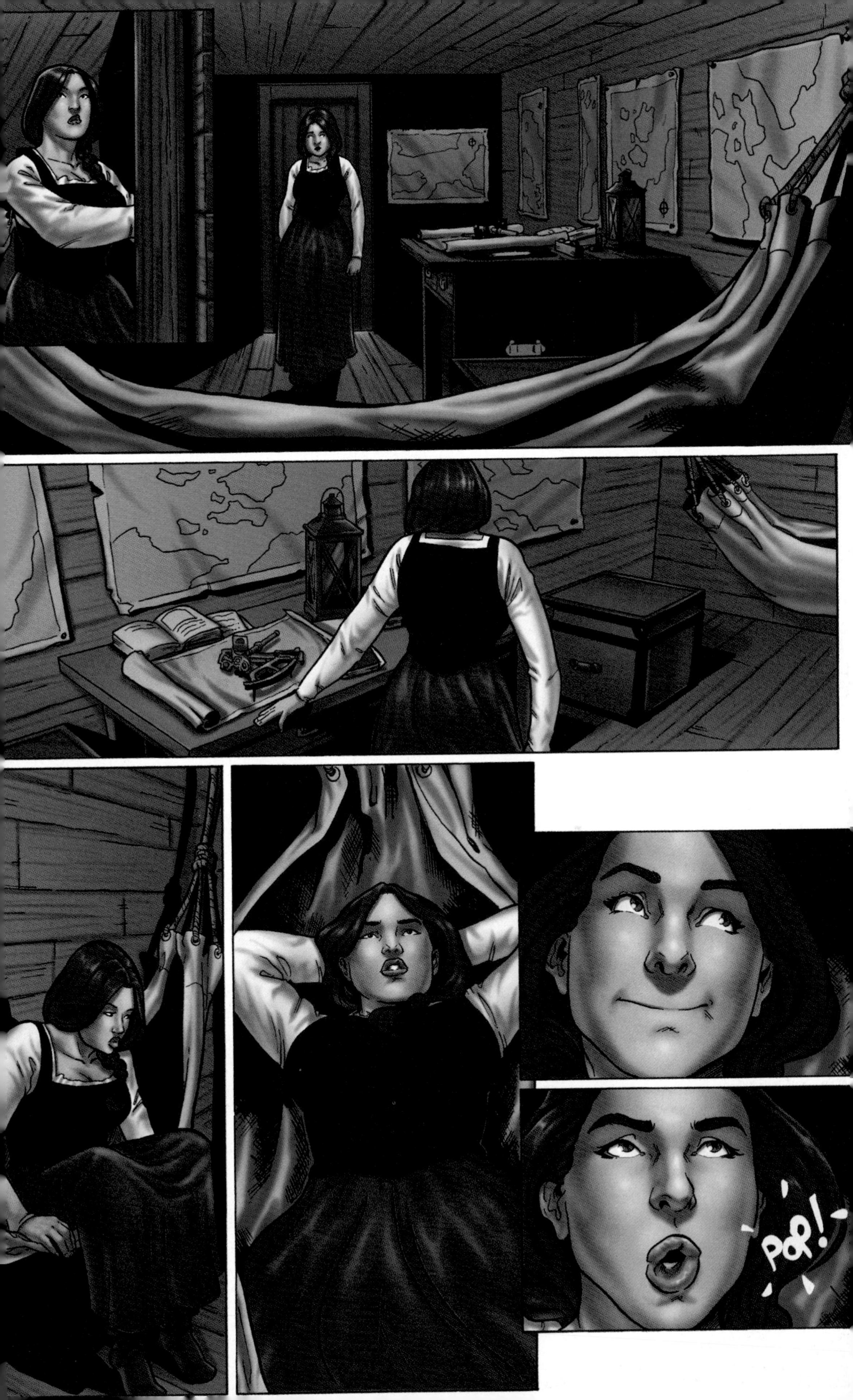
POP!

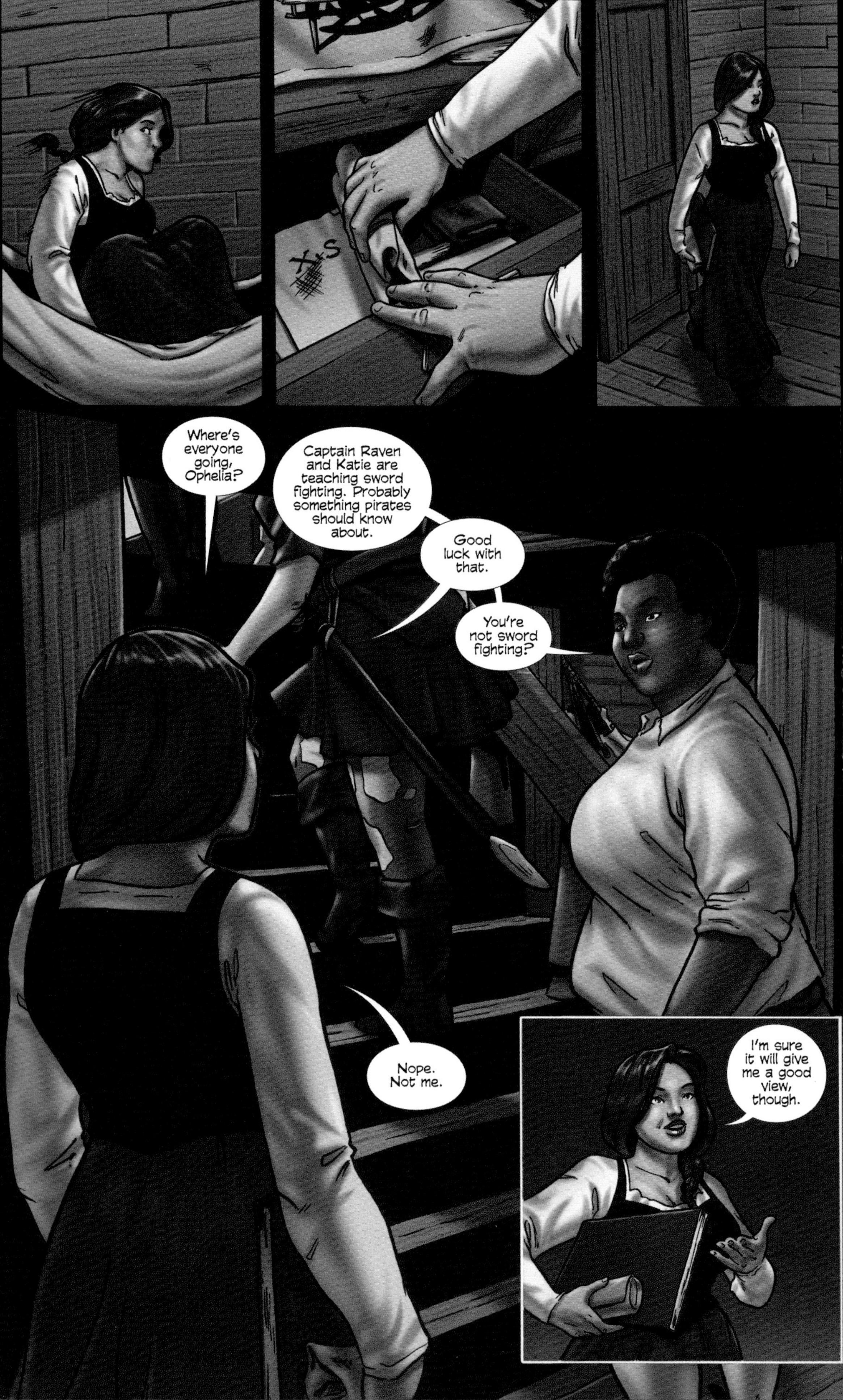
Where's everyone going, Ophelia?
Captain Raven and Katie are teaching sword fighting. Probably something pirates should know about.
Good luck with that.
You're not sword fighting?
Nope. Not me.
I'm sure it will give me a good view, though.

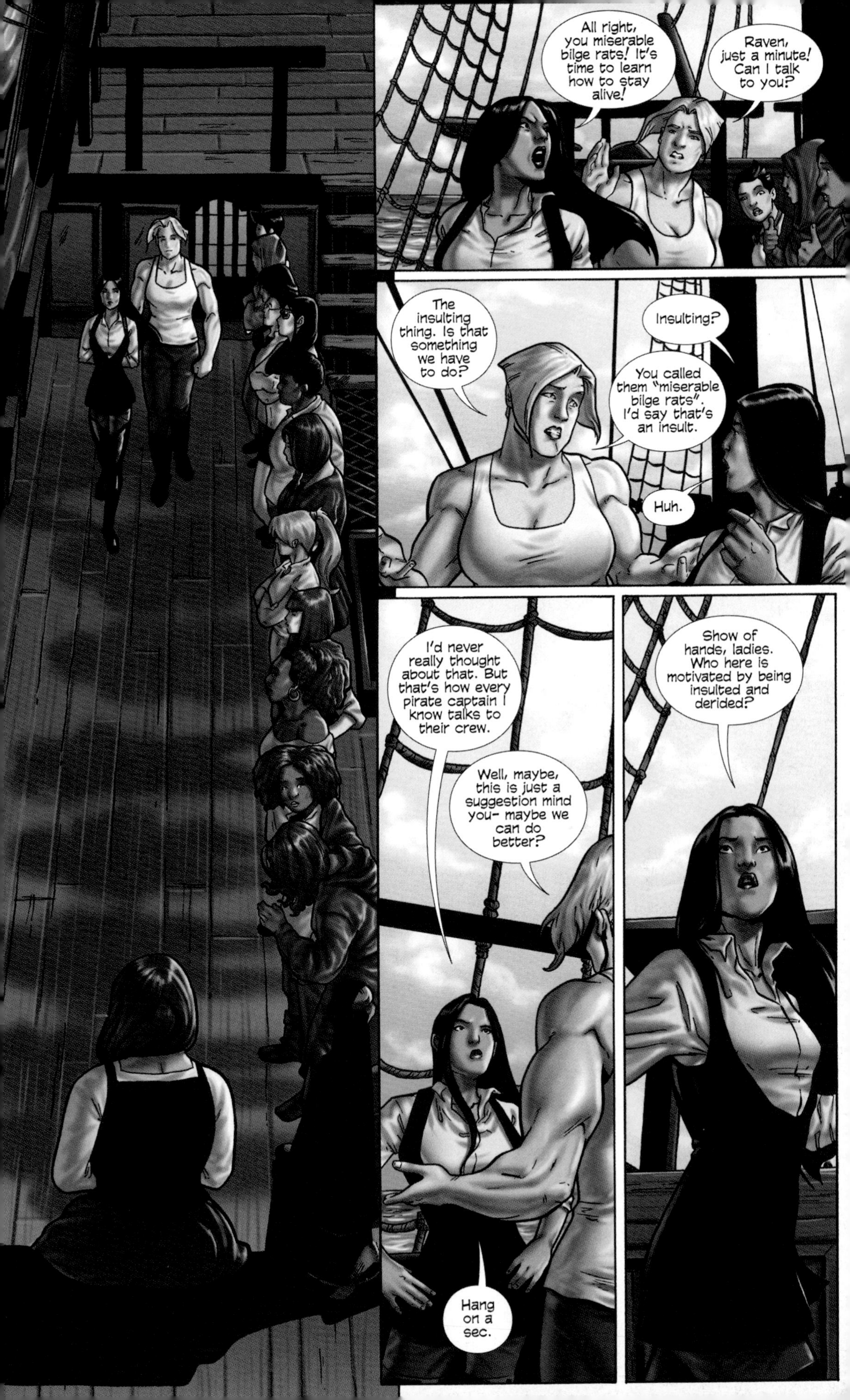
All right, you miserable bilge rats! It's time to learn how to stay alive!
Raven, just a minute! Can I talk to you?
The insulting thing. Is that something we have to do?
Insulting?
You called them "miserable bilge rats". I'd say that's an insult.
Huh.
I'd never really thought about that. But that's how every pirate captain I know talks to their crew.
Well, maybe, this is just a suggestion mind you- maybe we can do better?
Hang on a sec.
Show of hands, ladies. Who here is motivated by being insulted and derided?

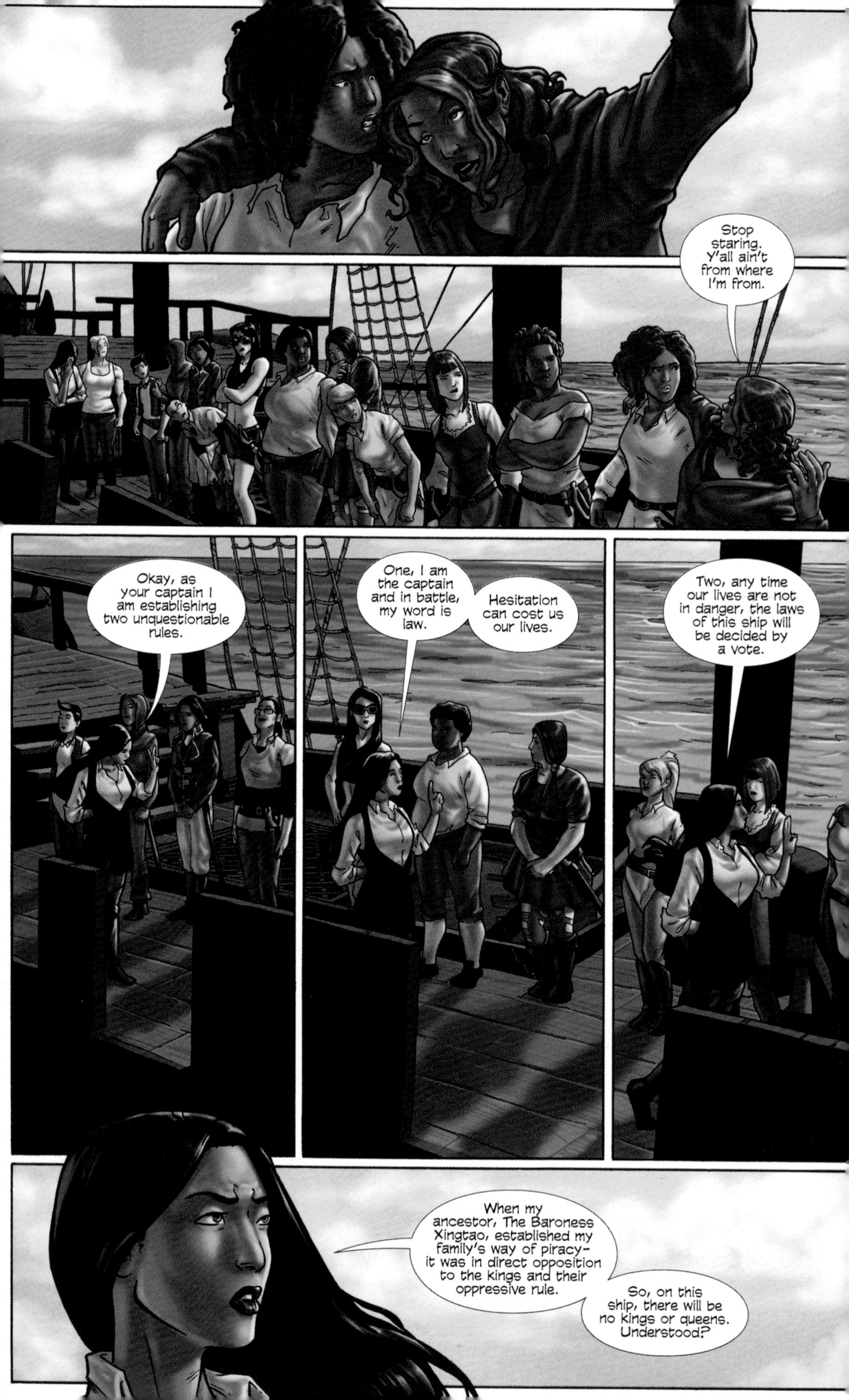

Stop staring. Y'all ain't from where I'm from.
Okay, as your captain I am establishing two unquestionable rules.
One, I am the captain and in battle, my word is law.
Hesitation can cost us our lives.
Two, any time our lives are not in danger, the laws of this ship will be decided by a vote.
When my ancestor, The Baroness Xingtao, established my family's way of piracy- it was in direct opposition to the kings and their oppressive rule.
So, on this ship, there will be no kings or queens. Understood?

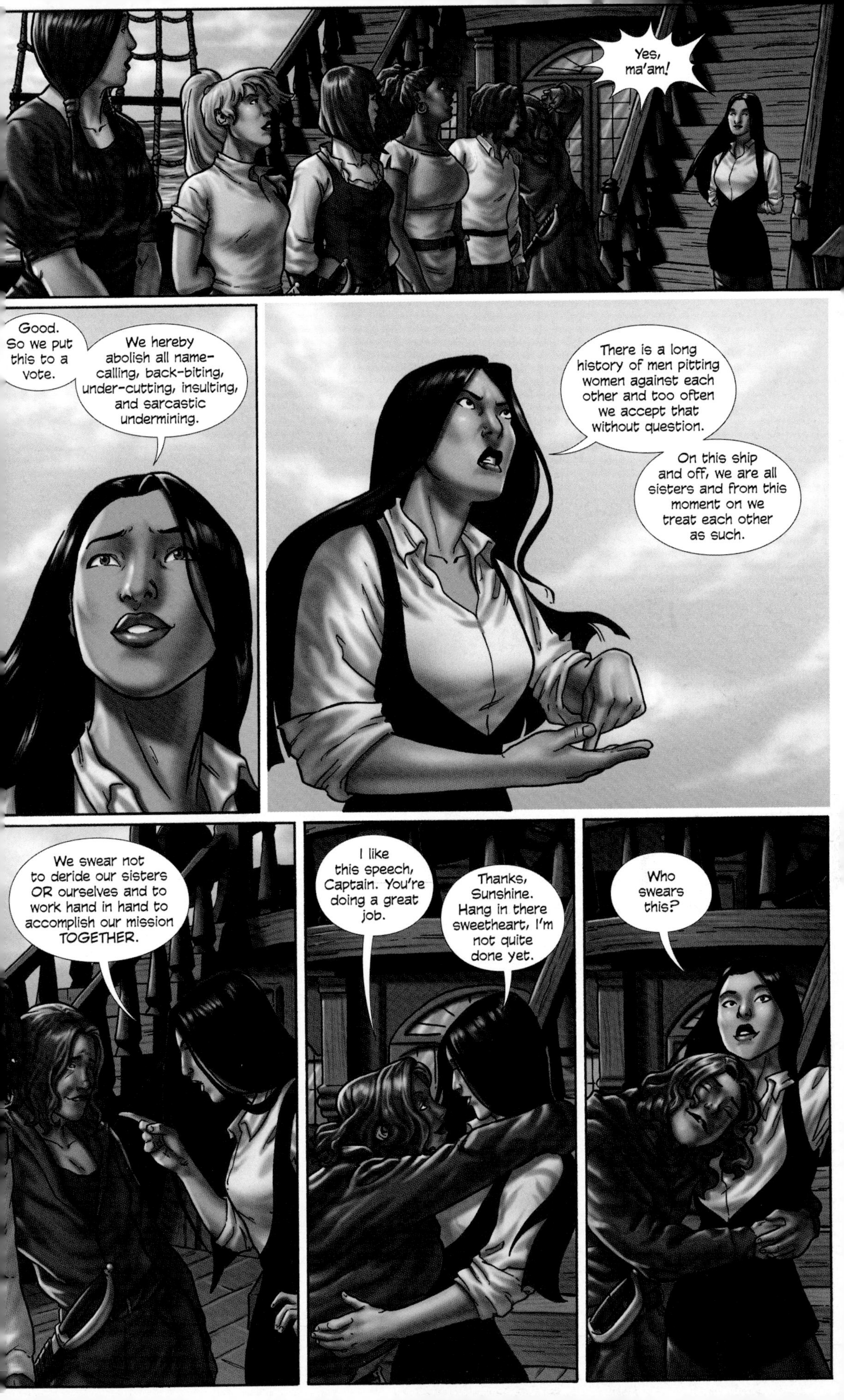
Yes, ma'am!
Good. So we put this to a vote.
We hereby abolish all name-calling, back-biting, under-cutting, insulting, and sarcastic undermining.
There is a long history of men pitting women against each other and too often we accept that without question.
On this ship and off, we are all sisters and from this moment on we treat each other as such.
We swear not to deride our sisters OR ourselves and to work hand in hand to accomplish our mission TOGETHER.
I like this speech, Captain. You're doing a great job.
Thanks, Sunshine. Hang in there sweetheart, I'm not quite done yet.
Who swears this?

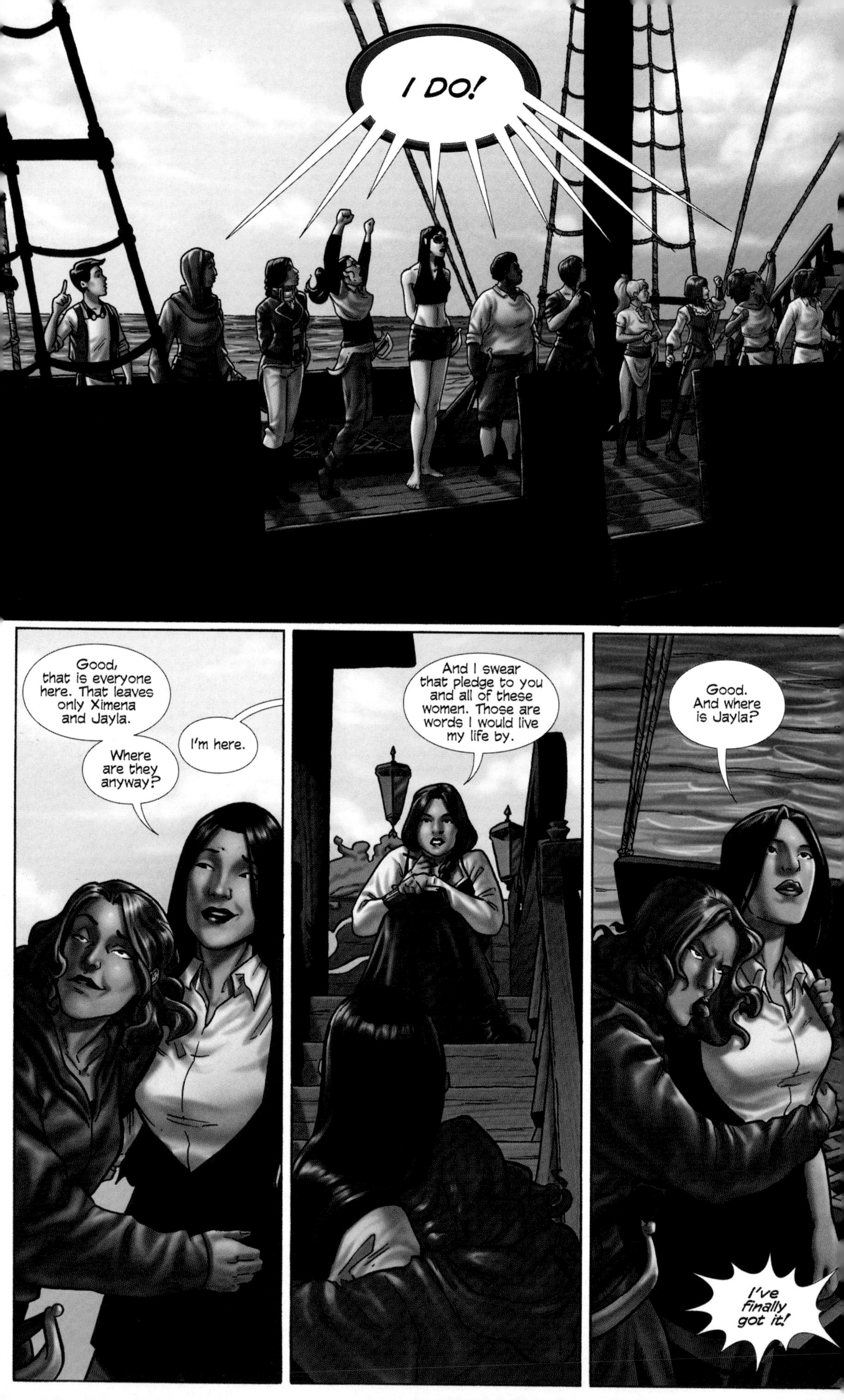
I DO!
Good, that is everyone here. That leaves only Ximena and Jayla.
Where are they anyway?
I'm here.
And I swear that pledge to you and all of these women. Those are words I would live my life by.
Good. And where is Jayla?
I've finally got it!

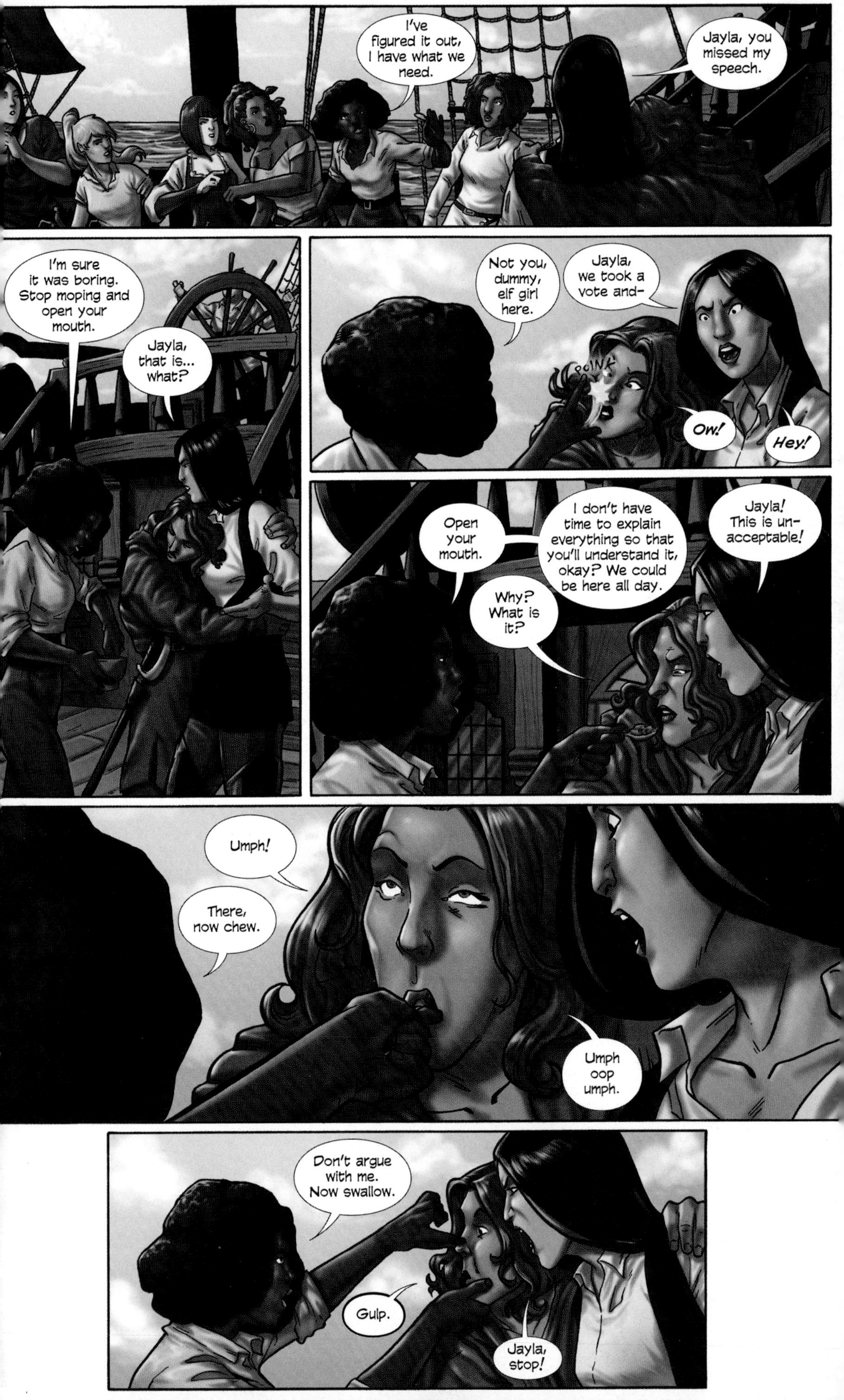
I've figured it out, I have what we need.
Jayla, you missed my speech.
I'm sure it was boring. Stop moping and open your mouth.
Jayla, that is... what?
Not you, dummy, elf girl here.
Jayla, we took a vote and–
BOINK
Ow!
Hey!
Open your mouth.
I don't have time to explain everything so that you'll understand it, okay? We could be here all day.
Jayla! This is un-acceptable!
Why? What is it?
Umph!
There, now chew.
Umph oop umph.
Don't argue with me. Now swallow.
Gulp.
Jayla, stop!

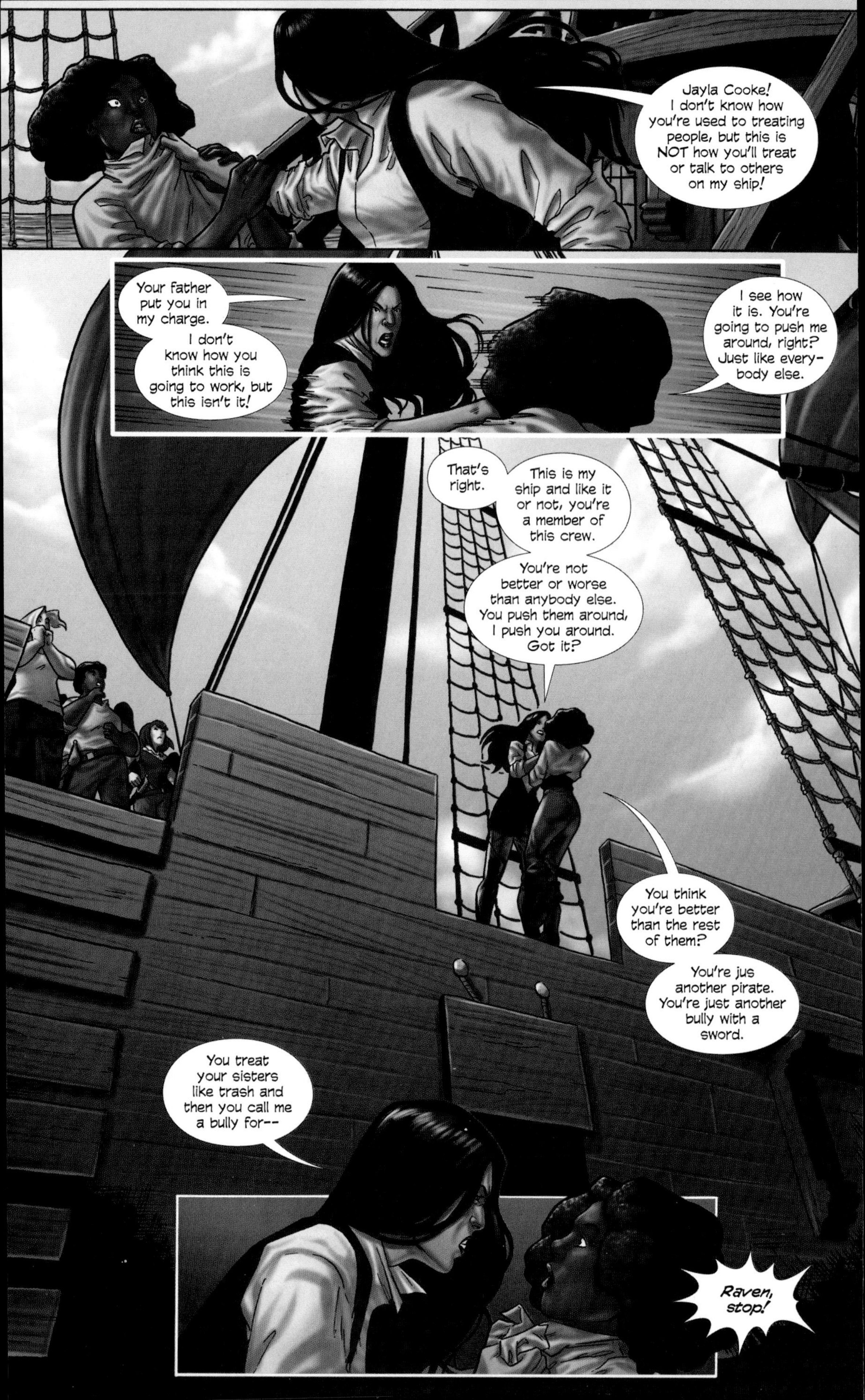
Jayla Cooke! I don't know how you're used to treating people, but this is NOT how you'll treat or talk to others on my ship!
Your father put you in my charge.
I don't know how you think this is going to work, but this isn't it!
I see how it is. You're going to push me around, right? Just like every-body else.
That's right.
This is my ship and like it or not, you're a member of this crew.
You're not better or worse than anybody else. You push them around, I push you around. Got it?
You think you're better than the rest of them?
You're jus another pirate. You're just another bully with a sword.
You treat your sisters like trash and then you call me a bully for--
Raven, stop!

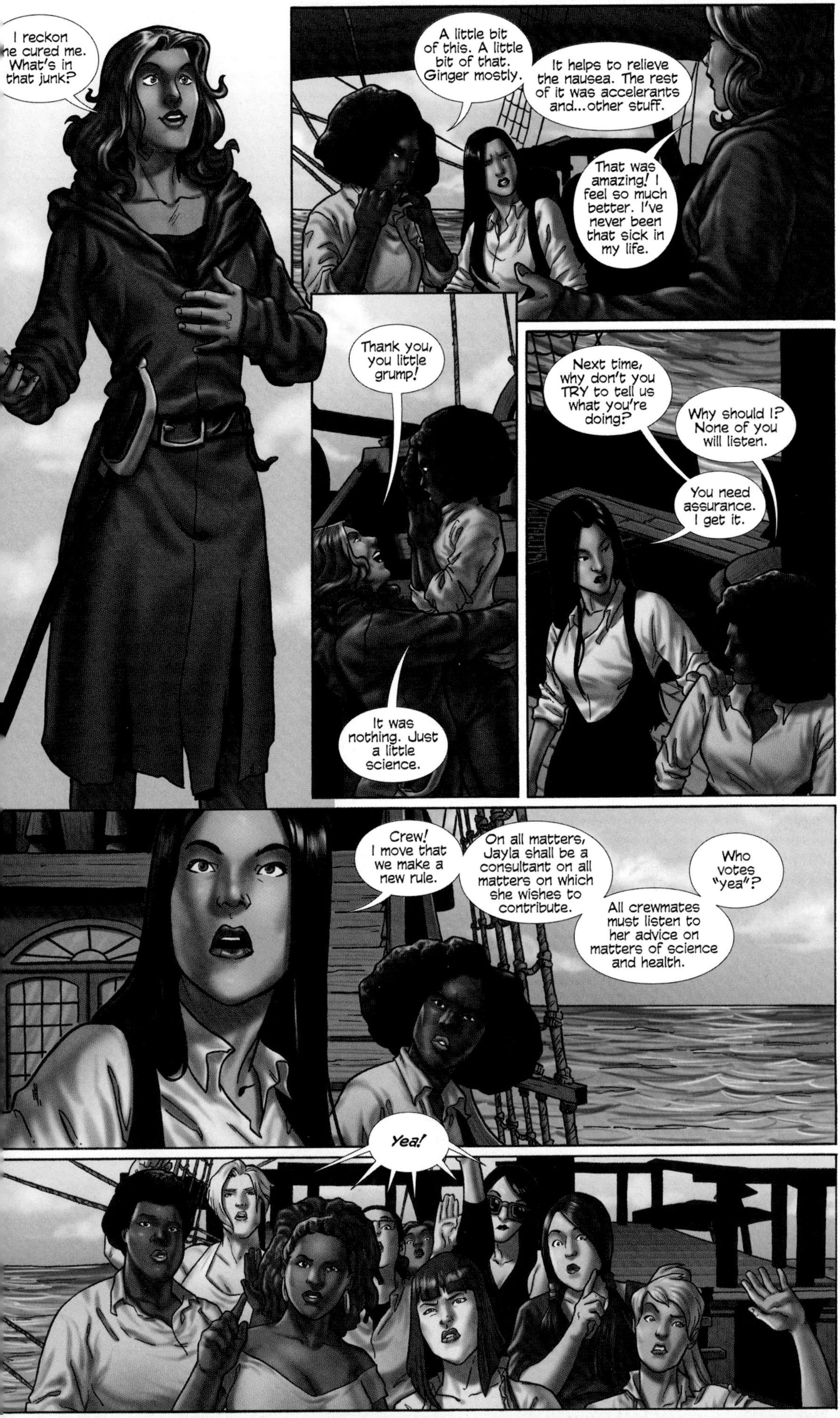
I reckon he cured me. What's in that junk?
A little bit of this. A little bit of that. Ginger mostly.
It helps to relieve the nausea. The rest of it was accelerants and...other stuff.
That was amazing! I feel so much better. I've never been that sick in my life.
Thank you, you little grump!
It was nothing. Just a little science.
Next time, why don't you TRY to tell us what you're doing?
Why should I? None of you will listen.
You need assurance. I get it.
Crew! I move that we make a new rule.
On all matters, Jayla shall be a consultant on all matters on which she wishes to contribute.
All crewmates must listen to her advice on matters of science and health.
Who votes "yea"?
Yea!

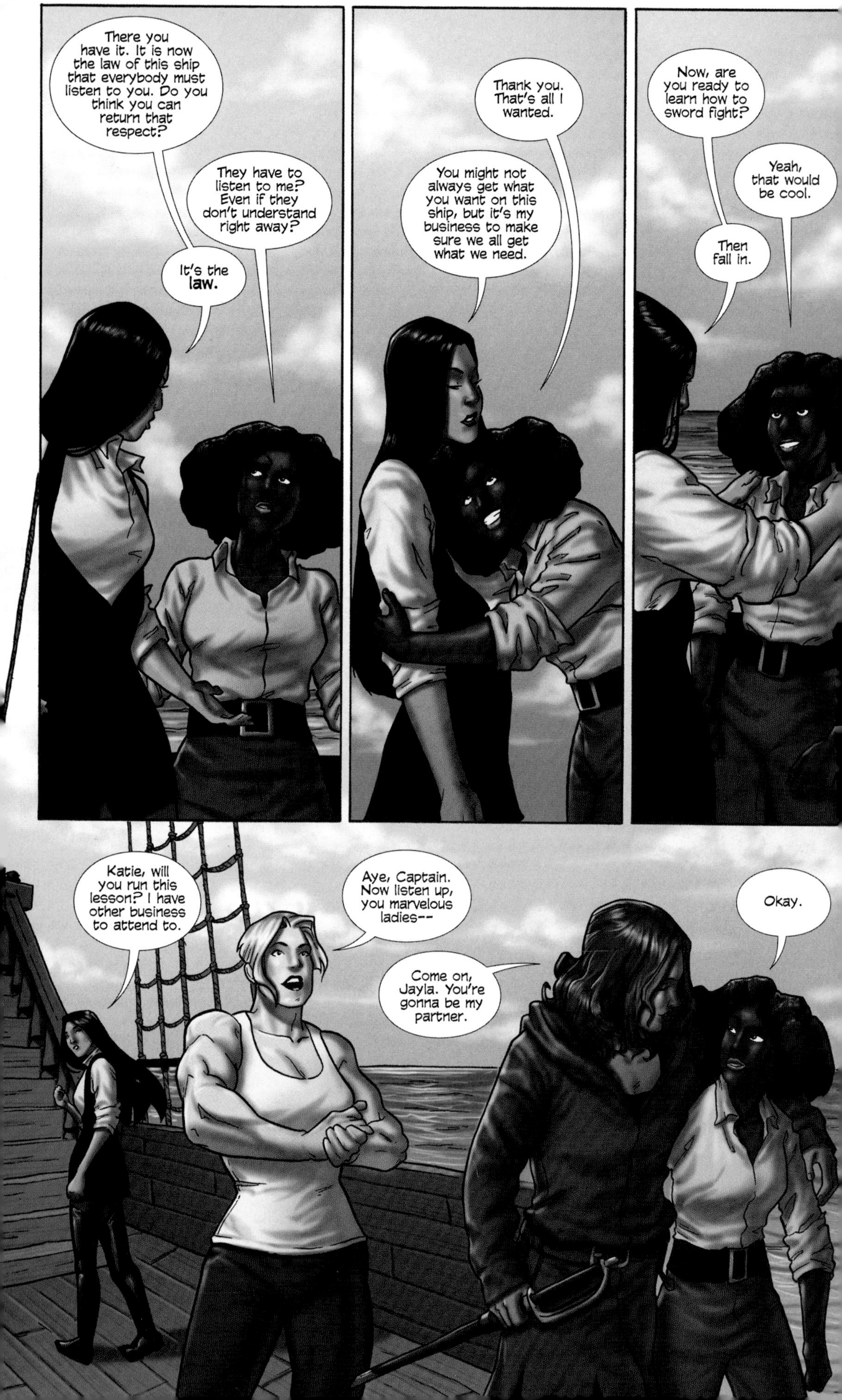

There you have it. It is now the law of this ship that everybody must listen to you. Do you think you can return that respect?
They have to listen to me? Even if they don't understand right away?
It's the law.
Thank you. That's all I wanted.
You might not always get what you want on this ship, but it's my business to make sure we all get what we need.
Now, are you ready to learn how to sword fight?
Yeah, that would be cool.
Then fall in.
Katie, will you run this lesson? I have other business to attend to.
Aye, Captain. Now listen up, you marvelous ladies--
Come on, Jayla. You're gonna be my partner.
Okay.

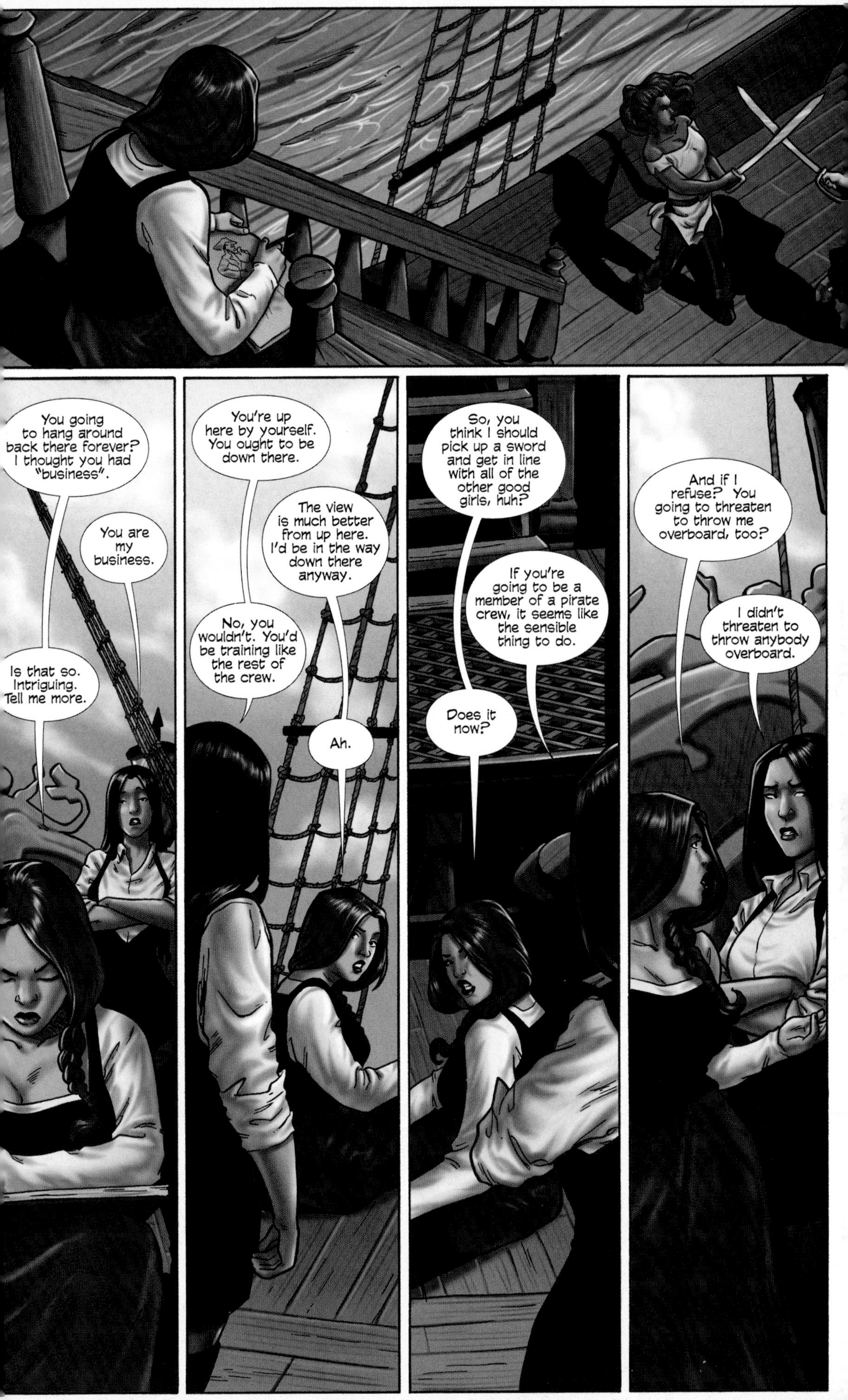
You going to hang around back there forever? I thought you had "business".
You are my business.
Is that so. Intriguing. Tell me more.
You're up here by yourself. You ought to be down there.
The view is much better from up here. I'd be in the way down there anyway.
No, you wouldn't. You'd be training like the rest of the crew.
Ah.
So, you think I should pick up a sword and get in line with all of the other good girls, huh?
If you're going to be a member of a pirate crew, it seems like the sensible thing to do.
Does it now?
And if I refuse? You going to threaten to throw me overboard, too?
I didn't threaten to throw anybody overboard.

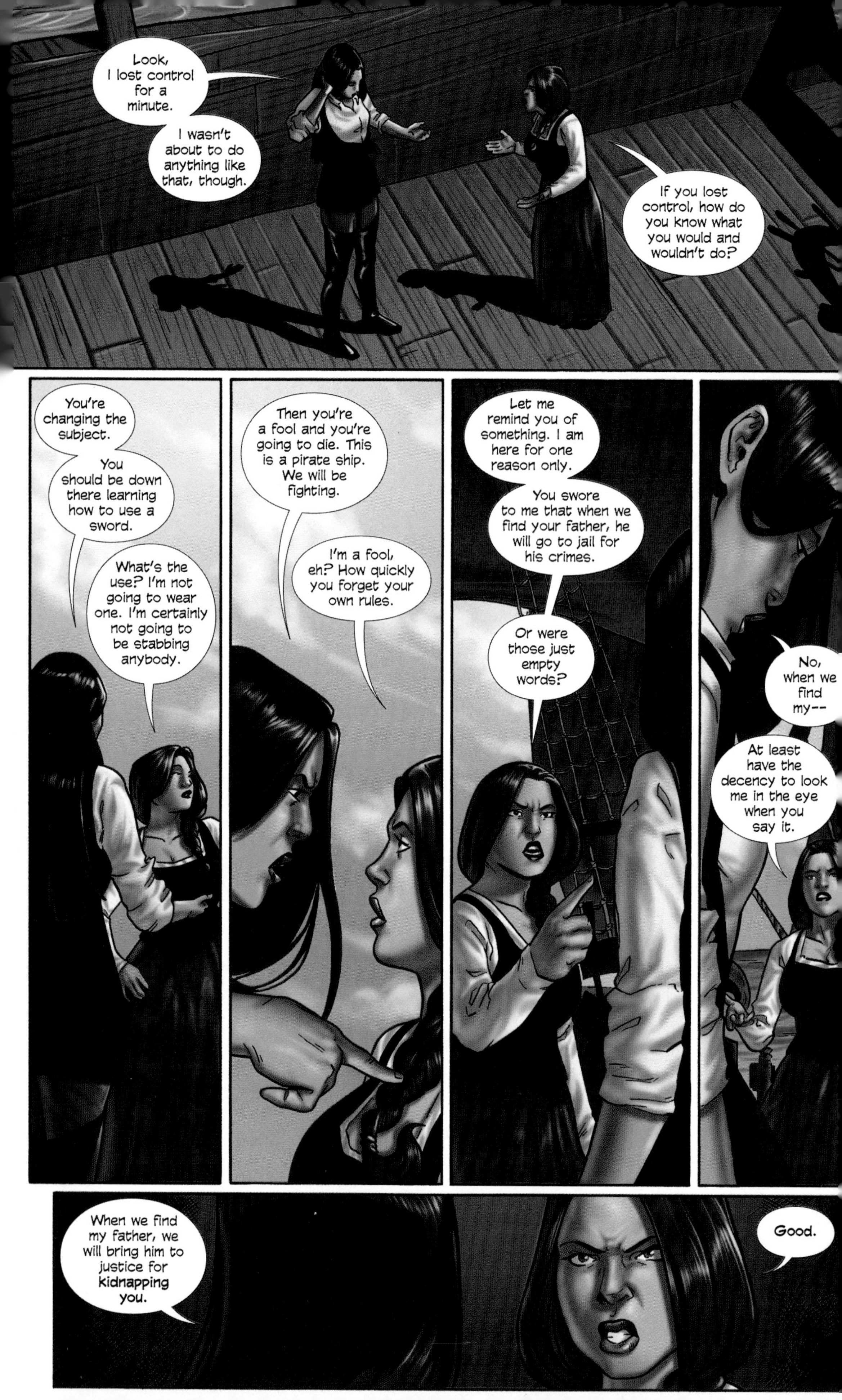
Look, I lost control for a minute.
I wasn't about to do anything like that, though.
If you lost control, how do you know what you would and wouldn't do?
You're changing the subject.
You should be down there learning how to use a sword.
What's the use? I'm not going to wear one. I'm certainly not going to be stabbing anybody.
Then you're a fool and you're going to die. This is a pirate ship. We will be fighting.
I'm a fool, eh? How quickly you forget your own rules.
Let me remind you of something. I am here for one reason only.
You swore to me that when we find your father, he will go to jail for his crimes.
Or were those just empty words?
No, when we find my--
At least have the decency to look me in the eye when you say it.
When we find my father, we will bring him to justice for **kidnapping** you.
Good.

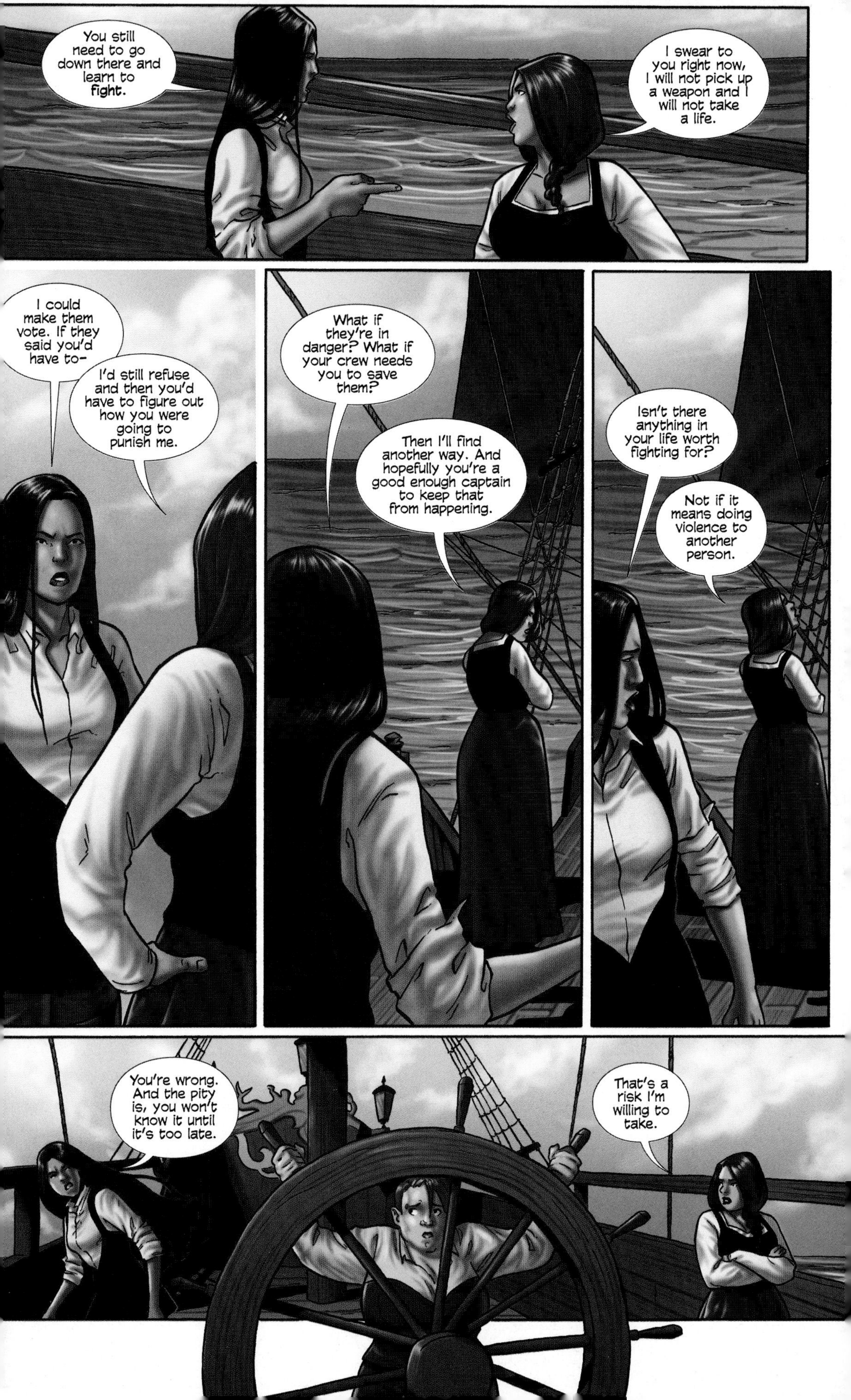
You still need to go down there and learn to fight.
I swear to you right now, I will not pick up a weapon and I will not take a life.
I could make them vote. If they said you'd have to-
I'd still refuse and then you'd have to figure out how you were going to punish me.
What if they're in danger? What if your crew needs you to save them?
Then I'll find another way. And hopefully you're a good enough captain to keep that from happening.
Isn't there anything in your life worth fighting for?
Not if it means doing violence to another person.
You're wrong. And the pity is, you won't know it until it's too late.
That's a risk I'm willing to take.

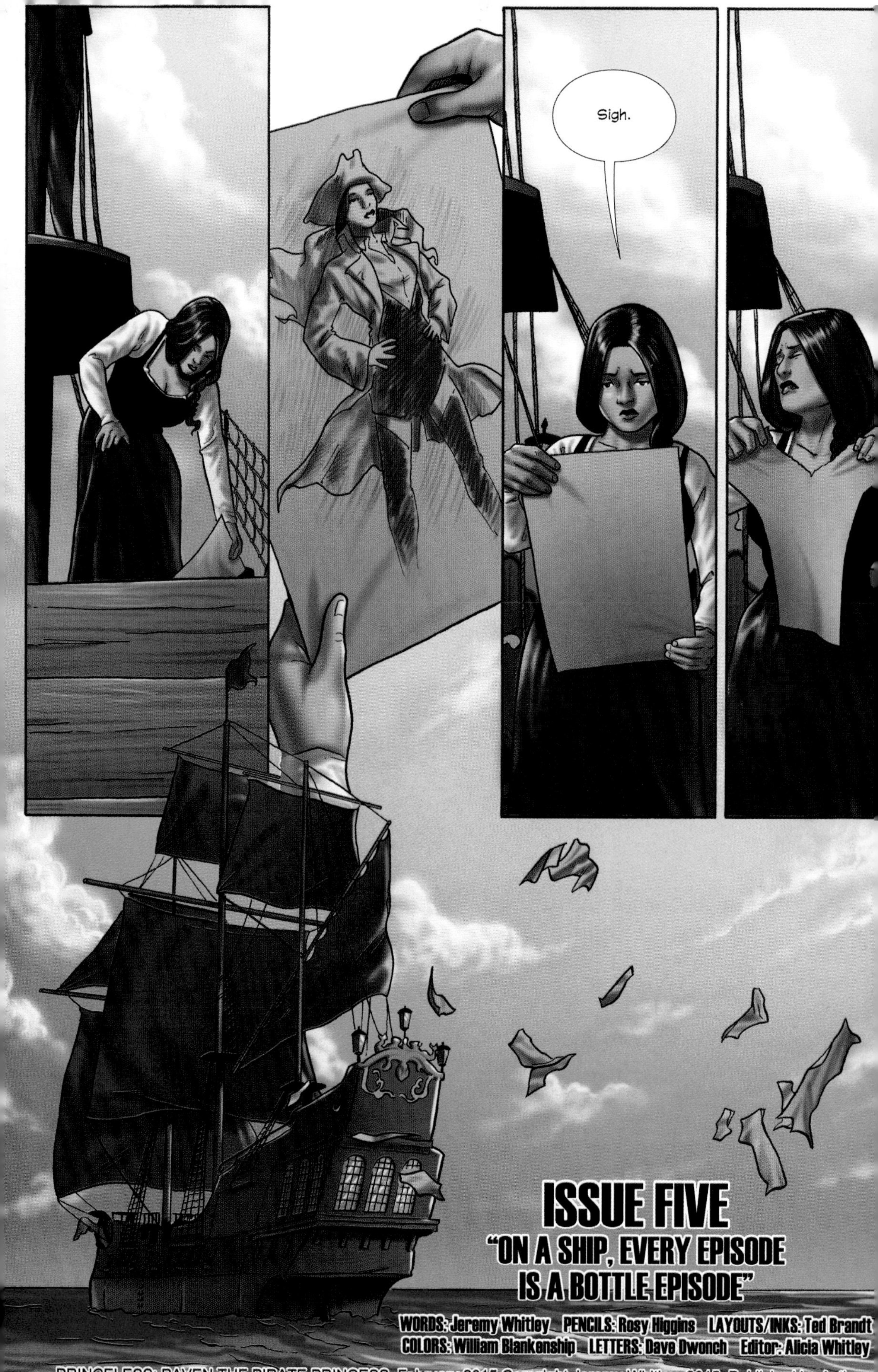
Sigh.

ISSUE FIVE
"ON A SHIP, EVERY EPISODE IS A BOTTLE EPISODE"

WORDS: Jeremy Whitley PENCILS: Rosy Higgins LAYOUTS/INKS: Ted Brandt
COLORS: William Blankenship LETTERS: Dave Dwonch Editor: Alicia Whitley

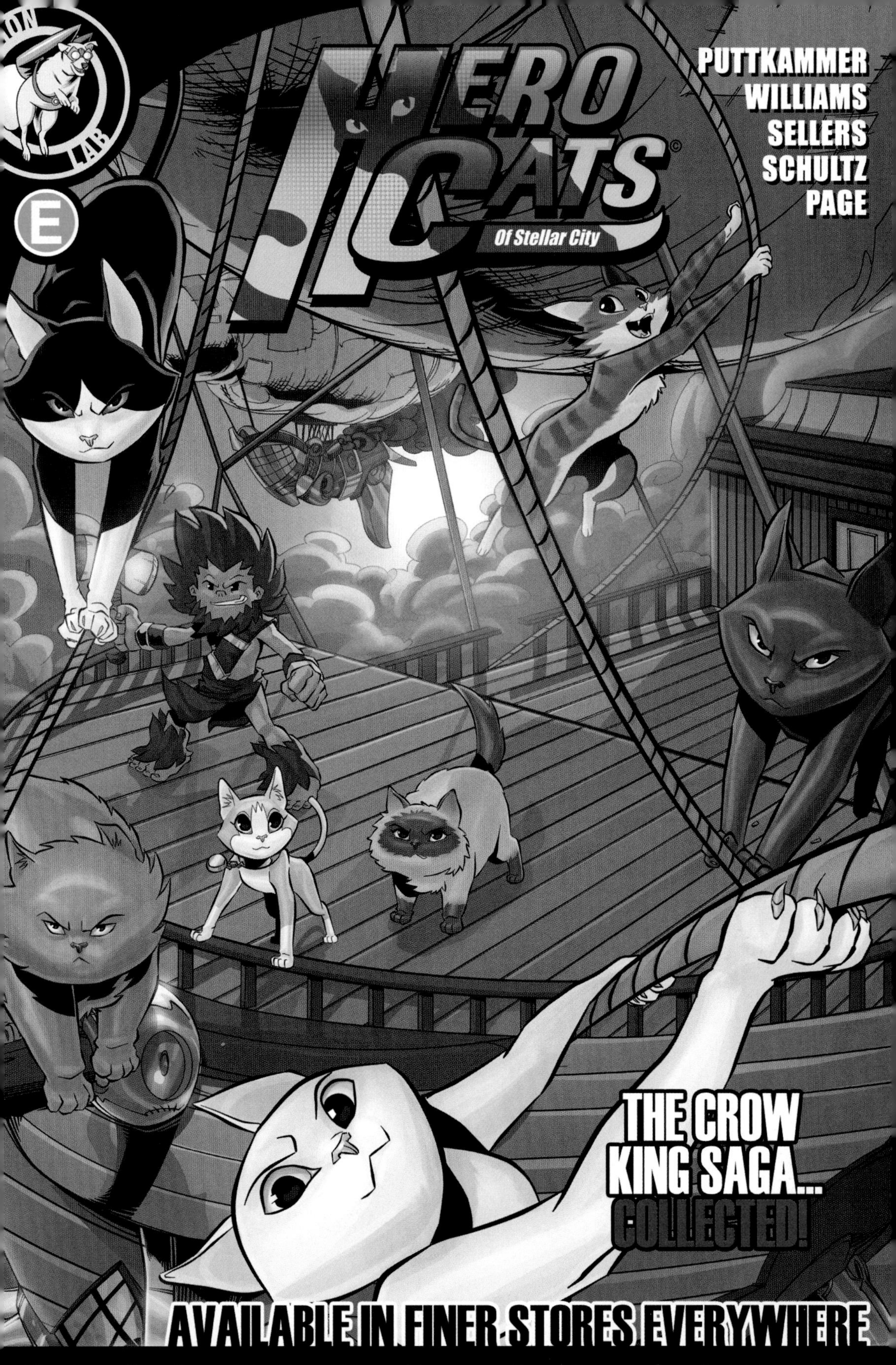
LAB
E
HERO CATS
Of Stellar City
PUTTKAMMER
WILLIAMS
SELLERS
SCHULTZ
PAGE
THE CROW KING SAGA...
COLLECTED!
AVAILABLE IN FINER STORES EVERYWHERE

The stunning conclusion to the most innovative crime noir in comics! Will Cyrus solve
Michael's murder? Will Michael finally get the peace he deserves? If you think you know
how the story ends, you are DEAD WRONG.

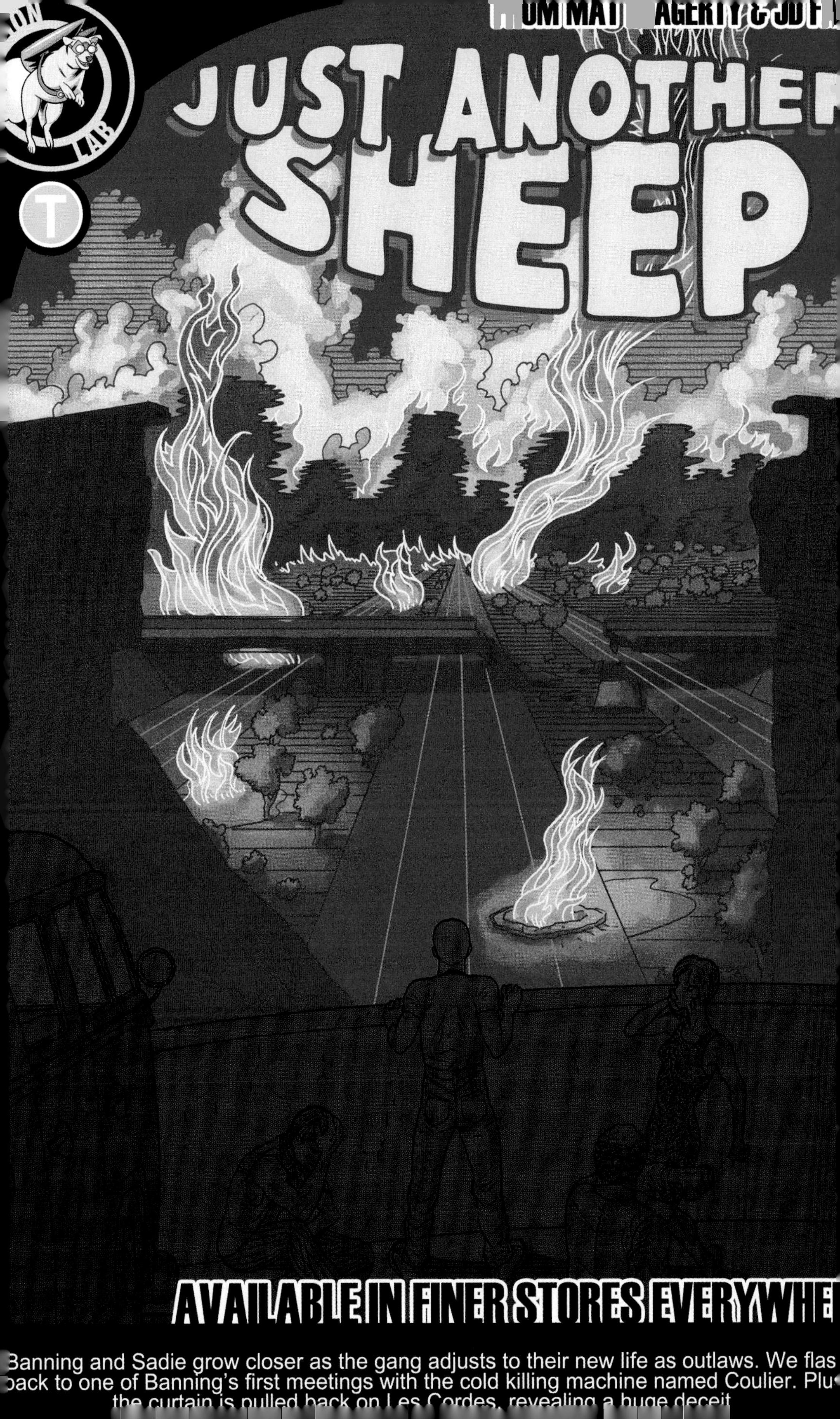
LAB
T
JUST ANOTHE
SHEEP
AVAILABLE IN FINER STORES EVERYWHE
Banning and Sadie grow closer as the gang adjusts to their new life as outlaws. We flas
back to one of Banning's first meetings with the cold killing machine named Coulier. Plu

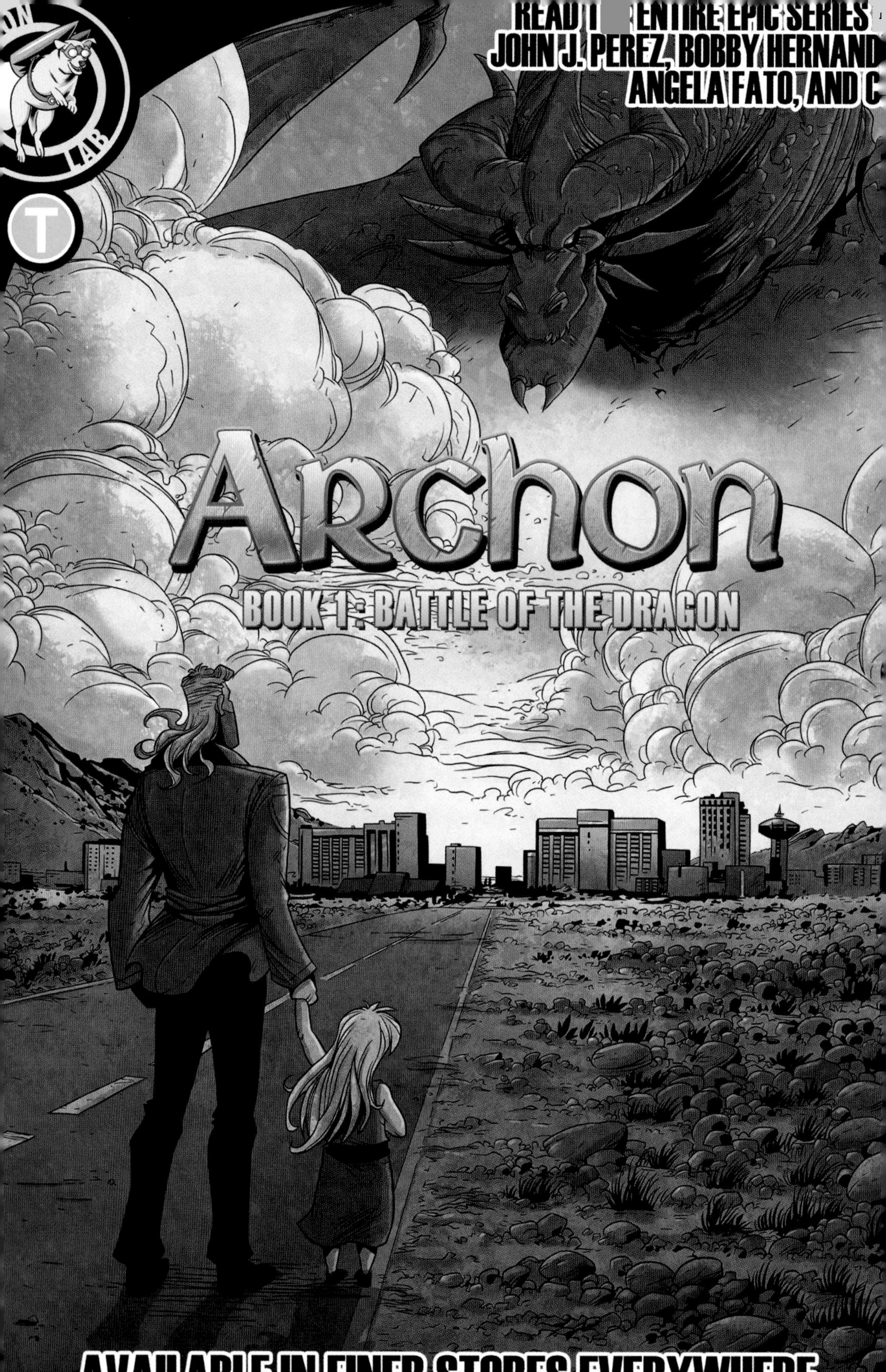
READ T ENTIRE EPIC SERIES
JOHN J. PEREZ, BOBBY HERNAND
ANGELA FATO, AND C
LAB
Archon
BOOK 1: BATTLE OF THE DRAGON
AVAILABLE IN FINER STORES EVERYWHERE

n 1981 Las Vegas is changing. The Mafia is being pushed out and Big Corporations are moving in. But something mysterious is taking up residency. Gareth Thompson, the rchon's new chief of security, will soon discover a mythical new world hidden behind the guise of a fantasy themed Hotel and Casino. Collects the adventure of ARCHON #1-5

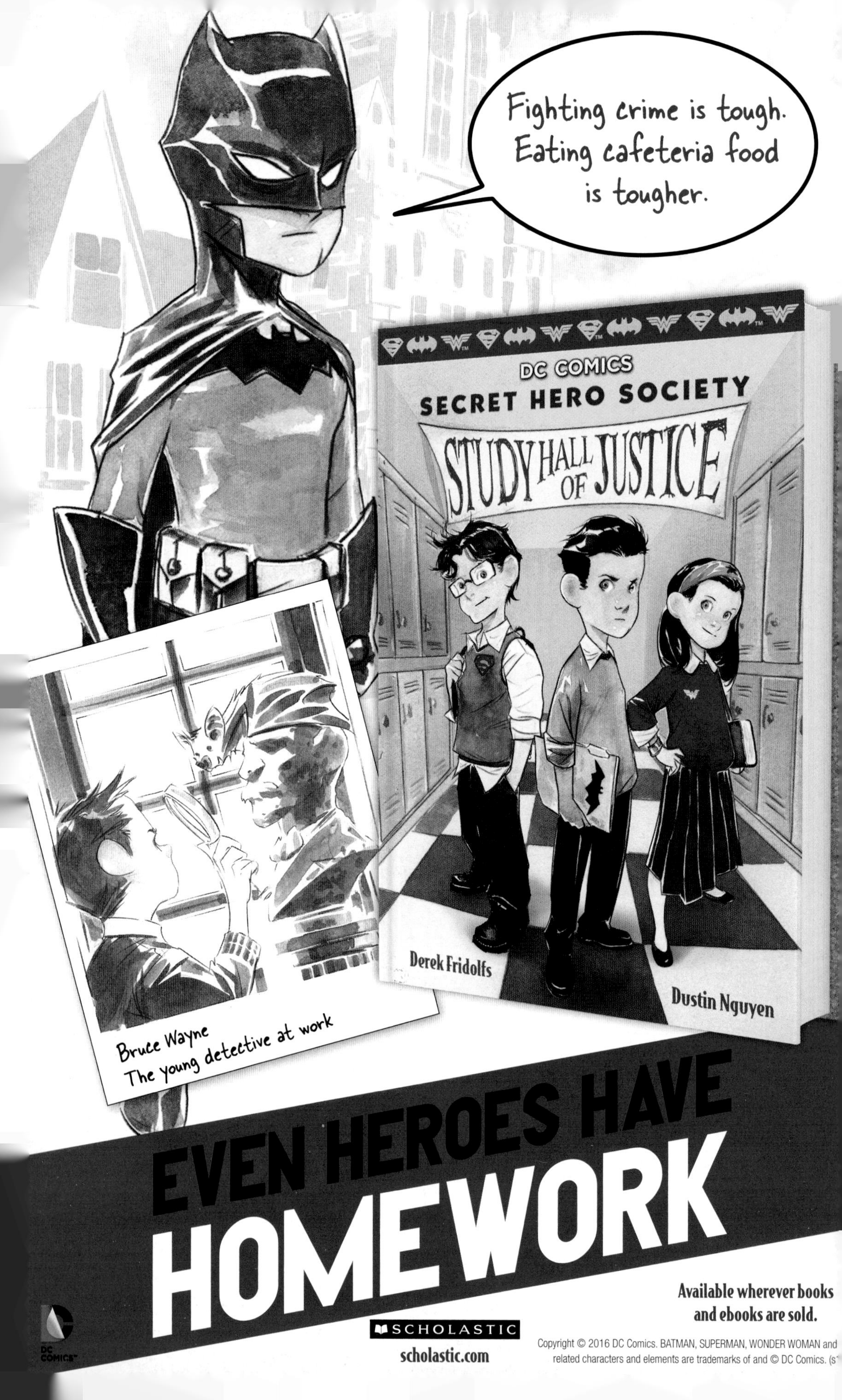

Fighting crime is tough. Eating cafeteria food is tougher.
DC COMICS
SECRET HERO SOCIETY
STUDY HALL OF JUSTICE
Derek Fridolfs
Dustin Nguyen
Bruce Wayne
The young detective at work
EVEN HEROES HAVE
HOMEWORK
Available wherever books and ebooks are sold.
SCHOLASTIC
scholastic.com
DC COMICS
Copyright © 2016 DC Comics. BATMAN, SUPERMAN, WONDER WOMAN and related characters and elements are trademarks of and © DC Comics. (s

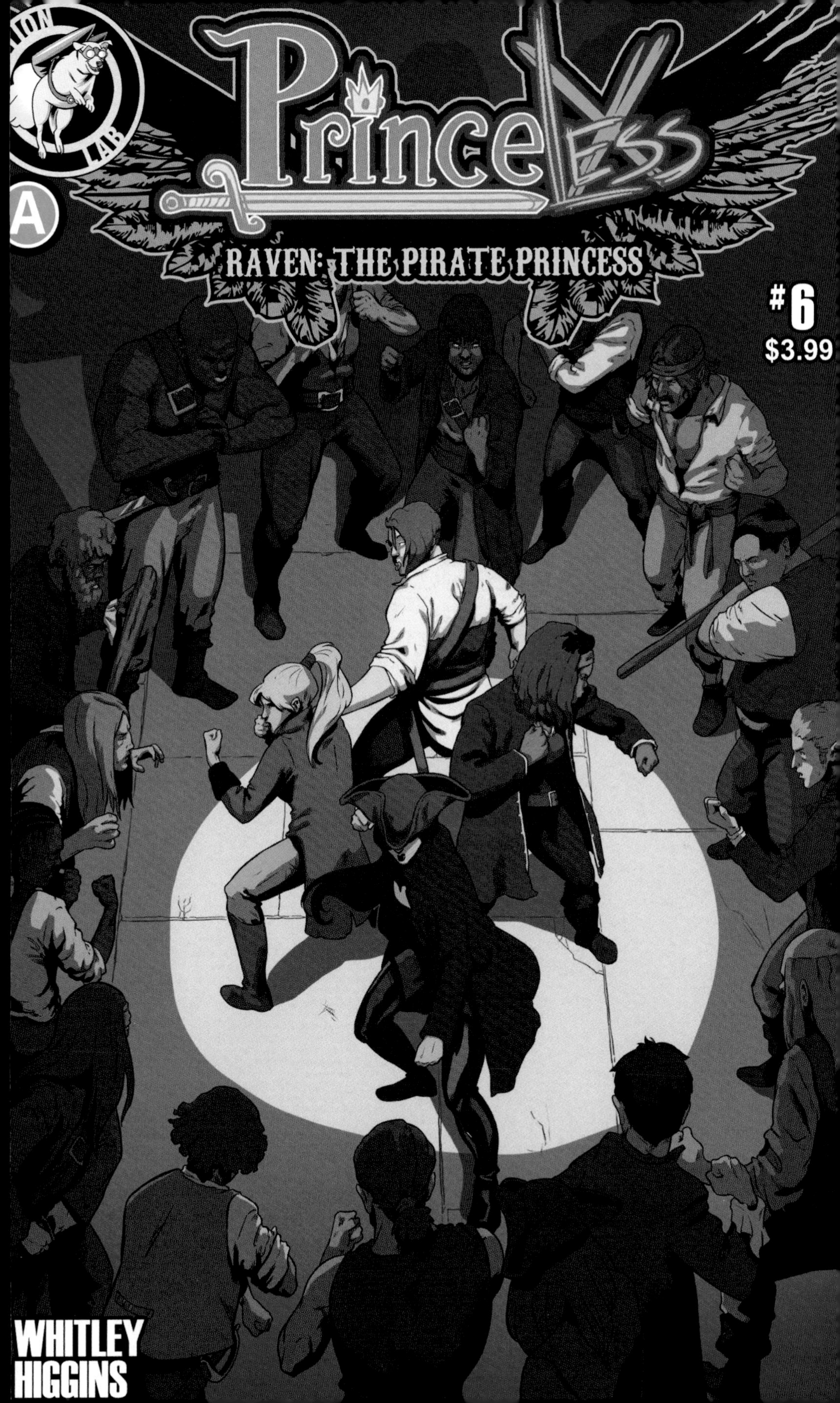

Princeless
RAVEN: THE PIRATE PRINCESS
#6
$3.99
WHITLEY
HIGGINS

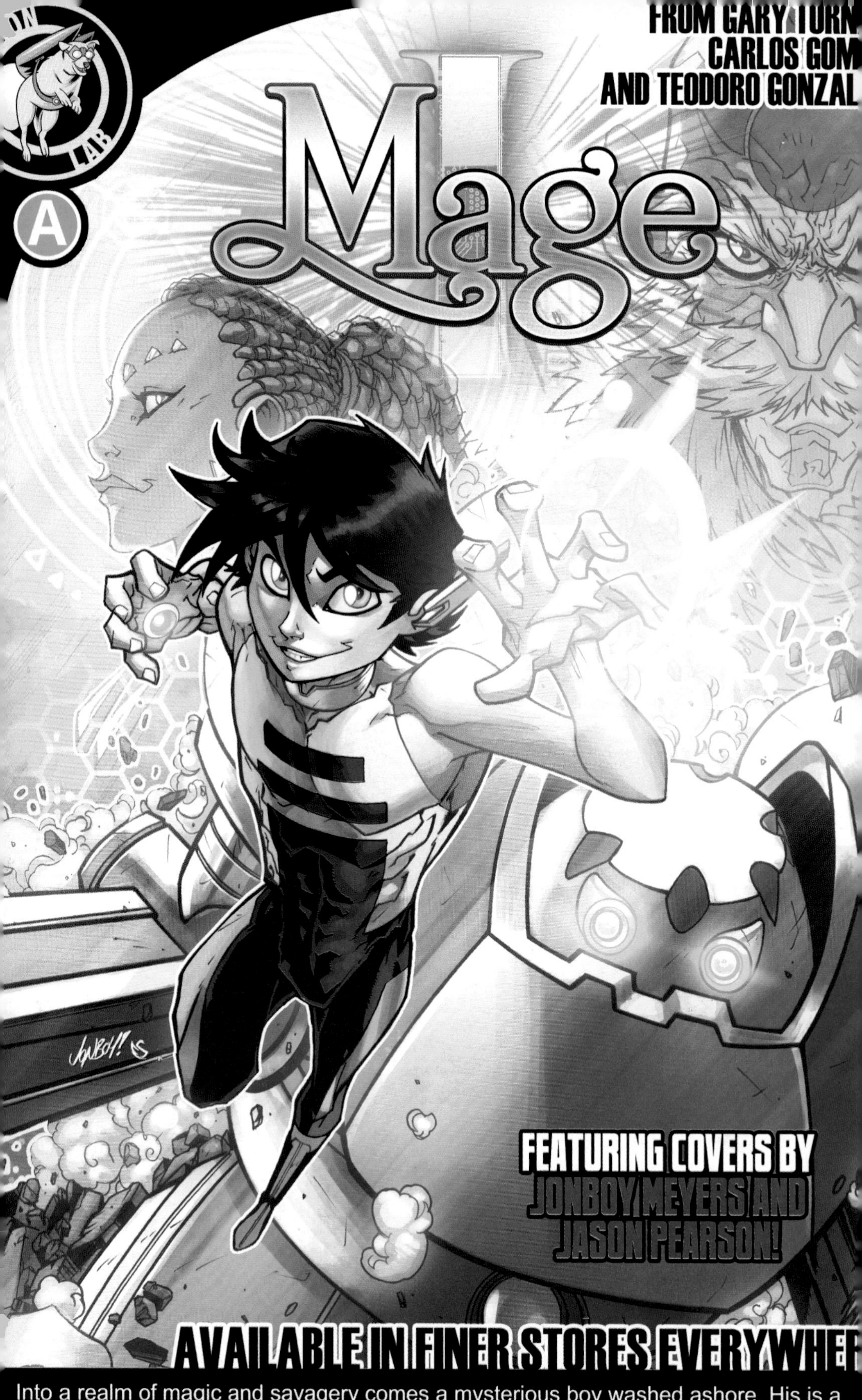
FROM GARY TURN
CARLOS GOM
AND TEODORO GONZAL
Mage
A
FEATURING COVERS BY
JONBOY MEYERS AND
JASON PEARSON!
AVAILABLE IN FINER STORES EVERYWHE

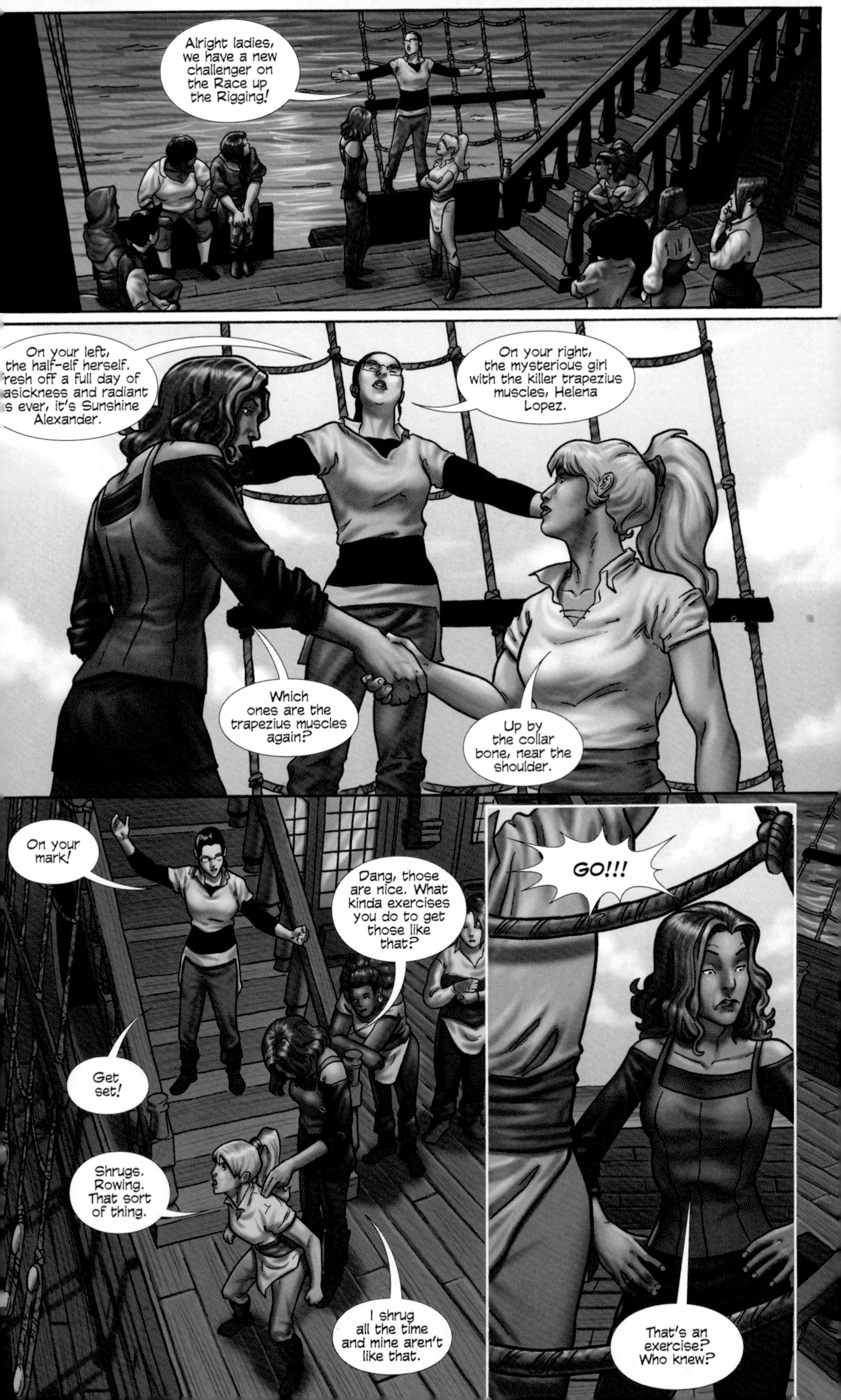

Alright ladies, we have a new challenger on the Race up the Rigging!
On your left, the half-elf herself. resh off a full day of asickness and radiant s ever, it's Sunshine Alexander.
On your right, the mysterious girl with the killer trapezius muscles, Helena Lopez.
Which ones are the trapezius muscles again?
Up by the collar bone, near the shoulder.
On your mark!
Dang, those are nice. What kinda exercises you do to get those like that?
Get set!
Shrugs. Rowing. That sort of thing.
I shrug all the time and mine aren't like that.
GO!!!
That's an exercise? Who knew?

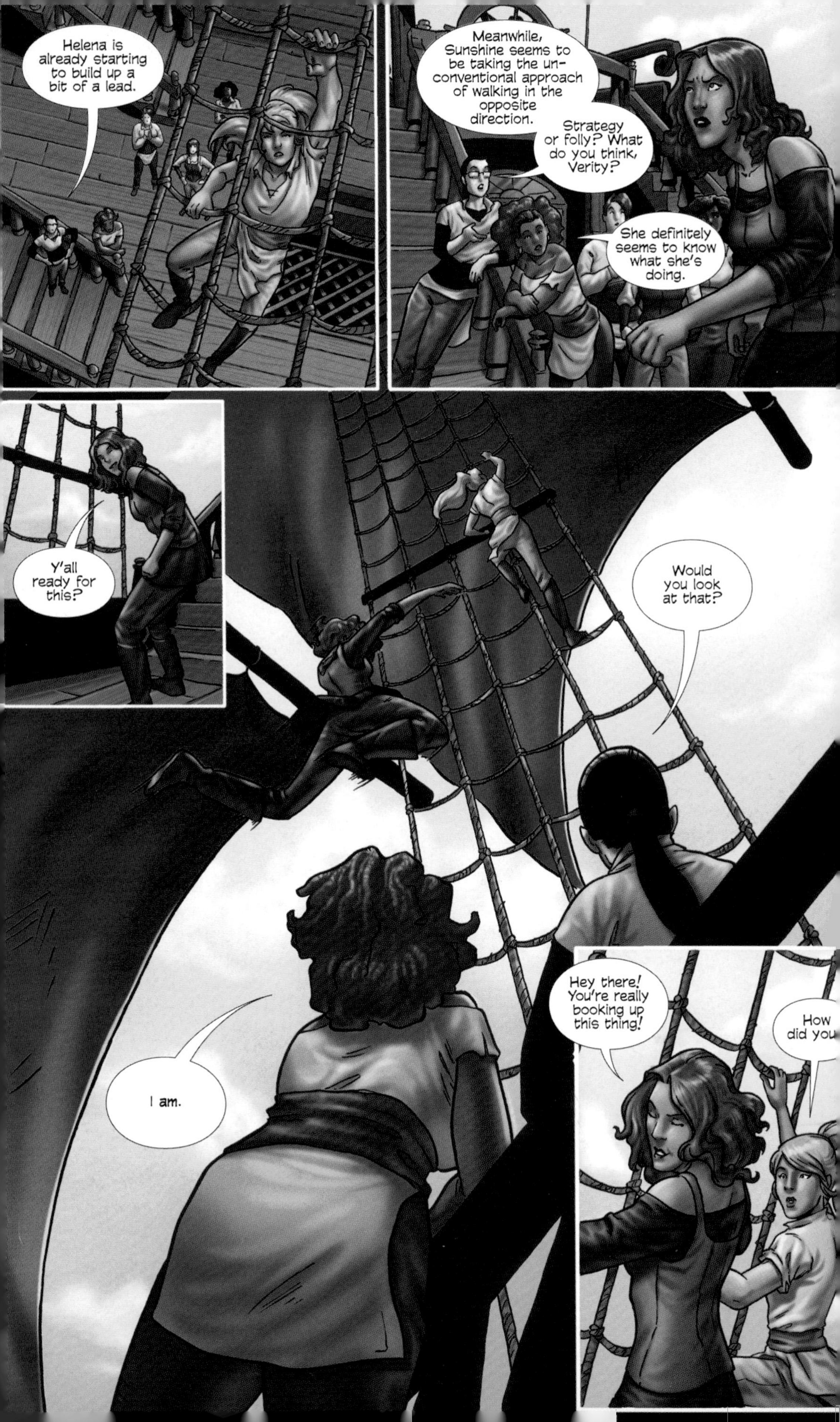

Helena is already starting to build up a bit of a lead.
Meanwhile, Sunshine seems to be taking the un-conventional approach of walking in the opposite direction.
Strategy or folly? What do you think, Verity?
She definitely seems to know what she's doing.
Y'all ready for this?
Would you look at that?
I am.
Hey there! You're really booking up this thing!
How did you

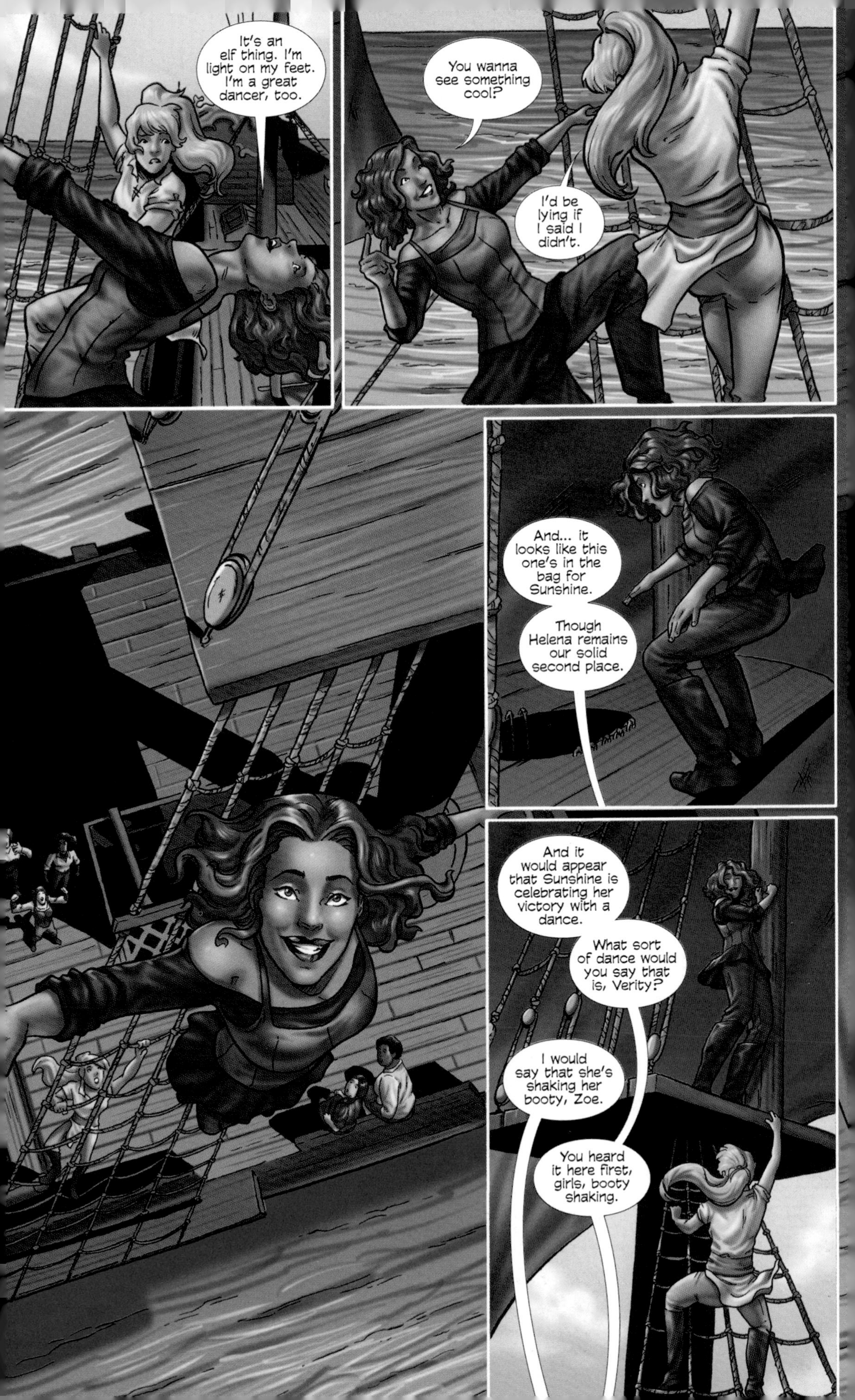
It's an elf thing. I'm light on my feet. I'm a great dancer, too.
You wanna see something cool?
I'd be lying if I said I didn't.
And... it looks like this one's in the bag for Sunshine.
Though Helena remains our solid second place.
And it would appear that Sunshine is celebrating her victory with a dance.
What sort of dance would you say that is, Verity?
I would say that she's shaking her booty, Zoe.
You heard it here first, girls, booty shaking.

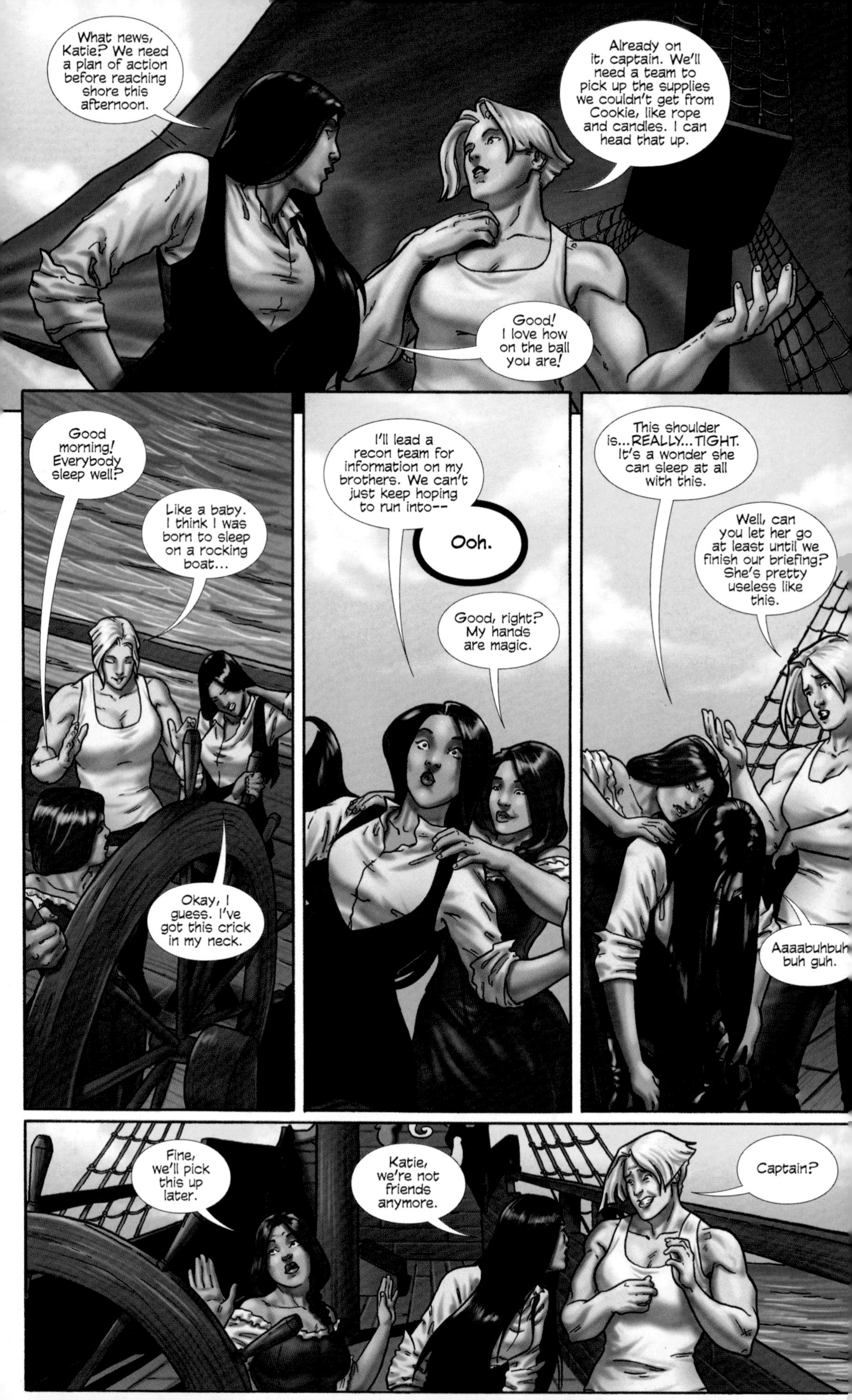
What news, Katie? We need a plan of action before reaching shore this afternoon.
Already on it, captain. We'll need a team to pick up the supplies we couldn't get from Cookie, like rope and candles. I can head that up.
Good! I love how on the ball you are!
Good morning! Everybody sleep well?
Like a baby. I think I was born to sleep on a rocking boat...
Okay, I guess. I've got this crick in my neck.
I'll lead a recon team for information on my brothers. We can't just keep hoping to run into--
Ooh.
Good, right? My hands are magic.
This shoulder is...REALLY...TIGHT. It's a wonder she can sleep at all with this.
Well, can you let her go at least until we finish our briefing? She's pretty useless like this.
Aaaabuhbuh buh guh.
Fine, we'll pick this up later.
Katie, we're not friends anymore.
Captain?

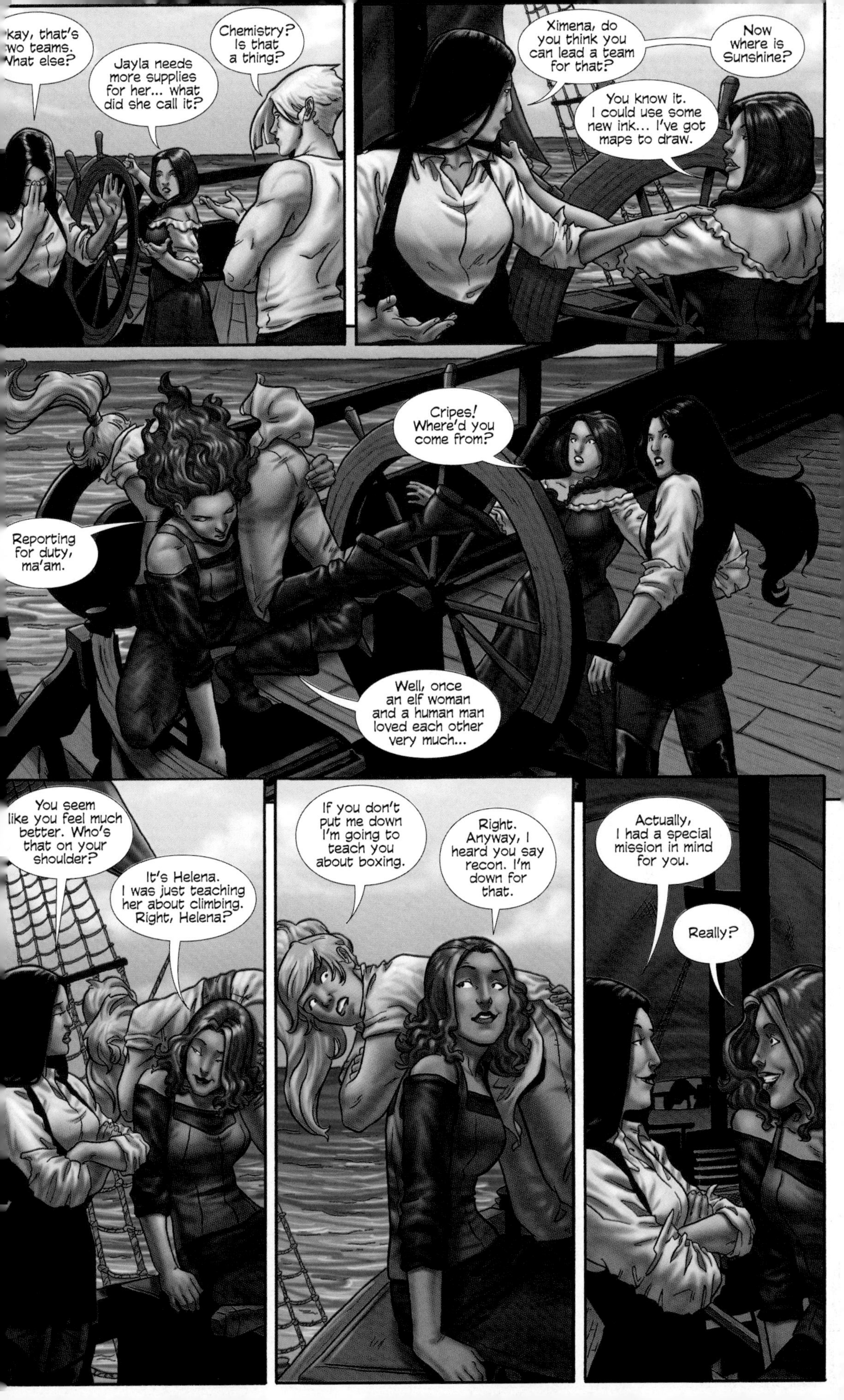

kay, that's
wo teams.
Vhat else?
Jayla needs more supplies for her... what did she call it?
Chemistry? Is that a thing?
Ximena, do you think you can lead a team for that?
Now where is Sunshine?
You know it. I could use some new ink... I've got maps to draw.
Cripes! Where'd you come from?
Reporting for duty, ma'am.
Well, once an elf woman and a human man loved each other very much...
You seem like you feel much better. Who's that on your shoulder?
It's Helena. I was just teaching her about climbing. Right, Helena?
If you don't put me down I'm going to teach you about boxing.
Right. Anyway, I heard you say recon. I'm down for that.
Actually, I had a special mission in mind for you.
Really?

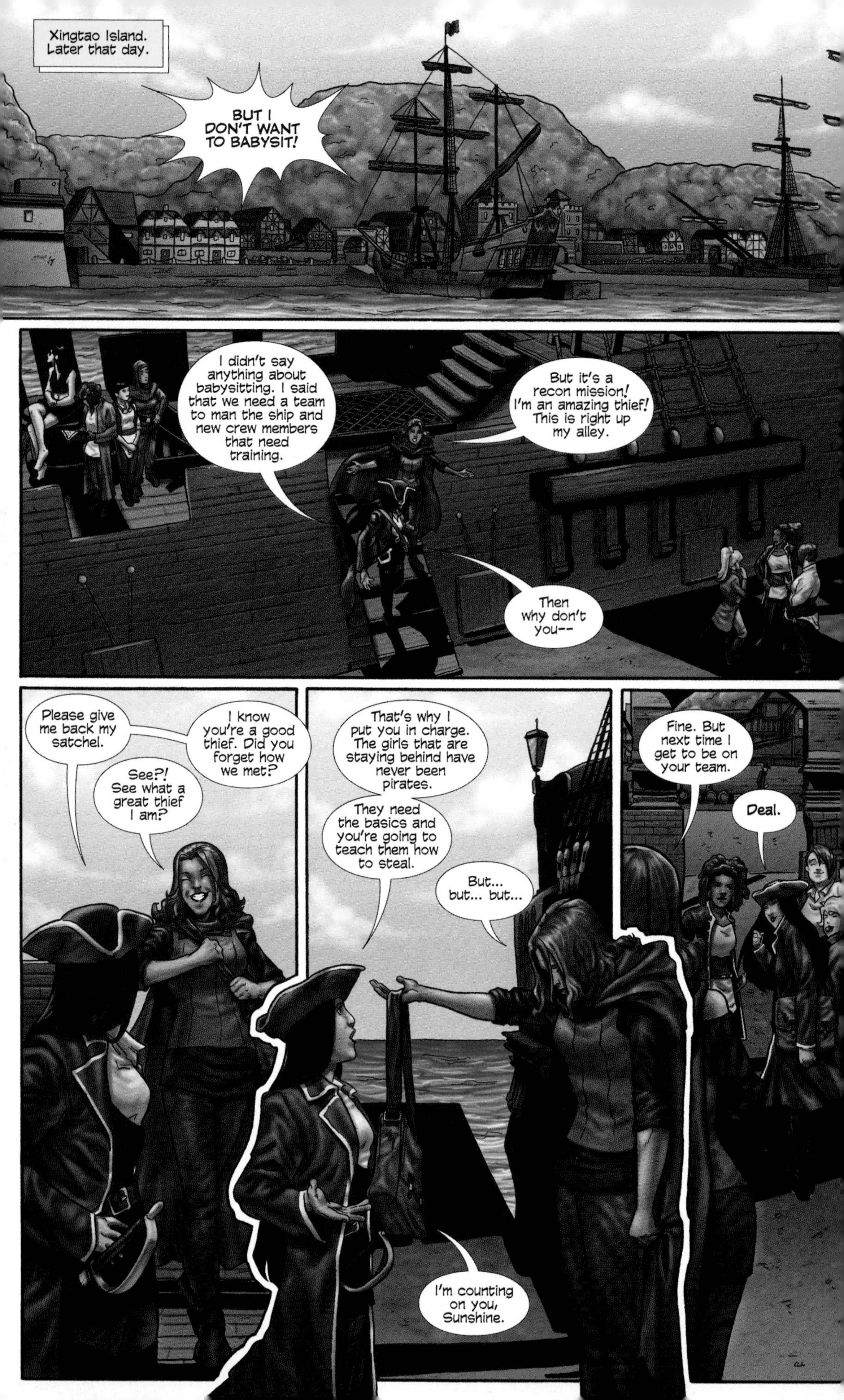
Xingtao Island. Later that day.
BUT I DON'T WANT TO BABYSIT!
I didn't say anything about babysitting. I said that we need a team to man the ship and new crew members that need training.
But it's a recon mission! I'm an amazing thief! This is right up my alley.
Then why don't you--
Please give me back my satchel.
I know you're a good thief. Did you forget how we met?
See?! See what a great thief I am?
That's why I put you in charge. The girls that are staying behind have never been pirates.
They need the basics and you're going to teach them how to steal.
But... but... but...
I'm counting on you, Sunshine.
Fine. But next time I get to be on your team.
Deal.

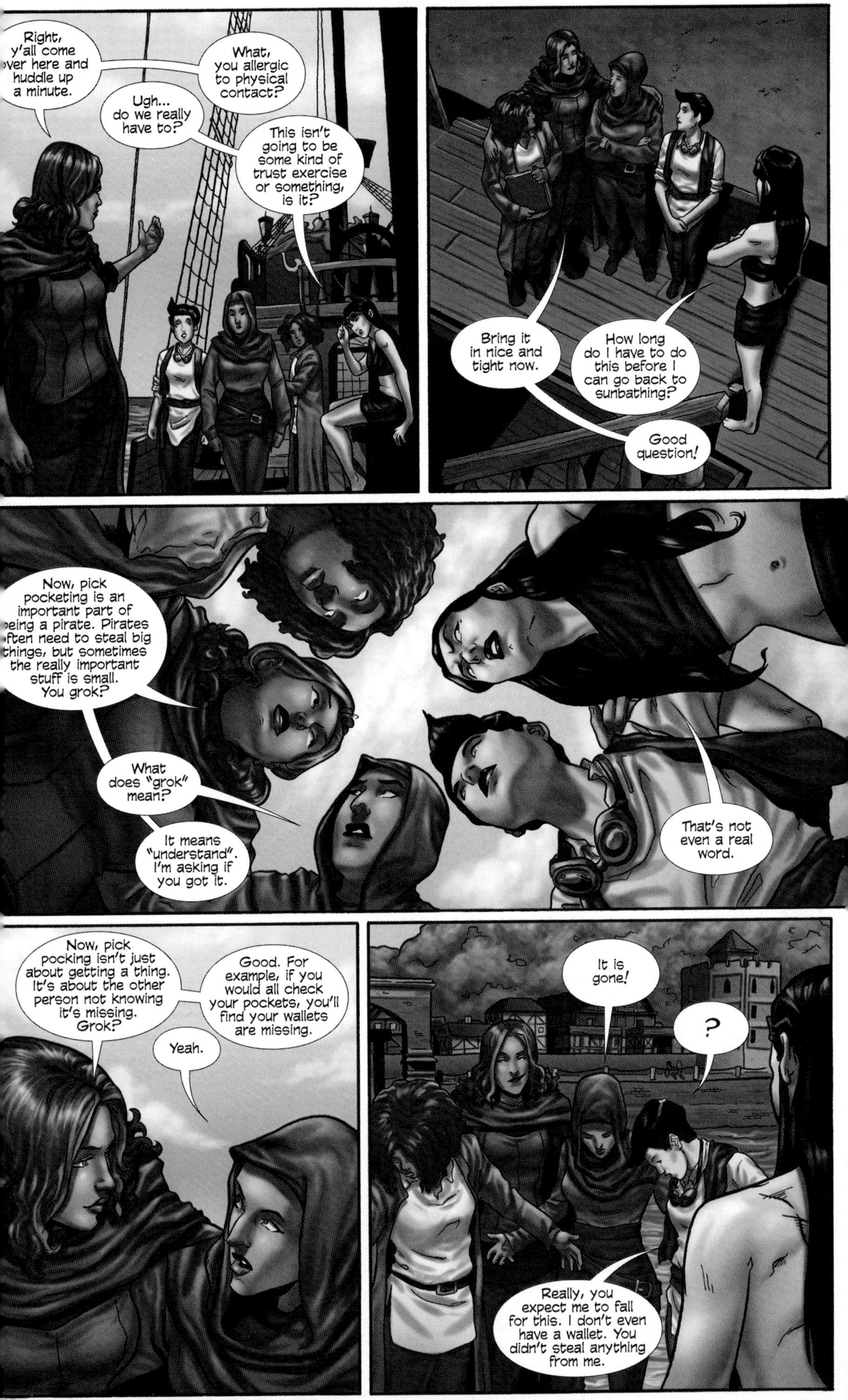
Right, y'all come over here and huddle up a minute.
What, you allergic to physical contact?
Ugh... do we really have to?
This isn't going to be some kind of trust exercise or something, is it?
Bring it in nice and tight now.
How long do I have to do this before I can go back to sunbathing?
Good question!
Now, pick pocketing is an important part of being a pirate. Pirates often need to steal big things, but sometimes the really important stuff is small. You grok?
What does "grok" mean?
It means "understand". I'm asking if you got it.
That's not even a real word.
Now, pick pocking isn't just about getting a thing. It's about the other person not knowing it's missing. Grok?
Yeah.
Good. For example, if you would all check your pockets, you'll find your wallets are missing.
It is gone!
?
Really, you expect me to fall for this. I don't even have a wallet. You didn't steal anything from me.

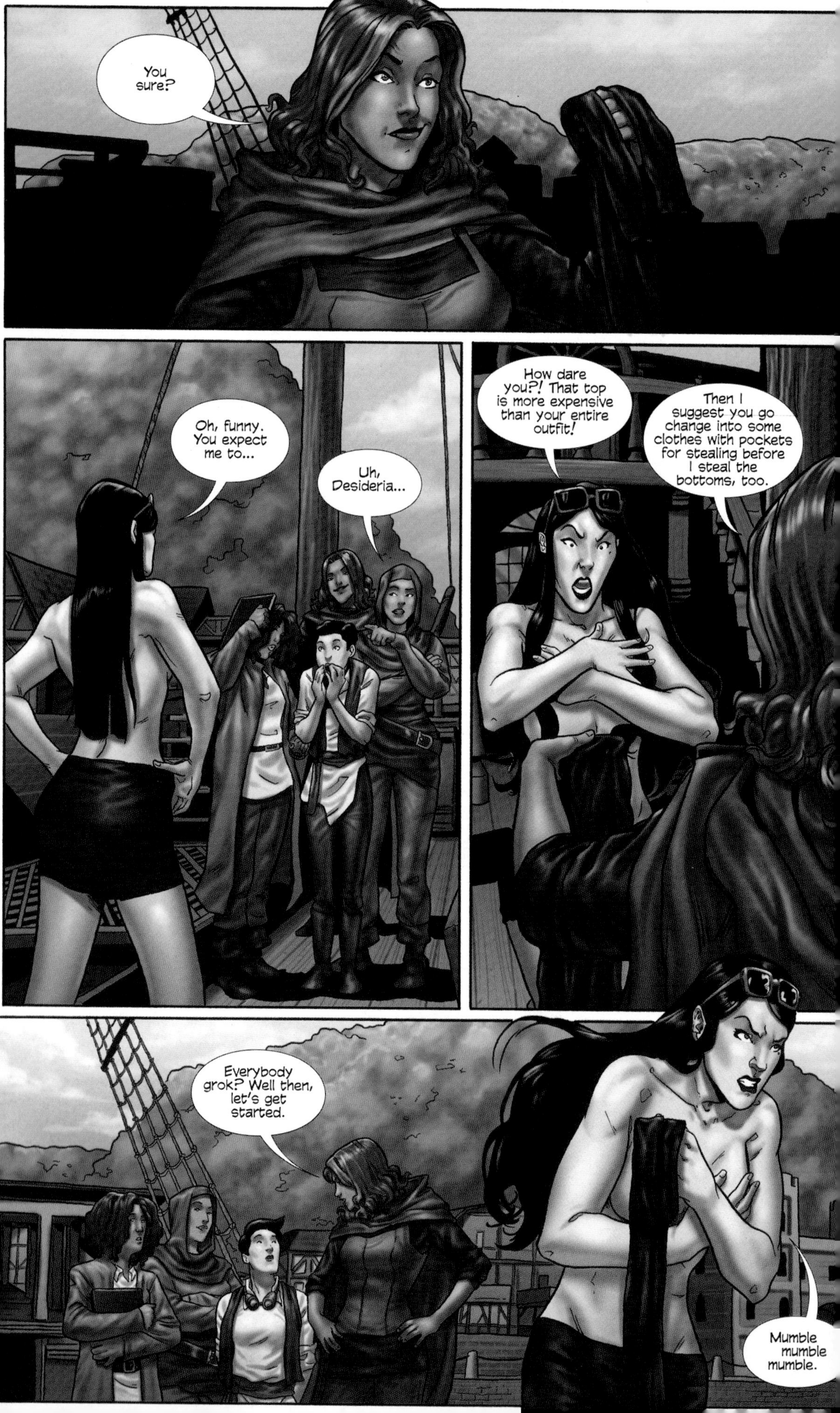

You sure?
Oh, funny. You expect me to...
Uh, Desideria...
How dare you?! That top is more expensive than your entire outfit!
Then I suggest you go change into some clothes with pockets for stealing before I steal the bottoms, too.
Everybody grok? Well then, let's get started.
Mumble mumble mumble.

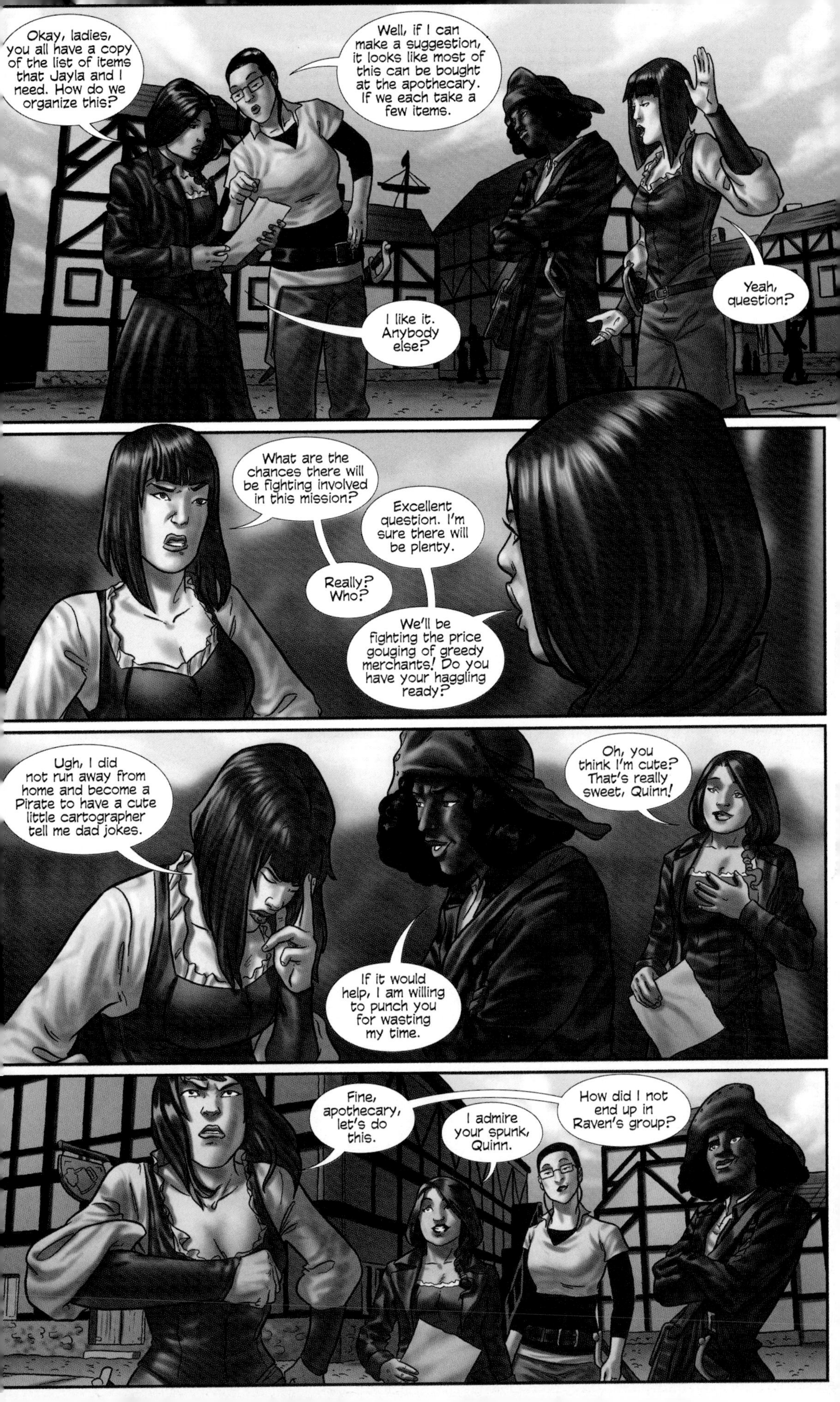
Okay, ladies, you all have a copy of the list of items that Jayla and I need. How do we organize this?
Well, if I can make a suggestion, it looks like most of this can be bought at the apothecary. If we each take a few items.
I like it. Anybody else?
Yeah, question?
What are the chances there will be fighting involved in this mission?
Excellent question. I'm sure there will be plenty.
Really? Who?
We'll be fighting the price gouging of greedy merchants! Do you have your haggling ready?
Ugh, I did not run away from home and become a Pirate to have a cute little cartographer tell me dad jokes.
Oh, you think I'm cute? That's really sweet, Quinn!
If it would help, I am willing to punch you for wasting my time.
Fine, apothecary, let's do this.
I admire your spunk, Quinn.
How did I not end up in Raven's group?

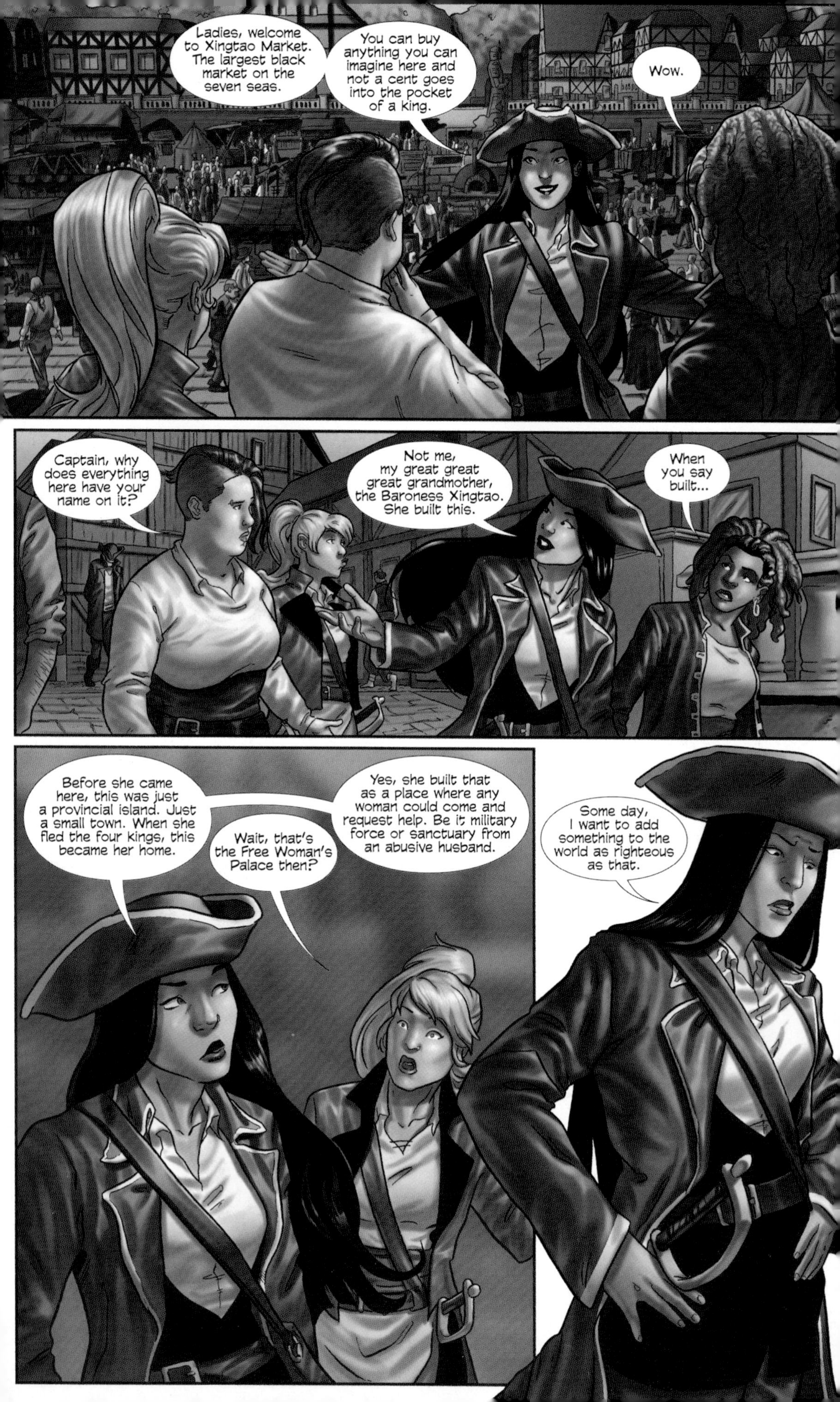
Ladies, welcome to Xingtao Market. The largest black market on the seven seas.
You can buy anything you can imagine here and not a cent goes into the pocket of a king.
Wow.
Captain, why does everything here have your name on it?
Not me, my great great great grandmother, the Baroness Xingtao. She built this.
When you say built...
Before she came here, this was just a provincial island. Just a small town. When she fled the four kings, this became her home.
Wait, that's the Free Woman's Palace then?
Yes, she built that as a place where any woman could come and request help. Be it military force or sanctuary from an abusive husband.
Some day, I want to add something to the world as righteous as that.

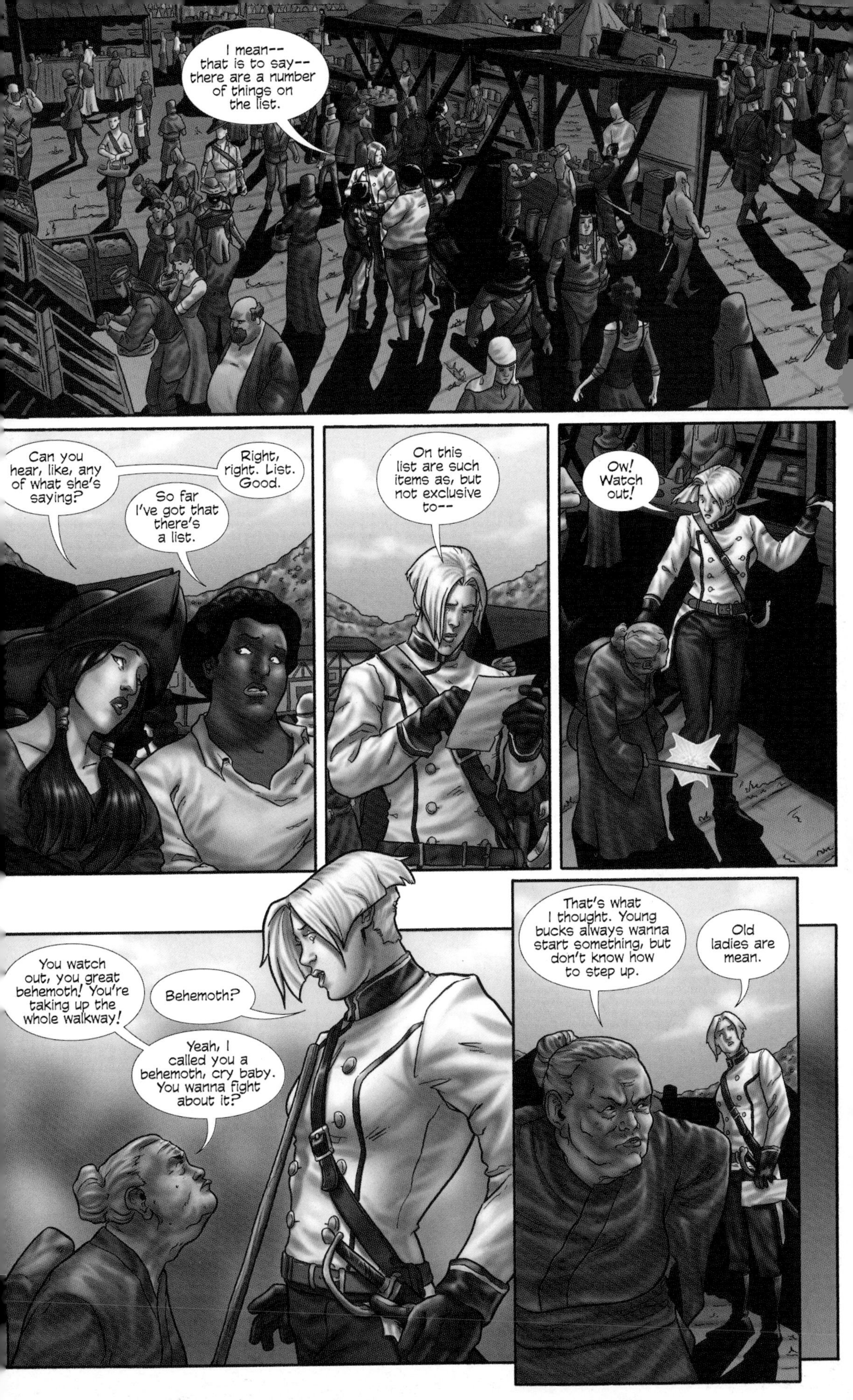
I mean-- that is to say-- there are a number of things on the list.
Can you hear, like, any of what she's saying?
Right, right. List. Good.
So far I've got that there's a list.
On this list are such items as, but not exclusive to--
Ow! Watch out!
You watch out, you great behemoth! You're taking up the whole walkway!
Behemoth?
Yeah, I called you a behemoth, cry baby. You wanna fight about it?
That's what I thought. Young bucks always wanna start something, but don't know how to step up.
Old ladies are mean.

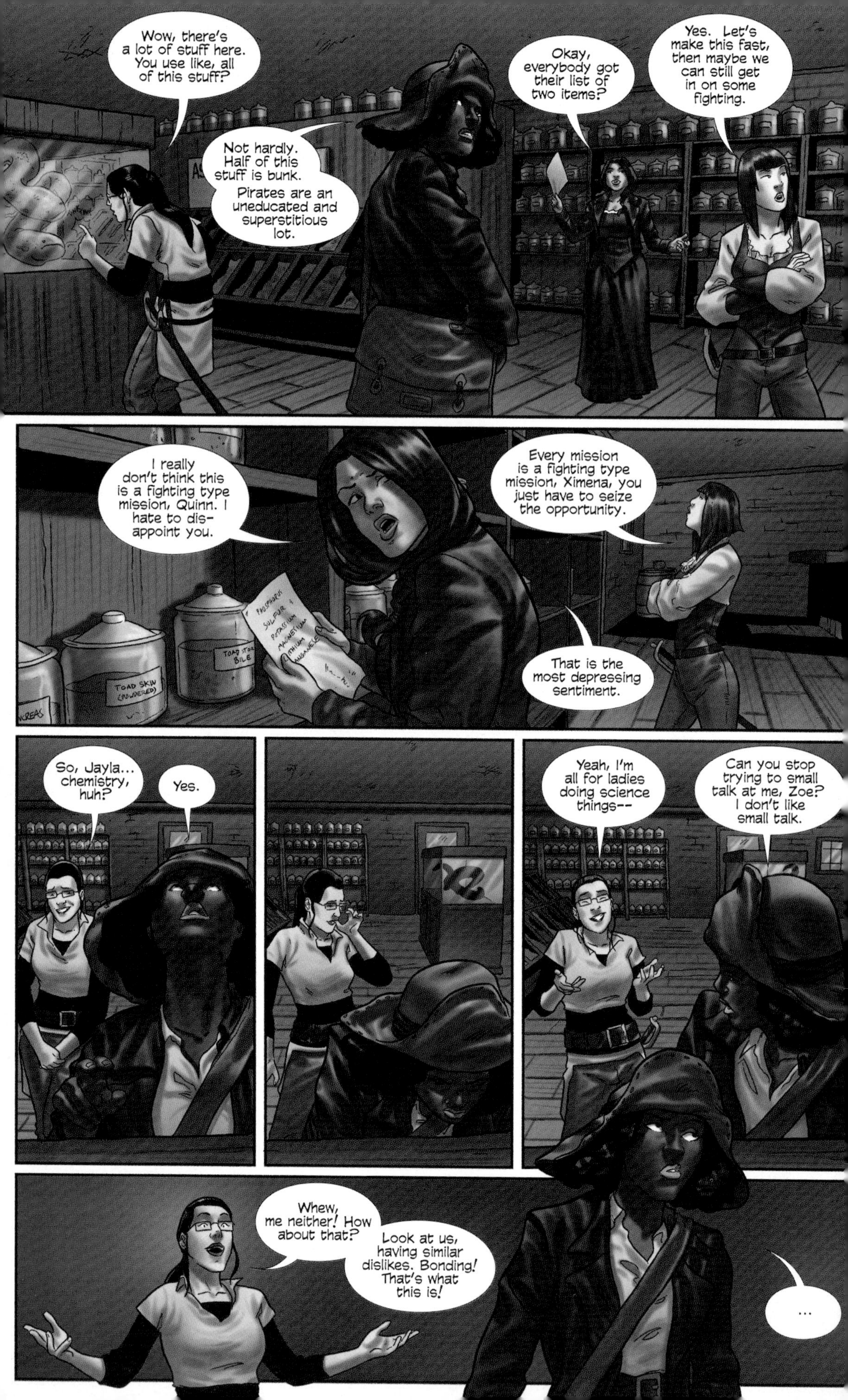
Wow, there's a lot of stuff here. You use like, all of this stuff?
Not hardly. Half of this stuff is bunk.
Pirates are an uneducated and superstitious lot.
Okay, everybody got their list of two items?
Yes. Let's make this fast, then maybe we can still get in on some fighting.
I really don't think this is a fighting type mission, Quinn. I hate to disappoint you.
Every mission is a fighting type mission, Ximena, you just have to seize the opportunity.
TOAD SKIN (POWDERED)
BILE
That is the most depressing sentiment.
So, Jayla... chemistry, huh?
Yes.
Yeah, I'm all for ladies doing science things--
Can you stop trying to small talk at me, Zoe? I don't like small talk.
Whew, me neither! How about that?
Look at us, having similar dislikes. Bonding! That's what this is!
...

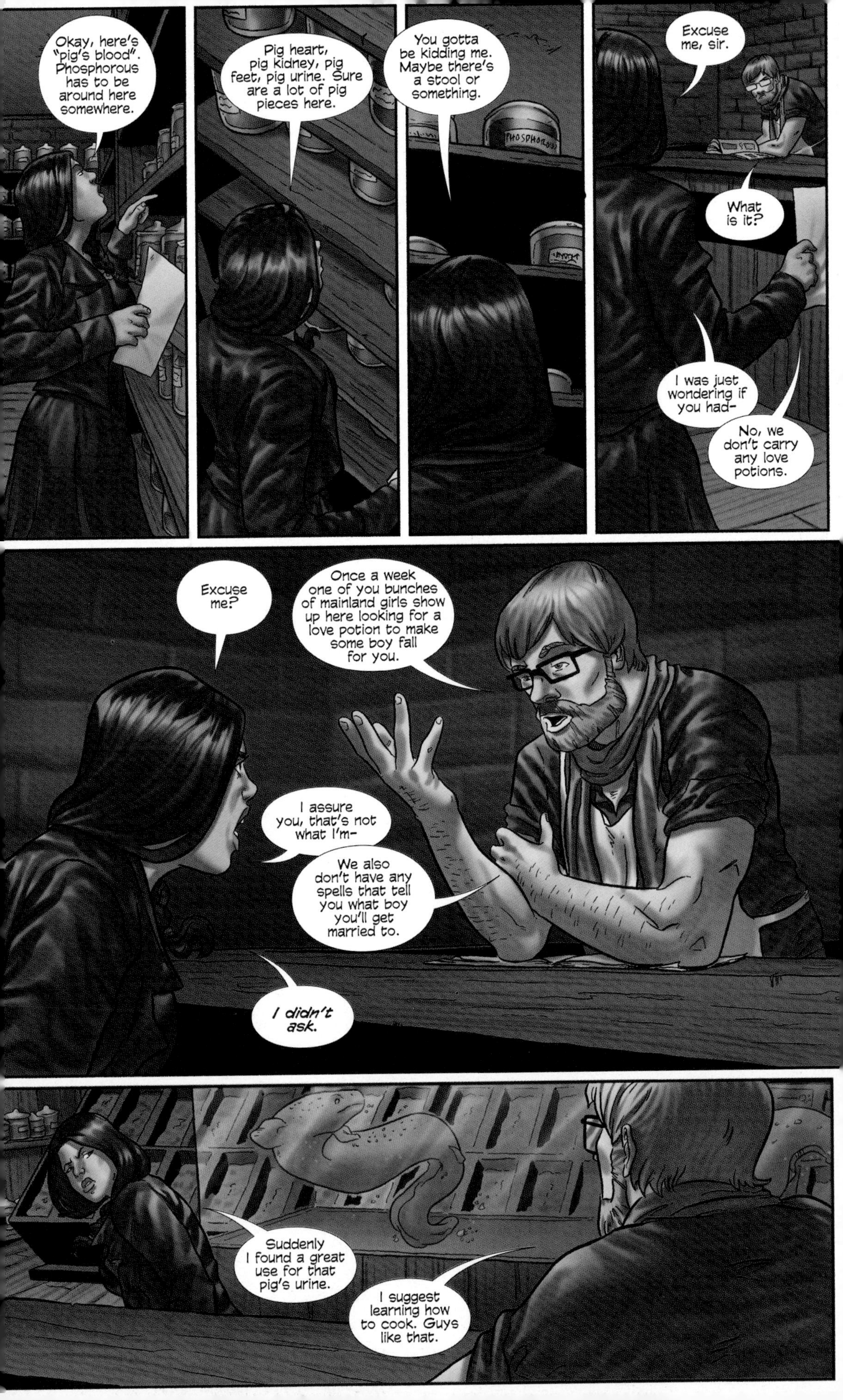
Okay, here's "pig's blood". Phosphorous has to be around here somewhere.
Pig heart, pig kidney, pig feet, pig urine. Sure are a lot of pig pieces here.
You gotta be kidding me. Maybe there's a stool or something.
PHOSPHOROUS
Excuse me, sir.
What is it?
I was just wondering if you had-
No, we don't carry any love potions.
Excuse me?
Once a week one of you bunches of mainland girls show up here looking for a love potion to make some boy fall for you.
I assure you, that's not what I'm-
We also don't have any spells that tell you what boy you'll get married to.
I didn't ask.
Suddenly I found a great use for that pig's urine.
I suggest learning how to cook. Guys like that.

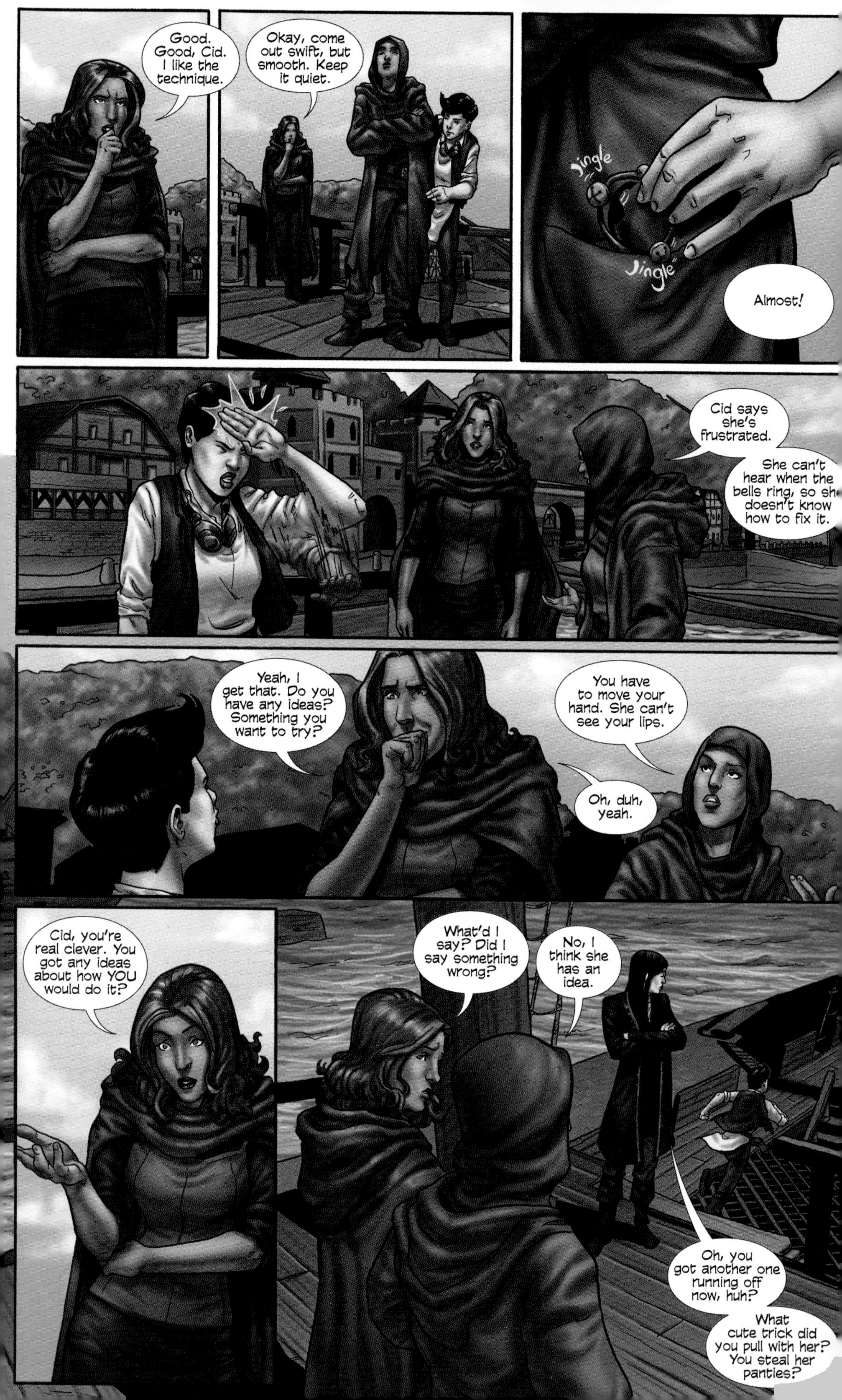

Good. Good, Cid. I like the technique.
Okay, come out swift, but smooth. Keep it quiet.
Jingle
Jingle
Almost!
Cid says she's frustrated.
She can't hear when the bells ring, so she doesn't know how to fix it.
Yeah, I get that. Do you have any ideas? Something you want to try?
You have to move your hand. She can't see your lips.
Oh, duh, yeah.
Cid, you're real clever. You got any ideas about how YOU would do it?
What'd I say? Did I say something wrong?
No, I think she has an idea.
Oh, you got another one running off now, huh?
What cute trick did you pull with her? You steal her panties?

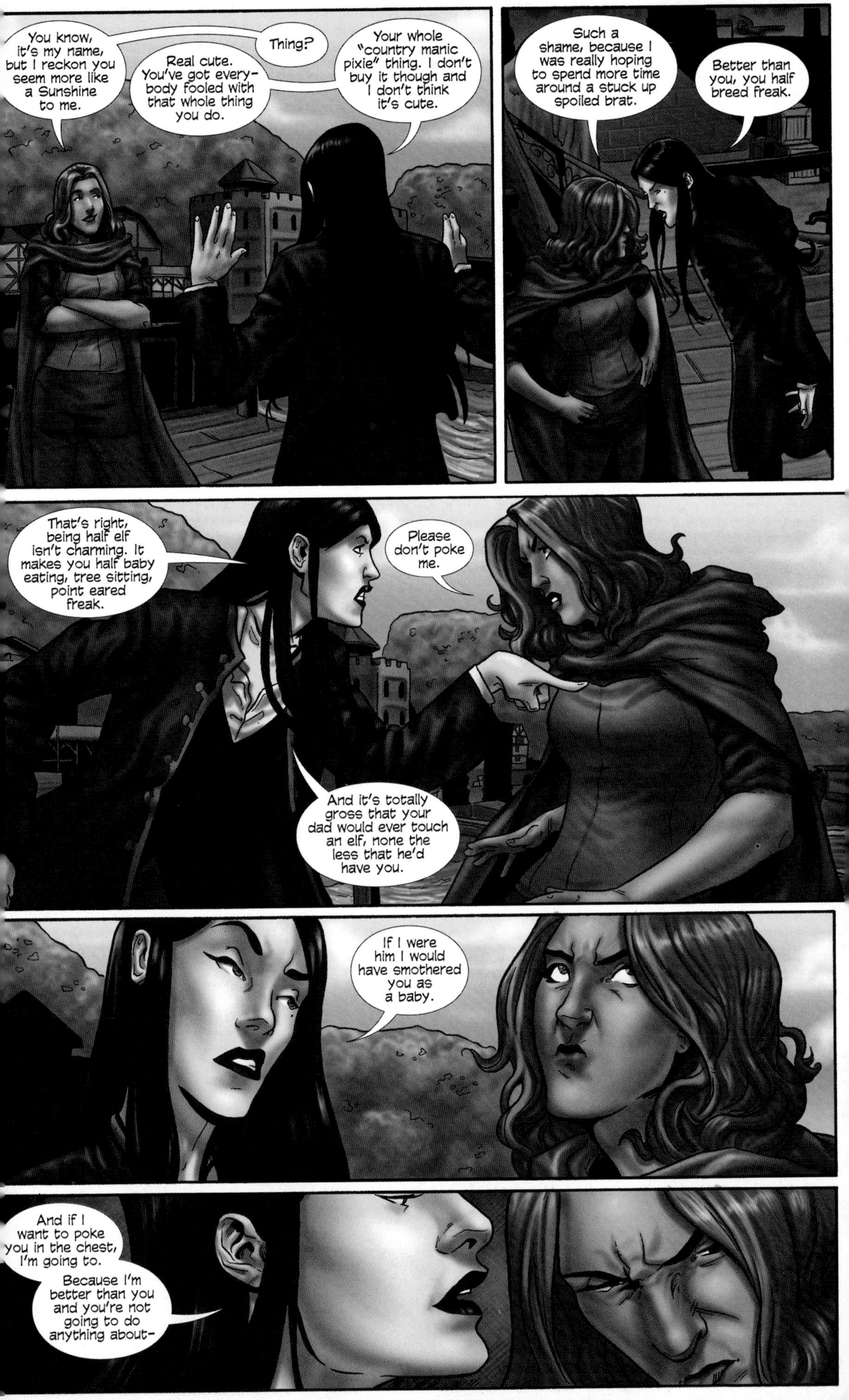
You know, it's my name, but I reckon you seem more like a Sunshine to me.
Thing?
Real cute. You've got every-body fooled with that whole thing you do.
Your whole "country manic pixie" thing. I don't buy it though and I don't think it's cute.
Such a shame, because I was really hoping to spend more time around a stuck up spoiled brat.
Better than you, you half breed freak.
That's right, being half elf isn't charming. It makes you half baby eating, tree sitting, point eared freak.
Please don't poke me.
And it's totally gross that your dad would ever touch an elf, none the less that he'd have you.
If I were him I would have smothered you as a baby.
And if I want to poke you in the chest, I'm going to.
Because I'm better than you and you're not going to do anything about-

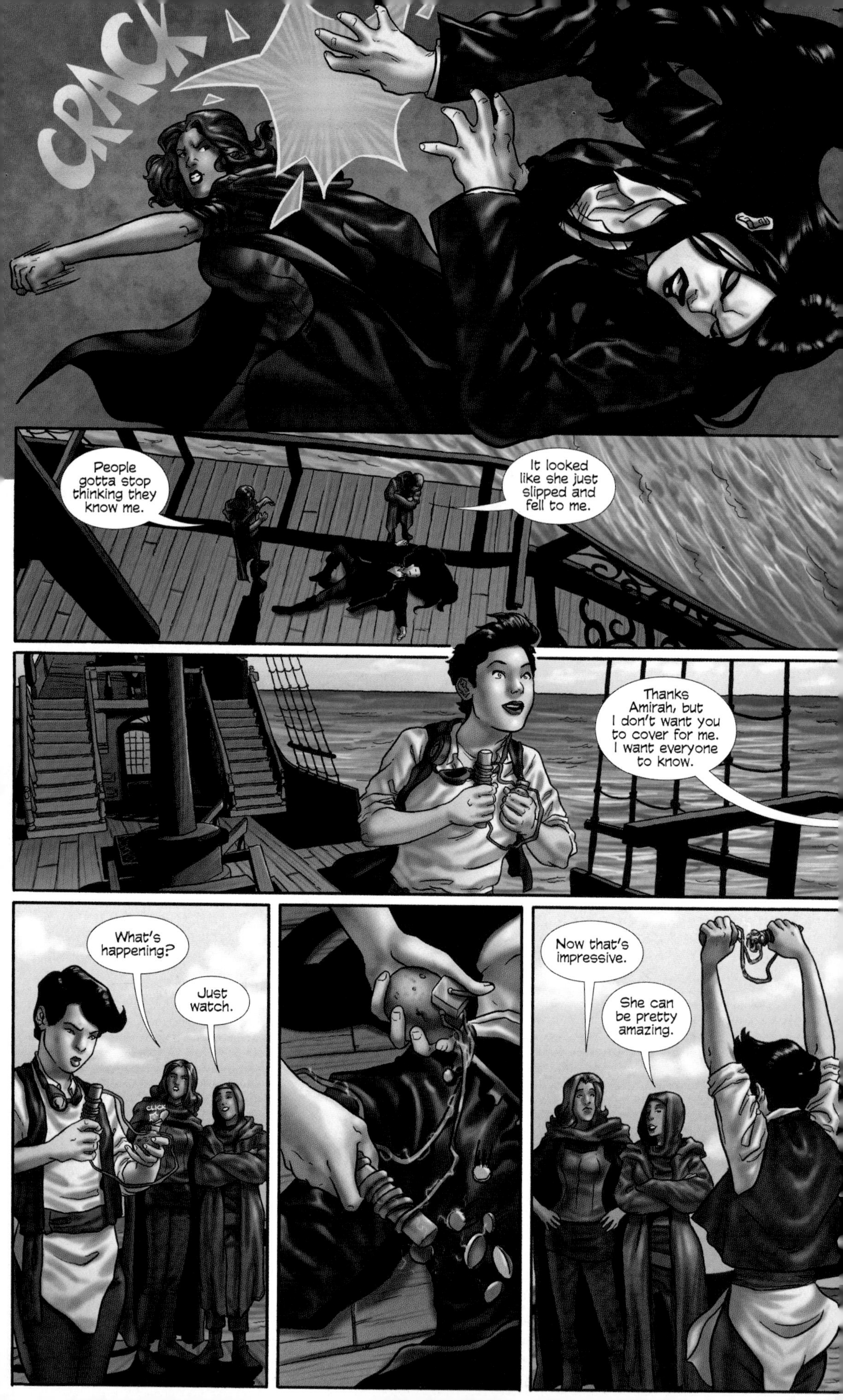
CRACK
People gotta stop thinking they know me.
It looked like she just slipped and fell to me.
Thanks Amirah, but I don't want you to cover for me. I want everyone to know.
What's happening?
Just watch.
CLICK
Now that's impressive.
She can be pretty amazing.

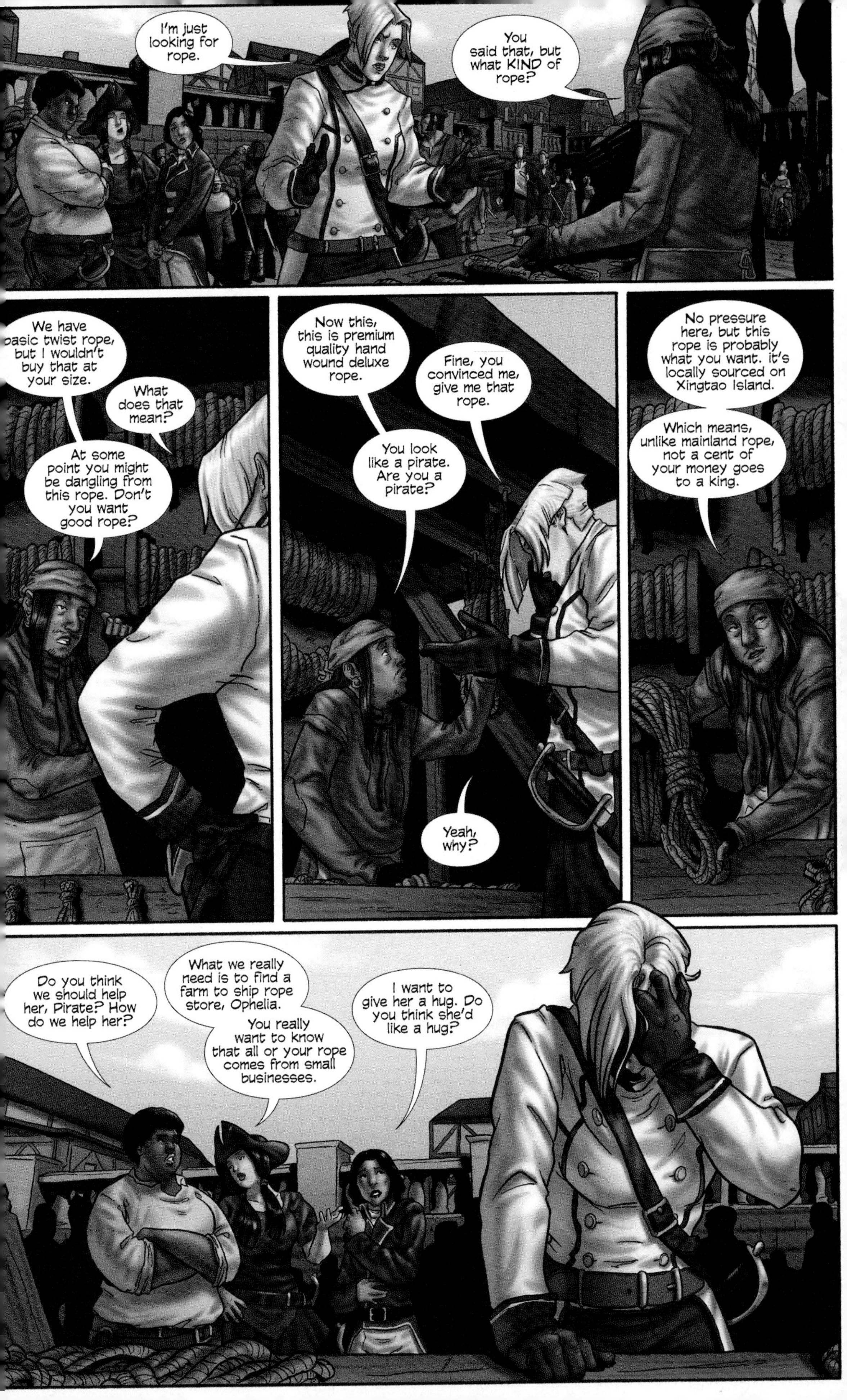
I'm just looking for rope.
You said that, but what KIND of rope?
We have basic twist rope, but I wouldn't buy that at your size.
What does that mean?
At some point you might be dangling from this rope. Don't you want good rope?
Now this, this is premium quality hand wound deluxe rope.
You look like a pirate. Are you a pirate?
Yeah, why?
Fine, you convinced me, give me that rope.
No pressure here, but this rope is probably what you want. it's locally sourced on Xingtao Island.
Which means, unlike mainland rope, not a cent of your money goes to a king.
Do you think we should help her, Pirate? How do we help her?
What we really need is to find a farm to ship rope store, Ophelia.
You really want to know that all or your rope comes from small businesses.
I want to give her a hug. Do you think she'd like a hug?

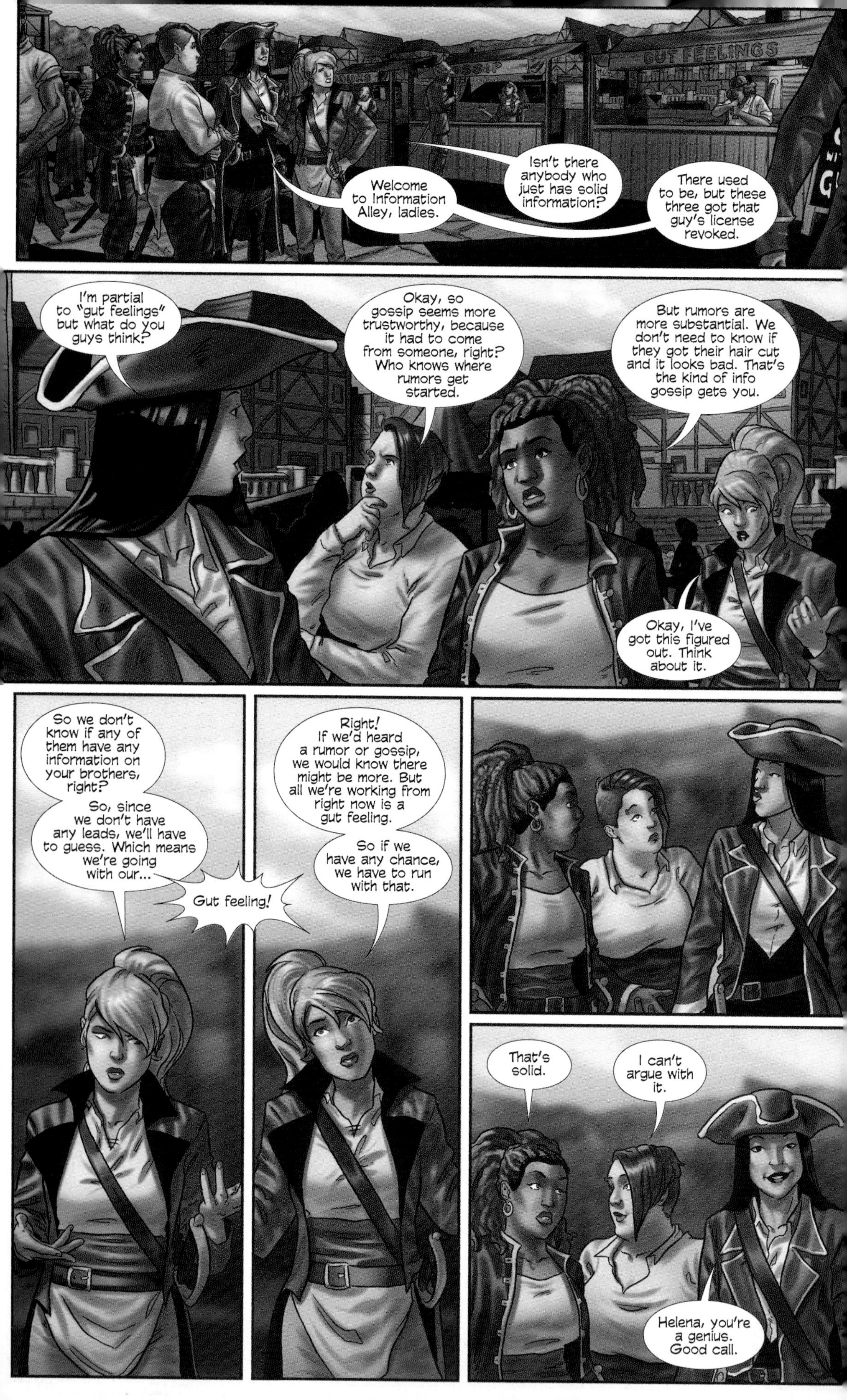
GUT FEELINGS
GOSSIP
Welcome to Information Alley, ladies.
Isn't there anybody who just has solid information?
There used to be, but these three got that guy's license revoked.
I'm partial to "gut feelings" but what do you guys think?
Okay, so gossip seems more trustworthy, because it had to come from someone, right? Who knows where rumors get started.
But rumors are more substantial. We don't need to know if they got their hair cut and it looks bad. That's the kind of info gossip gets you.
Okay, I've got this figured out. Think about it.
So we don't know if any of them have any information on your brothers, right?
So, since we don't have any leads, we'll have to guess. Which means we're going with our...
Gut feeling!
Right! If we'd heard a rumor or gossip, we would know there might be more. But all we're working from right now is a gut feeling.
So if we have any chance, we have to run with that.
That's solid.
I can't argue with it.
Helena, you're a genius. Good call.

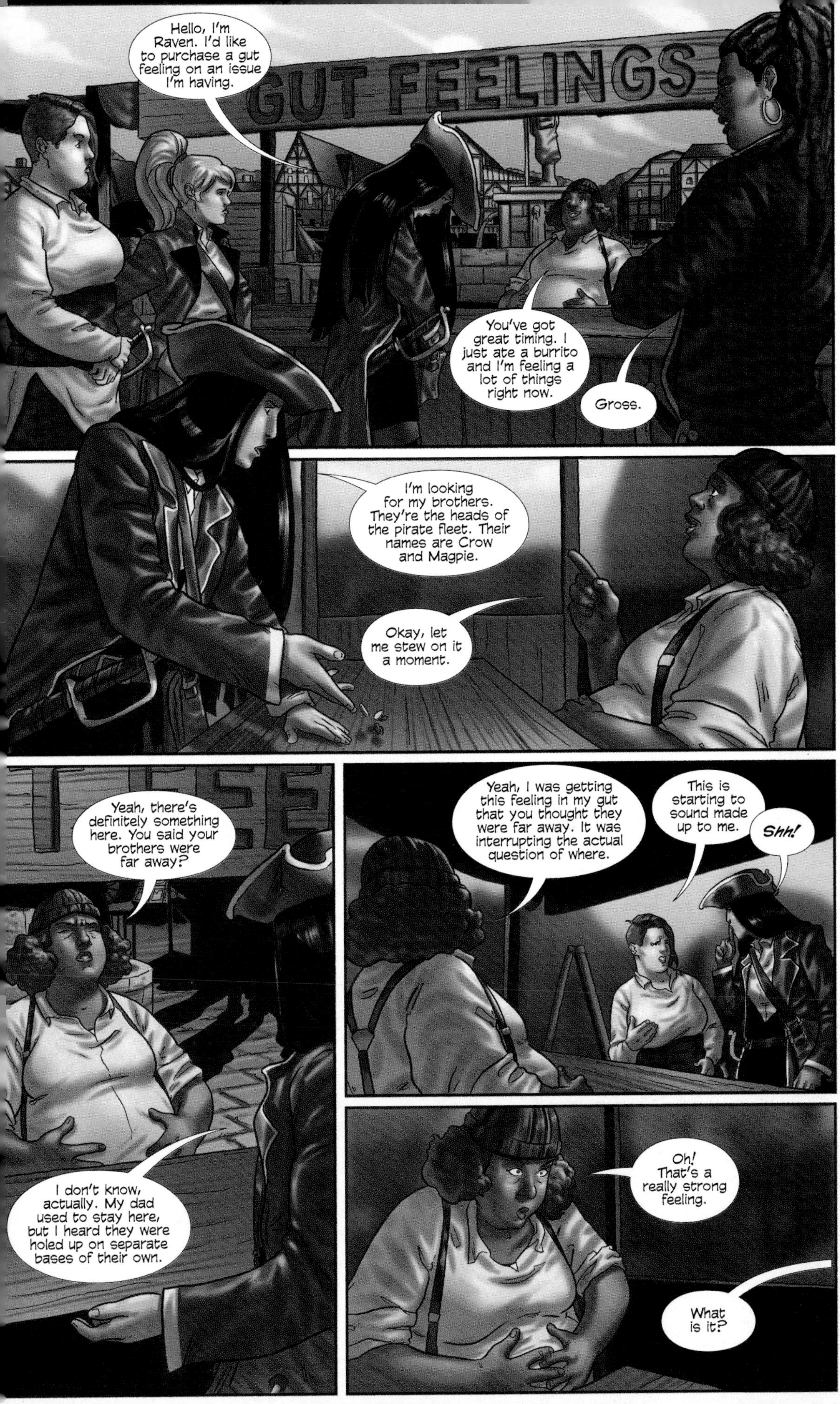
GUT FEELINGS
Hello, I'm Raven. I'd like to purchase a gut feeling on an issue I'm having.
You've got great timing. I just ate a burrito and I'm feeling a lot of things right now.
Gross.
I'm looking for my brothers. They're the heads of the pirate fleet. Their names are Crow and Magpie.
Okay, let me stew on it a moment.
Yeah, there's definitely something here. You said your brothers were far away?
I don't know, actually. My dad used to stay here, but I heard they were holed up on separate bases of their own.
Yeah, I was getting this feeling in my gut that you thought they were far away. It was interrupting the actual question of where.
This is starting to sound made up to me.
Shh!
Oh! That's a really strong feeling.
What is it?

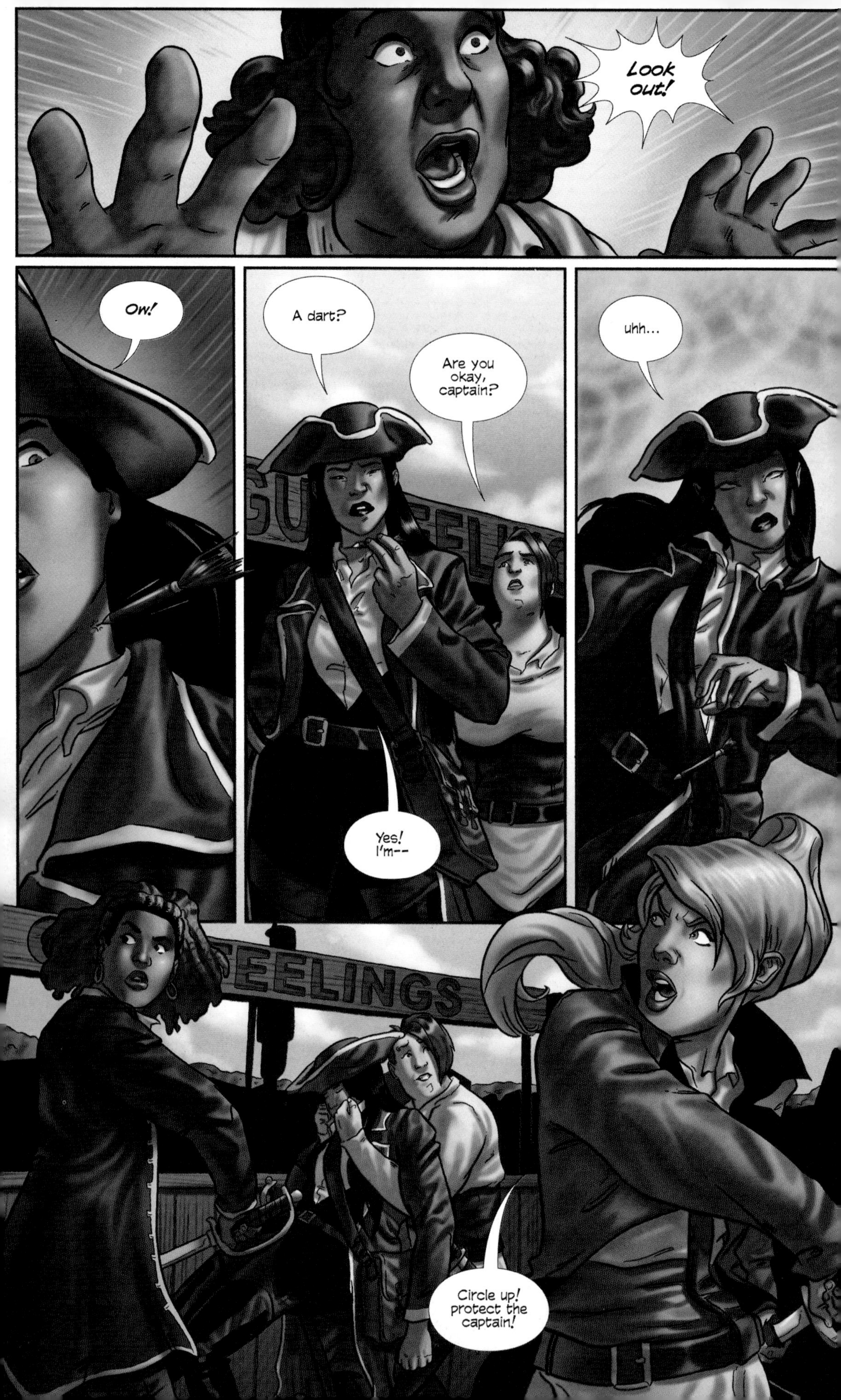
Look out!
Ow!
A dart?
Are you okay, captain?
Yes! I'm--
uhh...
GU
EELINGS
Circle up! protect the captain!

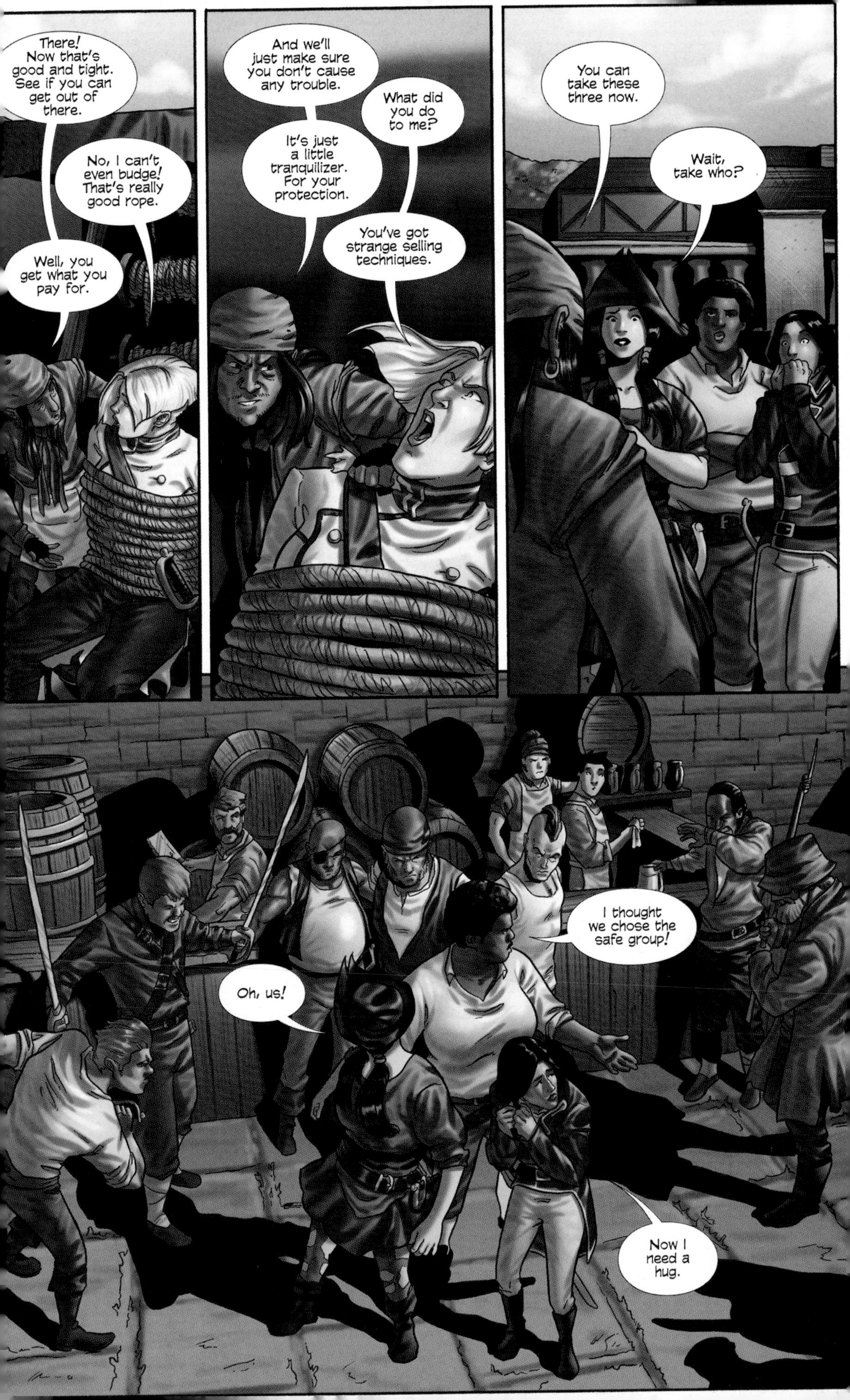
There! Now that's good and tight. See if you can get out of there.
No, I can't even budge! That's really good rope.
Well, you get what you pay for.
And we'll just make sure you don't cause any trouble.
What did you do to me?
It's just a little tranquilizer. For your protection.
You've got strange selling techniques.
You can take these three now.
Wait, take who?
I thought we chose the safe group!
Oh, us!
Now I need a hug.

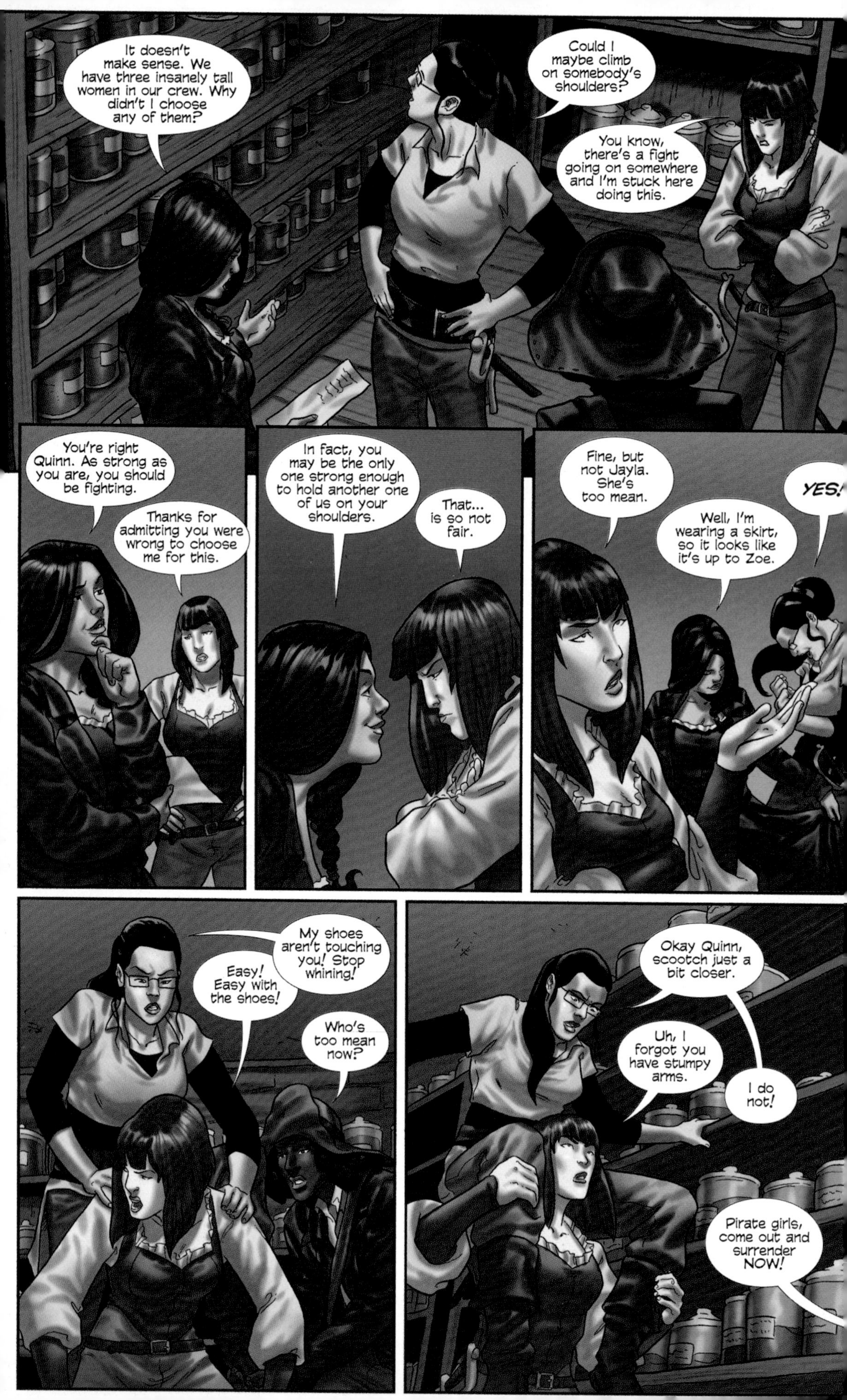

It doesn't make sense. We have three insanely tall women in our crew. Why didn't I choose any of them?
Could I maybe climb on somebody's shoulders?
You know, there's a fight going on somewhere and I'm stuck here doing this.
You're right Quinn. As strong as you are, you should be fighting.
Thanks for admitting you were wrong to choose me for this.
In fact, you may be the only one strong enough to hold another one of us on your shoulders.
That... is so not fair.
Fine, but not Jayla. She's too mean.
YES!
Well, I'm wearing a skirt, so it looks like it's up to Zoe.
My shoes aren't touching you! Stop whining!
Easy! Easy with the shoes!
Who's too mean now?
Okay Quinn, scootch just a bit closer.
Uh, I forgot you have stumpy arms.
I do not!
Pirate girls, come out and surrender NOW!

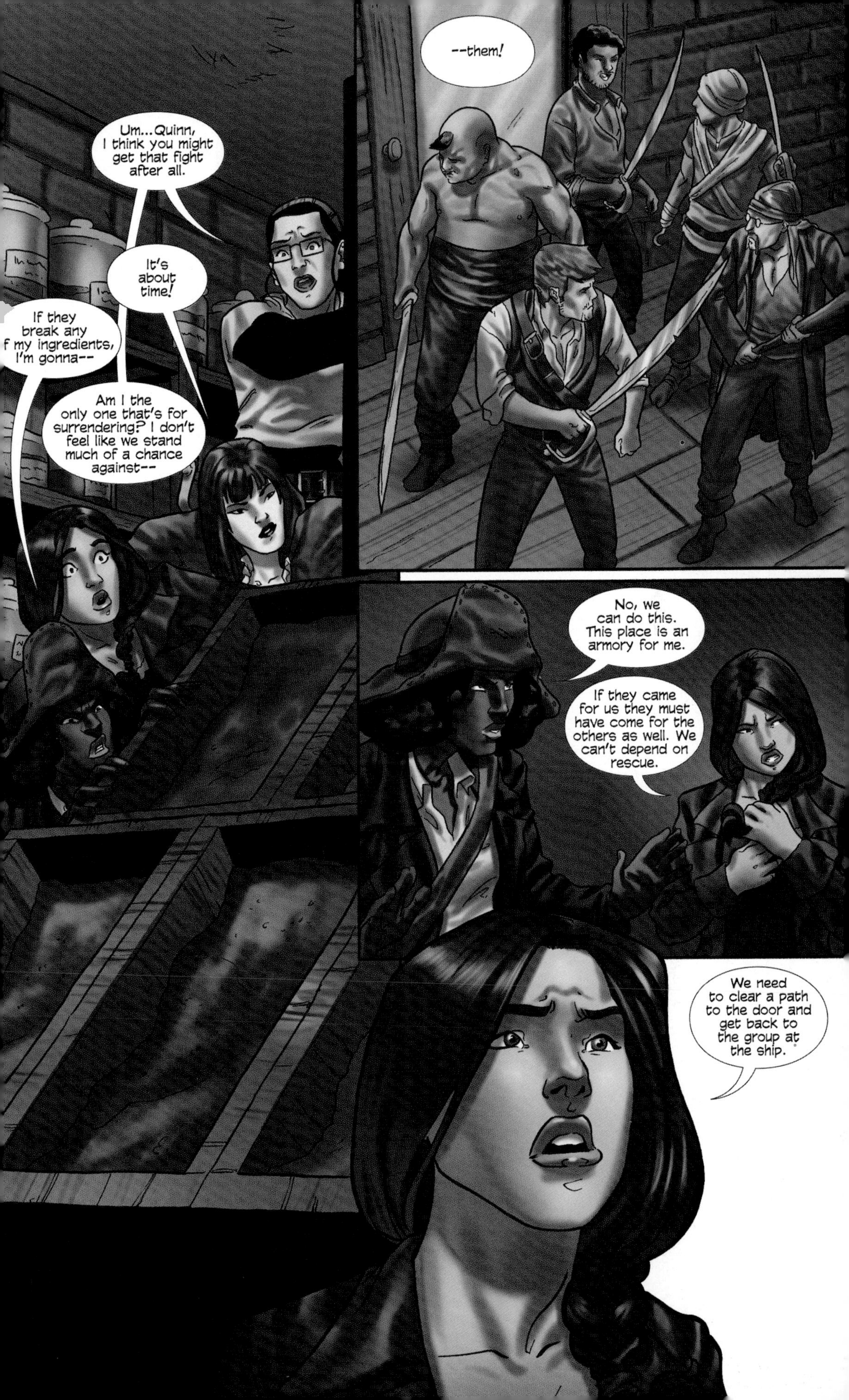
Um...Quinn, I think you might get that fight after all.
It's about time!
If they break any f my ingredients, I'm gonna--
Am I the only one that's for surrendering? I don't feel like we stand much of a chance against--
--them!
No, we can do this. This place is an armory for me.
If they came for us they must have come for the others as well. We can't depend on rescue.
We need to clear a path to the door and get back to the group at the ship.

"Hopefully, Sunshine will be in a better spot than we are."

ISSUE SIX
"THE ISLAND OF THE FREE WOMAN"

WORDS: Jeremy Whitley **PENCILS:** Rosy Higgins **LAYOUTS/INKS:** Ted Brandt
COLORS: William Blankenship **LETTERS:** Dave Dwonch **EDITOR:** Alicia Whitley

PRINCELESS: RAVEN THE PIRATE PRINCESS #6, March 2016 Copyright Jeremy Whitley, 2016. Published by Action Lab Entertainment. All rights reserved. All characters are fictional. Any likeness to anyone living or undead is purely coincidental. No part of this publication may be reproduced or transmitted without permission, except for small excerpts for review purposes. Printed in Canada. First Printing.

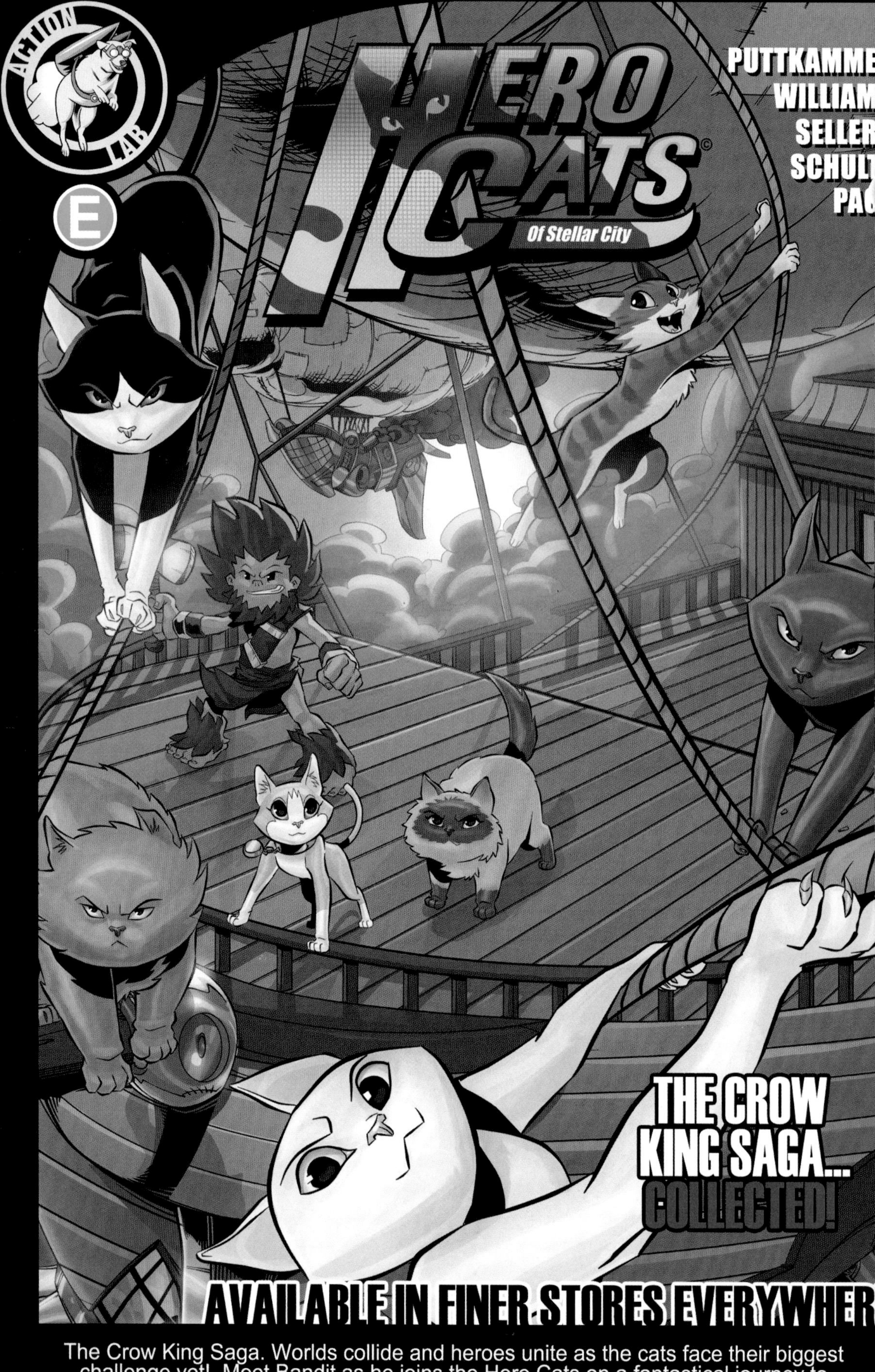
ACTION LAB
E
HERO CATS
Of Stellar City
PUTTKAMME
WILLIAM
SELLER
SCHULT
THE CROW KING SAGA... COLLECTED!
AVAILABLE IN FINER STORES EVERYWHER

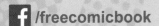

READ MORE NOW

Raven: Pirate Princess - Action Lab
www.actionlabcomics.com

ACTIONLABCOMICS.COM

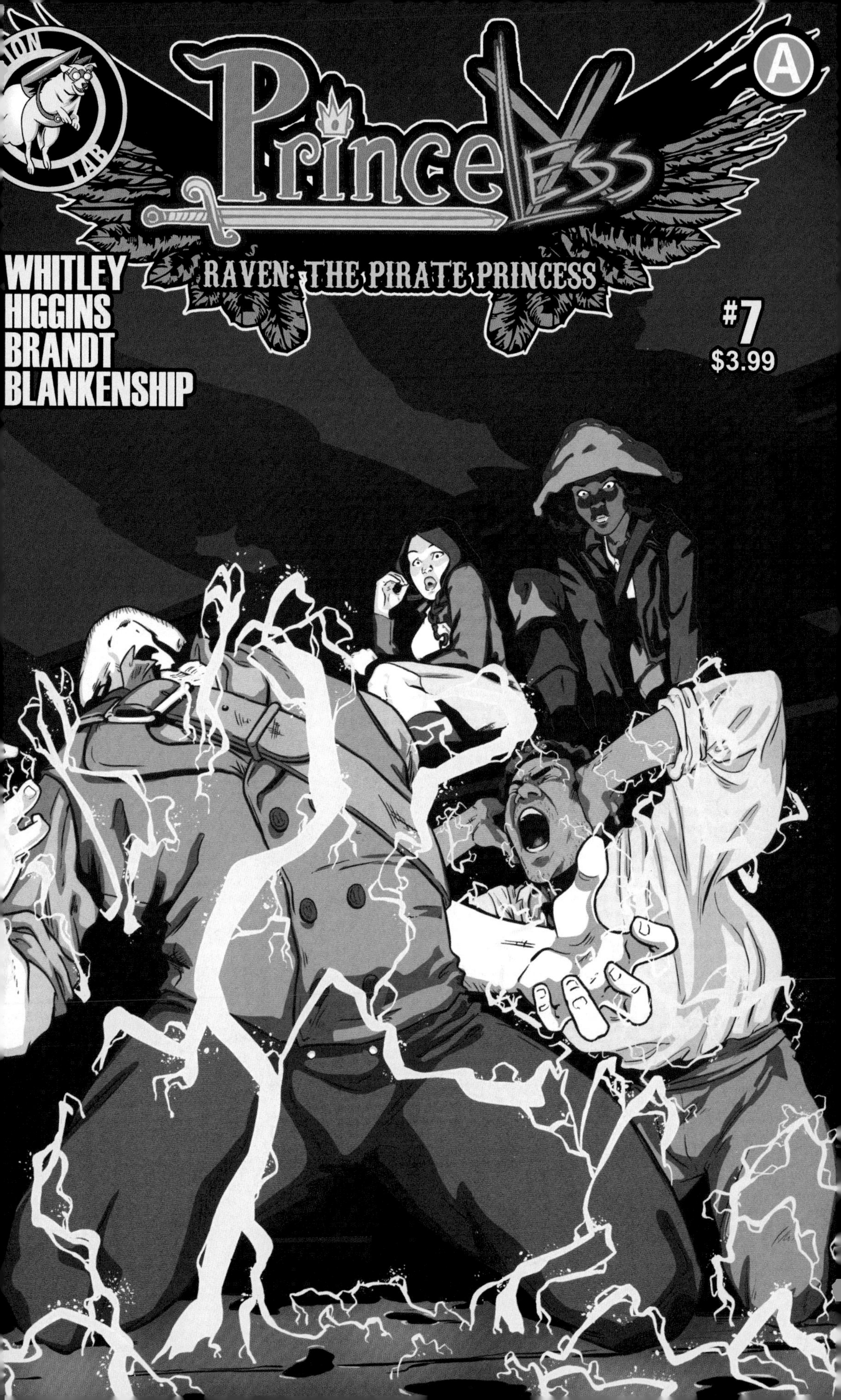
Princeless
RAVEN: THE PIRATE PRINCESS
A
WHITLEY
HIGGINS
BRANDT
BLANKENSHIP
#7
$3.99

FROM ALL-AGES TO MATURE READERS
ACTION LAB HAS YOU COVERED.

 **Appropriate for everyone.**

 **Appropriate for age 9 and up. Absent of profanity or adult content.**

 **Suggested for 12 and Up. Comics with this rating are comparable to a PG-13 movie rating. Recommended for our teen and young adult readers.**

 **Appropriate for older teens. Similar to Teen, but featuring more mature themes and/or more graphic imagery.**

 **Contains extreme violence and some nudity. Basically the Rated-R of comics.**

  FIND YOUR NEW FAVORITE COMICS.

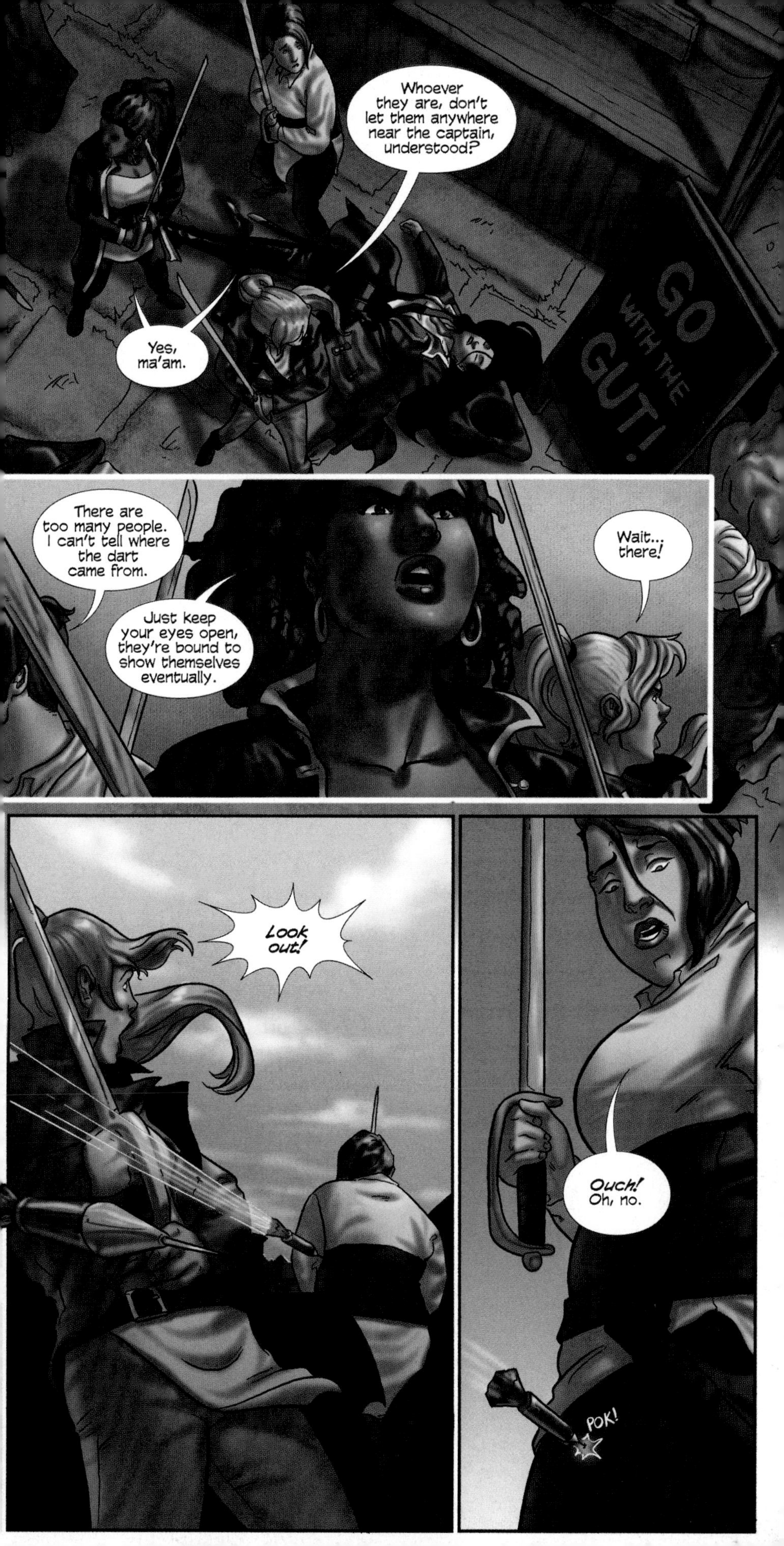
Whoever they are, don't let them anywhere near the captain, understood?
Yes, ma'am.
GO WITH THE GUT!
There are too many people. I can't tell where the dart came from.
Just keep your eyes open, they're bound to show themselves eventually.
Wait... there!
Look out!
Ouch! Oh, no.
POK!

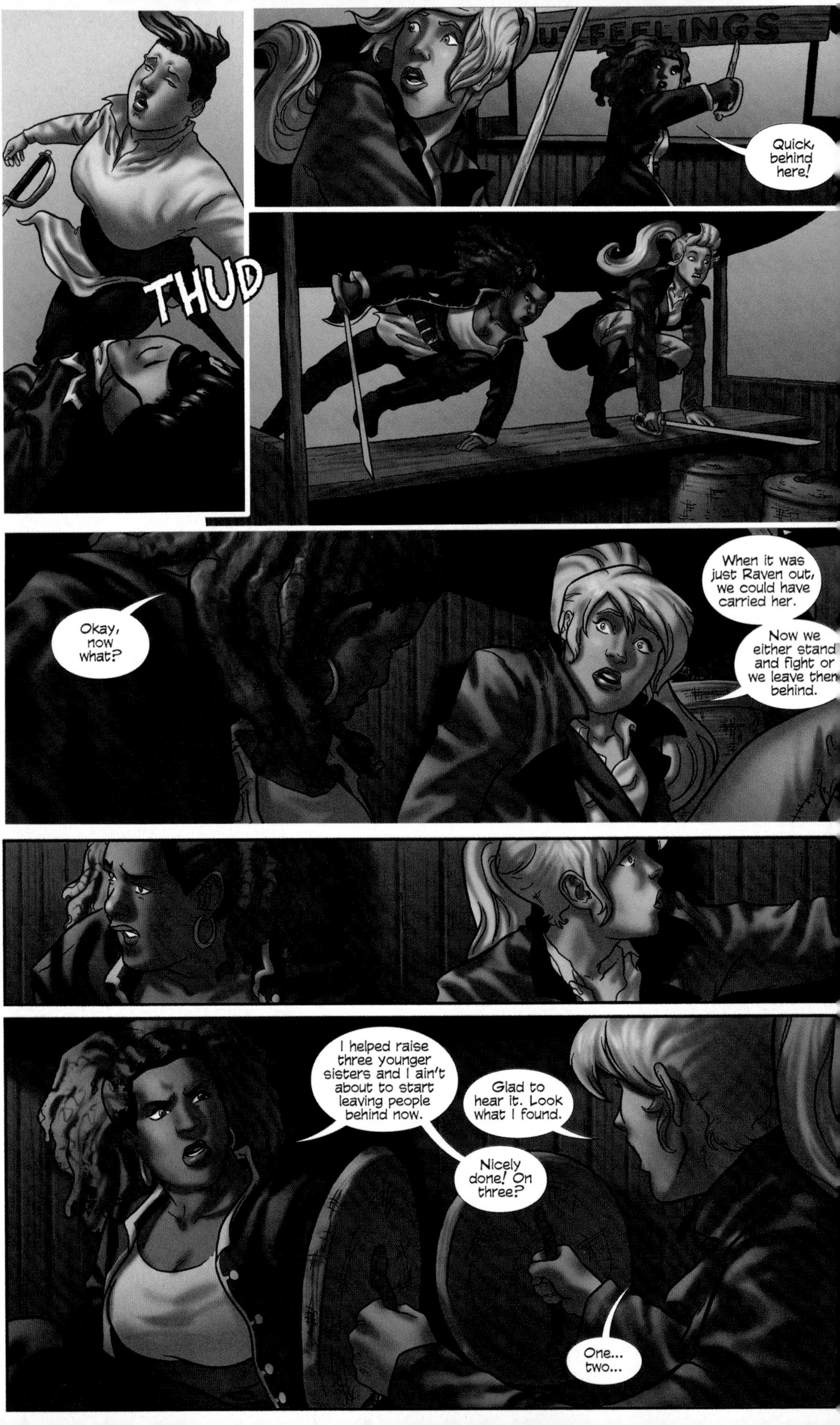
THUD
FEELINGS
Quick, behind here!
Okay, now what?
When it was just Raven out, we could have carried her.
Now we either stand and fight or we leave them behind.
I helped raise three younger sisters and I ain't about to start leaving people behind now.
Glad to hear it. Look what I found.
Nicely done! On three?
One... two...

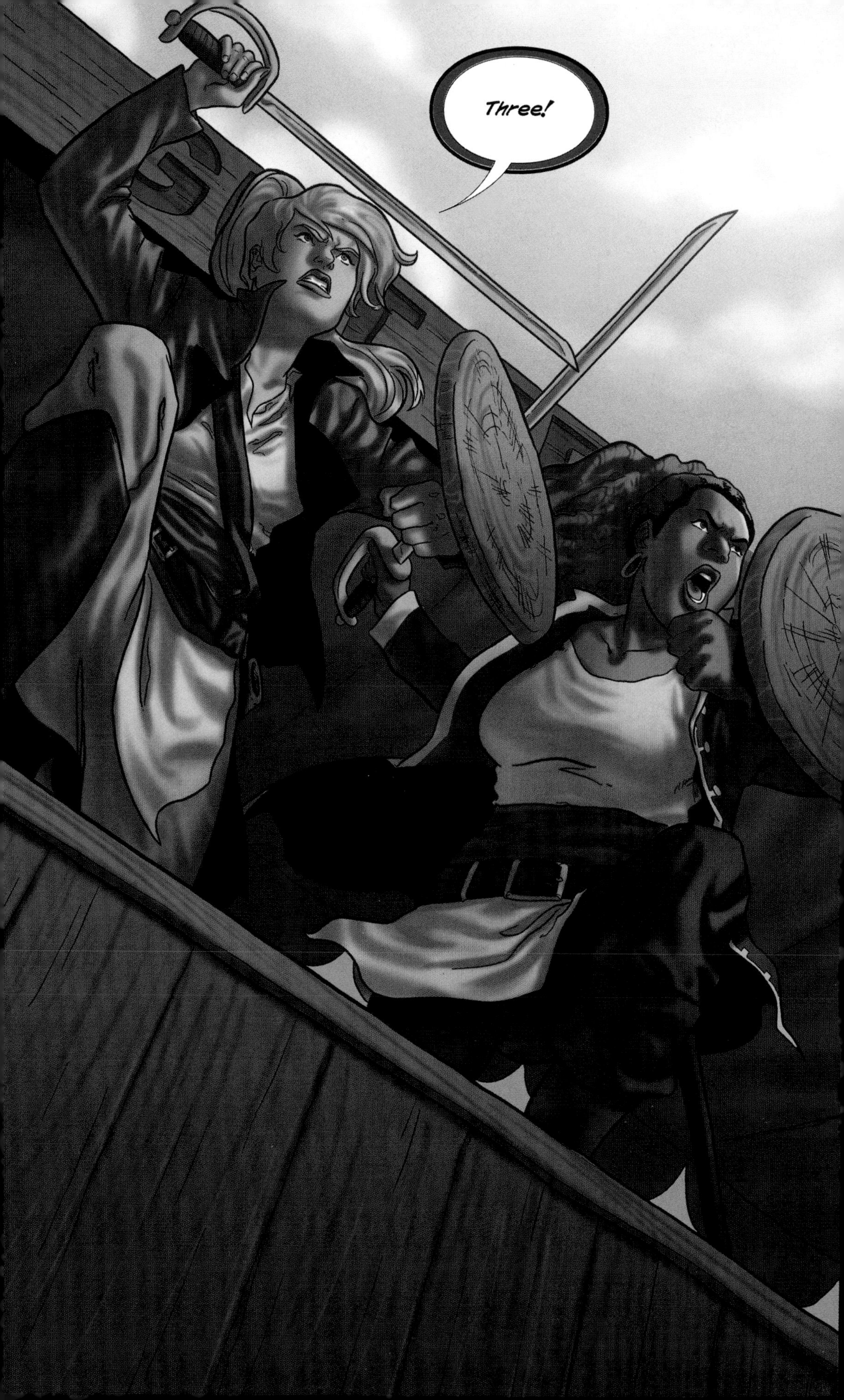
Three!

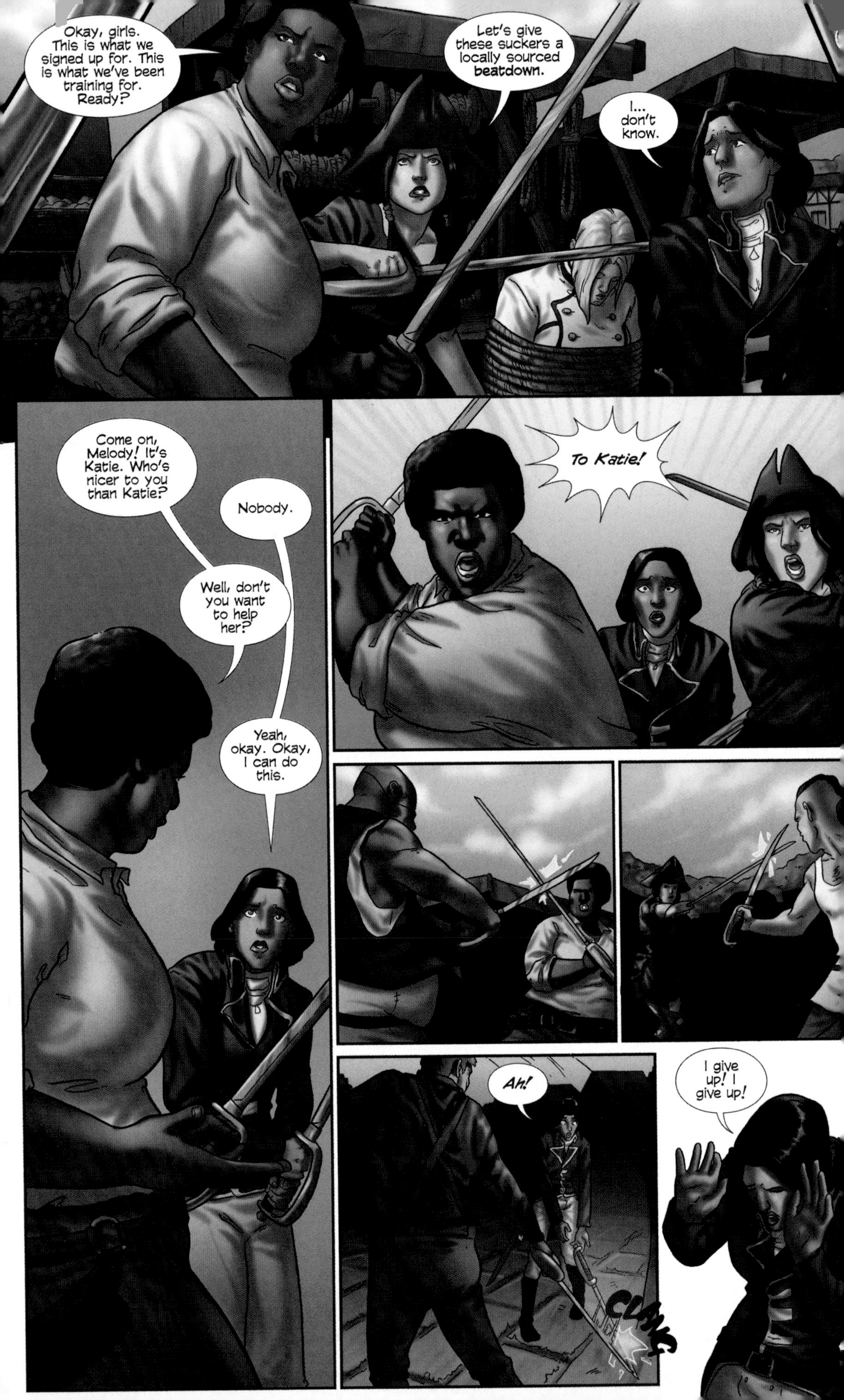
Okay, girls. This is what we signed up for. This is what we've been training for. Ready?
Let's give these suckers a locally sourced **beatdown.**
I... don't know.
Come on, Melody! It's Katie. Who's nicer to you than Katie?
Nobody.
Well, don't you want to help her?
Yeah, okay. Okay, I can do this.
To Katie!
Ah!
I give up! I give up!
CLANG

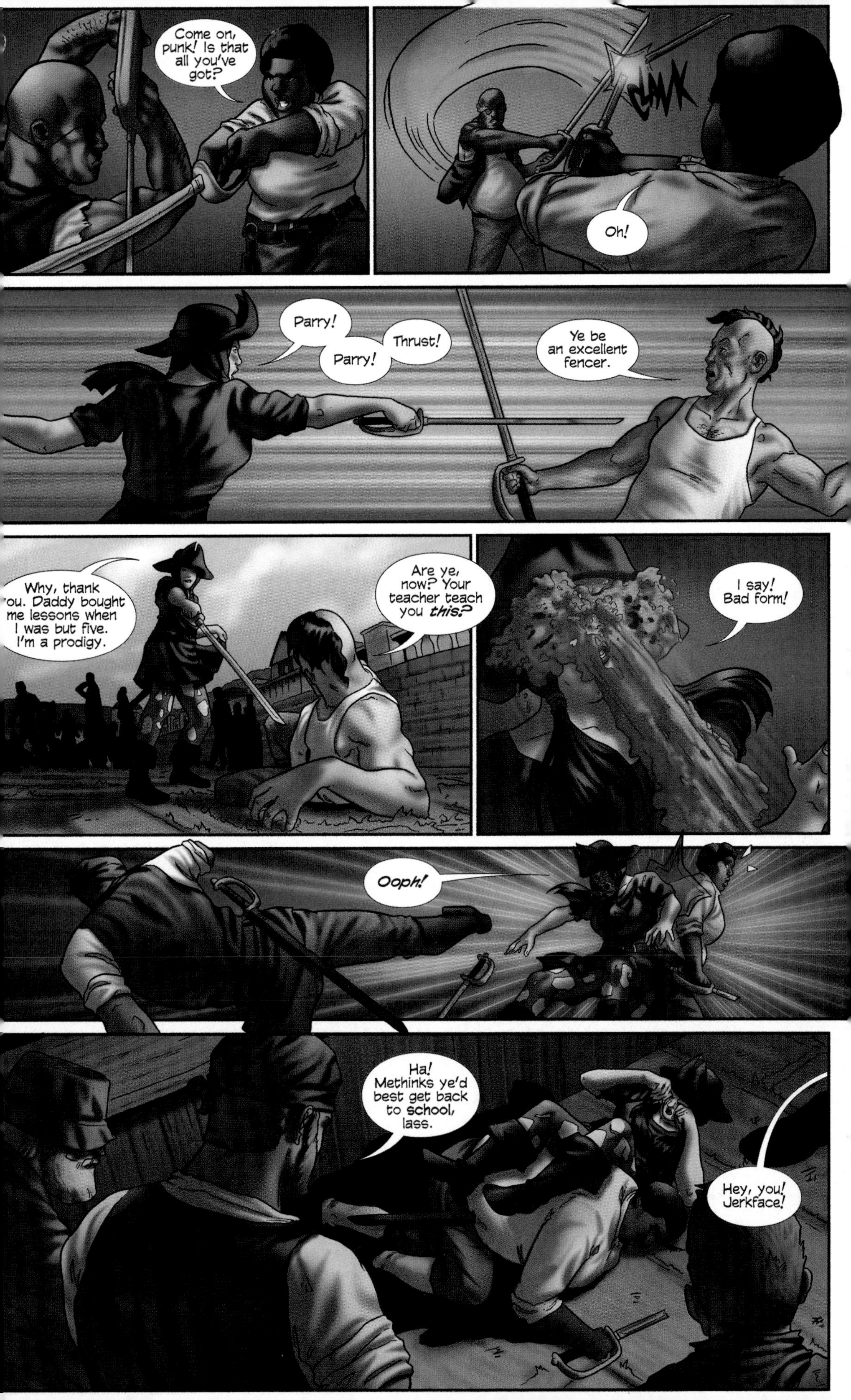
Come on, punk! Is that all you've got?
CLANK
Oh!
Parry!
Parry!
Thrust!
Ye be an excellent fencer.
Why, thank you. Daddy bought me lessons when I was but five. I'm a prodigy.
Are ye, now? Your teacher teach you *this?*
I say! Bad form!
Ooph!
Ha! Methinks ye'd best get back to **school,** lass.
Hey, you! Jerkface!

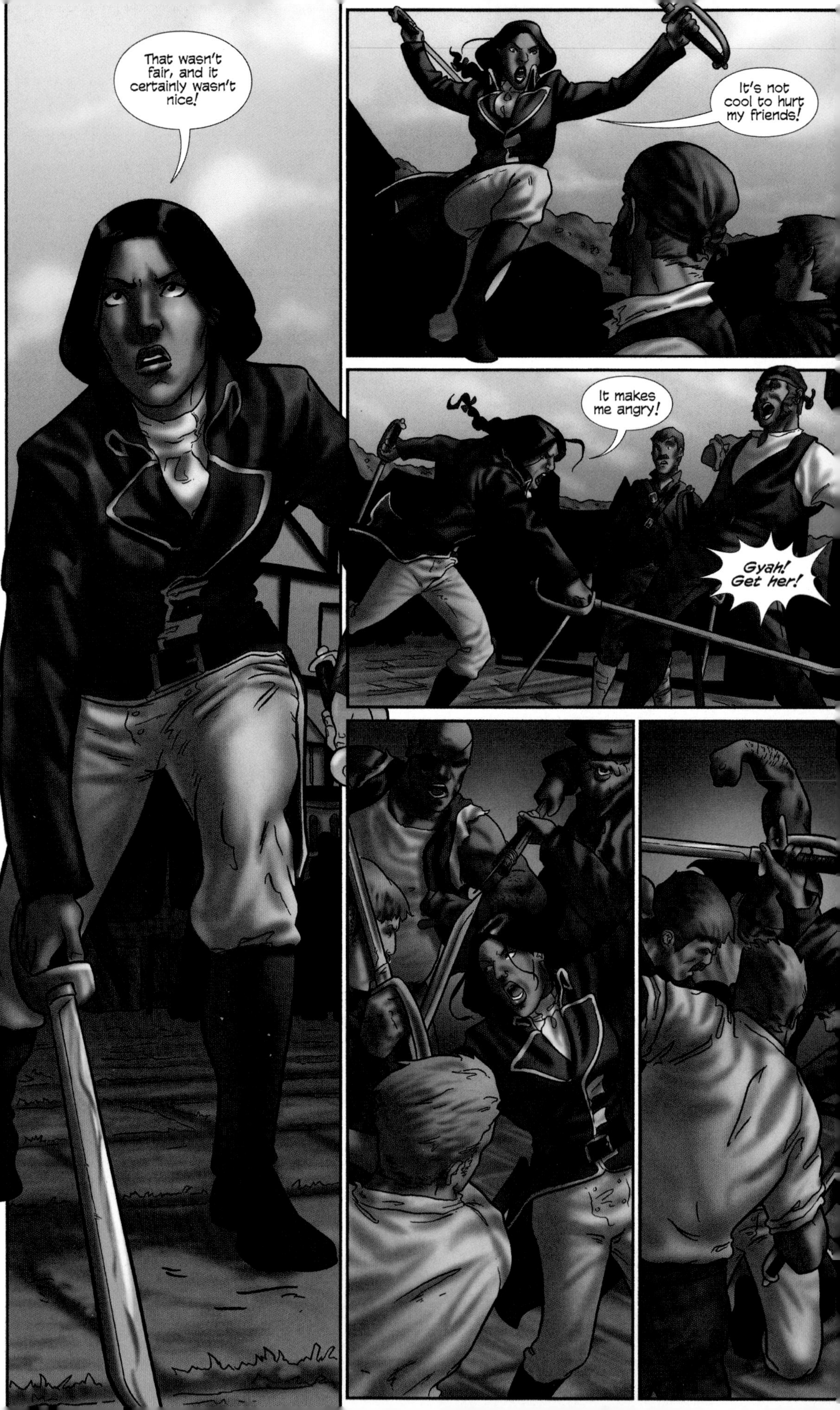
That wasn't fair, and it certainly wasn't nice!
It's not cool to hurt my friends!
It makes me angry!
Gyah! Get her!

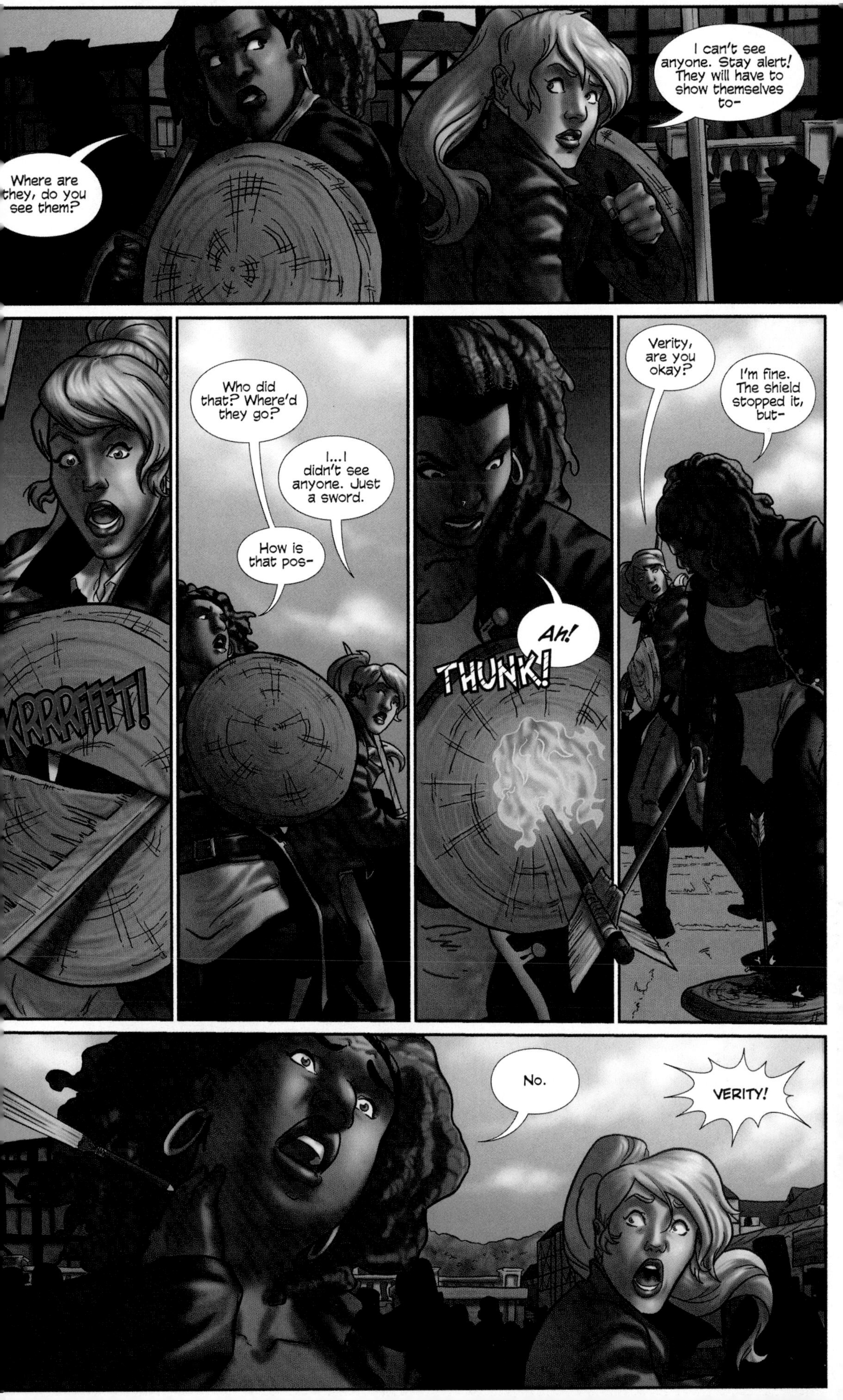

Where are they, do you see them?
I can't see anyone. Stay alert! They will have to show themselves to-
KRRRFFFT!
Who did that? Where'd they go?
I...I didn't see anyone. Just a sword.
How is that pos-
THUNK!
Ah!
Verity, are you okay?
I'm fine. The shield stopped it, but-
No.
VERITY!

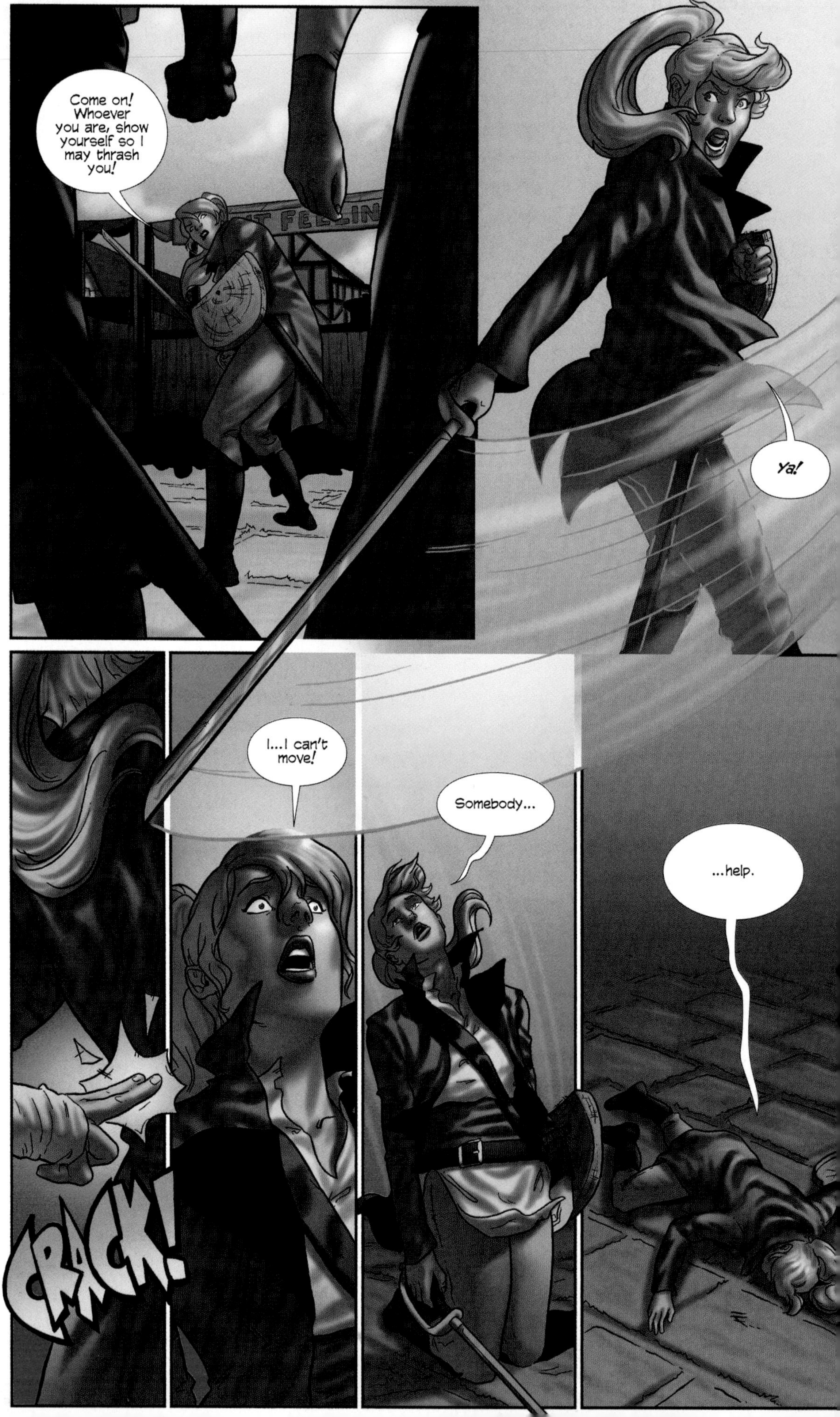
Come on! Whoever you are, show yourself so I may thrash you!
Ya!
I...I can't move!
Somebody...
...help.
CRACK!

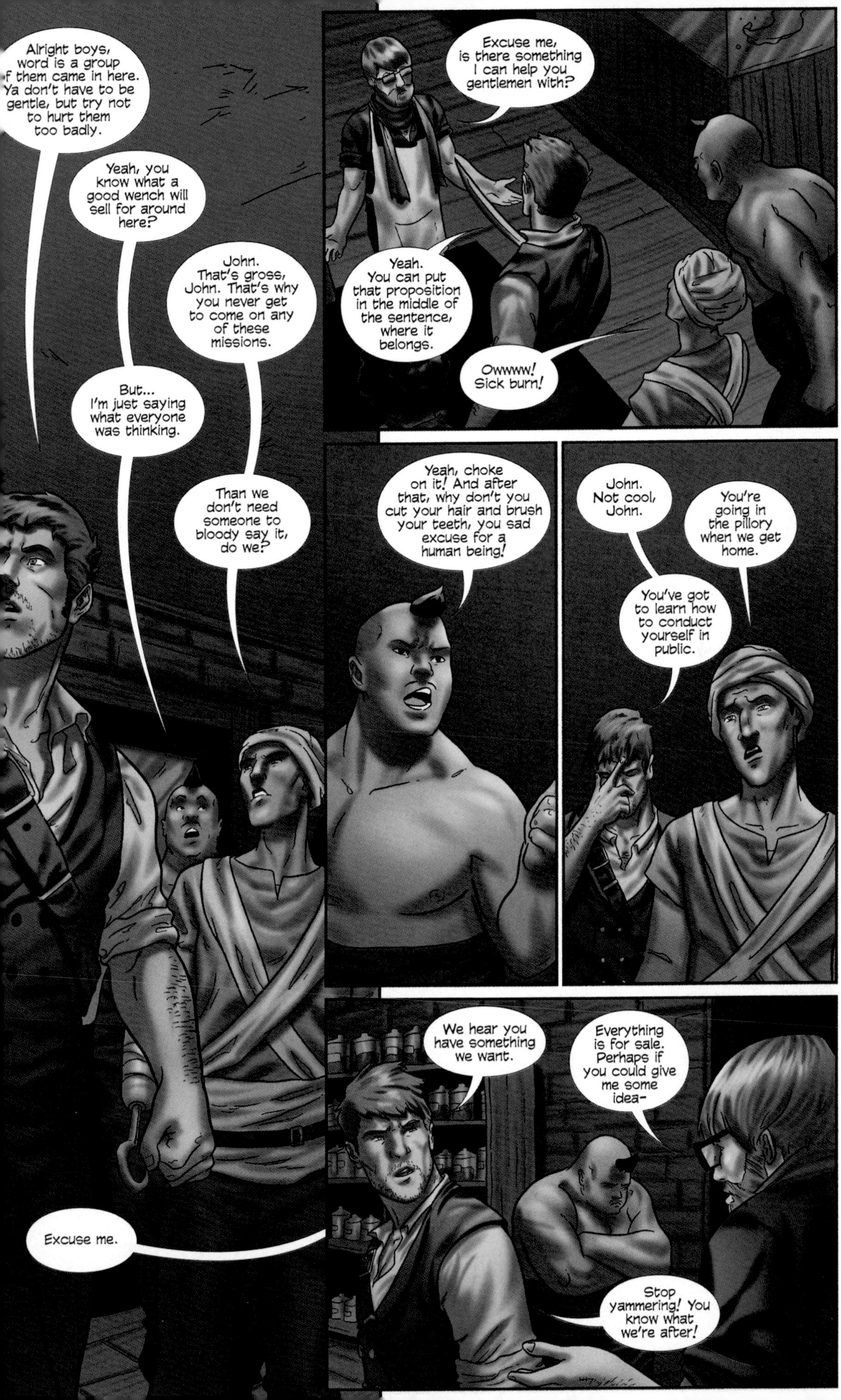

Alright boys, word is a group f them came in here. Ya don't have to be gentle, but try not to hurt them too badly.
Yeah, you know what a good wench will sell for around here?
John. That's gross, John. That's why you never get to come on any of these missions.
But... I'm just saying what everyone was thinking.
Than we don't need someone to bloody say it, do we?
Excuse me.
Excuse me, is there something I can help you gentlemen with?
Yeah. You can put that proposition in the middle of the sentence, where it belongs.
Owwww! Sick burn!
Yeah, choke on it! And after that, why don't you cut your hair and brush your teeth, you sad excuse for a human being!
John. Not cool, John.
You've got to learn how to conduct yourself in public.
You're going in the pillory when we get home.
We hear you have something we want.
Everything is for sale. Perhaps if you could give me some idea-
Stop yammering! You know what we're after!

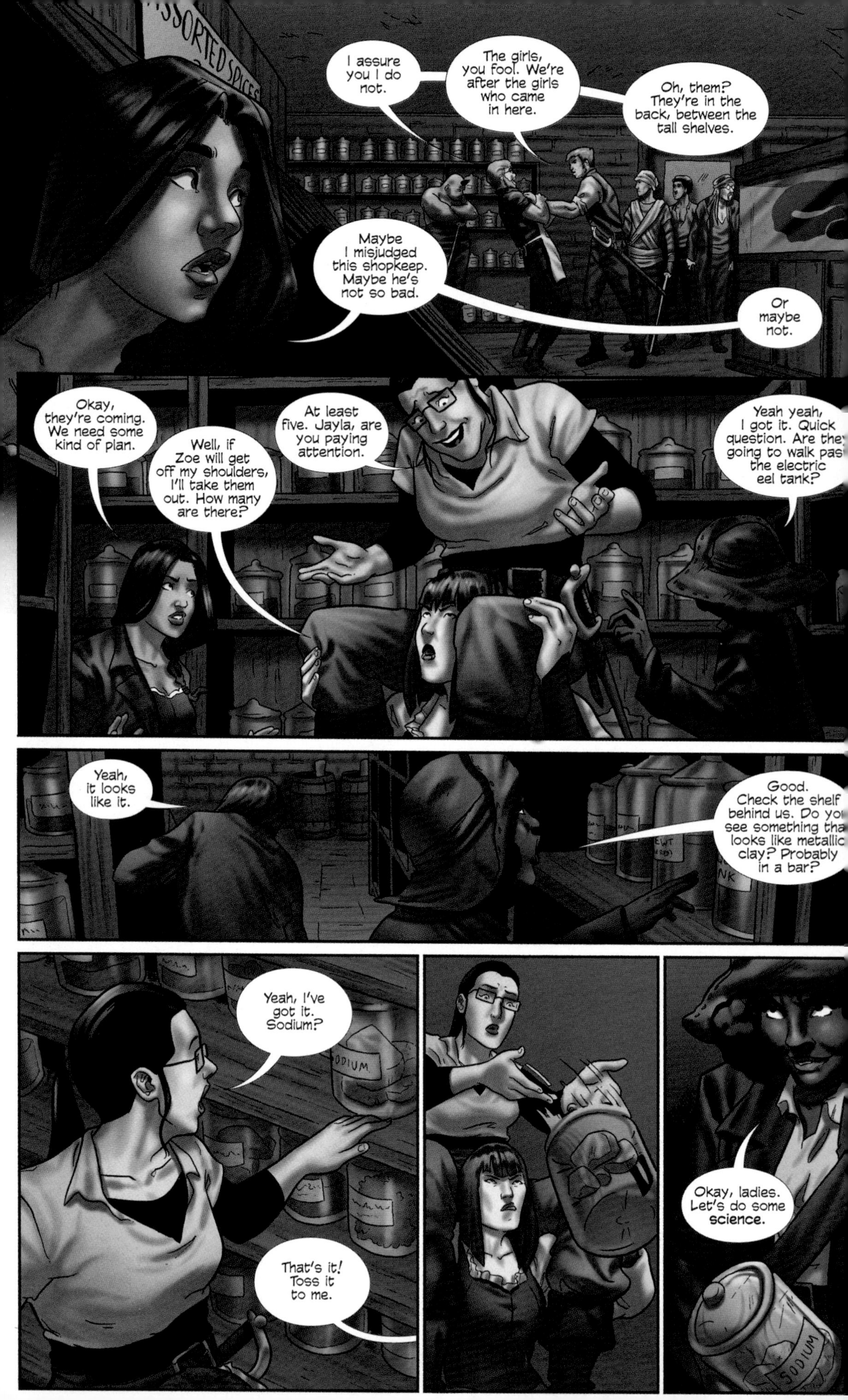
SSORTED SPICES
I assure you I do not.
The girls, you fool. We're after the girls who came in here.
Oh, them? They're in the back, between the tall shelves.
Maybe I misjudged this shopkeep. Maybe he's not so bad.
Or maybe not.
Okay, they're coming. We need some kind of plan.
Well, if Zoe will get off my shoulders, I'll take them out. How many are there?
At least five. Jayla, are you paying attention.
Yeah yeah, I got it. Quick question. Are the going to walk pas the electric eel tank?
Yeah, it looks like it.
Good. Check the shelf behind us. Do yo see something tha looks like metallic clay? Probably in a bar?
Yeah, I've got it. Sodium?
SODIUM
That's it! Toss it to me.
Okay, ladies. Let's do some science.
SODIUM

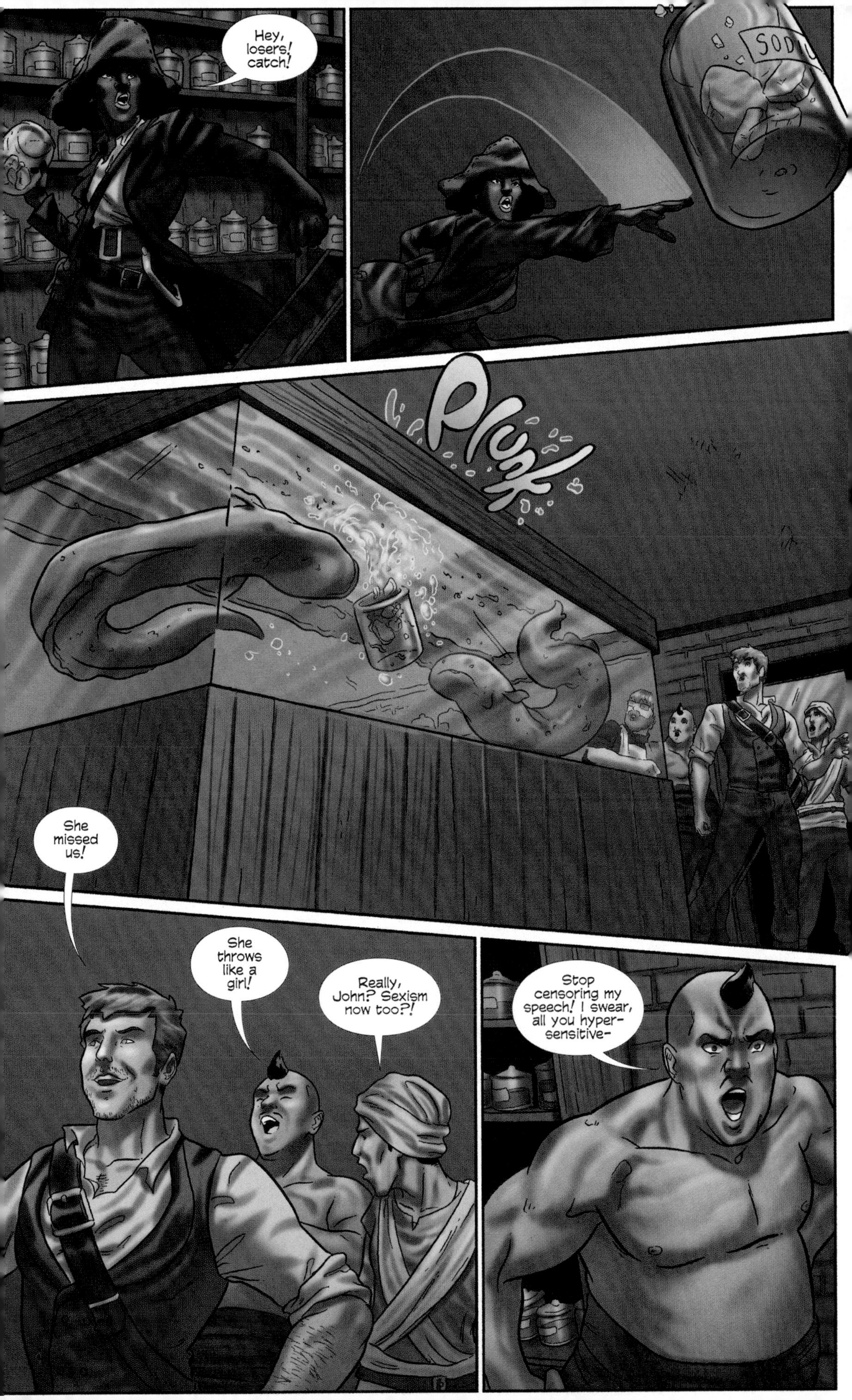
Hey, losers! catch!
SODIU
Plunk
She missed us!
She throws like a girl!
Really, John? Sexism now too?!
Stop censoring my speech! I swear, all you hyper-sensitive-

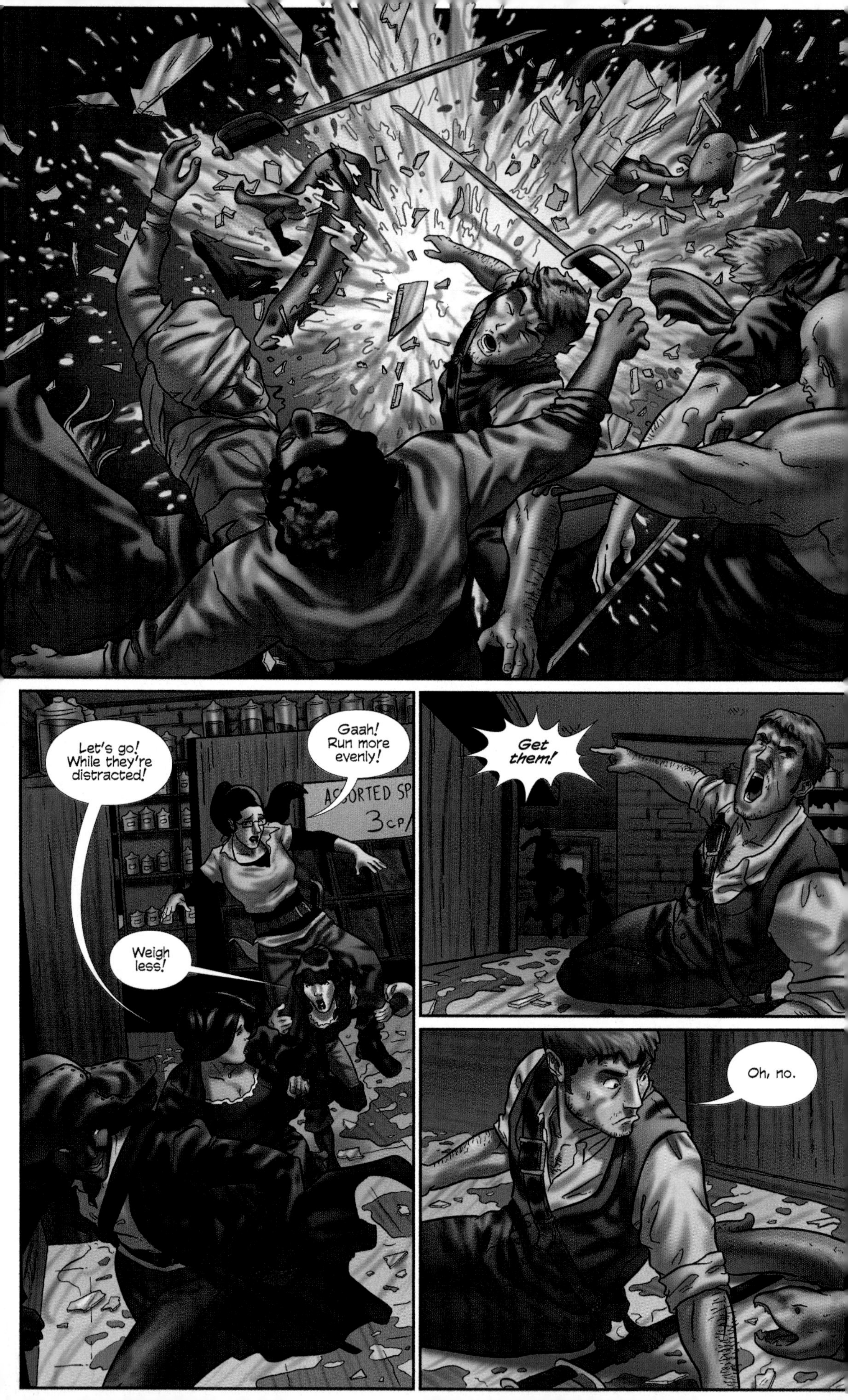
Let's go! While they're distracted!
Gaah! Run more evenly!
ASSORTED SP
3 CP
Weigh less!
Get them!
Oh, no.

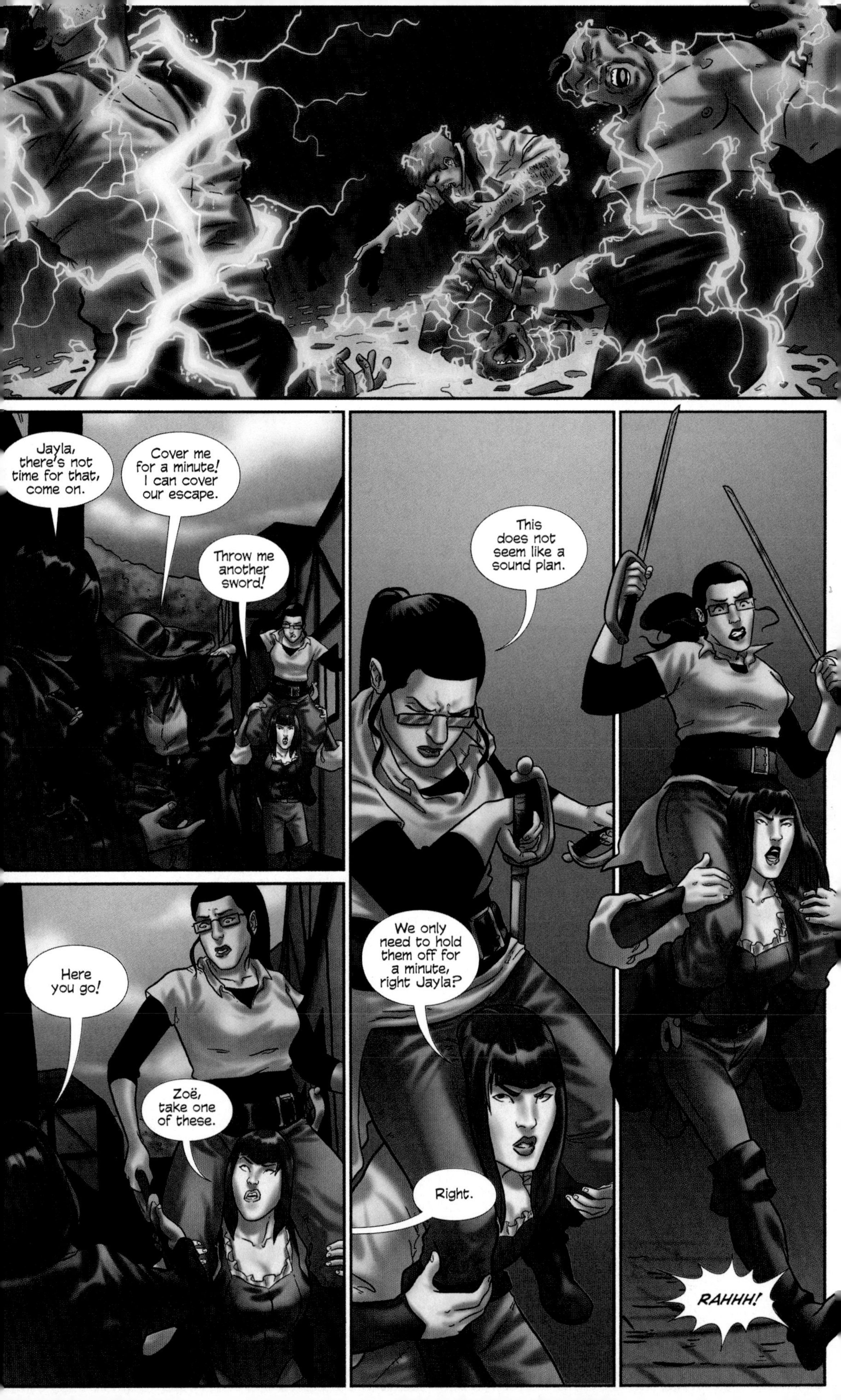
Jayla, there's not time for that, come on.
Cover me for a minute! I can cover our escape.
Throw me another sword!
Here you go!
Zoë, take one of these.
This does not seem like a sound plan.
We only need to hold them off for a minute, right Jayla?
Right.
RAHHH!

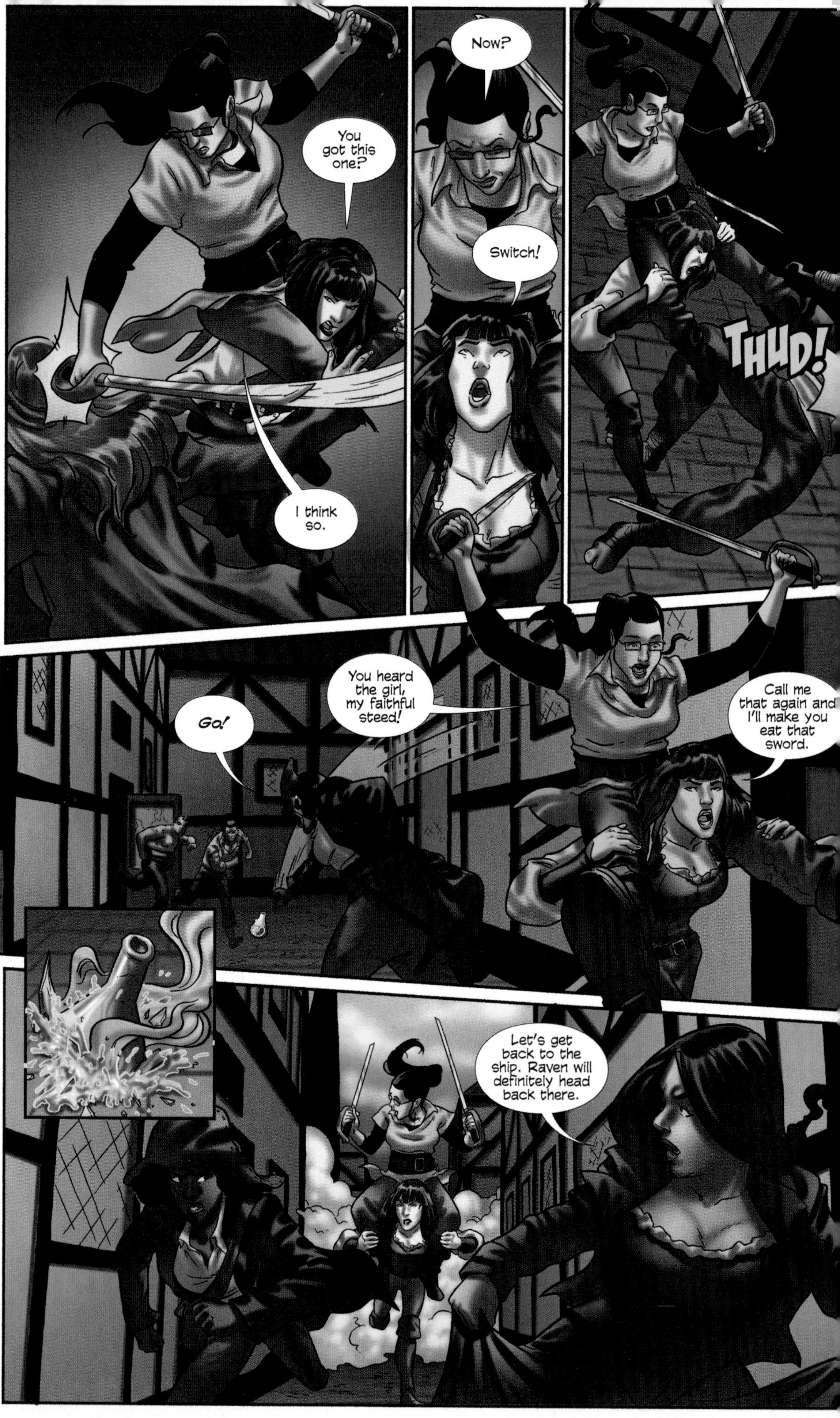
You got this one?
I think so.
Now?
Switch!
THUD!
Go!
You heard the girl, my faithful steed!
Call me that again and I'll make you eat that sword.
Let's get back to the ship. Raven will definitely head back there.

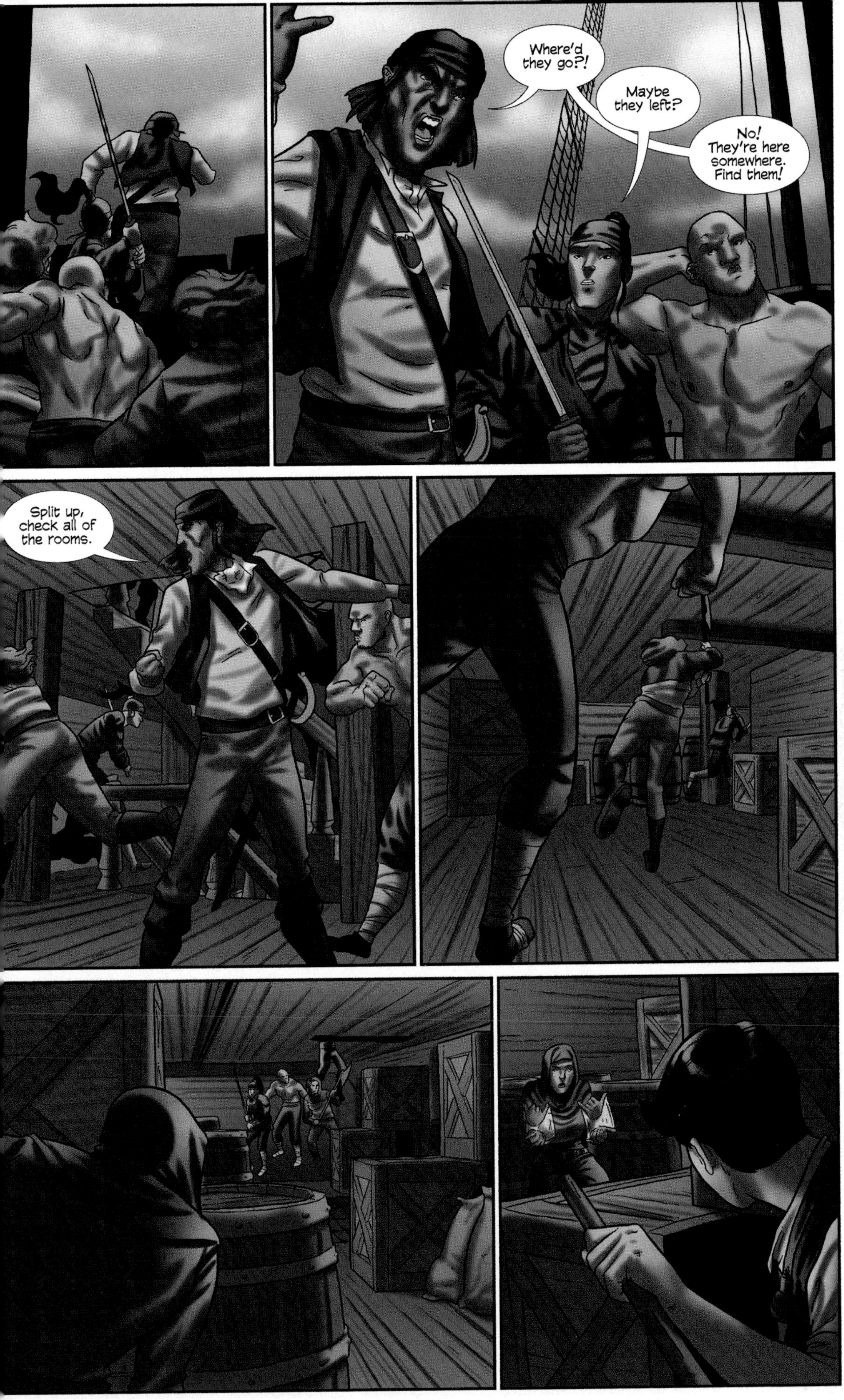
Where'd they go?!
Maybe they left?
No! They're here somewhere. Find them!
Split up, check all of the rooms.

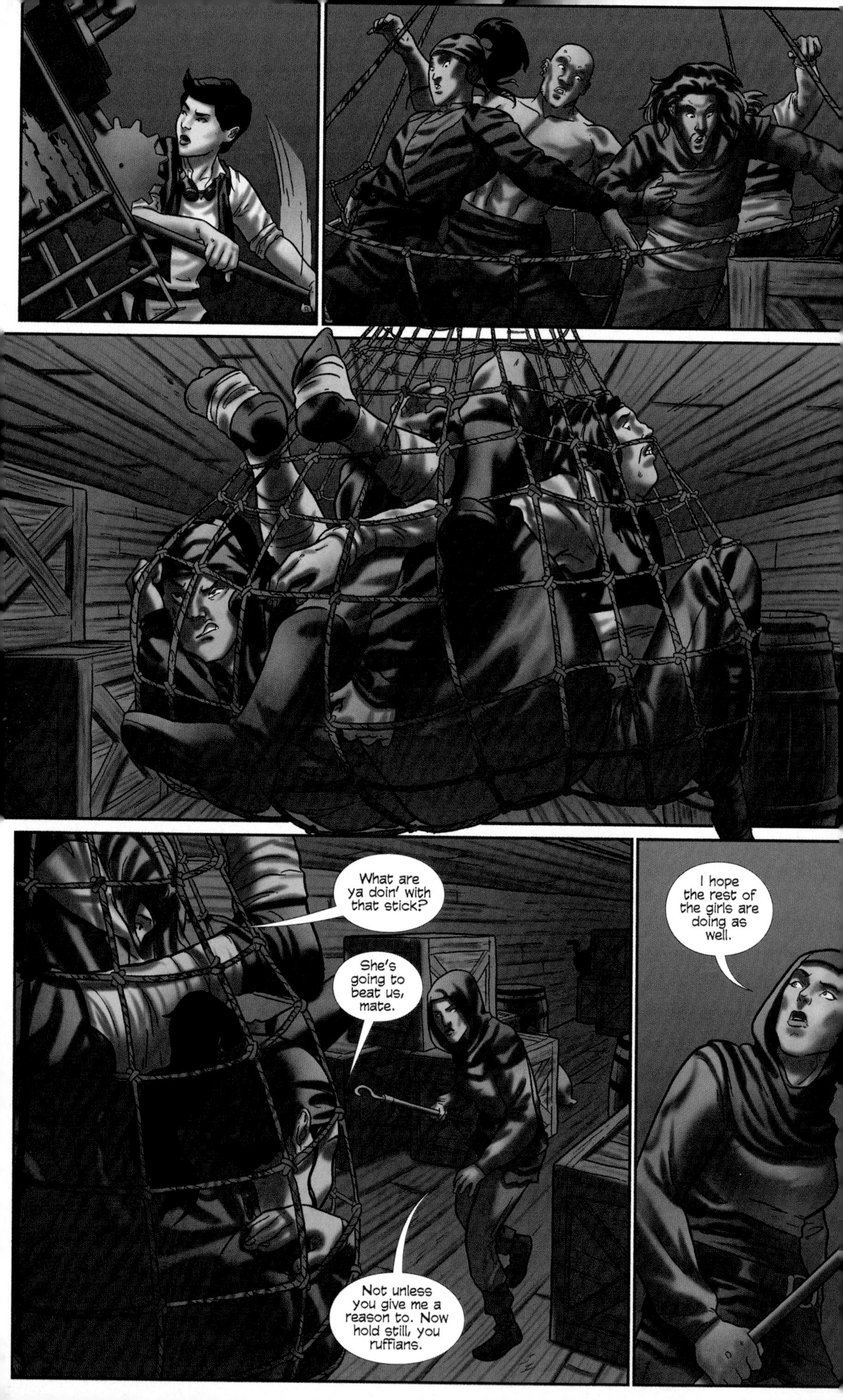
What are ya doin' with that stick?
She's going to beat us, mate.
Not unless you give me a reason to. Now hold still, you ruffians.
I hope the rest of the girls are doing as well.

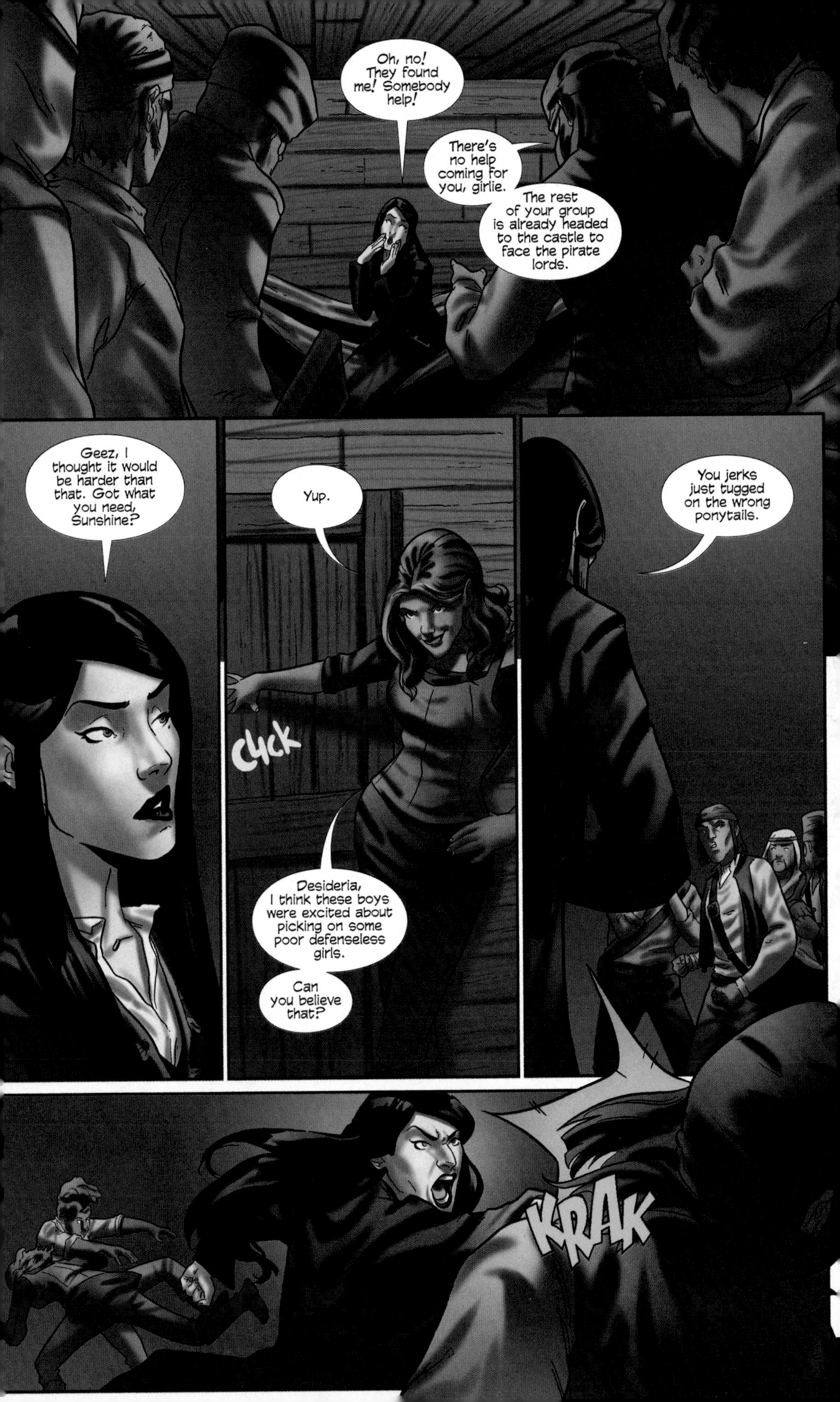

Oh, no! They found me! Somebody help!
There's no help coming for you, girlie.
The rest of your group is already headed to the castle to face the pirate lords.
Geez, I thought it would be harder than that. Got what you need, Sunshine?
Yup.
CLICK
Desideria, I think these boys were excited about picking on some poor defenseless girls.
Can you believe that?
You jerks just tugged on the wrong ponytails.
KRAK

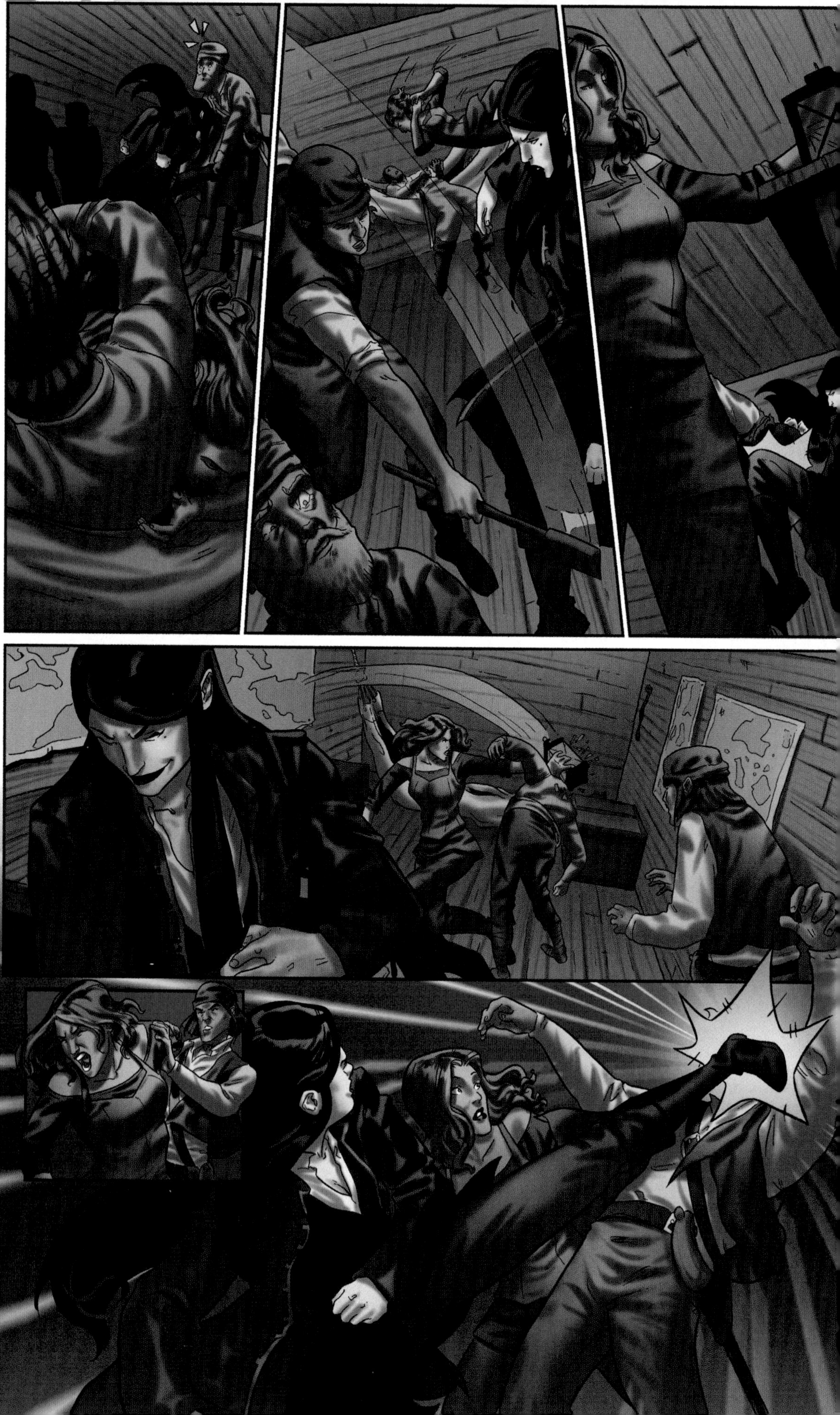

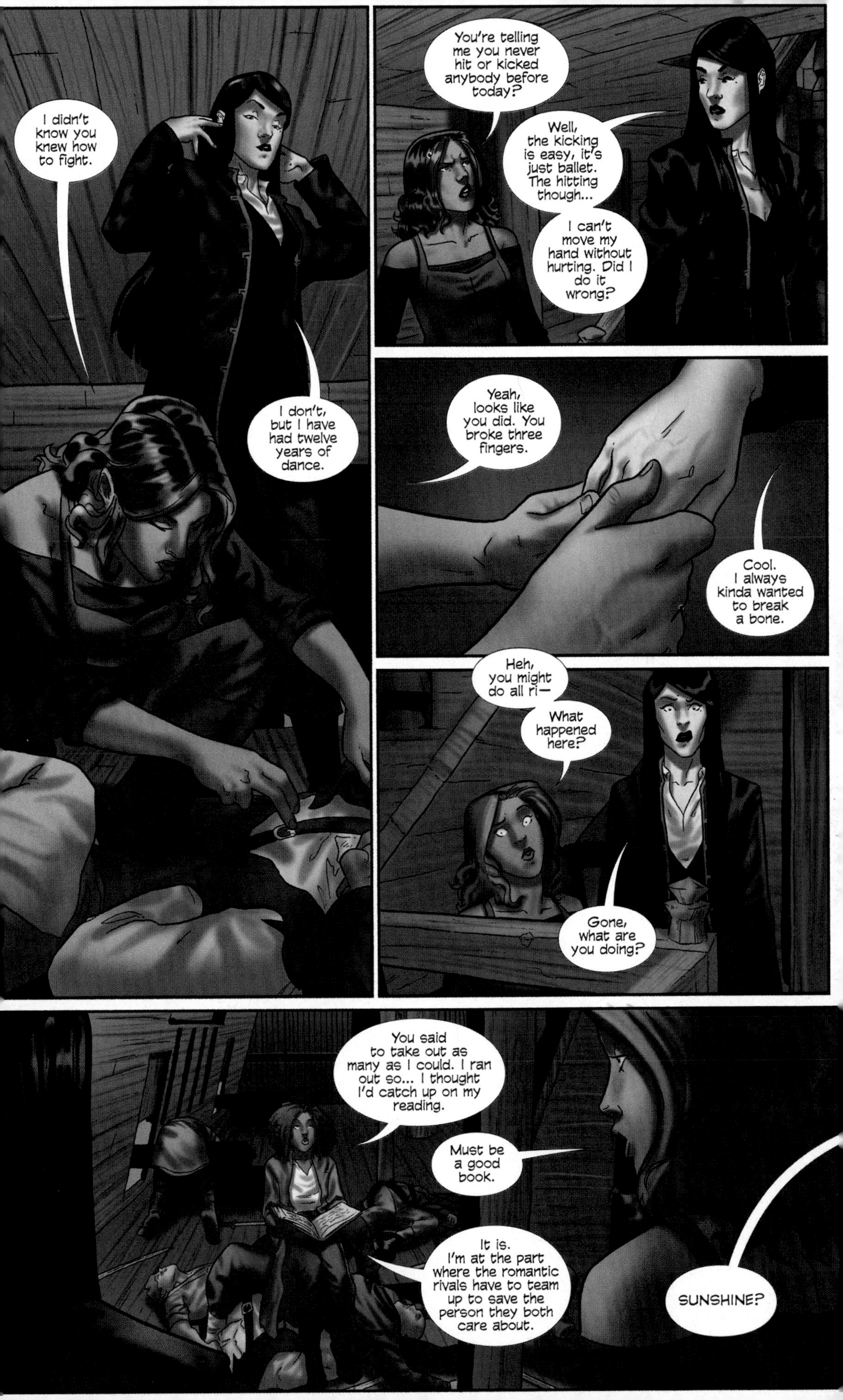

I didn't know you knew how to fight.
I don't, but I have had twelve years of dance.
You're telling me you never hit or kicked anybody before today?
Well, the kicking is easy, it's just ballet. The hitting though...
I can't move my hand without hurting. Did I do it wrong?
Yeah, looks like you did. You broke three fingers.
Cool. I always kinda wanted to break a bone.
Heh, you might do all ri—
What happened here?
Gone, what are you doing?
You said to take out as many as I could. I ran out so... I thought I'd catch up on my reading.
Must be a good book.
It is. I'm at the part where the romantic rivals have to team up to save the person they both care about.
SUNSHINE?

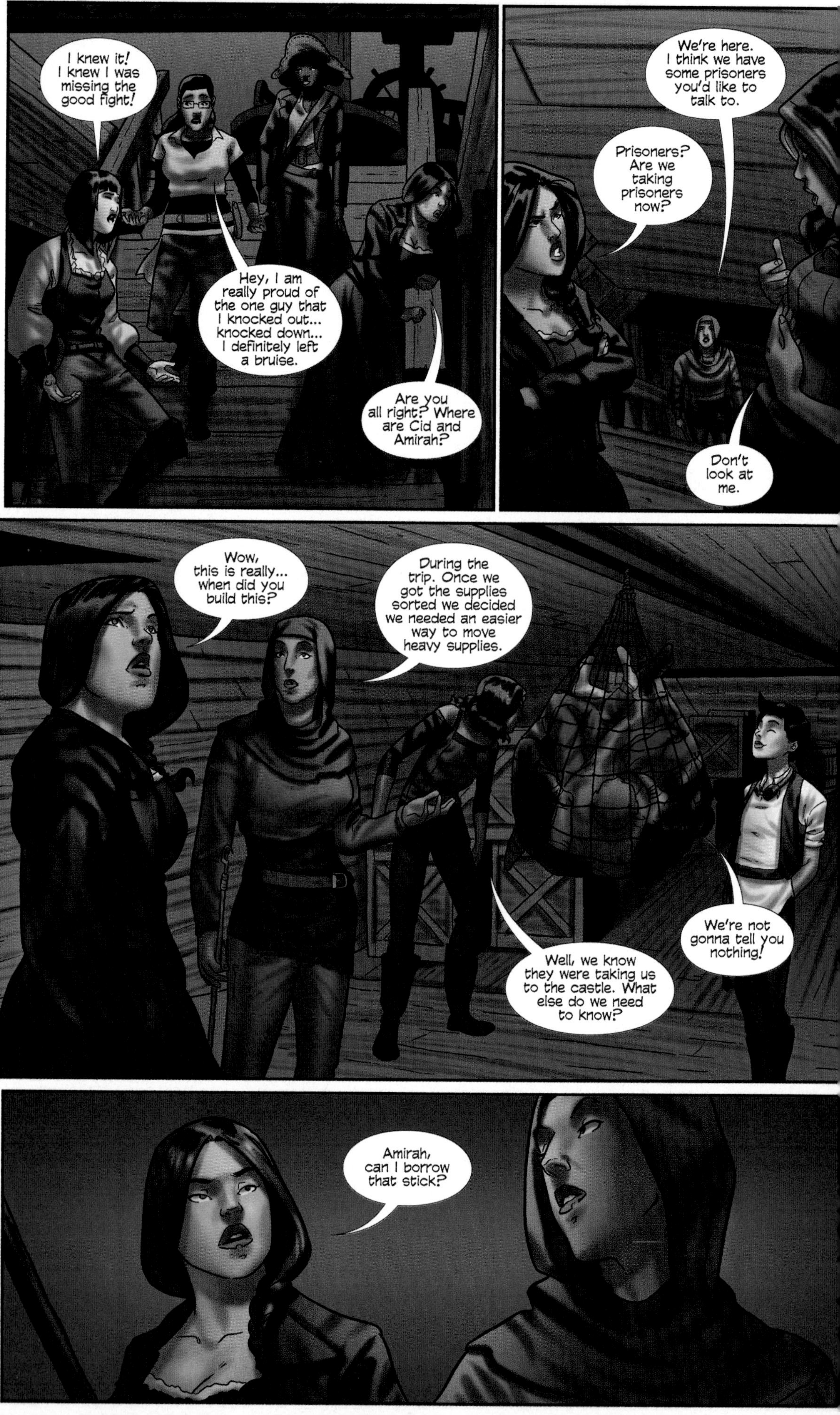
I knew it! I knew I was missing the good fight!
Hey, I am really proud of the one guy that I knocked out... knocked down... I definitely left a bruise.
Are you all right? Where are Cid and Amirah?
We're here. I think we have some prisoners you'd like to talk to.
Prisoners? Are we taking prisoners now?
Don't look at me.
Wow, this is really... when did you build this?
During the trip. Once we got the supplies sorted we decided we needed an easier way to move heavy supplies.
Well, we know they were taking us to the castle. What else do we need to know?
We're not gonna tell you nothing!
Amirah, can I borrow that stick?

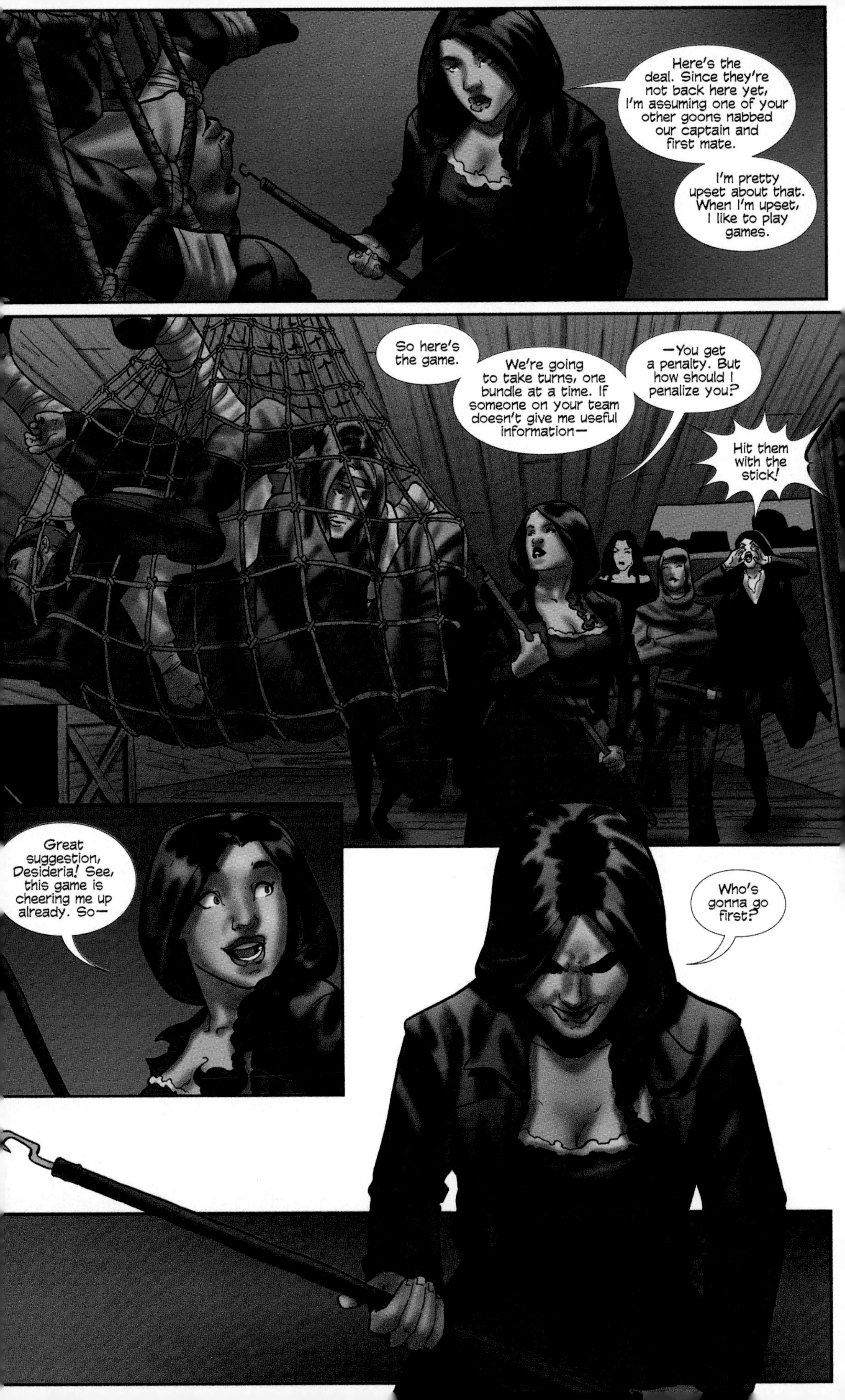
Here's the deal. Since they're not back here yet, I'm assuming one of your other goons nabbed our captain and first mate.
I'm pretty upset about that. When I'm upset, I like to play games.
So here's the game.
We're going to take turns, one bundle at a time. If someone on your team doesn't give me useful information—
—You get a penalty. But how should I penalize you?
Hit them with the stick!
Great suggestion, Desideria! See, this game is cheering me up already. So—
Who's gonna go first?

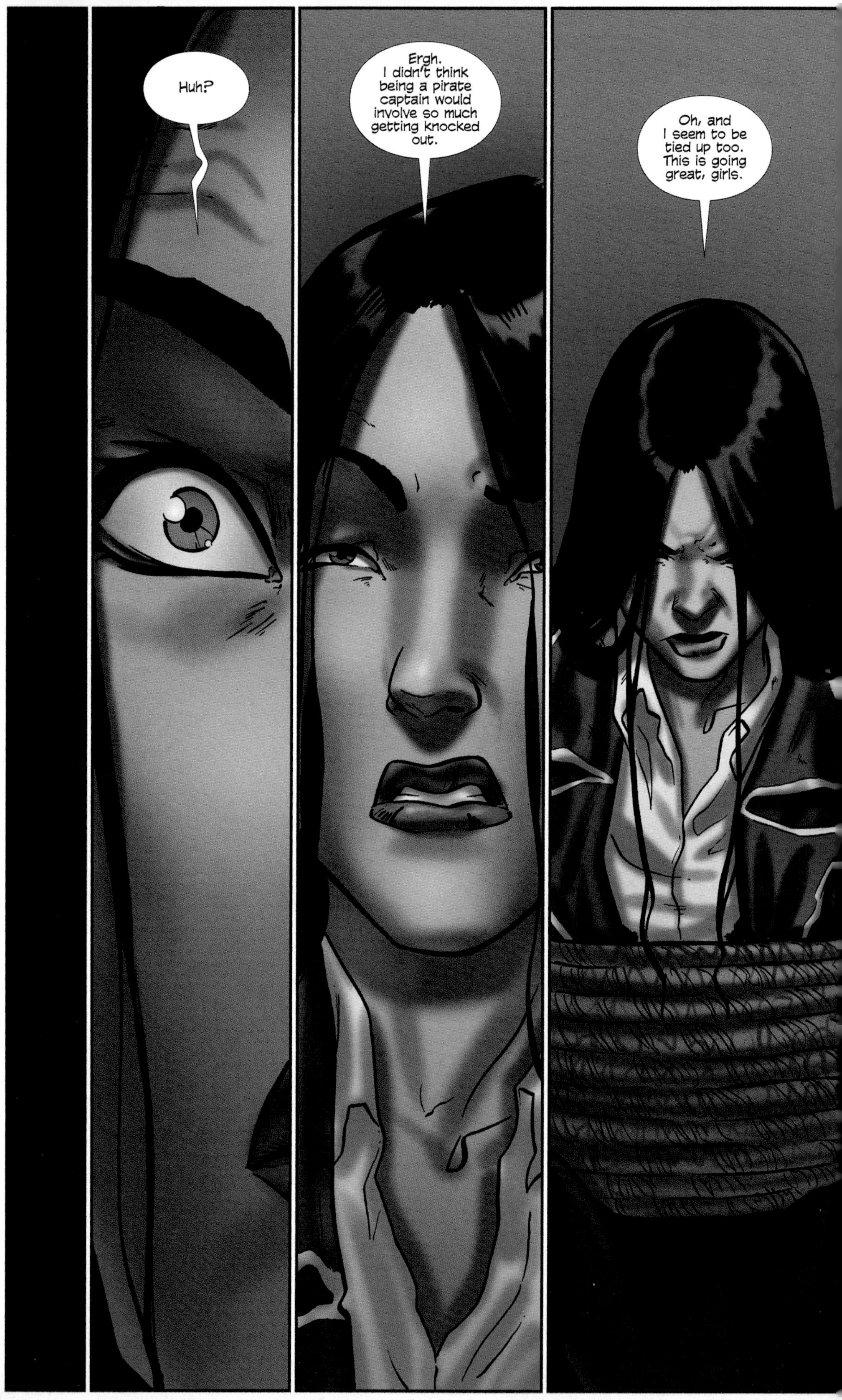
Huh?
Ergh. I didn't think being a pirate captain would involve so much getting knocked out.
Oh, and I seem to be tied up too. This is going great, girls.

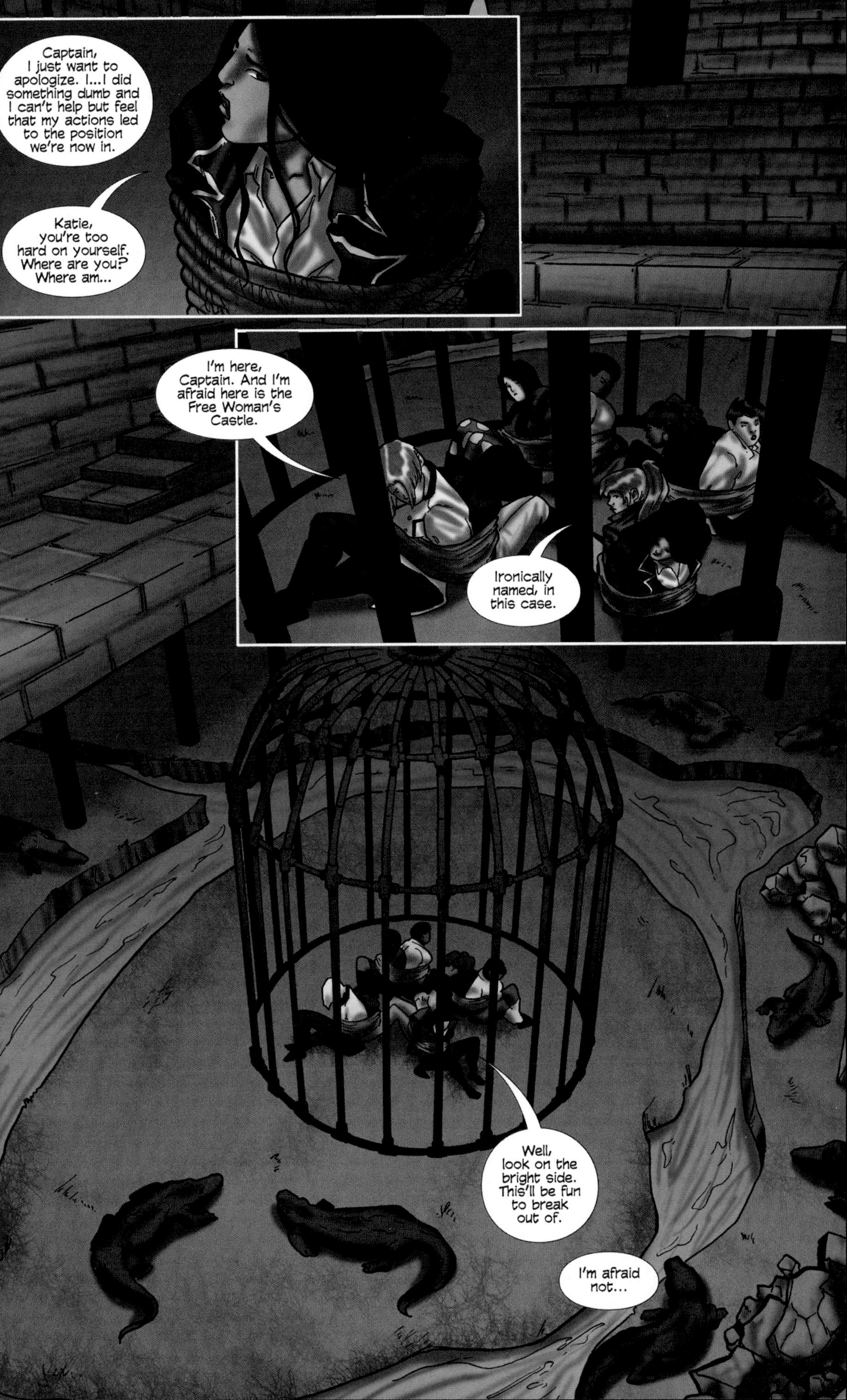
Captain, I just want to apologize. I...I did something dumb and I can't help but feel that my actions led to the position we're now in.
Katie, you're too hard on yourself. Where are you? Where am...
I'm here, Captain. And I'm afraid here is the Free Woman's Castle.
Ironically named, in this case.
Well, look on the bright side. This'll be fun to break out of.
I'm afraid not...

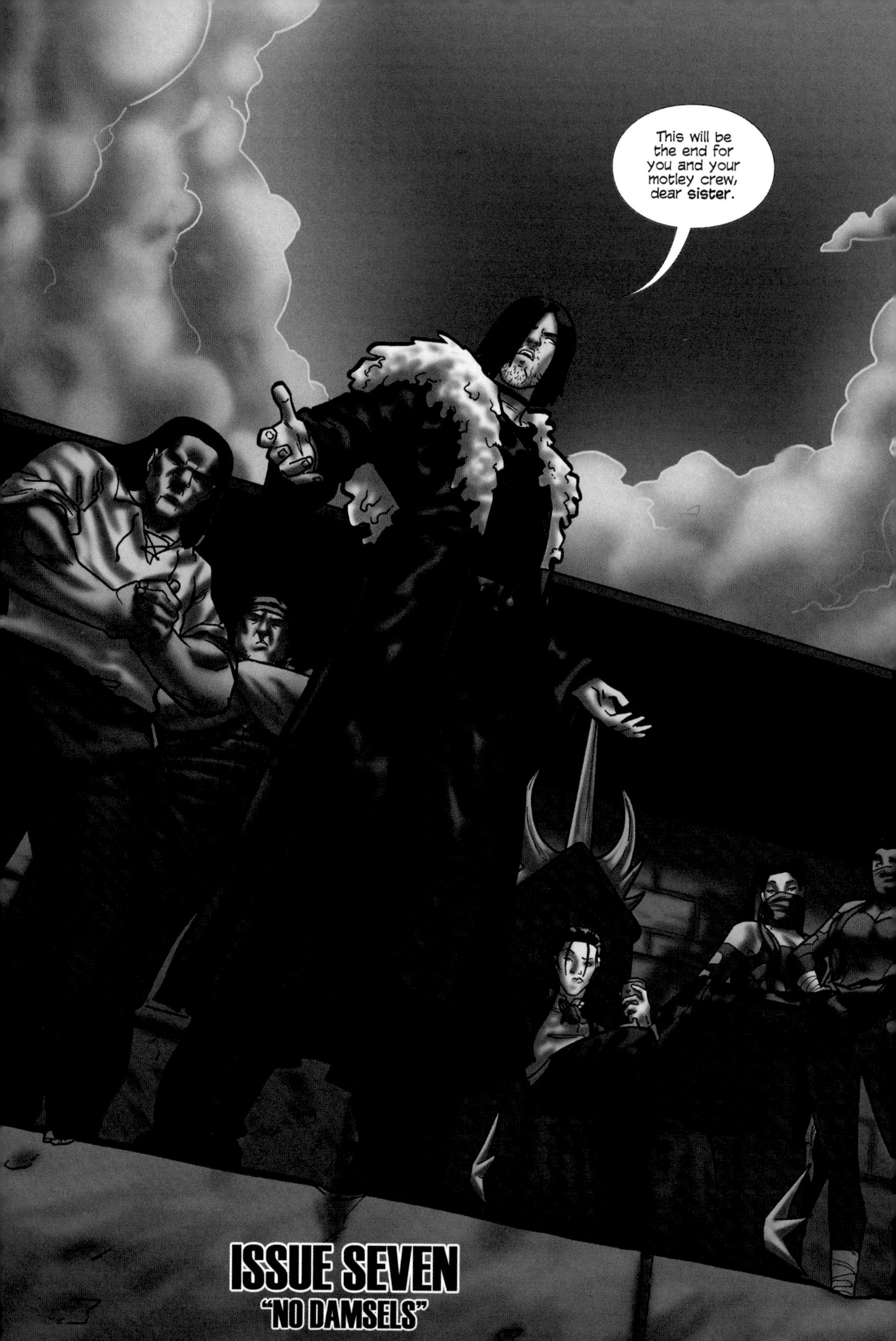
This will be the end for you and your motley crew, dear sister.

ISSUE SEVEN
"NO DAMSELS"

WORDS: Jeremy Whitley PENCILS: Rosy Higgins LAYOUTS/INKS: Ted Brandt
COLORS: William Blankenship LETTERS: Dave Dwonch EDITS: Alicia Whitley & Dave Dwonch

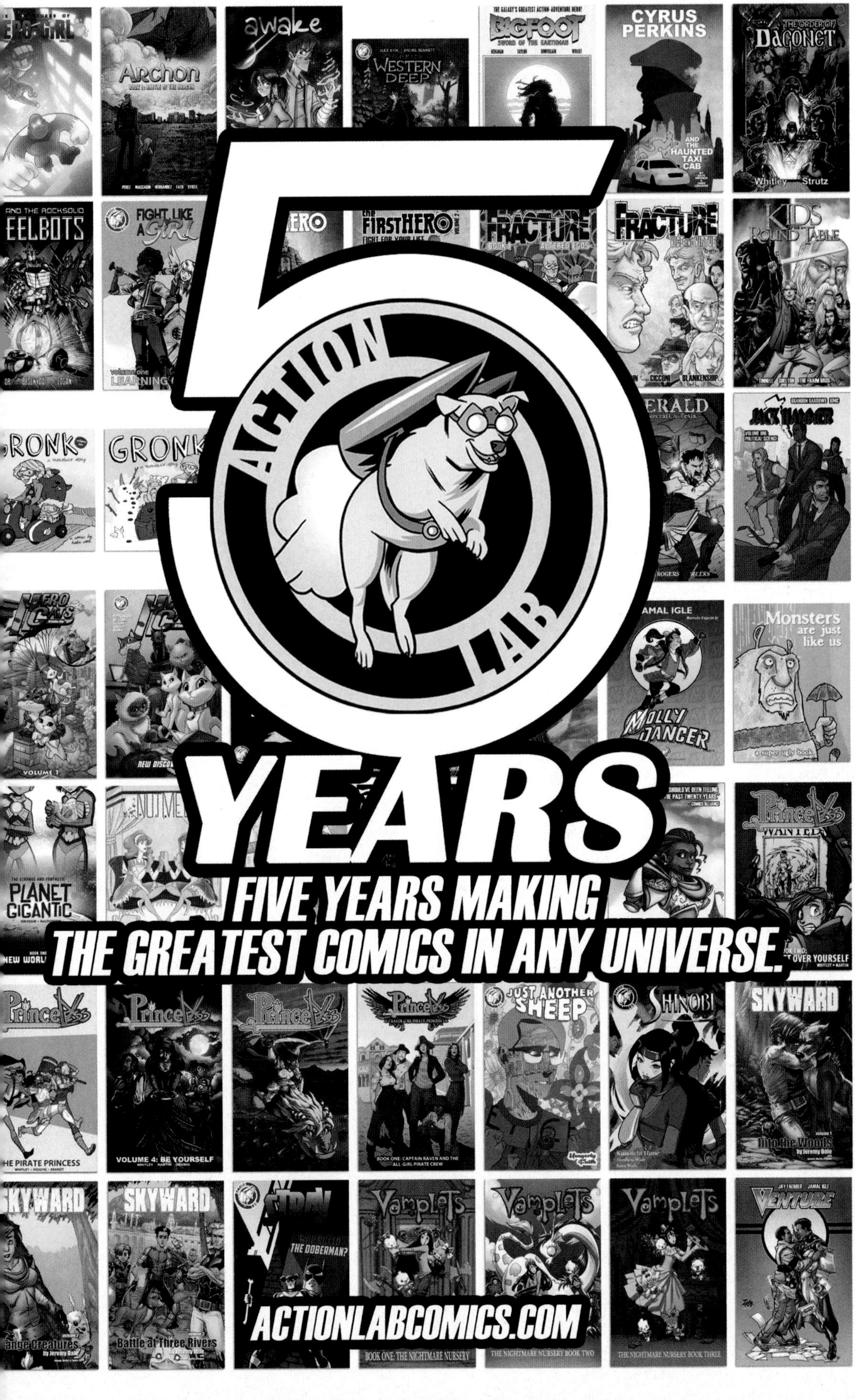

5
ACTION LAB
YEARS
FIVE YEARS MAKING
THE GREATEST COMICS IN ANY UNIVERSE.
ACTIONLABCOMICS.COM

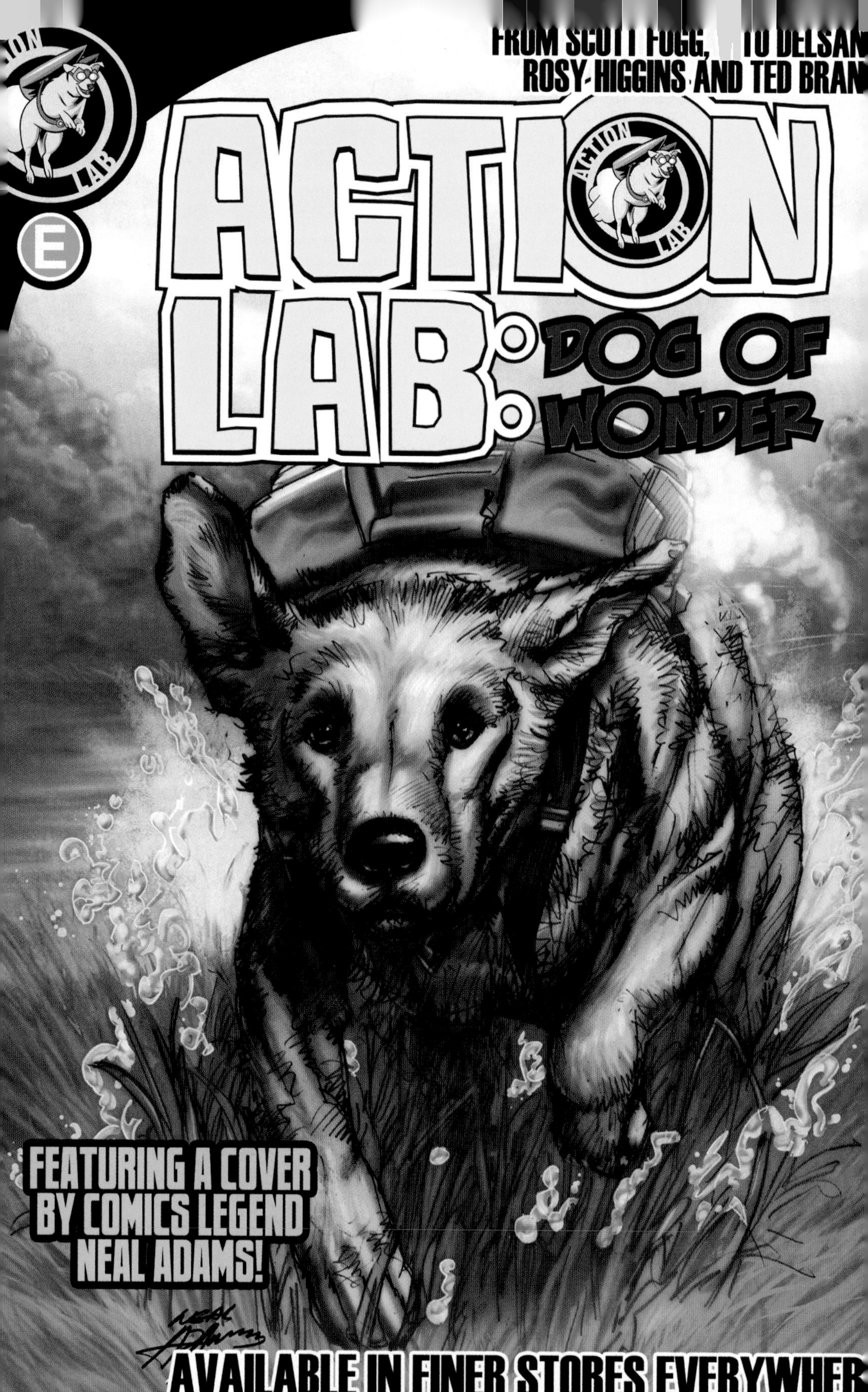
FROM SCOTT FOGG,
TO DELSAN
ROSY HIGGINS AND TED BRAN
ACTION LAB: DOG OF WONDER
FEATURING A COVER BY COMICS LEGEND NEAL ADAMS!
AVAILABLE IN FINER STORES EVERYWHER

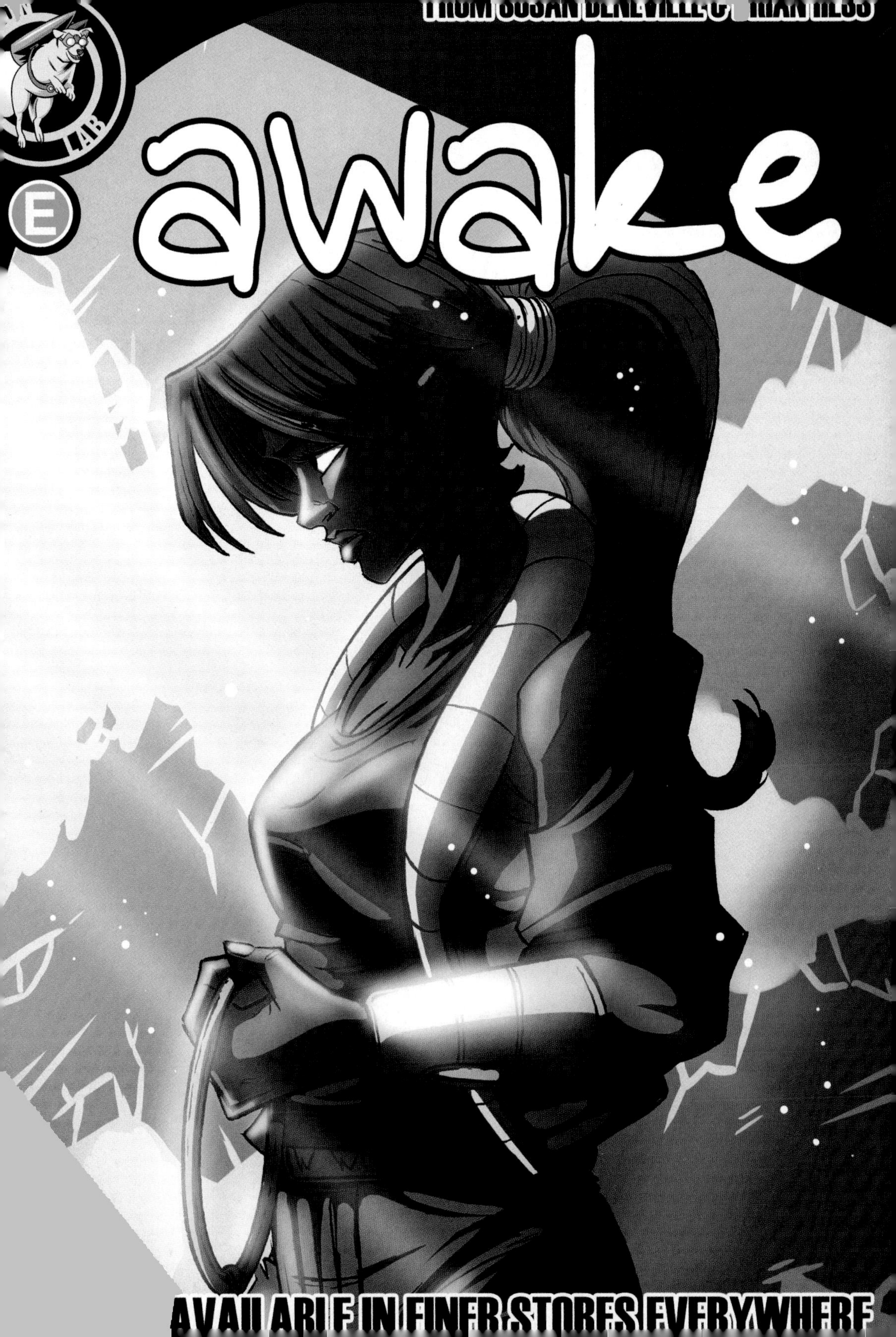

awake
E
AVAILABLE IN FINER STORES EVERYWHERE

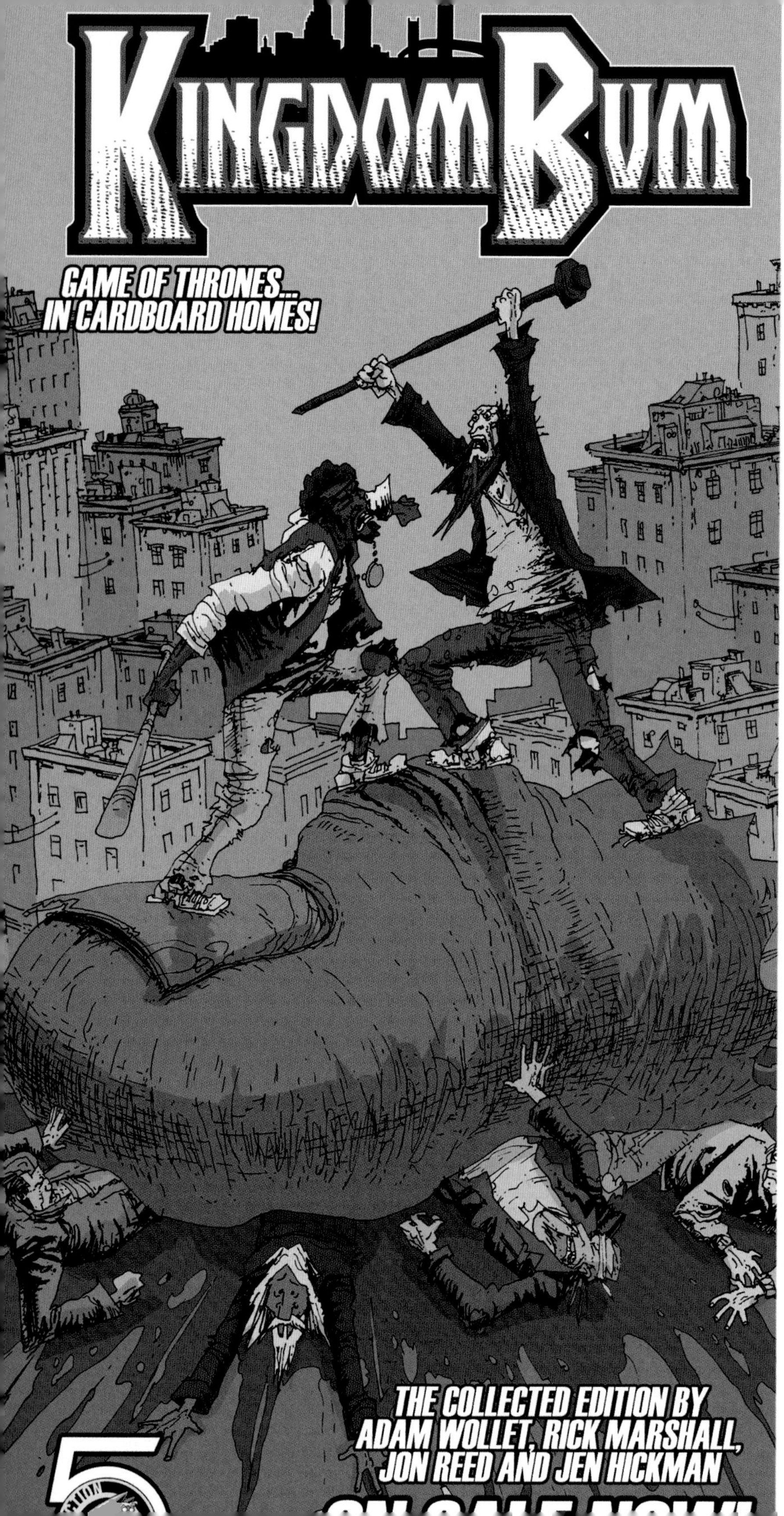
KINGDOM BUM
GAME OF THRONES...
IN CARDBOARD HOMES!
THE COLLECTED EDITION BY
ADAM WOLLET, RICK MARSHALL,
JON REED AND JEN HICKMAN

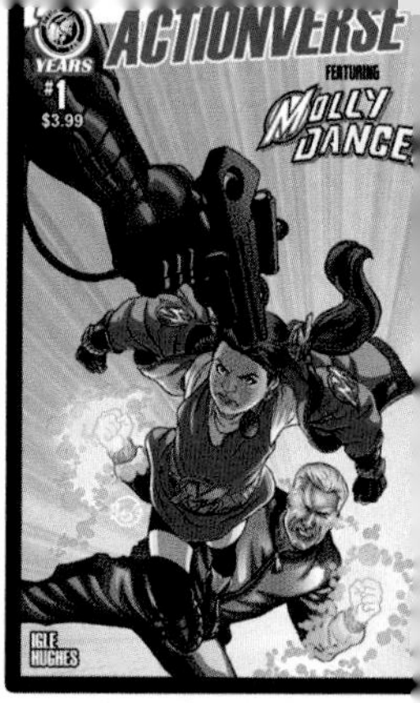
ACTIONVERSE
FEATURING
MOLLY DANGER
#1
$3.99
IGLE
HUGHES

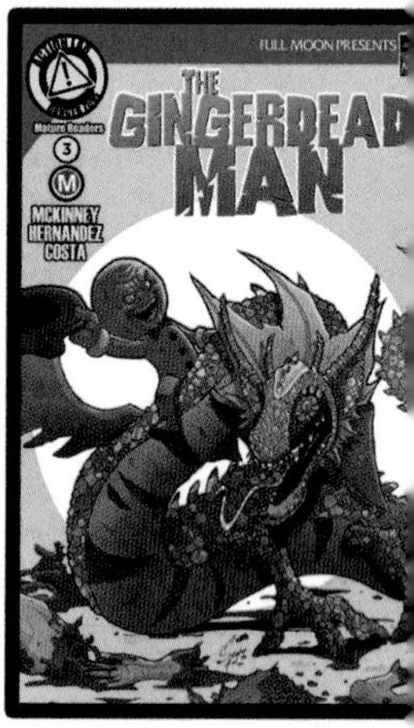
FULL MOON PRESENTS
THE GINGERDEAD MAN
3
MCKINNEY
HERNANDEZ
COSTA

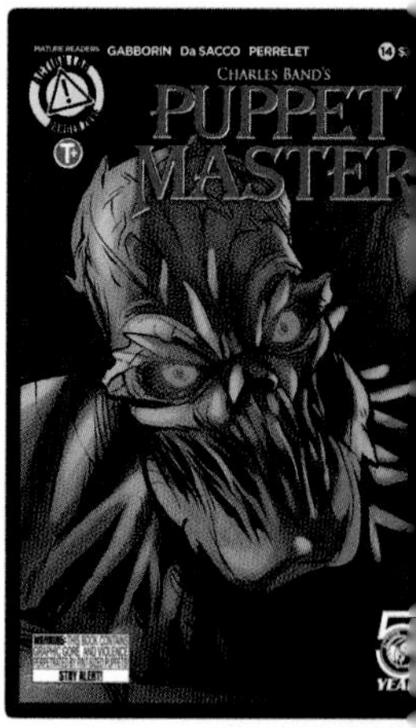
GABBORIN DaSACCO PERRELET
CHARLES BAND'S
PUPPET MASTER
STAY ALERT!

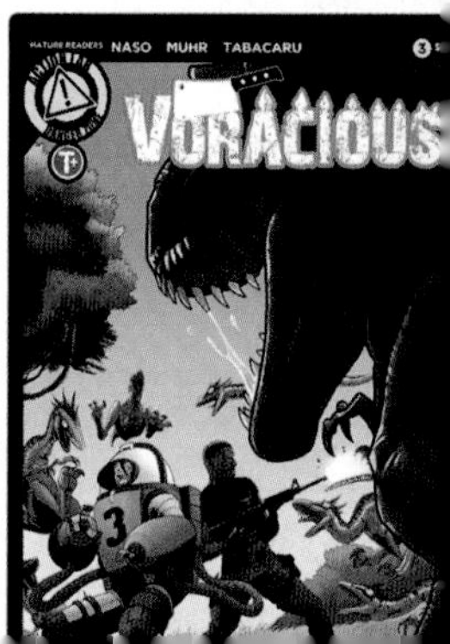
NASO MUHR TABACARU
VORACIOUS

SAVE THE DATE!

Celebrating 15 Years

FREE COMIC BOOK ·DAY·

1st SATURDAY IN MAY!

May 7, 2016
www.freecomicbookday.com

FREE COMICS FOR EVERYONE!

Details @ www.freecomicbookday.com

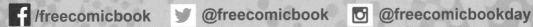
 /freecomicbook   @freecomicbook   @freecomicbookday

READ MORE NOW

Raven: Pirate Princess - Action Lab
www.actionlabcomics.com

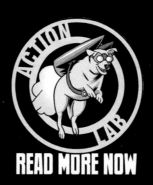

ACTIONLABCOMICS.COM

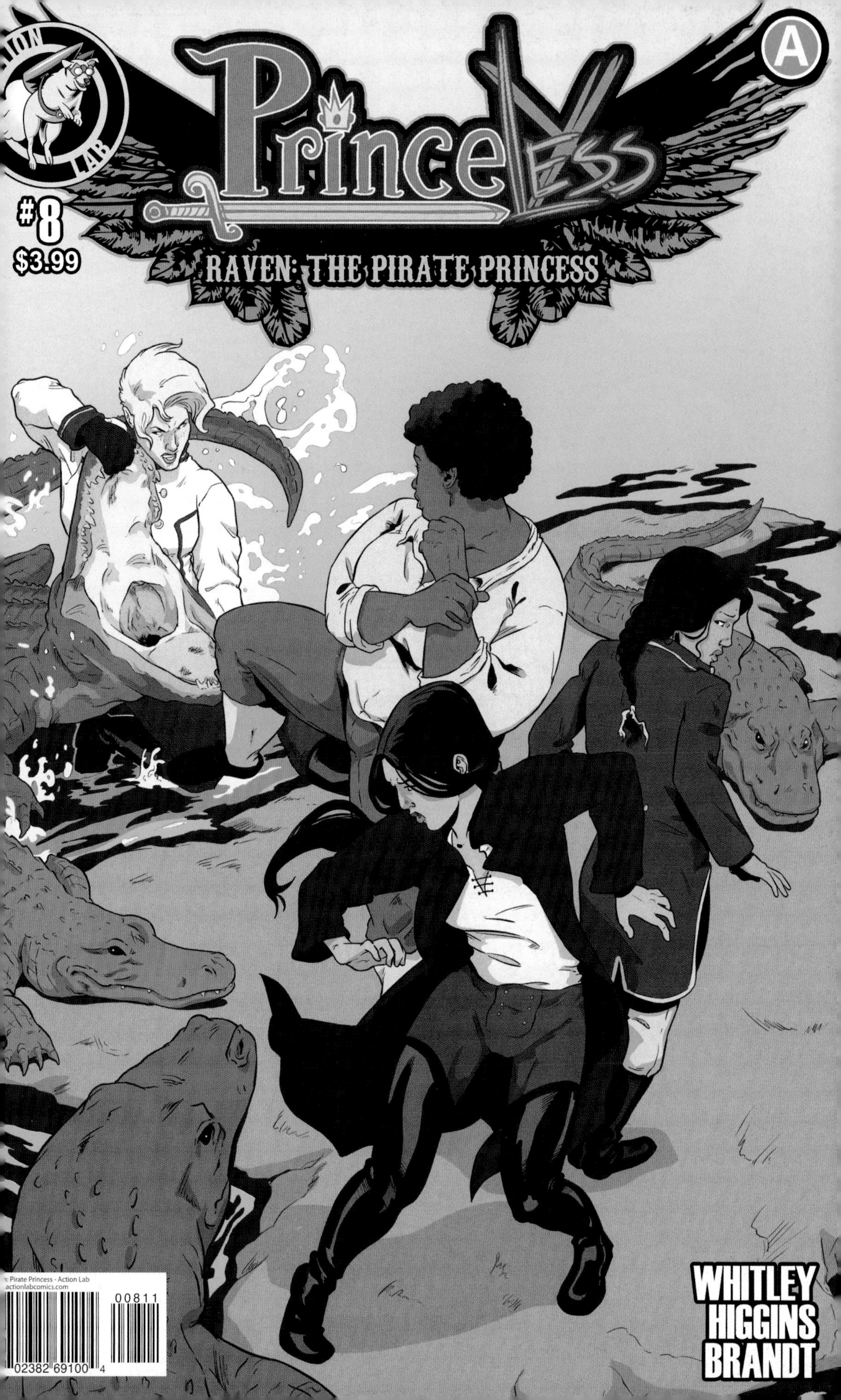

Princeless
#8
$3.99
RAVEN: THE PIRATE PRINCESS
actionlabcomics.com
WHITLEY
HIGGINS
BRANDT

FROM ALL-AGES TO MATURE READERS
ACTION LAB HAS YOU COVERED.

 **Appropriate for everyone.**

 **Appropriate for age 9 and up. Absent of profanity or adult content.**

 **Suggested for 12 and Up. Comics with this rating are comparable to a PG-13 movie rating. Recommended for our teen and young adult readers.**

 **Appropriate for older teens. Similar to Teen, but featuring more mature themes and/or more graphic imagery.**

 **Contains extreme violence and some nudity. Basically the Rated-R of comics.**

 FIND YOUR NEW FAVORITE COMICS.

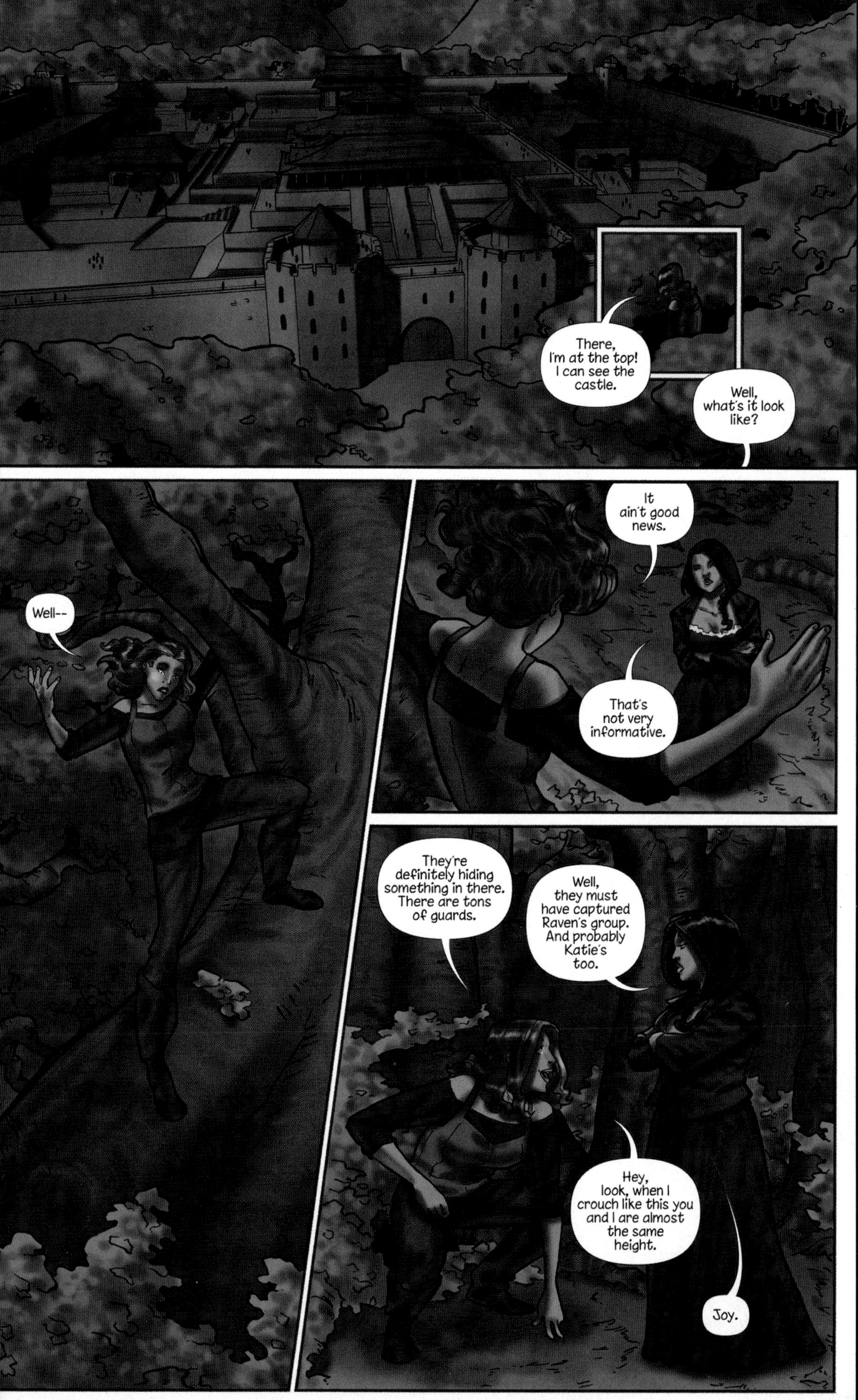
There, I'm at the top! I can see the castle.
Well, what's it look like?
Well--
It ain't good news.
That's not very informative.
They're definitely hiding something in there. There are tons of guards.
Well, they must have captured Raven's group. And probably Katie's too.
Hey, look, when I crouch like this you and I are almost the same height.
Joy.

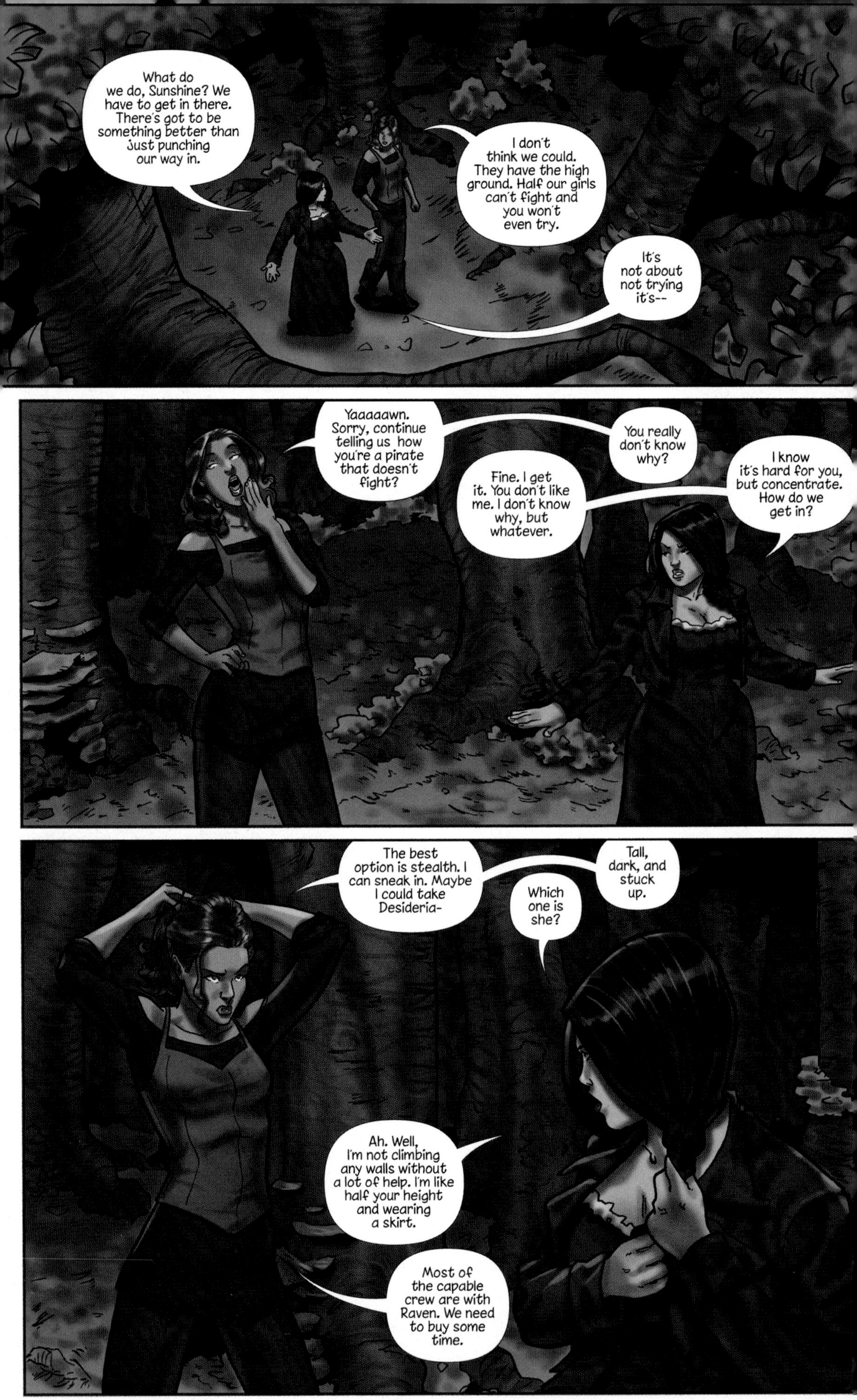
What do we do, Sunshine? We have to get in there. There's got to be something better than just punching our way in.
I don't think we could. They have the high ground. Half our girls can't fight and you won't even try.
It's not about not trying it's--
Yaaaaawn. Sorry, continue telling us how you're a pirate that doesn't fight?
You really don't know why?
Fine. I get it. You don't like me. I don't know why, but whatever.
I know it's hard for you, but concentrate. How do we get in?
The best option is stealth. I can sneak in. Maybe I could take Desideria-
Tall, dark, and stuck up.
Which one is she?
Ah. Well, I'm not climbing any walls without a lot of help. I'm like half your height and wearing a skirt.
Most of the capable crew are with Raven. We need to buy some time.

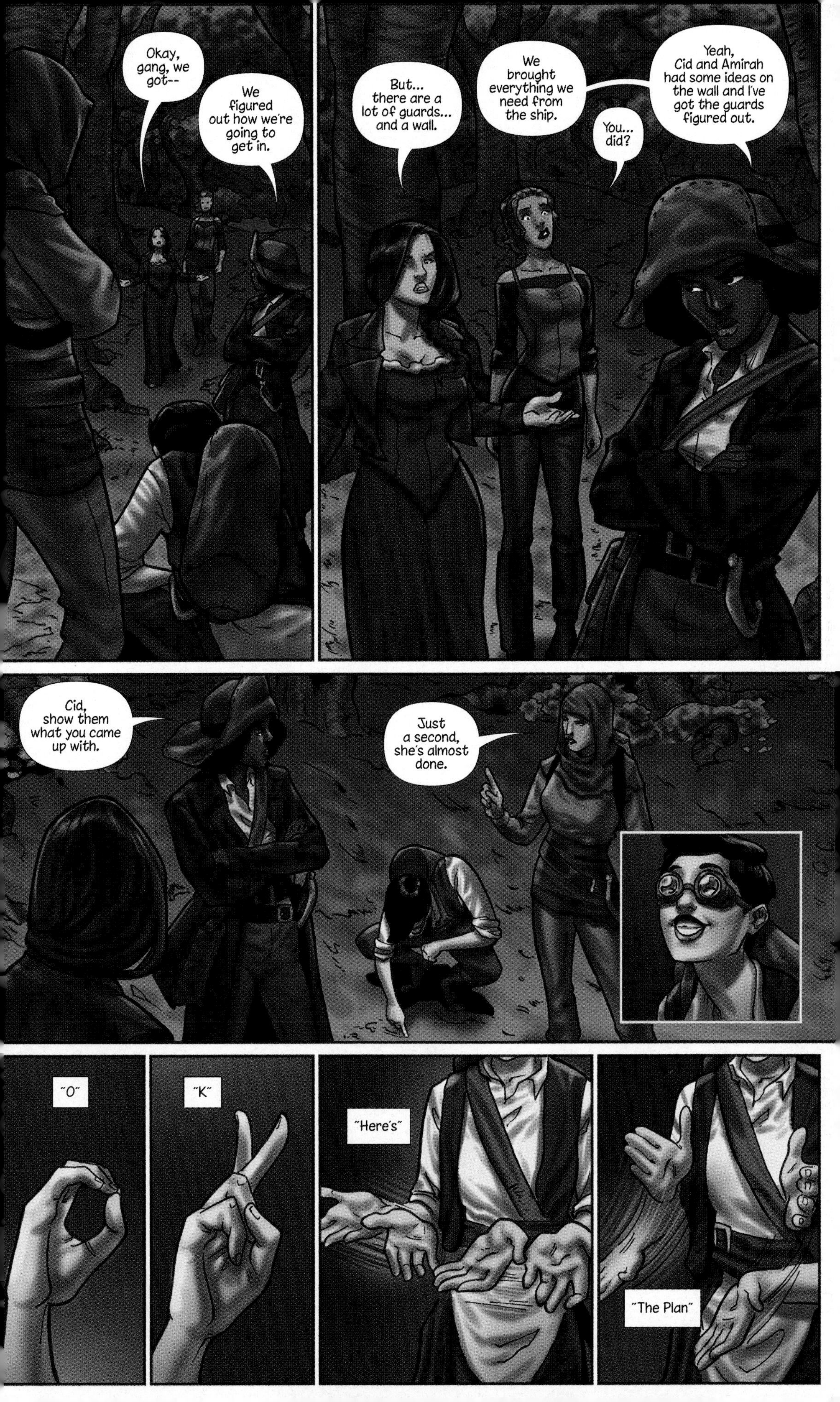
Okay, gang, we got--
We figured out how we're going to get in.
But... there are a lot of guards... and a wall.
We brought everything we need from the ship.
You... did?
Yeah, Cid and Amirah had some ideas on the wall and I've got the guards figured out.
Cid, show them what you came up with.
Just a second, she's almost done.
"O"
"K"
"Here's"
"The Plan"

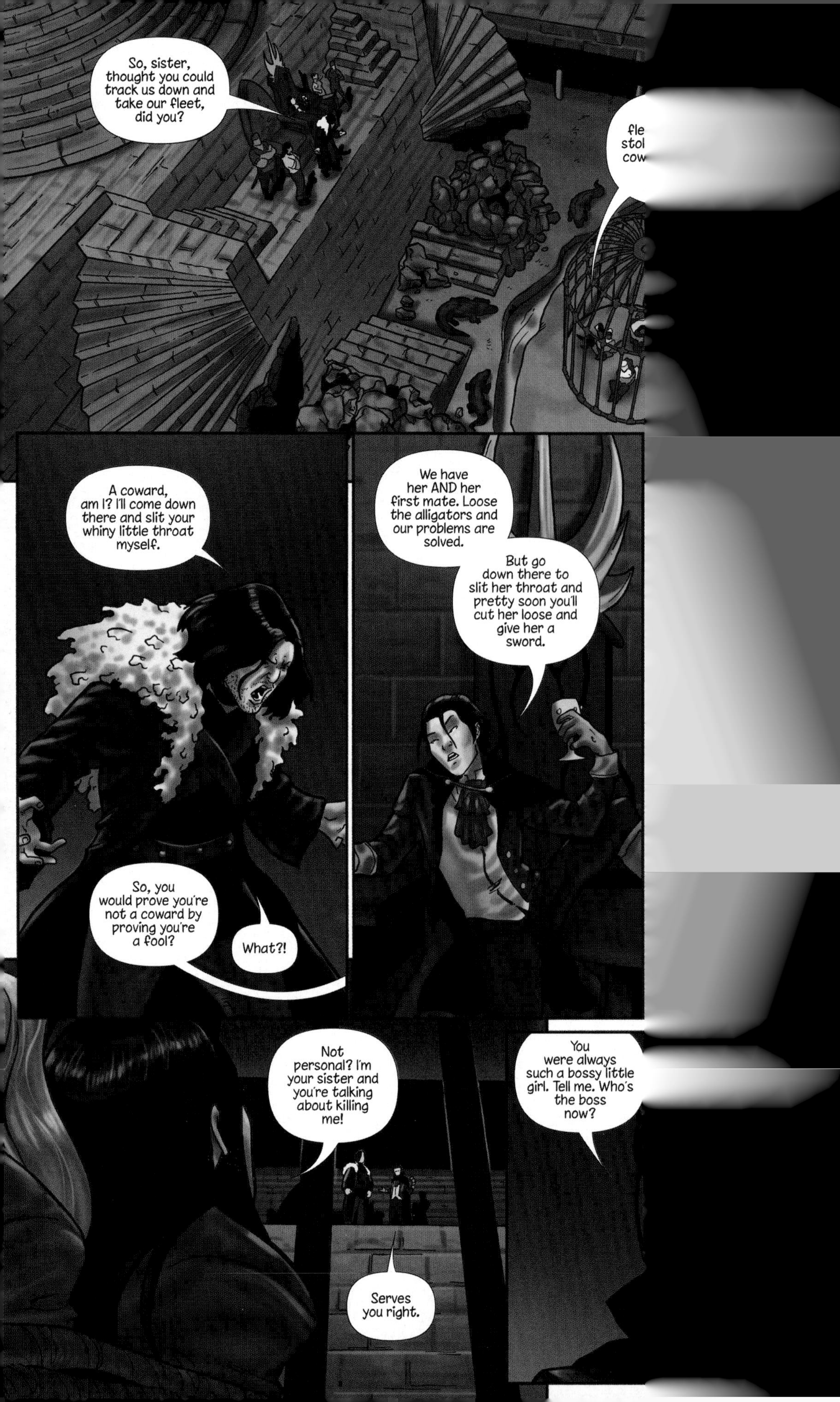
So, sister, thought you could track us down and take our fleet, did you?
fle stol cow
A coward, am I? I'll come down there and slit your whiny little throat myself.
We have her AND her first mate. Loose the alligators and our problems are solved.
But go down there to slit her throat and pretty soon you'll cut her loose and give her a sword.
So, you would prove you're not a coward by proving you're a fool?
What?!
Not personal? I'm your sister and you're talking about killing me!
You were always such a bossy little girl. Tell me. Who's the boss now?
Serves you right.

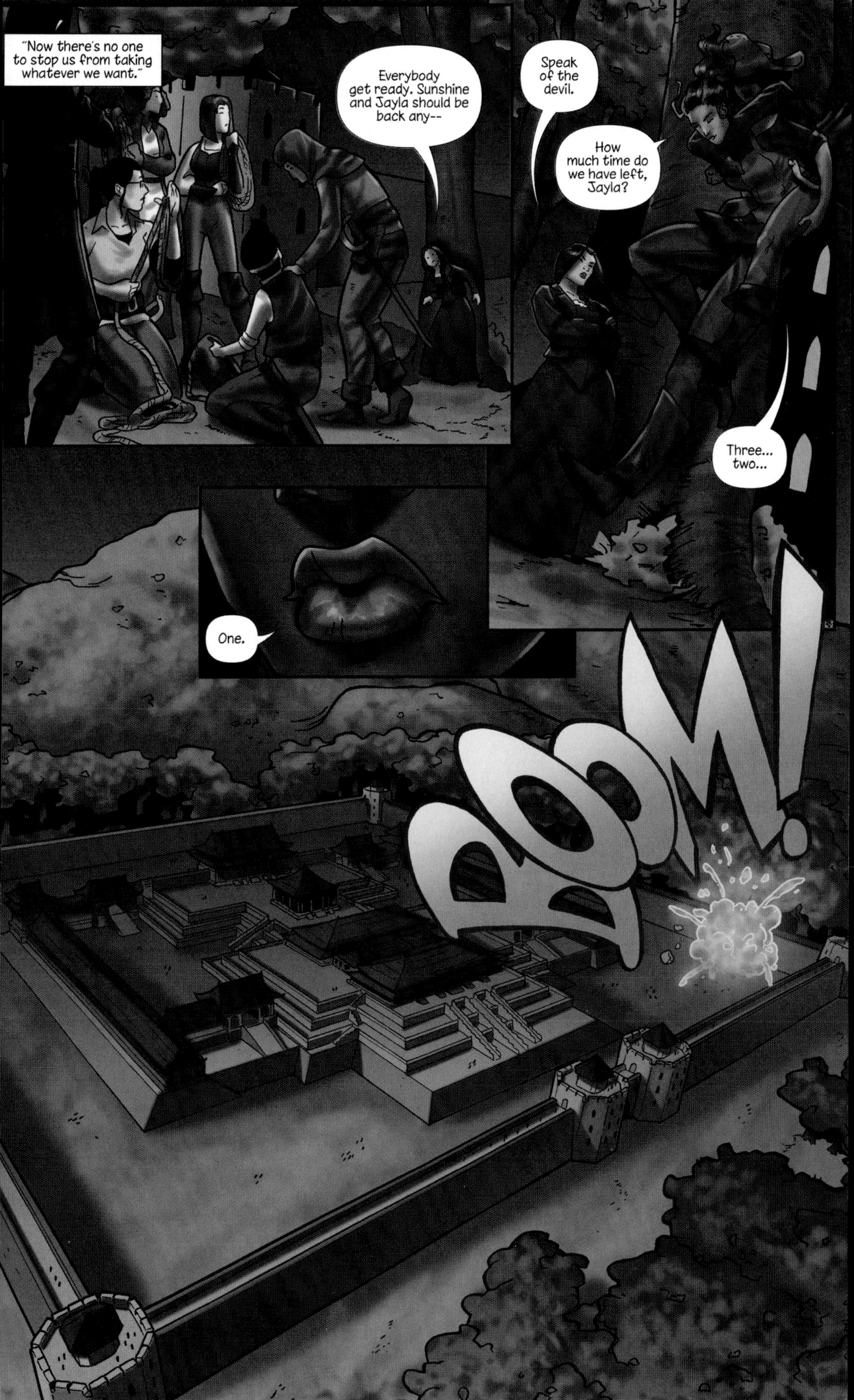
"Now there's no one to stop us from taking whatever we want."
Everybody get ready. Sunshine and Jayla should be back any--
Speak of the devil.
How much time do we have left, Jayla?
Three... two...
One.
BOOM!

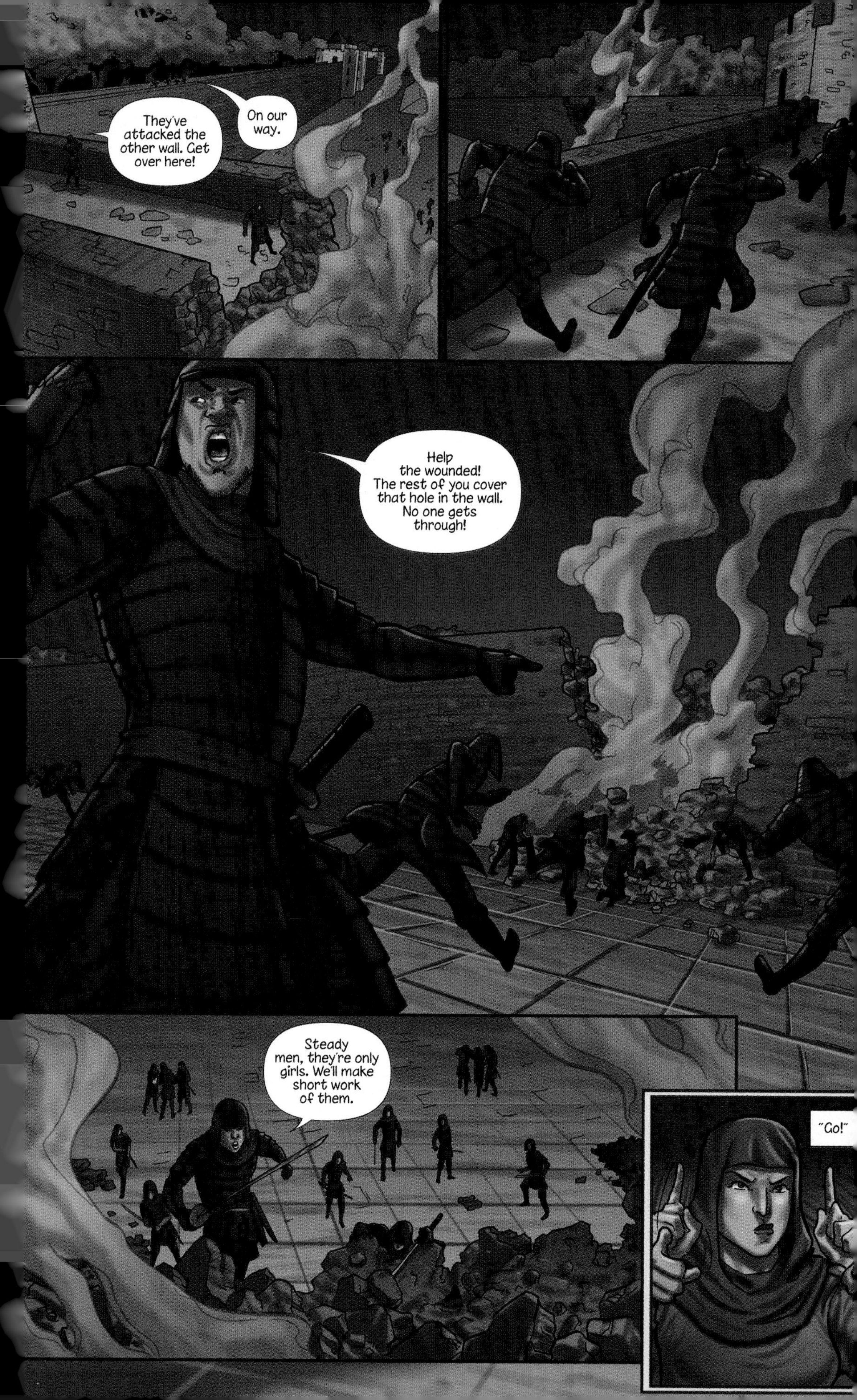
They've attacked the other wall. Get over here!
On our way.
Help the wounded! The rest of you cover that hole in the wall. No one gets through!
Steady men, they're only girls. We'll make short work of them.
"Go!"

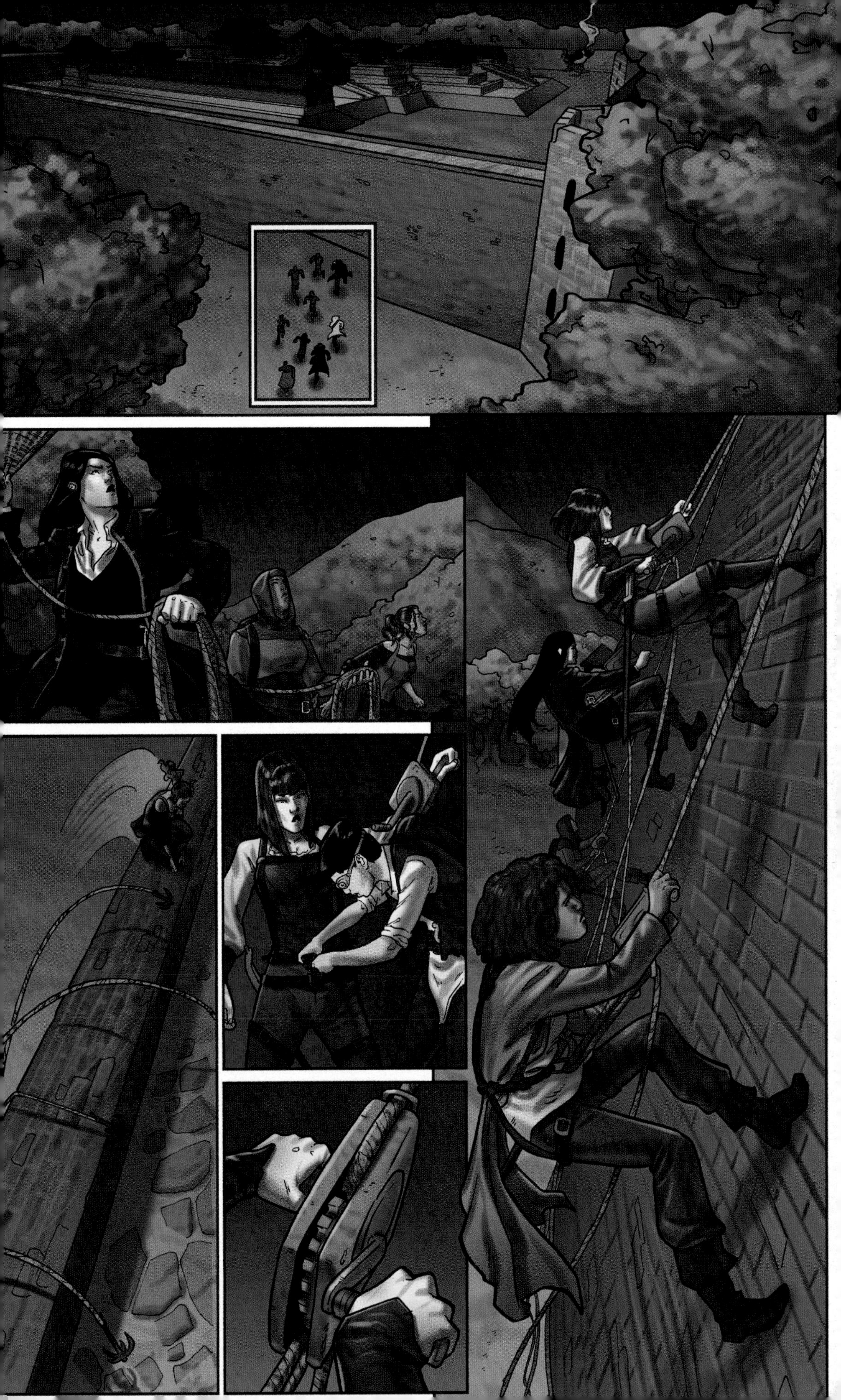

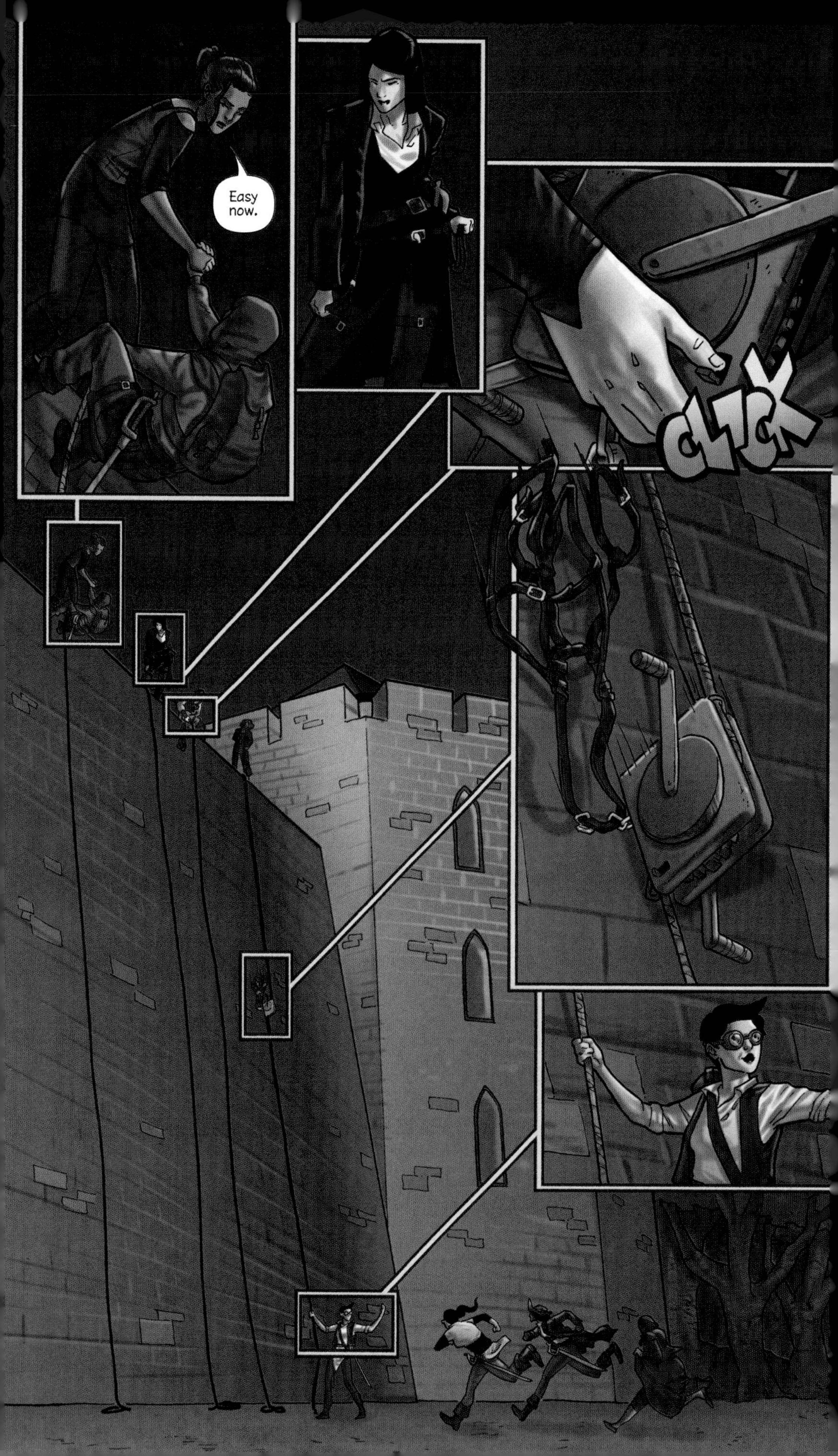
Easy now.
CLICK

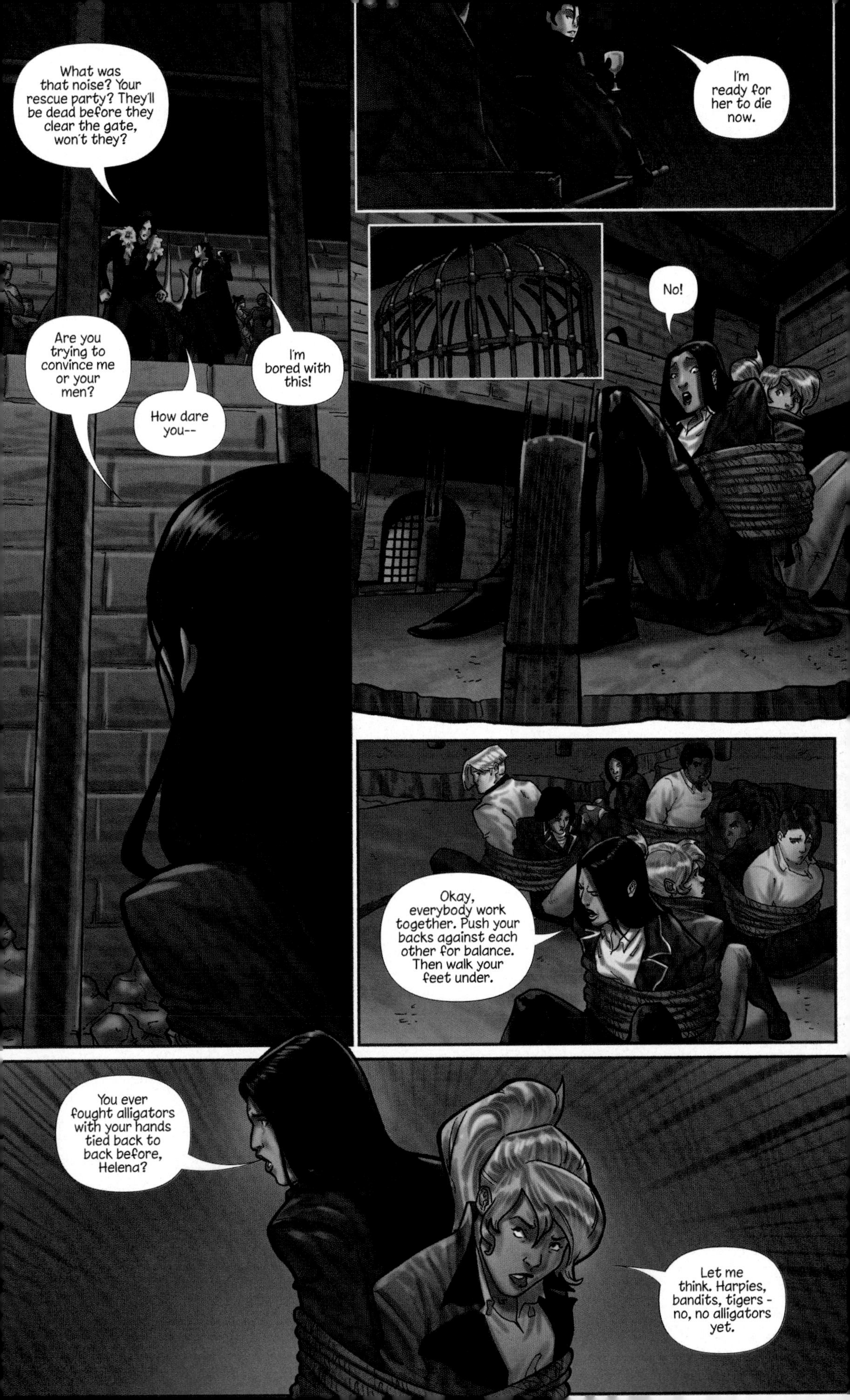
What was that noise? Your rescue party? They'll be dead before they clear the gate, won't they?
I'm ready for her to die now.
Are you trying to convince me or your men?
How dare you--
I'm bored with this!
No!
Okay, everybody work together. Push your backs against each other for balance. Then walk your feet under.
You ever fought alligators with your hands tied back to back before, Helena?
Let me think. Harpies, bandits, tigers - no, no alligators yet.

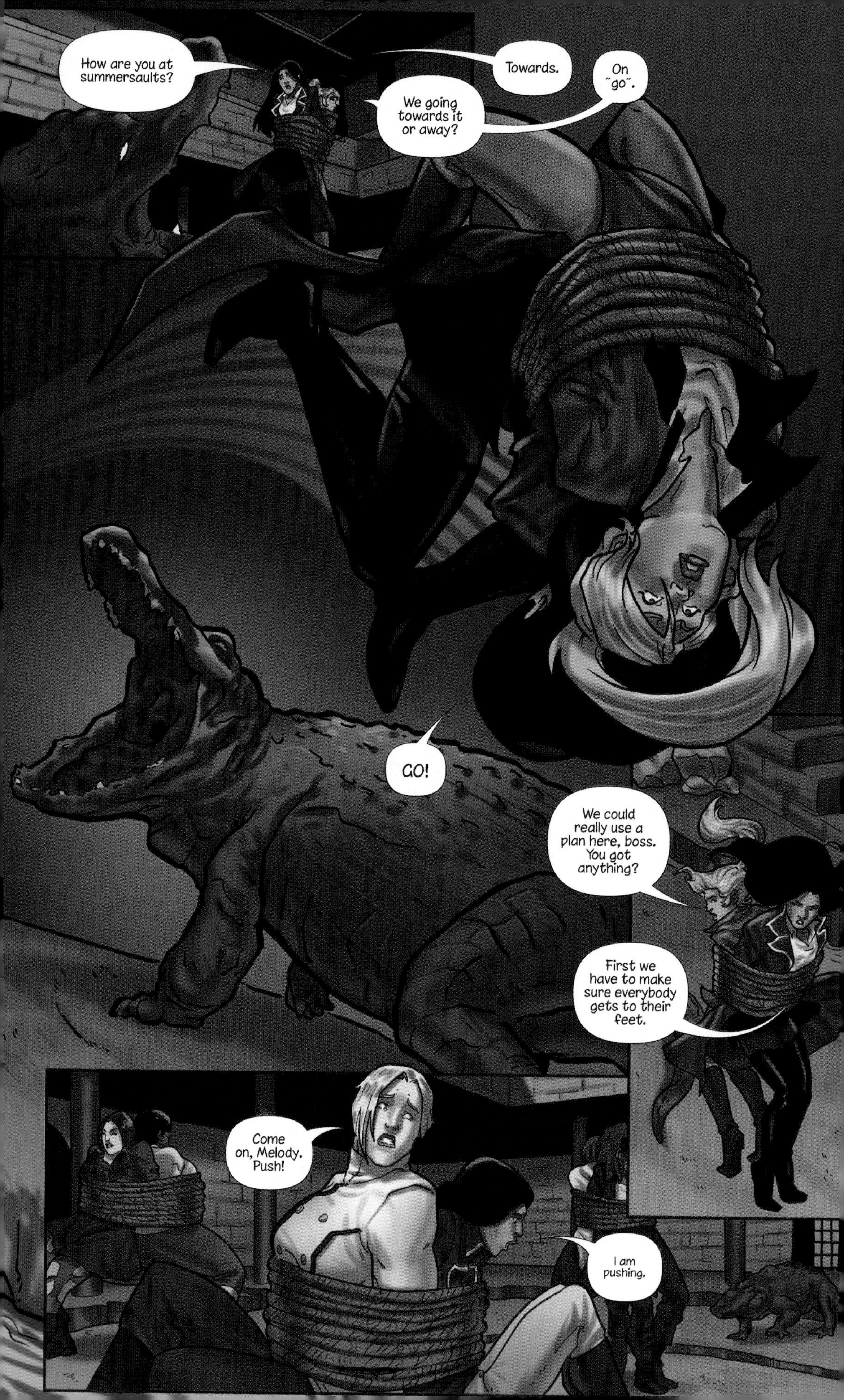
How are you at summersaults?
Towards.
We going towards it or away?
On "go".
GO!
We could really use a plan here, boss. You got anything?
First we have to make sure everybody gets to their feet.
Come on, Melody. Push!
I am pushing.

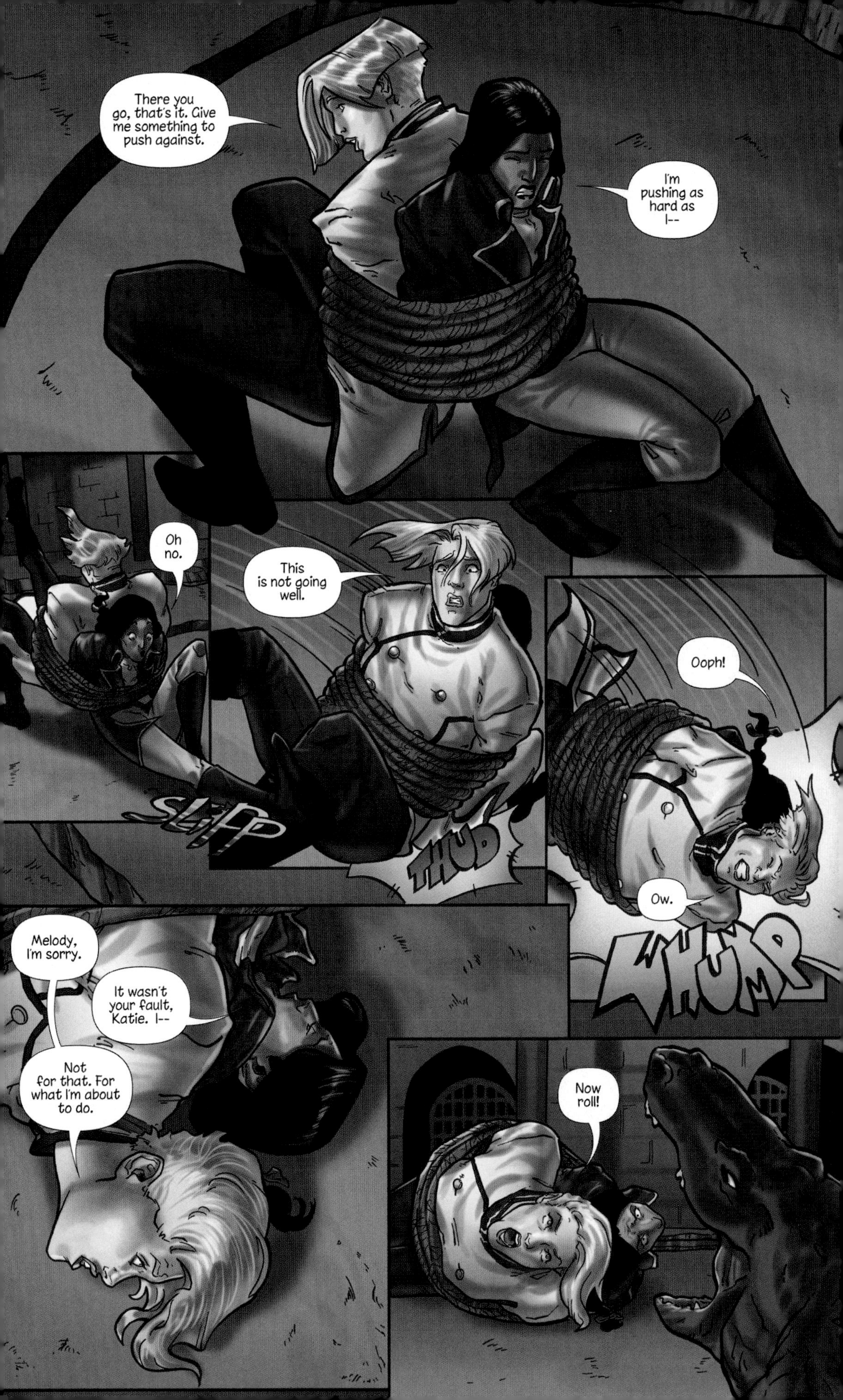
There you go, that's it. Give me something to push against.
I'm pushing as hard as I--
Oh no.
This is not going well.
SLIP
THUD
Ooph!
Ow.
WHUMP
Melody, I'm sorry.
It wasn't your fault, Katie. I--
Not for that. For what I'm about to do.
Now roll!

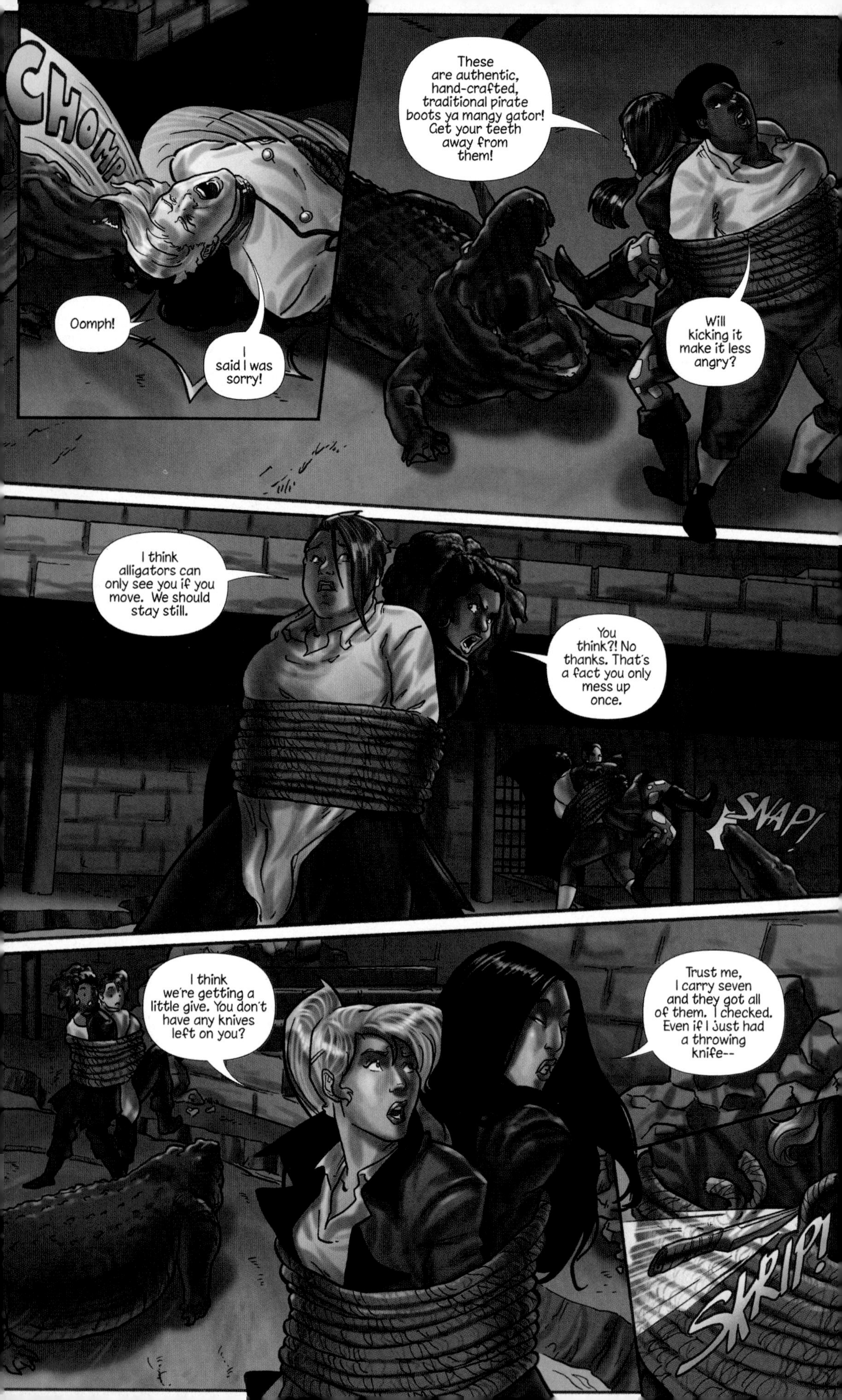
CHOMP
Oomph!
I said I was sorry!
These are authentic, hand-crafted, traditional pirate boots ya mangy gator! Get your teeth away from them!
Will kicking it make it less angry?
I think alligators can only see you if you move. We should stay still.
You think?! No thanks. That's a fact you only mess up once.
SNAP!
I think we're getting a little give. You don't have any knives left on you?
Trust me, I carry seven and they got all of them. I checked. Even if I just had a throwing knife--
SKRIP!

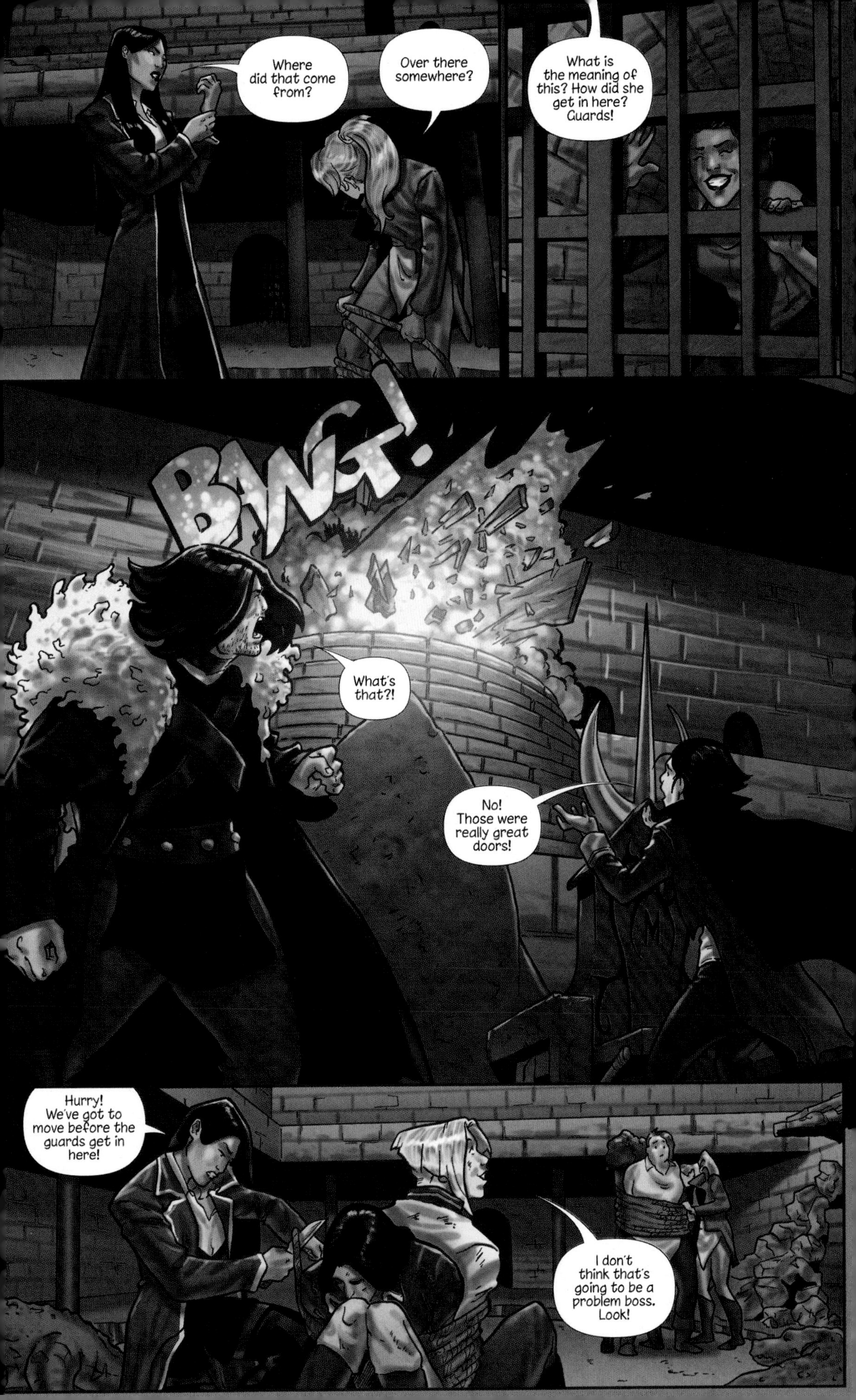
Where did that come from?
Over there somewhere?
What is the meaning of this? How did she get in here? Guards!
BANG!
What's that?!
No! Those were really great doors!
Hurry! We've got to move before the guards get in here!
I don't think that's going to be a problem boss. Look!

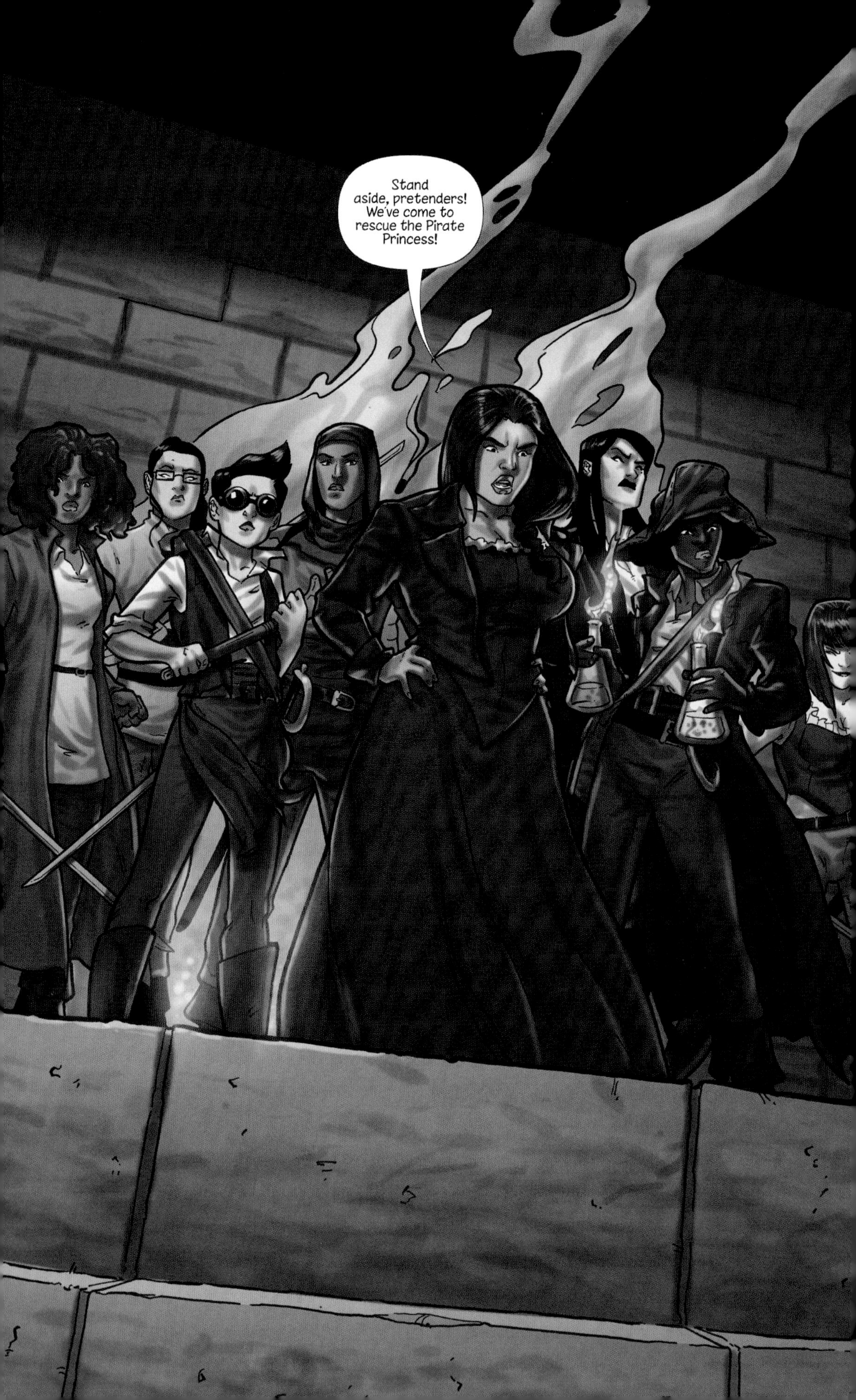
Stand aside, pretenders! We've come to rescue the Pirate Princess!

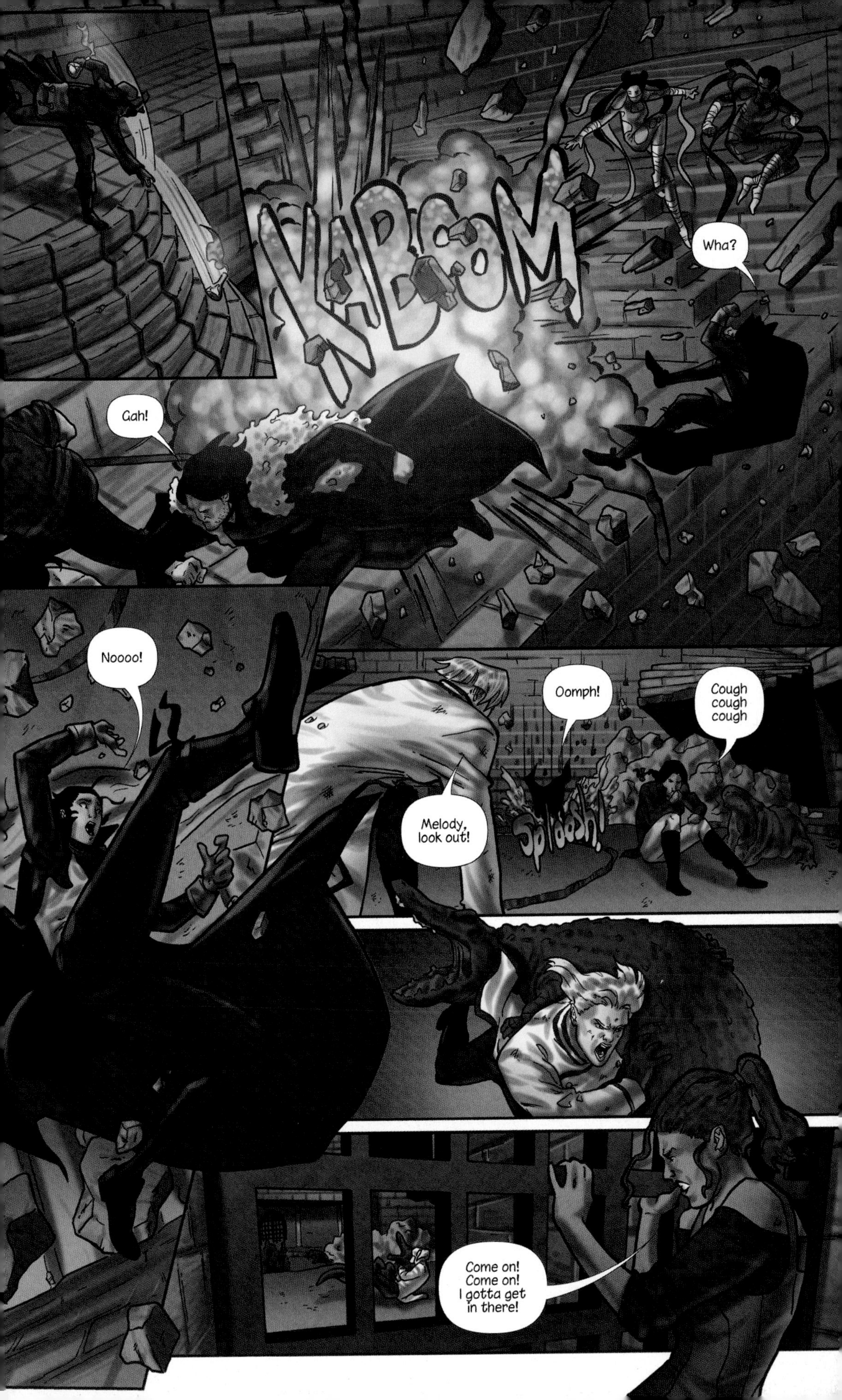
KABOOM
Wha?
Gah!
Noooo!
Melody, look out!
Oomph!
Sploosh!
Cough cough cough
Come on! Come on! I gotta get in there!

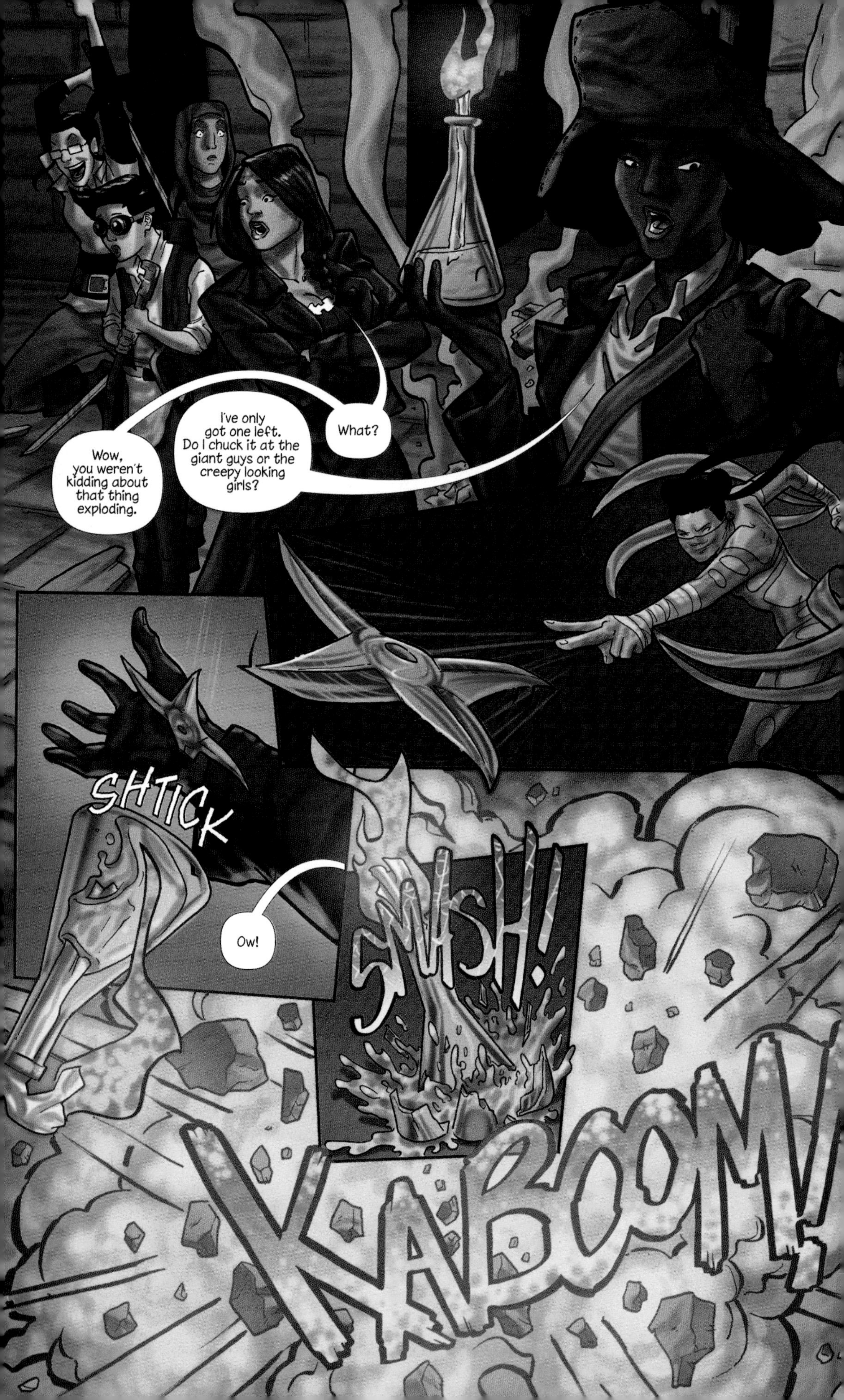
What?
I've only got one left. Do I chuck it at the giant guys or the creepy looking girls?
Wow, you weren't kidding about that thing exploding.
SHTICK
Ow!
SMASH!!
KABOOM!!

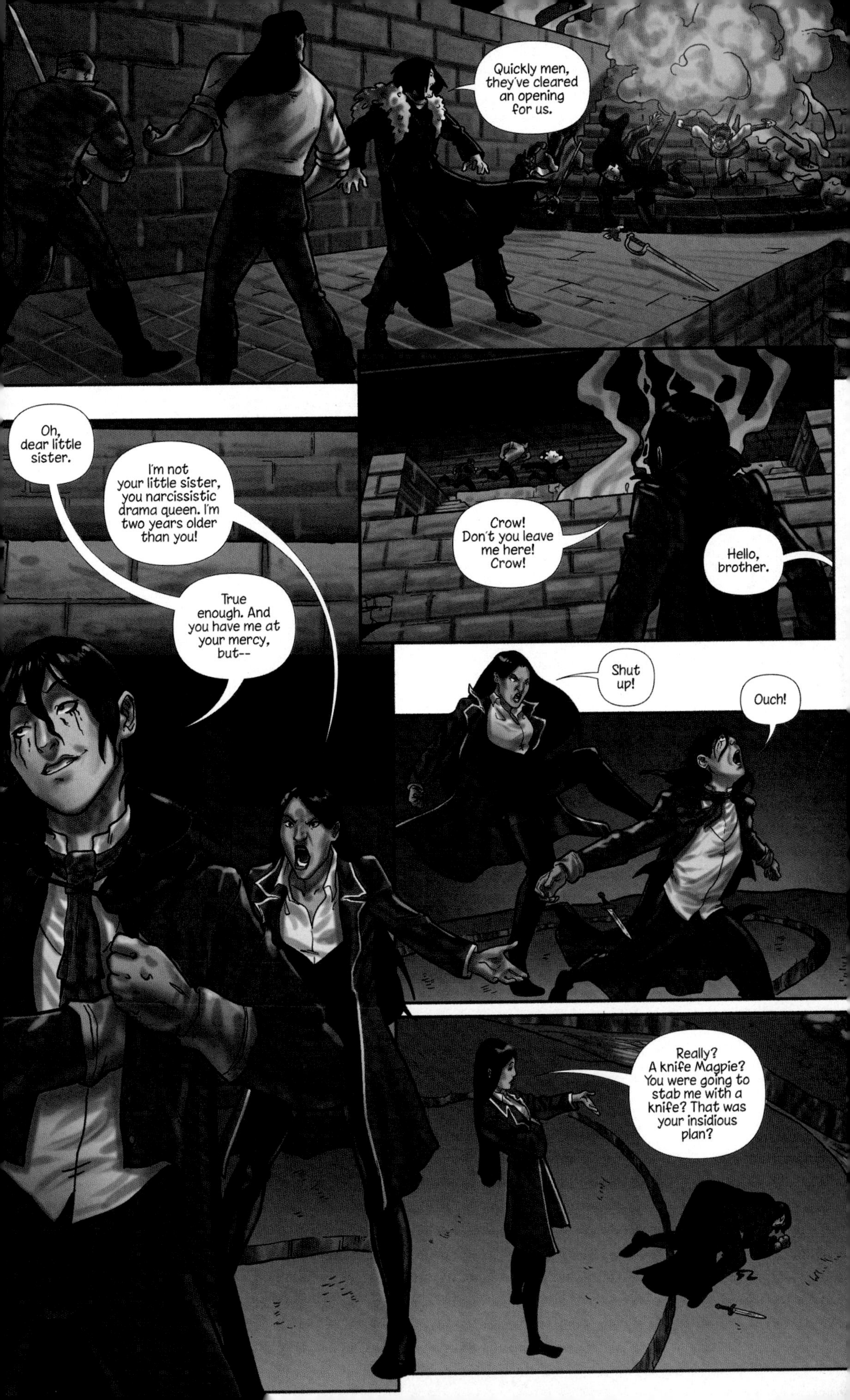
Quickly men, they've cleared an opening for us.
Crow! Don't you leave me here! Crow!
Hello, brother.
Oh, dear little sister.
I'm not your little sister, you narcissistic drama queen. I'm two years older than you!
True enough. And you have me at your mercy, but--
Shut up!
Ouch!
Really? A knife Magpie? You were going to stab me with a knife? That was your insidious plan?

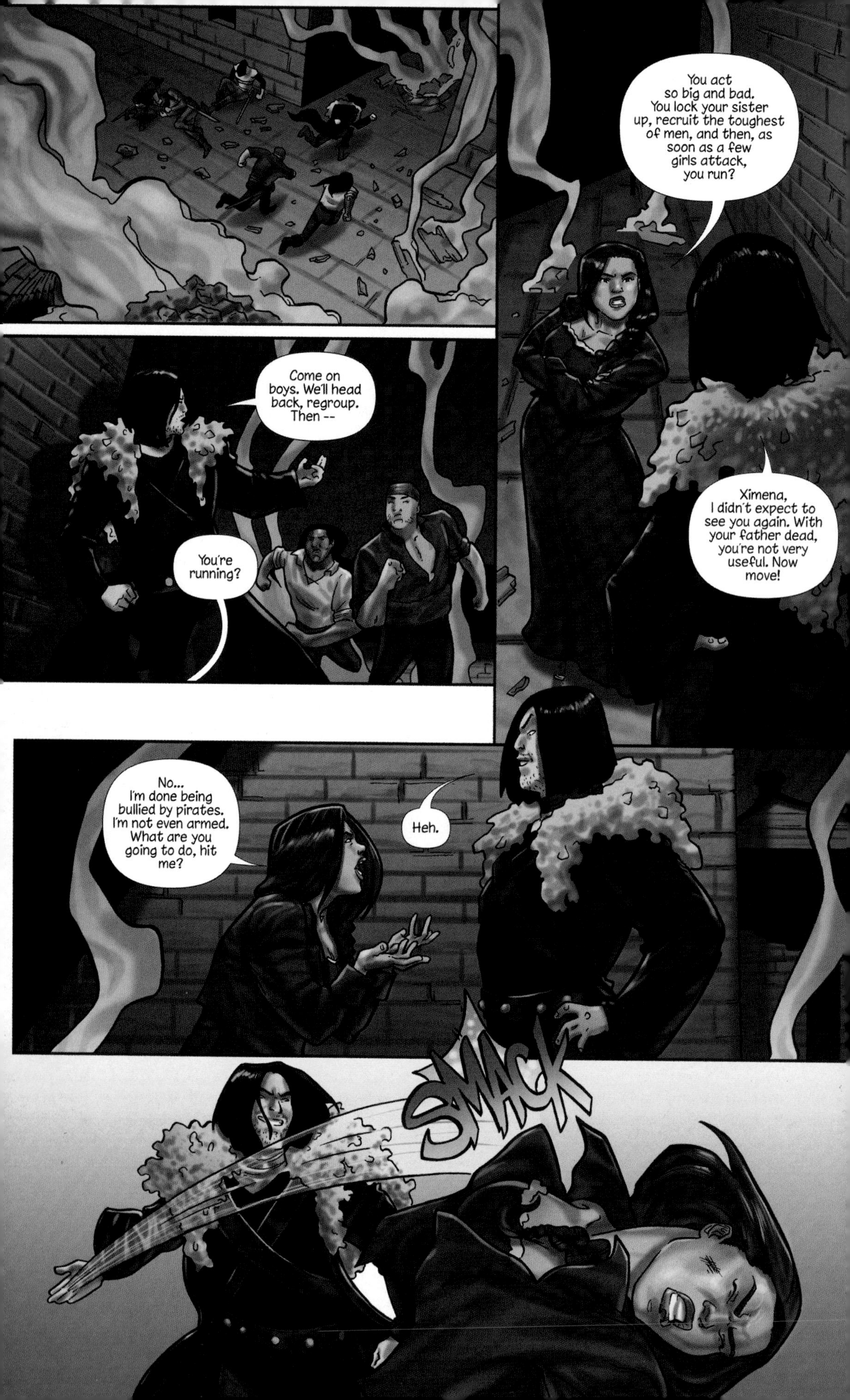
Come on boys. We'll head back, regroup. Then --
You're running?
You act so big and bad. You lock your sister up, recruit the toughest of men, and then, as soon as a few girls attack, you run?
Ximena, I didn't expect to see you again. With your father dead, you're not very useful. Now move!
No... I'm done being bullied by pirates. I'm not even armed. What are you going to do, hit me?
Heh.
SMACK

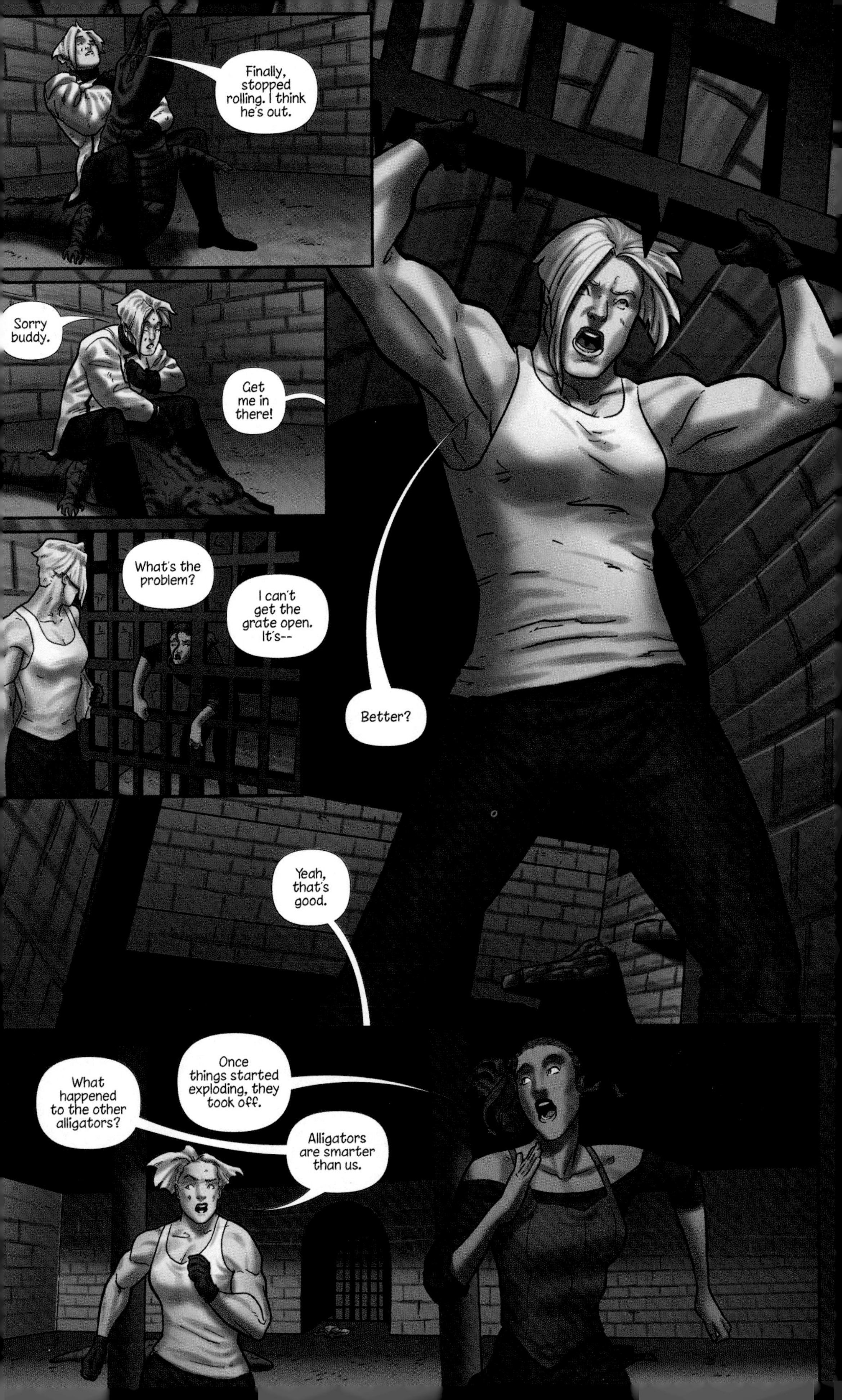
Finally, stopped rolling. I think he's out.
Sorry buddy.
Get me in there!
What's the problem?
I can't get the grate open. It's--
Better?
Yeah, that's good.
What happened to the other alligators?
Once things started exploding, they took off.
Alligators are smarter than us.

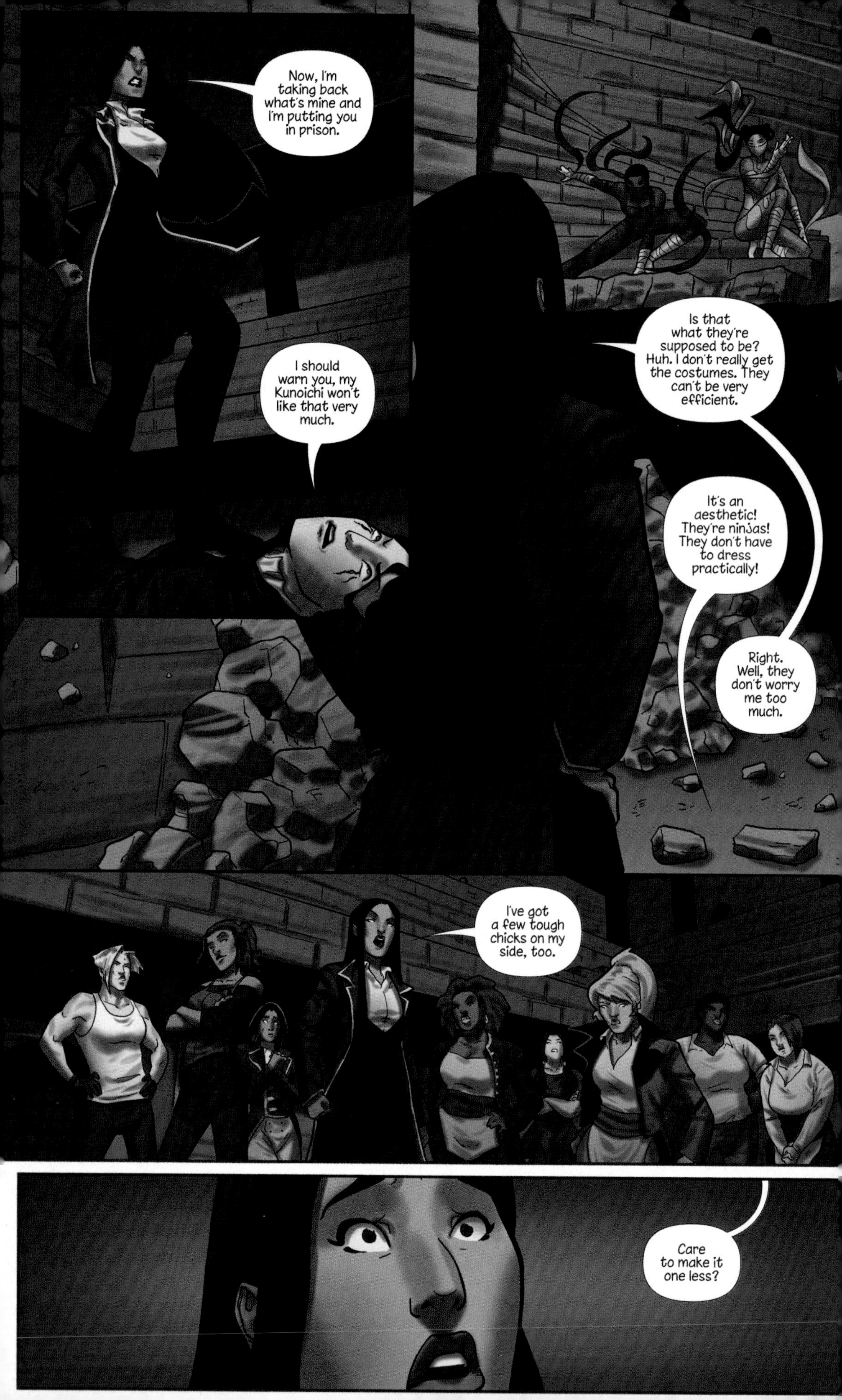
Now, I'm taking back what's mine and I'm putting you in prison.
I should warn you, my Kunoichi won't like that very much.
Is that what they're supposed to be? Huh. I don't really get the costumes. They can't be very efficient.
It's an aesthetic! They're ninjas! They don't have to dress practically!
Right. Well, they don't worry me too much.
I've got a few tough chicks on my side, too.
Care to make it one less?

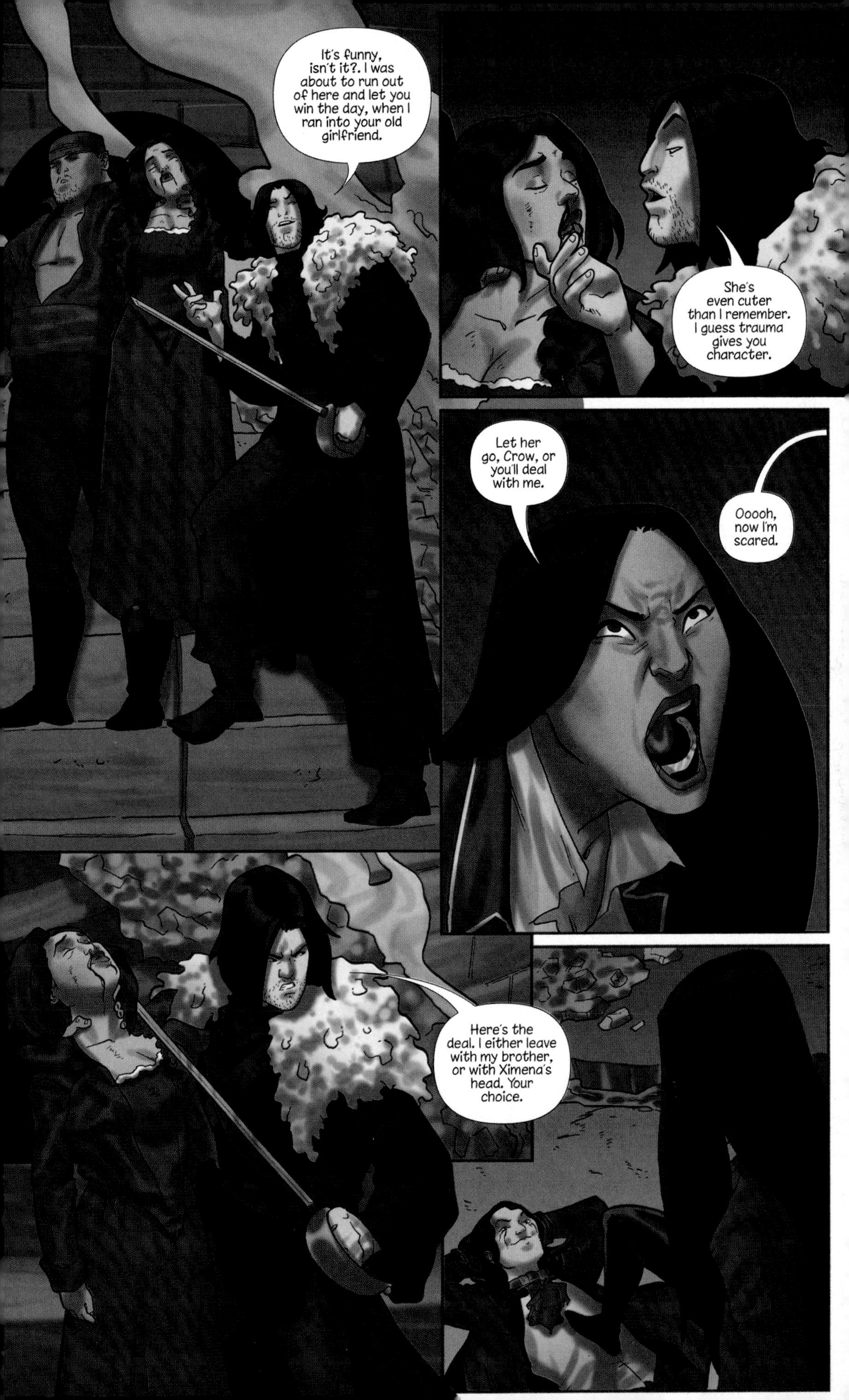
It's funny, isn't it?. I was about to run out of here and let you win the day, when I ran into your old girlfriend.
She's even cuter than I remember. I guess trauma gives you character.
Let her go, Crow, or you'll deal with me.
Ooooh, now I'm scared.
Here's the deal. I either leave with my brother, or with Ximena's head. Your choice.

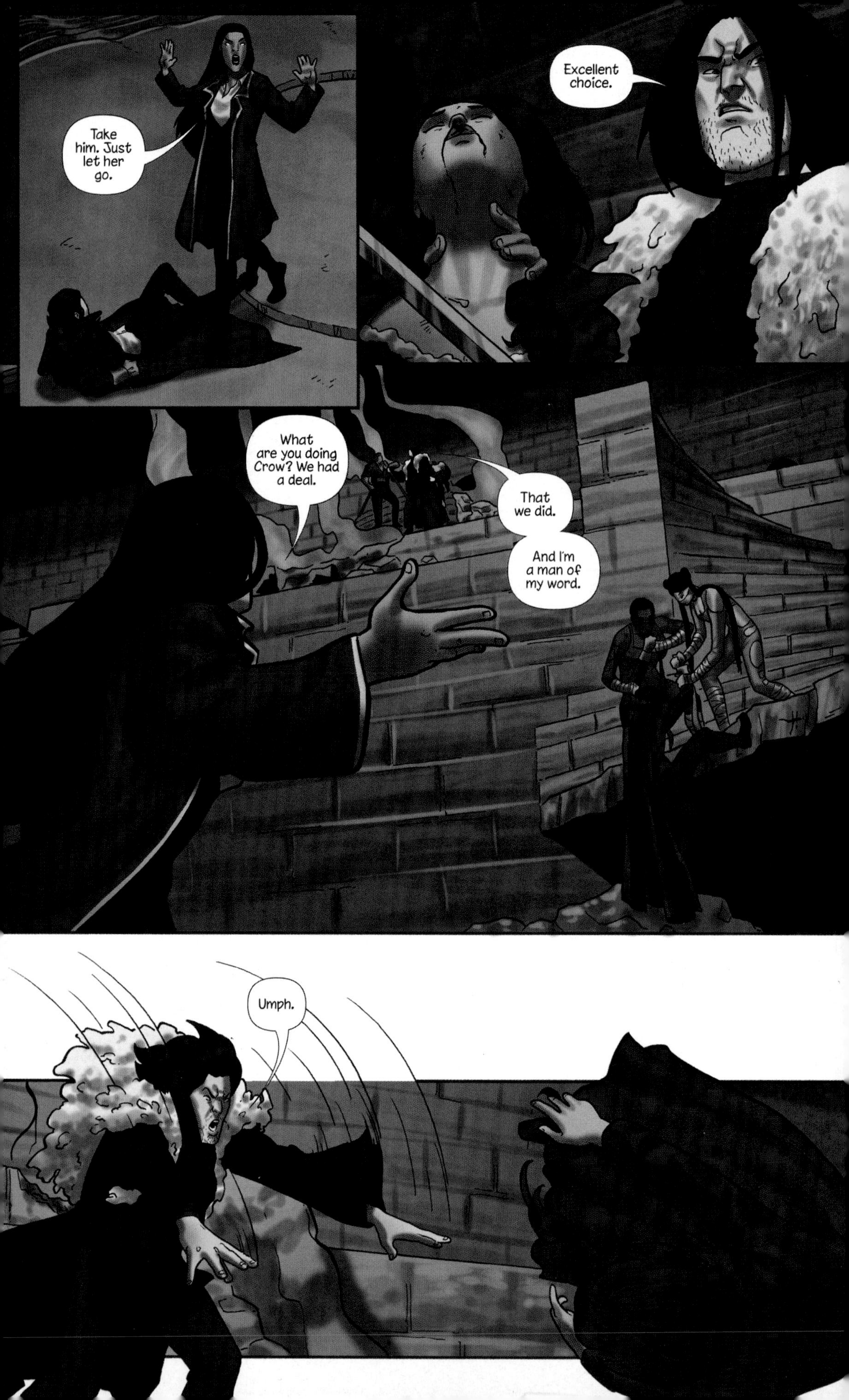
Take him. Just let her go.
Excellent choice.
What are you doing Crow? We had a deal.
That we did.
And I'm a man of my word.
Umph.

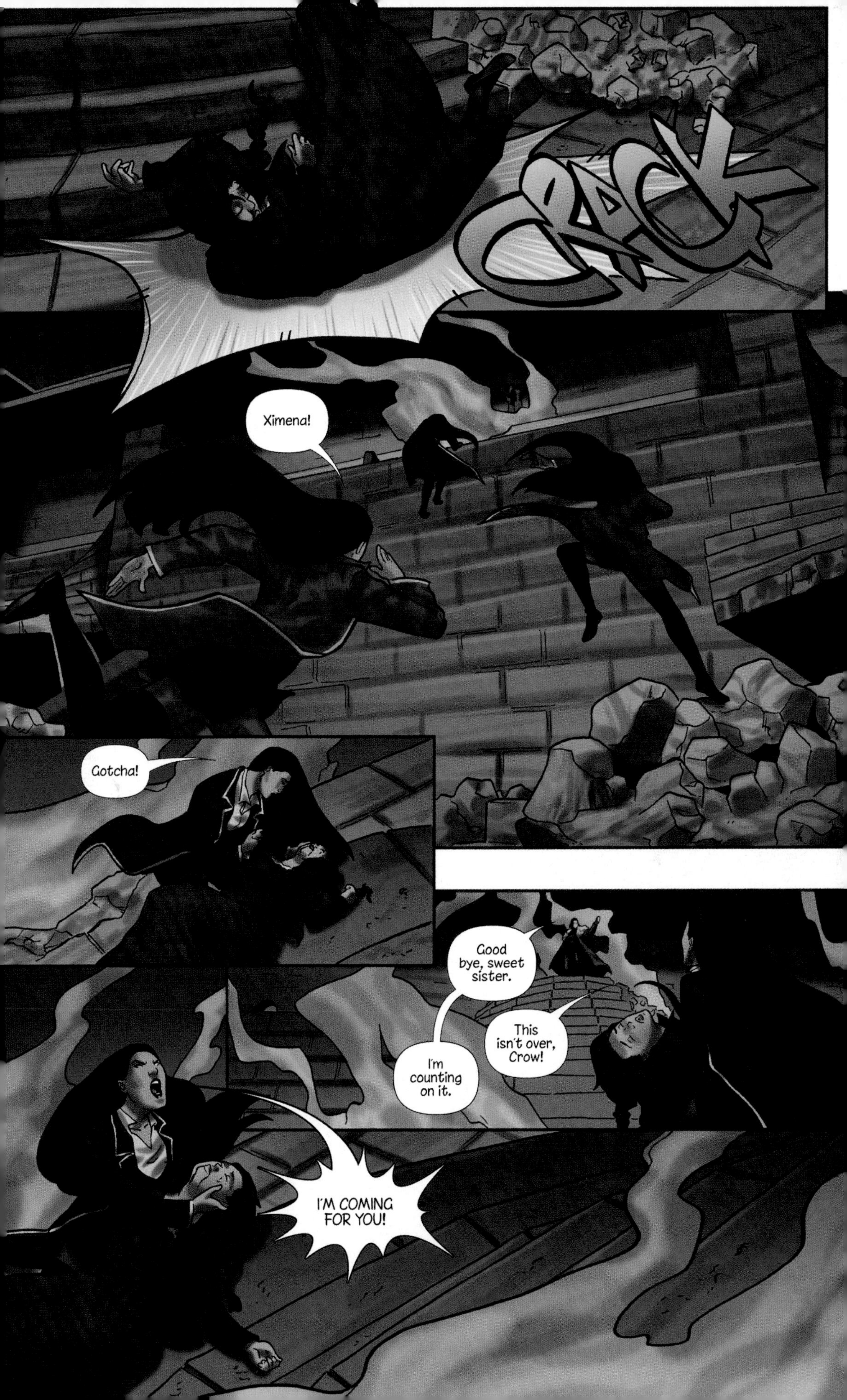
CRACK
Ximena!
Gotcha!
Good bye, sweet sister.
I'm counting on it.
This isn't over, Crow!
I'M COMING FOR YOU!

ISSUE EIGHT
"HAVE FUN STORMING THE CASTLE"

WORDS: Jeremy Whitley   PENCILS: Rosy Higgins   LAYOUTS/INKS: Ted Brandt
COLORS: William Blankenship   LETTERS: Justin Birch   EDITOR: Alicia Whitley

PRINCELESS: RAVEN THE PIRATE PRINCESS #8, May 2016 Copyright Jeremy Whitley, 2016. Published by Action Lab Entertainment. All rights reserved. All characters are fictional. Any likeness to anyone living or undead is purely coincidental. No part of this publication may be reproduced or transmitted without permission, except for small excerpts for review purposes. Printed in Canada. First Printing.

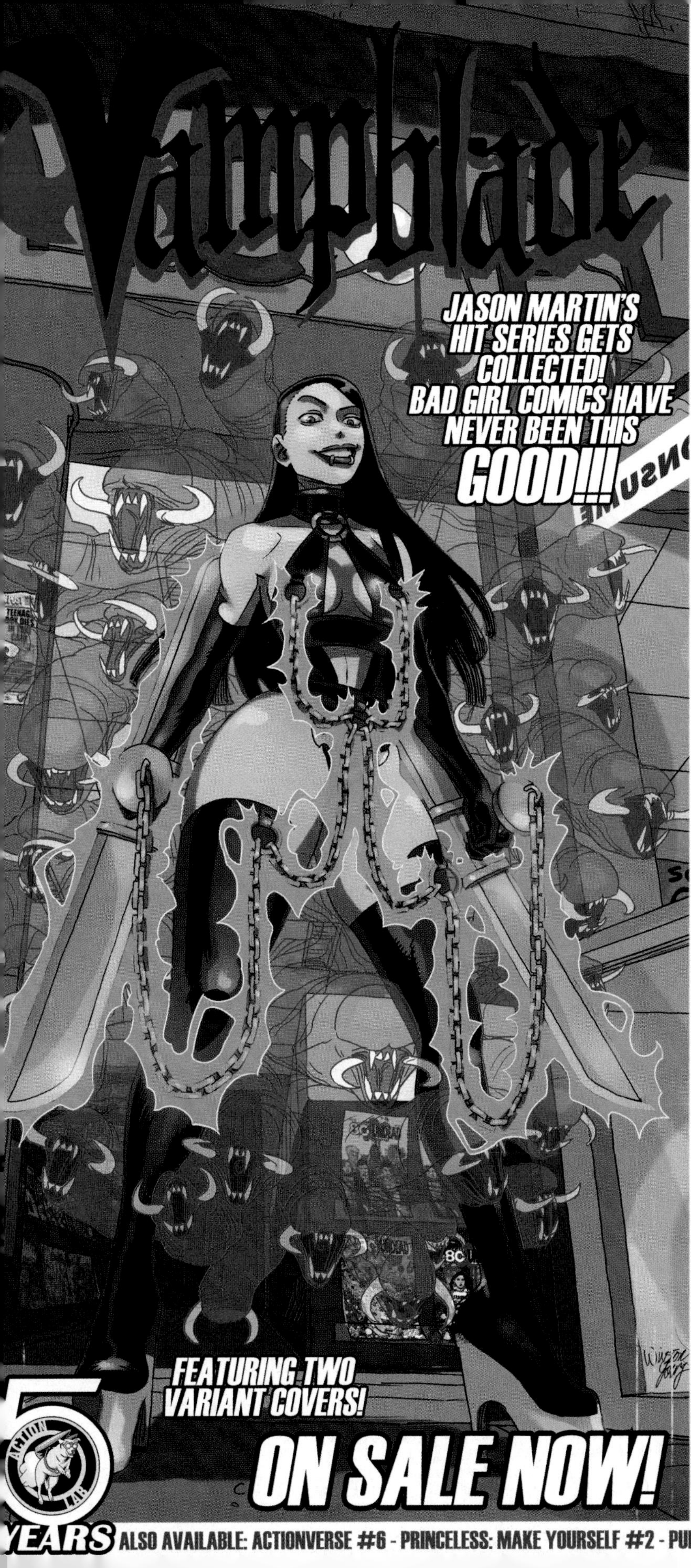
Vampblade
JASON MARTIN'S HIT SERIES GETS COLLECTED! BAD GIRL COMICS HAVE NEVER BEEN THIS GOOD!!!
FEATURING TWO VARIANT COVERS!
ON SALE NOW!
5 YEARS
ACTION LAB

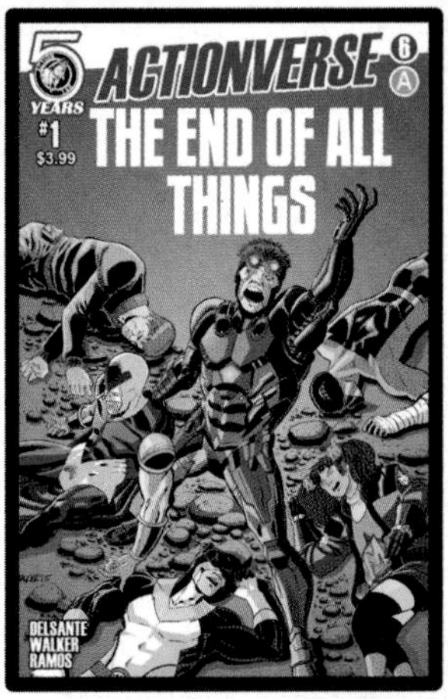
5 YEARS
ACTIONVERSE 6 A
#1
$3.99
THE END OF ALL THINGS
DELSANTE
WALKER
RAMOS

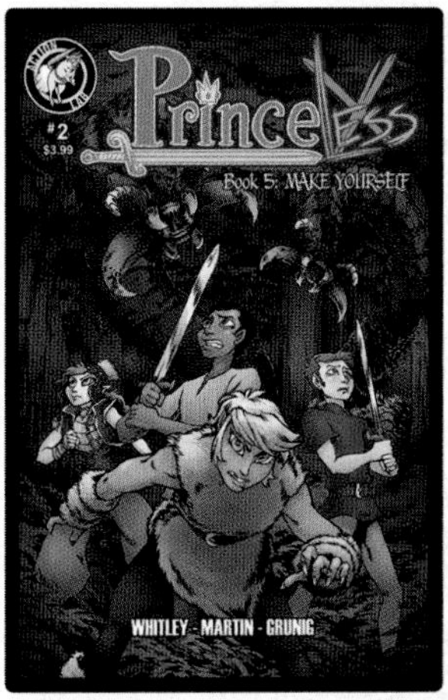
Princeless
#2
$3.99
Book 5: MAKE YOURSELF
WHITLEY - MARTIN - GRUNIG

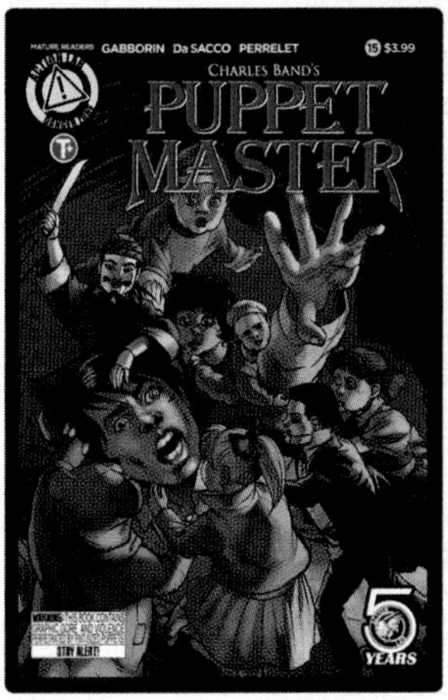
GABBORIN DaSACCO PERRELET
15 $3.99
CHARLES BAND'S
PUPPET MASTER
5 YEARS

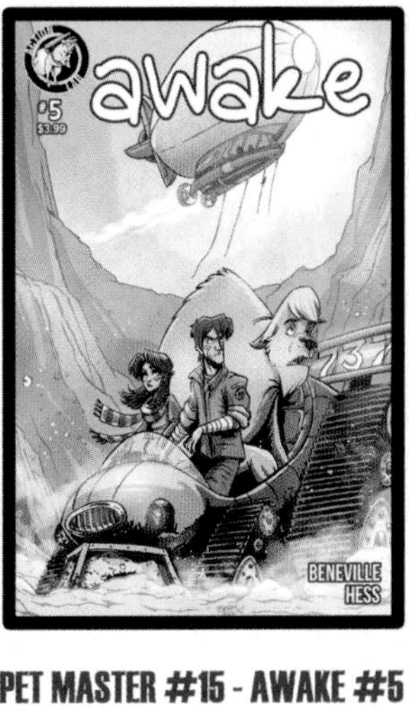
awake
#5
$3.99
BENEVILLE
HESS

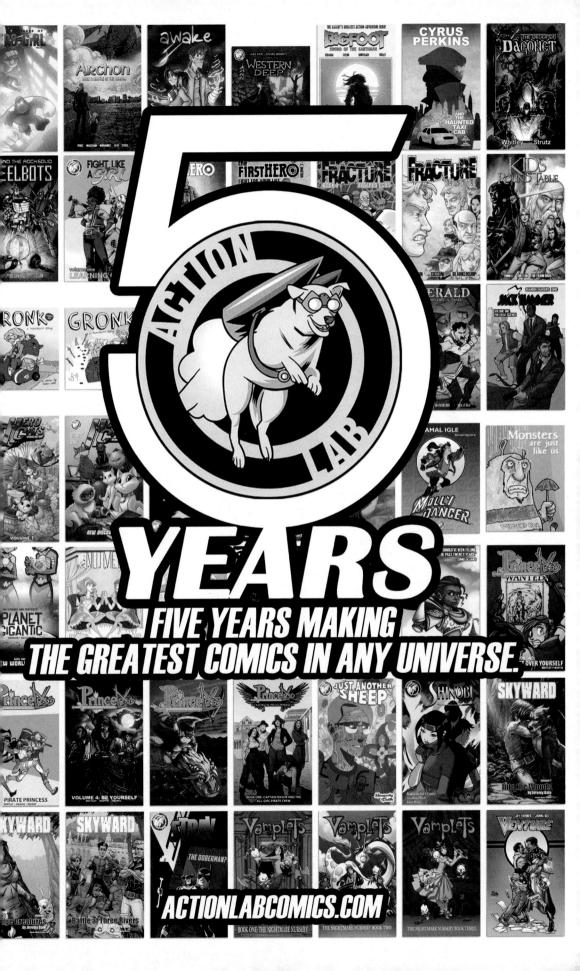

FIVE YEARS MAKING
THE GREATEST COMICS IN ANY UNIVERSE.

ACTIONLABCOMICS.COM

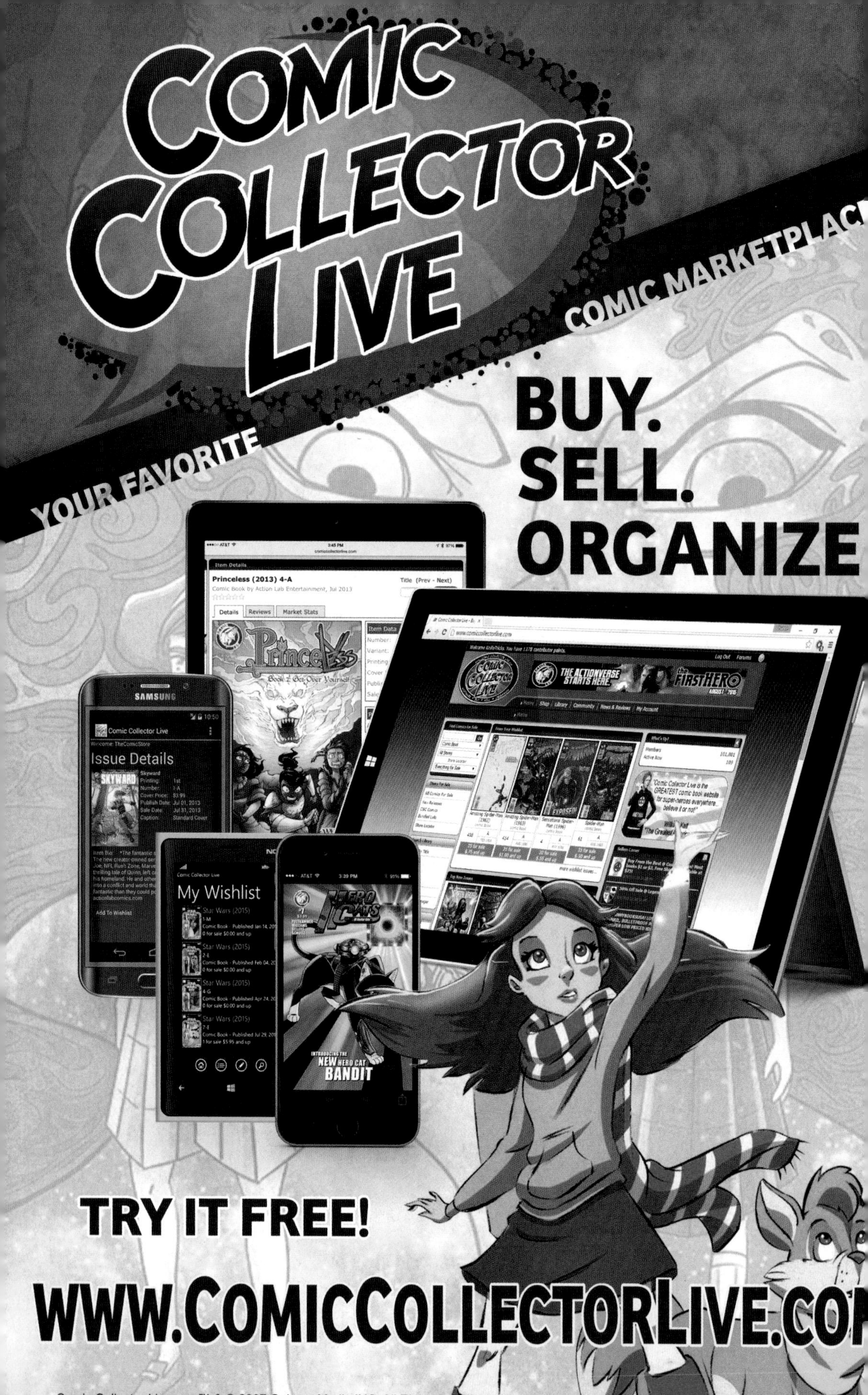

COMIC COLLECTOR LIVE
YOUR FAVORITE COMIC MARKETPLAC
BUY.
SELL.
ORGANIZE
TRY IT FREE!
WWW.COMICCOLLECTORLIVE.CO

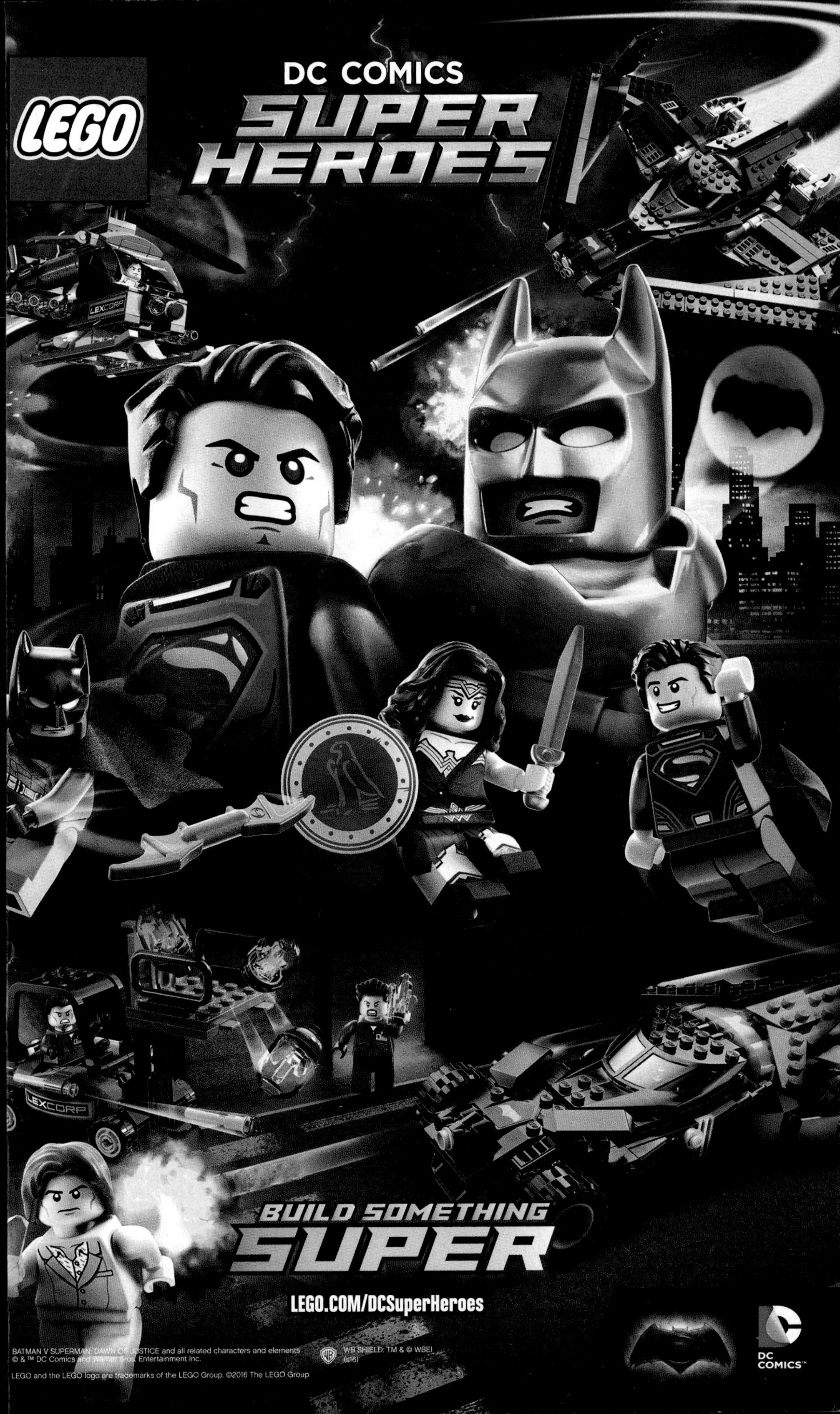

LEGO
DC COMICS
SUPER HEROES
LEXCORP
BUILD SOMETHING SUPER
LEGO.COM/DCSuperHeroes
BATMAN V SUPERMAN: DAWN OF JUSTICE and all related characters and elements © & ™ DC Comics and Warner Bros. Entertainment Inc.
WB SHIELD: TM & © WBEI (s16)
LEGO and the LEGO logo are trademarks of the LEGO Group. ©2016 The LEGO Group.
DC COMICS™

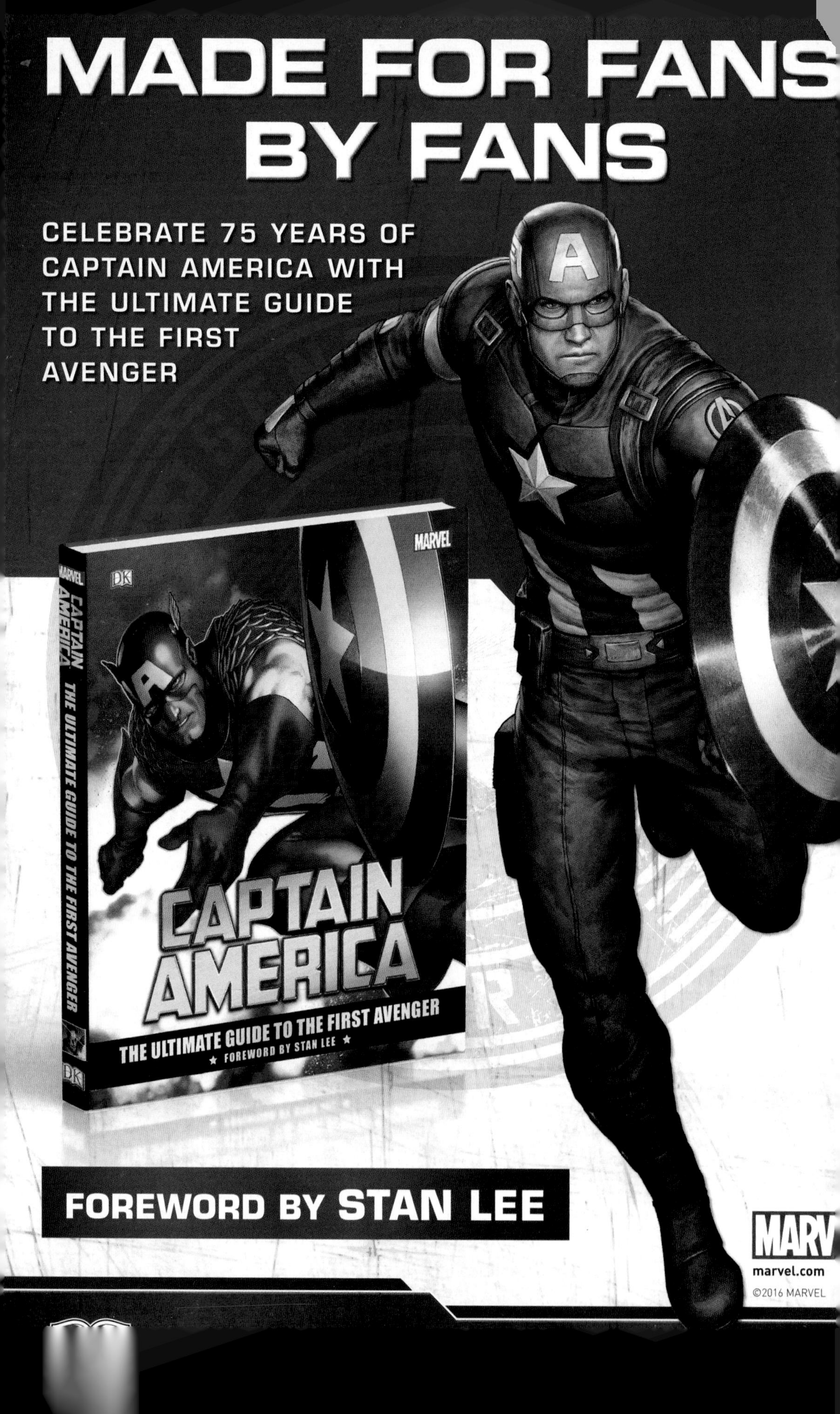
MADE FOR FANS BY FANS
CELEBRATE 75 YEARS OF CAPTAIN AMERICA WITH THE ULTIMATE GUIDE TO THE FIRST AVENGER
MARVEL
DK
CAPTAIN AMERICA
THE ULTIMATE GUIDE TO THE FIRST AVENGER
★ FOREWORD BY STAN LEE ★
FOREWORD BY STAN LEE
marvel.com
©2016 MARVEL